I0736071

BLOODLINE SERIES

# THE LOST QUEEN

BOOK 1

# GAIA LEWES

Copyright © 2023 Gaia Lewes.

All rights reserved. This book or any portion thereof may not be reproduced or used in any manner whatsoever without the express written permission of the publisher except for the use of brief quotation in a book review.

ISBN: 978-1-961017-46-7 (sc)
ISBN: 978-1-961017-47-4 (e)

Rev. date: 06/13/2023

# CONTENTS

# PROLOGUE

"Look good, Ma," Siward commented, admiring his pretty, petite mother in all her finery. "Just like those fancy aristos at the palace."

"I've told you not to call me Ma a thousand times," his mother reminded him. "It's common. I'm your Mother. Or Maman. Or Mamere. Or Mater. Not Ma." She smoothed her hair, glancing into the nearest mirror as she preened. Shifting her eyes from her own image, she allowed them to slide over her sons' forms. Slovenly in dress and posture, they slouched about the entry to their rather pretentious home, completely oblivious to the contrast between their own appearance and that of their mother. She shuddered, looking at them.

"It wouldn't hurt you to dress up a little," she commented, tipping her head to survey her husband. Even at something over fifty years of age, hard physical labor and clean living had kept him trim and muscular so that his dress suit fit over his shoulders, arms and legs the way a suit should.

Cassee Smith made his modest suit look expensive, the suit did not make the man. He wore his dress sword and poniard on his sash, and unlike the majority of the men they would join tonight, he not only knew how to use them, he knew how to use them well. He had been a handsome youth, and he had matured into a handsome man, the silvering of his hair only distinguishing him.

Marge' lowered her eyes, knowing that none of the men his age would be able to match him in looks, tonight, and that few of the younger men would manage it either. For a moment, she saw the military hero she had married so many years ago. Her husband might be a blacksmith, but dressed the way he was in this moment, he could stand beside any aristo in the city and look as if he belonged. She knew that he could dance as gracefully, and speak as well, as any man who would be at tonight's ball. Unfortunately—

"I have to admit that I'm grateful to Vere for staying behind to finish polishing those blades for Councilor Jiden," he commented now, "but it isn't right that she doesn't attend. She ought to be there, tonight. I'll hate to lose her help at the forge, but there's no denying she'd be an excellent catch for any young man in the city, right up to the aristos, with her money."

"What do you mean, her money?" Marge` protested. "That's our money. To pay us for taking the little bastard in and putting a roof over her head."

"Now," Cassee reminded her. "She isn't a bastard, she's an orphan, you know that. And that money rightfully belongs to her. It will have to go to her when she turns eighteen, to be her dowry and set her up however she wishes. We gave our word of honor about that. Those stones you're wearing belong to her. By rights, she should be wearing them tonight. She's old enough. She'll be seventeen near the end of Harvest." And he nodded at her before turning on his heel. "I'll bring up the carriage, shall I?"

It was a rhetorical question. He neither expected, nor received, an answer, but let himself out through the door and headed across the yard, leaving his wife clutching the cluster of diamonds sparkling above her cleavage and hating her husband's cold rectitude. He would be unyielding in it, she knew, no matter how little he cared for the girl. He had given his word. She knew he would hold to it.

She hadn't given her word, she thought to herself, quite viciously. She had intended to have the jewels the moment she had seen them and she had been willing to do whatever it took to lay hands on them, including give her word of honor. Never mind that she had no honor. Well, she had laid hands on those jewels. Now she would do whatever it took to keep them.

Her sons shook their heads.

"He means that, you know," her younger son, Liard, commented.

"And how much of that money is left, humm?" Siward twitted her. He had to know that he and his brother had a goodly number of the coins in the hoard that had come with the girl spent upon them through the years. "Father isn't going to like finding out how much of it is gone, these days," he pointed out, pretending helpfulness. "Touchy about his honor, the old man is, even if he doesn't like her above half."

"He's become more fond of her these days, now she's proven a help about the forge," Marge` mentioned faintly, her expression stricken, her eyes turned inwards.

"Going to have to do something about that," Liard offered slyly. "And fairly soon," Siward added.

Their mother grimaced. The much-maligned Vere had, all unknowingly, paid for the rich gown she wore and she had a feeling that, once the girl understood how much of her money had been used to support the household and her foster brothers, the worm she'd trodden underfoot all too often would turn on her, and with a vengeance.

Liard was right, she thought fleetingly. Something would have to be done, and soon. Because when Cassee found out how much of the girl's money she had spent, he was going to be angry. Very angry.

Cassee might not have treated the girl any better than she had, and he might not have cared two pins about her personally, but he did care about what he considered to be his 'honor'. What honor? Marge` sneered, just to herself. He'd made all kinds of promises about how the girl would be treated. He had sworn to love her and cherish her and teach her and to see that she had the ability to make the kind of marriage she wanted to the man she wanted and he had fulfilled none of them. He'd left all the work of raising the girl to her. All he'd done was use her to help him in the forge.

Marge` knew for a fact that he had lain hard hands upon the girl more than once through the years, and spoken more than his share of hard words to her as well so where did he get off on complaining because she had been known to knock the girl around now and again (particularly when she was younger, and helpless). One day when Marge` had picked up a whip to beat her with, the girl had taken it away from her—and easily! And Marge` knew—unhappily--that her days of beating the girl had passed.

The girl was bigger than she was, and stronger, her hours and days and years working at the forge having given her muscles to match her height and breadth, none of which Marge` had. (The girl was unnatural! Or at least, unfeminine, by Marge`'s lights.) Her husband's 'honor' certainly hadn't balked at any of that!

But when it came to the money, and the jewels left for the girl, well, that was a different story! Marge` sneered, just to herself. She knew very well that the girl didn't like either one of them above half. Oh, she worked in the forge, all right, and willingly, at that, an eventuality that Marge` found completely inexplicable. And she liked her lessons in the temple—the scholars were always praising her and agitating for her to join their ranks--something Marge` couldn't understand any better. Her own sons had avoided their lessons in any manner and by any method they could, and she had considered that no more than amusing at worst. She, herself, had never been any better than an indifferent scholar, so they had come by their dislike of study naturally.

Marge` considered her sons merely a pair of 'high spirited' boys, watching them turn into rogues and useless lay-abouts with complete equanimity. She didn't understand her husband's impatience with their lack of either education or a job. To her, their refusal to work at the forge was nothing worse than perfectly natural. After all, who would wish to do the dirty, sweaty, hard work of smithing when they didn't have to? And as far as the satisfaction in creating something went, where was the satisfaction in forging a shovel? Or a hoe?

How often did anyone commission a blade? Not very. Only aristos could afford them! No, she just made very sure that her sons didn't have to.

But when it came to the money and the jewels, well, Marge` had no intention of parting with any of them. Her fingers closed spasmodically about the ropes of diamonds hanging from her neck. Five glittering strands showcased a large center stone cut in tear-drop fashion, with two more matching stones at her ears and an equally ostentatious bracelet on her wrist.

She didn't care what her husband said, he wasn't taking these jewels away from her. Not the diamonds, not the rubies, and not the combined diamond and ruby set. The stupid girl could have that insipid pearl set with the moonstones, and the opals. She didn't care about those. Well, they were not nearly as valuable and not at all fashionable. But no one was taking the jewels away from her. No one.

Marge` didn't care that the stones didn't rightfully belong to her. She'd taken them, and she had them hidden away where her husband wouldn't find them. She thought, malevolently, of the adoptive daughter she'd sworn to love and cherish, the girl child she'd coaxed so assiduously and so successfully to get in the hope of stealing her dowry and acquiring a useful house slave. The girl was an unnatural; she labored at the forge, designing and making plebian things, as well as beautiful, working over the bellows, swinging a hammer, skillful, strong, and, in Marge`'s eyes, wholly unfeminine.

Incomprehensibly, the girl liked to read and to study, and even more inexplicably, she liked to work at the forge. Not even Cassee's abuse, thinly disguised as teaching, had discouraged her. She even consented to wear her foster brothers' hand-me-downs when she worked at the forge; she'd rather work over a finely crafted sword or dagger with an inlaid hilt or fashion a lacy, filigree chain than attend a party and flirt with boys.

It never occurred to her that for all the hours the girl labored in their service, neither of her foster parents ever paid her a fair wage for all her efforts, despite the fat rolls of gold and silver coin that had been left for her. Marge` never admitted to herself that she kept the girl dressed as a servant, rather than as a daughter of her house and that as a result, her adoptive daughter had less clothing than the meanest servant in the city. They, at least, had wages with which to purchase their one Temple-day dress, and her daughter, who possessed a king's ransom in coin of the realm and jewels yet had not a brass farthing in hand with which to purchase herself better dress than the cast-offs they provided.

The sound of the carriage disrupted her reverie, and Marge`
frowned.

"Better think of something pretty quick," her son Siward advised
her, as he opened the door and ushered her towards the arriving
carriage. "Time is running out."

Marge` remembered, entirely too well, the time before her adoptive
daughter had arrived, when she and Cassee could not afford a carriage.
Siward was right, she thought. She had better think of something, and
quickly. Something had to be done, before the girl turned eighteen
and Cassee insisted upon giving her the coin and the jewels Marge`
had come to consider her own. She doubted that the girl liked her
above half and she was fairly certain that it was entirely too late for
her to change the girl's mind. She might be stupid, but Marge` had a
feeling it was too late for fine words or fine fabrics to carry the day.

She let Cassee hand her up into the carriage and took her seat.
Maybe, she thought, she'd have a word or two with Freddy. The son
of the king ought to know some way the pestilent girl could be gotten
rid of—not that she'd let him know that was what she wanted. No,
she'd have to be more subtle than that.

But Freddy. . . well, the boy was a bit of a fool, thinking that he
could pull the wool over her eyes. As if he could come around her
boys all these years without her finding out that he was the king's
youngest son!

She glanced fondly over at her sons in the dimness of the carriage,
seeing them in her mind's eye as far more handsome than they, in
reality, were. Her sons were the confidants of a prince! That ought to
be worth something.

# I

# VERE

THE DAY THAT I FIRST met the Crown Prince Nehl Aurelius Mariano, I was making deliveries for my foster father. At the moment that he stopped me, I was approaching the tradesmen's entrance to Privy Council member Jiden Malone Malorca Medinos' home, carrying four matched daggers that I had made to Privy Council Member Jiden's order. Each one of them had been a work of art, and the cloth bag which held the daggers and their handmade leather sheaths was heavy in my arms.

I never even reached for my sword. I never imagined I might have to; I recognized both the Crown Prince and his brother Freddy immediately and never dreamed that they meant me harm. Freddy had been my brothers' buddy—the three of them had gotten into trouble together more than once, but the city guard all knew Freddy by sight and so they had always gotten out of trouble as easily as they found it. And, of course, everyone in the city knew his oldest brother, the Crown Prince. The girls all swooned over him, though I had always thought he looked far too arrogant to be really handsome.

He kept asking me about rebels. I knew nothing about rebels. As far as I knew, there weren't any. But when he put his dagger to my throat and Freddy took the blades from the cloth bag I was carrying and showed them off, saying that they were symbols of the rebellion (what rebellion?) I knew I was in trouble. I might have fought, but how could I raise a blade against Freddy, my foster brothers' buddy? (I could raise a blade against him now! And kill him with it, too.)

The city guards manacled my hands behind my back while the prince held me at blade's edge, and when they had secured me, Freddy explained to the Crown Prince, who was evidently not too bright, how delivering the daggers implicated me as a rebel. I understood then, when it was far too late to get away, what had happened. Privy Council Member Jiden had commissioned those blades from my foster father and I had designed and made them, meaning that if anyone was a rebel, if you could call a Privy Council Member a rebel— more like a plotter in a plan to pull off a coup, if you ask me. To cover him and keep him from suspicion, my foster family had been put on the hook. In their turn, and with Freddy's connivance, my foster family had schemed to pass the guilt on to me, and now here I was, on my way to the palace dungeon, thrust into a nightmare from which the only end might be my death.

I had no idea how bad it would become, or how I would welcome death before my time in the dungeon was over. I could not have imagined then, in my worst nightmares, what was to come to me. They believed nothing of my truth. The Crown Prince himself struck me, and not once, but over and over, while I sat in a blood-stained chair, chained in place to his abuse. Soon, my blood stained the chair along with all the other blood.

He called it an interrogation, though why he bothered asking me questions he refused to believe the answers to, I would never understand. After I passed out, I was taken from the chair and chained to the wall in a dungeon cell in my bloody clothing. The Crown Prince ordered—I had roused enough to hear him—the window opened so that I would have no protection from the rain the wind blowing into the cell brought with it. The cell had no straw, no privacy, and only a bucket for relief.

I received a small loaf of bread and one cup of water every twenty-four hours and not one drop of water or crumb more.      T h e Crown Prince ordered that, too. I heard him. And periodically, once or twice a day, I was taken from my cell and chained to the chair in the interrogation cell, and beaten. After the second day the Crown Prince didn't even bother asking questions. He just beat me.

I would never have imagined that the king had such a place in the kingdom.

For it was the classic dungeon of stories, dark and dank and dirty, bare stone walls, iron bars and clanking chains. Men moaned in pain through the nights and screamed, too, and the days were so dark you could disappear into the shadows that filled the place to overflowing. Nights were dark and cold and drafty and filled with pain.

In the beginning of my time there, I wondered how many of the men there were like me, innocent. After a while, I thought of nothing at all. The Crown Prince grew bored and stopped coming.

Then one day (I had lost count) one of the men who 'interrogated' me in partnership with the Crown Prince hung me from the ceiling beam by my manacled wrists and proceeded to alternate beating me with his fists and a club and cutting me up with a knife. He enjoyed it a lot.

I don't think any of the cuts were deep or life threatening by themselves, but altogether, I lost a lot of blood, and he broke several of my ribs, my collarbone, my jaw and my cheekbone and my nose (for the second time). While he did it, he threatened me with even worse tortures. After a while, he actually started carrying them through, heating a poker and burning me with it. When he raised it towards my face, and I saw his gleaming eyes—he was enjoying what he was doing a lot! And the men with him were enjoying it as well. My agony was their finest entertainment—I lost it.

Something burst in my mind—he'd touched me with the heated end of the poker again—I screamed and passed out. Just as I blacked out, with my last conscious breath, I saw the men burst into flame. After that, I might as well have died.

I came to in a bed in what I later came to know as the palace infirmary. I would rather have died. The pain was indescribable. My right arm had been tied down under my breasts to hold my collarbone in place. My jaw had been tied to a piece of carved wood to keep it still. They hadn't bothered to do anything with my cheek.

Instinctively, without quite knowing what I did, I nudged at my unanchored cheekbone with my mind until it somehow slipped into place. When it did, that little, tiny bit of relief from the agony in which I drowned dropped me back into unconsciousness. I had no idea that I had used magic. I lacked the level of consciousness to understand what I was doing, I just reacted to the pain. My attempt to ease my pain by quieting the movement of the bones was as simple and unthinking as the way you stop moving a finger when it hurts.

The next time I awakened, someone was attempting to tease a sip of broth down my throat through my abused mouth, making the bones in my jaw grate. I didn't even think about it. I simply fit the grating bones together until they locked into place, and then dropped back into unconsciousness. I didn't knowingly heal myself. I only fit the bones together so they'd stop hurting, but in fitting them, and locking them into place, I allowed them to heal cleanly, without dislocation.

The next time I came to, it was my collarbone giving me fits. Automatically, without the slightest thought, I eased the bones into position, locked them into place, and then allowed myself to drop back into unconsciousness. I woke up coughing. That made my ribs hurt and the muscles in my back feel as if they were being torn apart; I mended one of my ribs as much as I could, following the source of my pain, and then slipped back into nothingness again.

My awareness of my surroundings remained, through those days, virtually nil. The only awareness I had was that I no longer languished in the dungeon. Beyond that, I didn't really care. The healing I wasn't actually aware I was doing took all of what little strength I garnered during my unconsciousness periods. I awakened, corrected the fit of whatever bone hurt me the most in that moment, and then dropped back into the kind darkness.

In those days it was usually coughing that awakened me, coughing and the pain it created. I didn't stay awake long enough to think; if I had, I would have known I had pneumonia. Well, the Crown Prince had deliberately arranged to give me pneumonia, so no one should have been surprised that he had succeeded.

Once all the bones were settled into place and on their way to healing, the worst of the pain eased up, and I became more aware of where I was and the woman taking care of me. Her name, I learned, was Lara, and she was an apprentice healer. She did her best for me, though I gathered she was not particularly knowledgeable, nor at all powerful in her healing talent. She did keep me propped upright, which helped with my lungs somewhat, and she fought to get broth down me every couple of hours, and to keep me swaddled in clean rags, which was a real accomplishment. I found her heroic.

Soon enough, when I could convince her to bring me a commode to sit beside the cot upon which I had been propped semi-upright, I relieved her of the worst of her chores, but it took more days before I could utilize my as yet unrealized healing skills to push the infection from my lungs. At first, I only managed to unload a small amount of the infection my poor lungs were carrying; the process was painful and debilitating. But as my strength grew, I managed to rid myself of more and more of the fluid on my lungs, until at last, I could breathe almost freely. I had no idea how I found myself where I was, and less notion of why. I was too weak even to be suspicious. I simply didn't care.

I don't know quite when I realized that the King himself dozed in the chair beside my bed, giving poor Lara a much needed break. I didn't know why he was there. Everybody knew that King Marc was not like other aristos; his unusual humanity was commonly credited to his Nogaynos mother. It was well known that Nogaynos Mages were not in the common way. It made the King and his mother incalculable, and not just to me.

If he meant to ask me any more questions, he was out of luck; I had no answers for anyone, least of all myself. The next time I awakened Lara was there instead of the king, making me wonder—vaguely—if I had imagined his presence. I coughed up more crap from out of my lungs and went back to sleep as soon as Lara had managed to get more broth down me.

The day came when she started soaking bread in the broth for me to tongue— my jaw had yet to completely mend—and hot chocolate followed. I started to gain enough strength to at least look around the infirmary where I presently lived. The place didn't impress me a whole lot. It was clean, with bunches of herbs and leaves everywhere, dried and fresh—the fresh were being steeped for teas—with a fire in the hearth and a kettle on the hob. The walls and ceiling of the room had been painted an unremarkable white, as had the stone floor.

Windows and a door opened out into a garden where the herbs and vegetables grew, and there was a sink under one of the windows.

I saw nothing startling in that until the King walked through the garden door and smiled at me. Everyone who lived in the city knew who King Marc was, and I was no exception. I stared at him, stunned. Then I thought, they're bringing out the big guns now. And I still didn't know anything. I wondered what they were going to do to me now.

"I know you don't," King Marc said, which told me I'd been thinking aloud.

He sighed. "This should never have happened."

He was right about that. I tried out my voice. It came out scratchy and hoarse, but it worked, even if I had to keep clearing it and coughing now and again.

"I did a lot of thinking, when you first put me in the dungeon, to try to figure it out," I told him, hacking away. "What was going on. I don't believe there is a rebellion. I've never heard anything about one. But if there is something going on, then it is Counsellor Jiden who is mixed up in it, because he is the one who ordered the daggers, and he is the one who drew up the design for them that I copied. So if you mean to torture me some more so you can cover his involvement in whatever it is, don't bother. You might as well just go to killing me. It would be a lot kinder."

Not, I imagined, that he cared about being kind to some lowly smith's apprentice.

"Don't worry about that," King Marc told me. "You just get well. I just came by to check on you and see how you were doing."

And he expected me to believe that? After what his sons had done to me? Either he was mad or I was. Or maybe I was dreaming and he wasn't here, I thought. That made more sense than what he was saying. (In my dream?)

"If you keep getting better," King Marc said, "we'll be moving you to a room of your own in a couple of weeks. Would you like that?"

A room of my own? More likely another cell in the dungeons, I thought. And more interrogations for the amusement of the men conducting them. It wasn't as though they really expected to get anything out of me but what they already had, because I didn't have anything else to tell them.

Very carefully, I didn't glance towards the gardens. I needed clothes and my weapons if I was to get out of here, and some supplies. In a pinch, I could manage without weapons. All I had to do was to get myself back to the smithy. I had weapons and clothing there, and once I had collected those, I could head into the northern forest towards the border with Mahdi and find a place to hide where I could build myself a den to keep me through the winter.

I'd spent every spare minute I could come by in those forests as a youth.

With a few tools from the smithy and my weapons, and some decent clothing, I could get by. I knew how. The smith owed me quite a bit of money, not that he would ever admit of it, and I had made the tools myself.

"Well," King Marc said, patting my leg under the covers (I flinched back away from him. It hurt.) He lifted his hand. "I'll see you tomorrow and check on how you're doing. Maybe bring you some books, if you'd like. I'm told you're well-educated. All right?"

He was asking me? Like I had anything to say about it. I just watched him warily. He moved over to Lara and ducked his head to her, making her flinch away from him almost as much as I had.

"How is she doing, really?" he wanted to know.

"Better than anyone has any right to expect, given all the broken bones and burns and cuts she has," Lara told him.

This time it was King Marc who flinched. I wondered what I looked like now. Maybe I'd better make that visit to the smithy in the middle of the night, I told myself.

"I cannot believe that any man of mine would do such things to anyone, never mind a young girl!" King Marc complained.

Lara all but sneered at him.

"The proof of the pudding," she reminded him. Her voice was flat. She clearly wasn't happy with him. Or, it sounded to me, as if men in general displeased her right then. She didn't tell him that his son had been the ring leader, and that he had done his share of the damage himself, with his own hands. Probably she didn't know it.

"I know," he said. He actually sounded remorseful.

Good actor, I thought. Well, being a good actor would be a good skill for a king to possess, I considered, thinking about it.

# II

# GARVE`

GARVE` REGARDED HIS FATHER ANXIOUSLY, an anxiety he attempted to hide. If his father allowed his brother Nehl to even so much as suspect that he, Garve` had brought the girl's condition to the king's attention, he was as good as dead. He had to act as if he had no idea what his father was about, as if the entire matter was a mystery to him. The appearance of unspotted ignorance was his only hope. Good thing he had long ago perfected the persona he so badly needed now.

Garve` knew he lacked the good looks that characterized both of his brothers, the arrogance and elegance of his older brother and the charm possessed by his younger brother had passed him by. Instead, he looked plain and solid, with big shoulders and hands made for heavy labor—not that he did any. His brothers had long been accepted as the 'brains' of the trio of them. He willingly shouldered the burden of being the 'brawn,' even acknowledging internally that he was far from the most accomplished fighter he had ever seen.

Oh, he could hold his own against either of his brothers—singly—but he was well aware that didn't mean much. If he was hardly better than mediocre with either his fists or a sword, he had to admit that his brothers hardly aspired to mediocrity—mostly because they both thought themselves excellent fighters, having been assured of as much by all their trainers through the years, but almost as much because of their own arrogance. The trainers had been lying through their teeth, and Garve` knew it.

The 'spare' heir, he had been raised in a sort of mental and physical stasis, always ready to take over for his older, more 'gifted' brother, yet never to have or do anything for himself. Like his brothers, he played at fighting, but would never be a general. Being the 'spare' heir had made him an observer at life, and very aware of the limitations under which he lived.

He was given ample money with which to indulge his every want or wish, but he had none of his own. Women laid down for him in order to gain his influence with his father and his brother, but none of them desired him for himself; for them, he was merely a path by which to achieve influence or an alliance with either his father or his brother. Yet somehow, the hopelessness and meaninglessness of his life had not—so far—soured him.

"There is no excuse for what you allowed to happen to that girl," his father said now, to all three of them. "No excuse whatsoever. Even if she had been guilty of something—which she is NOT! It would not have excused what you allowed to happen to her. At least I hope it's no more than that," Marc tempered suddenly. "I would not like to think that you had an actual hand in what was done to that girl."

"No, no," Freddy hurried to assure him, his expression one of unspotted innocence, "we had no idea that would happen to the girl. No idea at ALL!"

"The idea was for her to spend the night in gaol, be a little bit uncomfortable," Nehl added, catching on.

"Make her more willing to talk."

"About what?" King Marc demanded. "How to make fine daggers for Councilor Jiden?"

Garve` didn't like the way his father's head snaked about as he turned to his older son.

"That guttersnipe?" Nehl sneered, from his other side. The expression on his father's face convinced Garve` that he needed to find something to say to defuse the situation before his father and his brother came to physical blows. If that happened, there was no telling what his father would do to his brother. Unlike Nehl, his father worked out seriously with his palace guard, and it showed.

"She is no guttersnipe," Garve` told him thoughtfully, "and only a real artisan could have fashioned those blades."

"And you were wrong that she was dissident," Freddy added, certainly, changing his coat about as if he had not been the first to posit her connection to the nonexistent rebels.

"I don't care," Nehl told them both, but the knife edge the moment had been poised upon eased. "And are you sure those daggers were truly ordered by the Councilor?"

"I'm sure," King Marc assured him. "I've seen the diagrams, in the Councilor's own hand, and the written directions for them—also in the Councilor's own hand. Unlike you," it was the king's turn to do the sneering, "I do my homework."

"So," Nehl returned. "What?"

"So you're going to Quattar," the king told him. "You and Freddy. I'm giving you over to General Meric's charge. Maybe he can make a decent man of you. I have certainly failed at it." He shook his head. "I should never have given you over to Margrete D'Arcy to raise. She turned you into the same kind of arrogant, despicable lout all the rest of the D'Arcy men are." He stared down at his sons enigmatically. "You will stay in Quattar until you can prove you're fit to return. I have no idea whether you can learn to behave better, whether you can become better men. We'll find out."

"Why not Garve`?" Freddy wanted to know, his tones a bit resentful.

"Because Garve` didn't have anything to do with brutalizing that girl," King Marc told him flatly. "That was all on you two." He smiled at them. It was not a reassuring smile. "As I believe I mentioned, I do my homework. I know which of you did what."

The words sounded more threat than otherwise. Nehl stared back at his father, his gaze unflinching. They would see, he considered, who was the better man. Neither one of them saw the light go on behind Freddy's eyes, but Garve` saw it.

What did that mean? he wondered. Freddy had thought of something. What?

He watched as Freddy elbowed Nehl, breaking his concentration.

"When?" Freddy wanted to know. And, at his father's inquisitive glance, he repeated his question. "When do we go?"

"As soon as the trireme gets back from delivering my message to General Meric," King Marc told them. "So start thinking about what you want to take with you. It should be here in a matter of days." He turned his attention from one son to the other. "There won't be a lot of room," he warned them. "Better get busy."

Garve` followed them out of the room, Nehl muttering, mostly to himself, about his father's high-handedness in exiling them to the south. The sound of his growls held defiance. Freddy followed along after him, hurrying his steps to keep up, tugging at his brother's arm to get his attention, like a persistent puppy.

"But this is good," Garve` heard Freddy saying, as he dropped back out of their sight. "If we're gone, they'll never suspect--"

Freddy's voice dropped below Garve`'s ability to hear him. Nehl's response, however, he clearly heard.

"You might have something there," Nehl said. "But how to get hold of Jiden?"

"Leave that to me," Freddy returned firmly, clearly audible around the curve of the corridor.

Garve` slipped away completely.

So there Was some kind of a plot with Councilor Jiden, he thought, as he left his brothers to their own devices. Whatever they were up to, he wanted no part of it. He did an about face in the corridor and headed back to his father's library. For the next month or so, he decided, as he walked, he would live in his father's pocket. When the time came, he wanted to be there to lift his sword in his father's defense.

Freddy and Nehl might consider him big and dumb and not much good for anything, but when his father looked around to see who was there on his side to be counted, Garve` wanted his father to see him standing there with his arm raised in defense. His father had been deeply unhappy when he'd found out about the girl and that unhappiness with his sons had pushed him to the verge of making some very serious decisions about the succession. If he disinherited

Nehl and Freddy. . . well, if he did, Garve` didn't intend, not for one moment, to be disinherited right along with them.

Nehl hadn't noticed it, because Nehl didn't notice much of anything other men said, but with the situation with the Caelian ramping up, it wasn't doing any of King Marc's three sons by his Caelian wife any good. Freddy and Nehl suffered even more from their appearance, not that they ever noticed it. They looked Caelian, so much so, that they would be indistinguishable from any other Caelian warrior, had they dressed the part, but fortunately for them, they affected Amadean court dress and stayed clean-shaven pretty much at all times. The few times Freddy had allowed his beard to grow and joined his two buddies in their habitual slovenly dress, he'd been taken for a Caelian peasant.

Freddy had thought it a great joke at the time, but Garve` had a feeling that if things got much worse on the Caelian border, that Freddy's little jokes might turn dangerous—for everyone. And as for Nehl—well, Garve` had long admitted, if only to himself, that his older brother had a streak of cruel a yard wide running up his back. It did not do to get on Nehl's bad side, and Garve` knew it. Whispers about their uncle, King Bane, indicated that Nehl's cruel streak had been honestly acquired.

Maybe, Garve` admitted, in the privacy of his mind, his father would be right to disinherit Nehl. His brother would not make a good ruler. Dumb or not, even Garve` understood that! Nehl wouldn't be interested in justice, or fairness, or honor, or decency, or any of those things. He wouldn't care about the country or the people in it. Nehl would only care about himself; whatever he wanted, however he wanted it, and why-ever he wanted it. He wouldn't care about women or children, he wouldn't care if any of his people starved, or if they suffered. A king, Garve` thought dimly, ought to care about those things. He needed to care about them. Like his father did.

But then he wondered—did he actually care about any of those things?

Really? The question stayed with him as he reached the library and went in, finding his father there studying a stack of reports cluttering his desk. He sat down and regarded his father thoughtfully.

"They're up to something," he told his father. He didn't have to specify who 'they' were. They both knew who he was talking about.

"Of course they are," King Marc agreed with him. "We'll have to make sure they have the opportunity to confer with Jiden before they leave," he added.

This comment perplexed Garve`. "Why?" he wanted to know.

"It will be much better to control when the coup Nehl and Jiden are planning happens than to allow them to dictate its terms," his father told him. "This way, we know it won't happen until Freddy and Nehl are gone, and that gives us a little time to prepare. And, since we know it will happen not too long after they're gone, we won't have to wait for them to strike, day after dragging day until we lose our edge and our awareness."

Garve` considered it and decided that his father knew what he was about. He nodded.

"How long will you make them stay in the south?" he wanted to know. "Years, if I can manage it," King Marc returned. "I certainly don't want them here. It will be a lot harder for Nehl to stir up trouble down in the south. They have enough trouble of their own without his."

Garve` reflected on that.

"Nehl won't like it," he concluded. His father shrugged.

"I don't like Nehl. We're stuck with each other." He tipped his head. "What about Freddy?" he wanted to know.

"Freddy can always amuse himself," Garve` assured him. "He'll have Bardons and D'Arcys eating out of his hand, give him time."

"No doubt," his father frowned. "There will be a Bardon and a D'Arcy in on this attempt at a coup," he added.

Garve` raised his brows. "You think so?"

"Of course. Who do you think murdered your mother?"

"Bardons?" Garve` gasped. "D'Arcys?"

"Yes."

"But—" Garve` tried to protest, lost the impetus. Things started making sense to him. It felt sort of as if he had been stumbling through the murk when suddenly a tree emerged from the fog, givin g him something to hold on to.

"Yes," his father said again, reading his face.

Garve thought back over the years. He'd been eight when his mother died.

Nehl had been ten, Freddy barely five. "Nehl knows?" he only half asked.

"Yes, I think he does," his father nodded.

"And that's why he never really liked Margrete," Garve` commented wonderingly.

"Probably," his father allowed. Then he frowned. "He liked what she taught you boys well enough."

"Yes," Garve` agreed, because his brother had. Then he added, "Nehl likes being kowtowed to." His brother liked flatterers and toadeaters, Garve` had to admit, if only to himself.

"And that's why he'll never make a decent king," his father pointed out. "Good men, decent men, don't kowtow to anyone."

Garve` wasn't so sure of that, but he didn't challenge his father. "What are you going to do about the girl?" he asked, instead.

"Keep her until she's fully healed," his father told him. "As long as she likes. She won't have an easy time of it with those facial scars, and we owe her."

Garve` considered that. He suspected his father was right about the scars, but he wasn't sure that he agreed that they owed her. After all, it had been Nehl and Freddy who had scarred her, not he or his father. And, then again, what was she but some nothing of a girl? Perhaps not the guttersnipe that Nehl had called her, but certainly not a person of note.

"For a long time," King Marc mused, "I've known that something was very wrong with Nehl, but I didn't want to face it." He shook his head. "And she paid for my cowardice. My sins. And because she paid, I can no longer deny what my son has become. It is my duty to my country to make certain Nehl never comes to the throne." He said again, "I owe her."

All right, if that was the way he felt about it, Garve` thought, then let him owe her. He shrugged.

"Then settle a manor on her somewhere. Give her servants. Find her a husband. Whatever."

His father tipped his head to him.

"I don't suppose you'd care to marry her," he offered.

"Me?" Garve` knew he sounded shocked. He was shocked.

"If she'll have you," his father maundered on, as if oblivious to his astonishment.

To Garve` such a concept was unthinkable. No woman found him unacceptable; all the daughters of his father's privy council and of the noble class sought him out and prostituted themselves to him. They curried his favor, debased themselves before him, courted his attention, tried to seduce him and in every way they could imagine, attempted to inveigle themselves into matrimony with him. Women flattered him; they didn't tell him home truths about himself and they certainly didn't deny him.

"Or perhaps I'll ask her myself," his father mused on, increasing his amazement. "Maybe she wouldn't mind an old geezer like me."

Maybe she wouldn't. The idea burst, in full bloom, into his mind. Garve` stumbled into speech.

"Maybe she wouldn't," he fumbled. Added, clumsily, "You're not an old geezer."

"I will be to her," his father assured him. "She is still very young. But," he added, musingly, "we shall see, shall we?" Leaving Garve` speechless.

# III

# FREDDY

"AH, COUNCILOR JIDEN, JUST THE man I wanted to see," Nehl greeted, jerking Freddy out of his thoughts. He stared, horrified, as his brother tossed an arm over the older man's narrow shoulders and guided him into an ante-chamber without a by-your-leave, other than a significant glance over his shoulder for Freddy. If anybody saw them--!

But no one appeared to. Freddy closed the door and stood by it with his back against it so no one would come in, watching their co-conspirator carefully.

Councilor Jiden's weaselly face looked as horrified as Freddy felt. "About that bridge proposal of yours," Nehl began.

"What about it?" Jiden quavered.

Freddy had a notion that the old man had just realized that he had a tiger by the tail and the perception of his error shocked him. He had thought, Freddy recognized, that he could control Nehl. More fool him. No one controlled Nehl. They just thought they did. If they were stupid enough.

"It's getting close to time to making a start on it," Nehl informed the old man. "We ought to be heading out on a trireme for Quattar in a couple of weeks. I suggest you give us two more weeks to get out on the open sea before you start laying the foundations. That ought to work out about right."

The old Councilor's weaselly face squinched up in thought. "Oh, yes?" he more asked than answered.

"Oh, yes," Nehl assured him. "And make certain you take care of Del and Hubare when you do," he warned Jiden. "I'll take care of Margrete, myself, but I want Hubare's and Del's heads on pikes before I get back." And he slapped the old man on the back, none too gently.

Jiden's eyes flared as he realized Nehl was threatening him, however subtly.

This surprised him a little. Nehl was seldom subtle. He didn't need to be.

"Four weeks," he repeated, more to himself than to either Nehl or Freddy.

"And five days," Nehl reminded him.

Jiden repeated it, his narrow, pointed little nose twitching.

"Don't forget," Nehl warned him, in pretended bonhomie that was, in itself, a threat.

"No," Jiden made the only response he could. "No, of course not. We'll be ready."

"You'll do it," Nehl assured him firmly.

"Of course," Jiden agreed, and, as Freddy opened the door, hurried out. Freddy closed the door after him.

"Think he'll do it?" he asked Nehl.

"He'd better," Nehl said grimly. His smile was not reassuring. "He can always take the other old man's place, if necessary." This time he clapped

Freddy on the back. "C'mon," he invited. "We'd better start getting packed up. "Two weeks to departure, remember?"

Freddy frowned to himself all the way back to their rooms. It was a good thing they weren't in danger of being attacked; Freddy wasn't paying any attention to their surroundings. He just walked beside his brother, hardly seeing where they were going, not that his brother was paying any more attention than he was. Freddy didn't understand it.

Oh, he knew where they had gone wrong, but that was what he didn't understand. The girl was nothing but an orphan, and a Nogaynos orphan at that. Why did his father care about what they did with her?

Or to her, either, when it came right down to it? They were princes. Margrete had taught them that, taught them their unfettered impunity to do whatever they felt like doing to whomever they felt like doing it to. It wasn't, after all, as if the law applied to them!

As far as the plot to take over the government of the country from their father, why, he didn't worry about that. He and Nehl wouldn't be implicated in that! Not now that they had been sent to Quattar. Jiden would take care of it while they were traveling the high seas and no wind of blame would ever attach to them. All they had to do was to wait for the news to reach them in Quattar and then come back to the palace and take over. And get rid of Jiden, of course.

Freddy already had plans in place for trumped up evidence to be presented to the Council implicating Jiden in the coup and the evidence had already been planted. If it hadn't come to light by the time they got back from Quattar, all Freddy had to do was to see that it did. It wasn't as if Nehl wasn't the rightful inheritor of the crown. It would be a simple matter of 'the king is dead, long live the king'!

Freddy glanced over at his brother. Nehl could be difficult upon occasion, and no one knew better than Freddy how dangerous he could be. Well, his brother Nehl's particular combination of stupidity and stubbornness always provided the possibility of danger, but Freddy had been handling him for years without getting burned. He'd manage it once again.

Nehl had lost himself in thought, a rare condition for him. He wasn't well accustomed to introspection. It didn't come naturally to him, and he hadn't been trained to it, either. He seldom actually thought. He had been, though he wouldn't have called it that, programed to respond in certain ways to certain words and certain situations. Raise a sword against him and he would fight. Shove papers in front of him and he would read them and sign them. Well, sign them, anyway. Read them? Maybe. If he felt like it. He believed his country held rebel factions because he had been raised by the D'Arcy family to believe in the possibility of rebels, whether they existed or not (the D'Arcys were nothing if not paranoid) and since Freddy had been raised with him, by the same people, he knew what buttons to push.

In Nehl's view, the one both he and Freddy had been taught, kings did not admit to doing wrong. They didn't say sorry, they didn't take responsibility and they didn't, for the most part, change things. It would have never occurred to him to punish the man who had tortured an innocent girl, and he never admitted, even to himself, what he had done when he had tortured her. It never occurred to him that his father might have sought to bring him to justice for his crimes.

Neither would it ever have occurred to Nehl to attempt to identify the man who had tortured her. He had never looked for the man who had finished what he had started, he did not separate himself from the man who had done as he suggested. He did not order that man taken up and imprisoned for his crimes, did not, in fact, do anything at all about him, because he did not think of him at all. The man was simply extraneous to him. Thus he had no idea that the man was missing, or that the men who had joined in on the torture with him were missing as well. If he had given any thought to the man or his associates, he would have assumed that the man had run away, knowing that he had done wrong and fearing retribution for his wrong-doing. Freddy, who had given all this some thought, assumed the same.

If the dungeon master had said something to him regarding the man's absence, he had forgotten it. The man simply wasn't important to him. Neither was the dungeon master, whom he had forgotten along with the rest of the torturers. Theoretically, Freddy knew that torture was wrong in general, and that it was particularly abhorrent when used on innocents, but that knowledge lacked any meaning for him. Oh, he knew it had upset his father, but he simply did not care about it, nor did he care about some young girl, regardless of whether she was his buddies' foster sister or not. She simply didn't matter to him.

Well, really, no one outside of his immediate family was of any significant importance to him. Even the nobles on his privy council were only important to him within the scope of their functions. Replacing one of the Council might inconvenience him (well, not him. Maybe the country, and maybe his father or Nehl, but not him) and he liked a couple of them, but he had no deep ties to any of them. He didn't actually care about any of them, even the couple of them he liked. Pretty much everybody was expendable, from his standpoint, well, other than his brothers.

Freddy felt no remorse for what he had done or what he had set in motion; in his view the girl's torture had been a regrettable mistake (not that he regretted it, he didn't) that shouldn't have happened. It made him look bad to his father. He didn't like looking bad to his father. He found it difficult to accept that she was innocent.

He had decided, right back in the beginning, to present her as a rebel as the best way of furthering Nehl's and his schemes, and being held up by his father as being wrong about it stuck in his craw, so to speak. For his purposes, reality was what he said it was, and he said she was guilty, so in his mind, she was, and nothing anyone else said, particularly her, made any significant difference as to how he felt. He didn't like it when his father and Garve` kept saying the girl was innocent. He accepted it grudgingly, because they held to it and thus he had to, but their attitude grated on him.

His acceptance was only a surface veneer and he was aware that Nehl had difficulty even attempting that much. How Nehl felt about the girl and how he treated her would always be based on his inner conviction that he was superior to her and that she was guilty of being a rebel, merely because he said so.

Freddy understood that. He knew that he could use it. That he would use it.

Judiciously. Because ever since he had tortured the girl, his older brother had been coming unraveled, in ways that Freddy didn't understand. It worried him.

Nehl had always been something of a loose cannon. He'd never been what anyone could call trustworthy. He had a cruel streak and a cowardly streak, all intertwined in his psyche in odd ways but Freddy had grown up with him. He'd always understood that there were ways to manipulate his brother, yet times when it was better to go along with him, because he wouldn't be influenced by much of anything.

Now he felt those ways changing. He didn't like it. Those changes boded ill for the future, unless he could get hold of them and use them as reins in guiding the monster that lived at the center of his brother's being. So far, he hadn't managed it, and that boded ill for the future unless he could catch hold of those reins' flapping ends and make use of them.

Now he looked forward to their time on the trireme and Quattar with anticipation mixed with real apprehension. He wasn't at all sure how Nehl would react to Quattar, with its opulent, brightly colored bazaars, its rich food, balmy air, redolent of spices and sea kelp, its lush vegetation and ornate mansions. In Quattar, they'd be in the territory of the Bardons and the D'Arcys, aristos who used their people as if they were slaves and treated their peers as if they were their servants.

Nehl already despised the D'Arcys for murdering their mother. What would their aristocratic privilege drive him to do? How many of Nehl's few inhibitions would the sensual, passionate air of Quattar release? What would the new tensions Freddy more felt than saw drive his brother to do? He didn't like the speculative way Nehl looked at the people around him, as if he was wondering what their screams would sound like, or what kind of noise their bones would make when they broke. Freddy didn't like those thoughts. What if Nehl decided to make him scream, to break his bones? He might. Freddy had a very bad feeling that nothing could be put past his brother now.

Freddy felt foreboding settle over him as he let himself into his room in the palace and faced the task of deciding what to take with him on the journey.

Even by sea, it was a long way to Quattar.

# IV

# KING MARC

MARC EYED HIS SECOND SON with interest as he re-entered the library. He looked to be scowling to himself over something or other. He wondered what had furrowed his son's brow so deeply. The boy, as he still thought of his second son, despite his attainment of his majority and then some, gave some indications of a modicum of intelligence in his handling of the girl from the dungeons. It was the first light of brains the boy had ever evinced. It intrigued him and gave him hope for the boy.

Freddy was supposed to be the spy, but it had been Garve` who had understood the implications of the order of the daggers by Councilor Jiden. And, he mustn't forget, it had been Garve` who had the courage to go over Nehl's head to save Vere, though he had to know that his older brother was vindictive and would surely find a way to get his own back if he ever learned of it. Too, he had also shown the courage to bring the matter of his brother's involvement with Jiden to his attention.

These were not qualities his son had ever displayed before. Were they meaningful? Did they hint at deep waters at the center of his middle son's character? Or were they merely a momentary flash in the pan, meaningless in the general order of things?

He tried out alternative solutions in his mind. Maybe there was hope for at least one of his sons. Maybe something could be made of Garve`, if he could find a way to do it subtly enough. If he couldn't,

Marc admitted, just to himself, he might just get the boy killed. His brothers were certainly murderous enough!

He turned his thoughts to his oldest son. He had no more illusions regarding Nehl. He had lost them when he had learned that Nehl had ordered a young girl starved and tortured. If he had to take the boy's life with his own hand, he had to make certain that Nehl did not succeed him on the throne. No torturer could be allowed to be the leader of a country, never mind a son who plotted the murder of his father.

If the boy had just shown the least bit of remorse, he cried within the confines of his own heart. If he'd even admitted that he had done wrong! But he hadn't. And he wouldn't, if he hadn't done it by now. Marc admitted, in his own mind and heart, the monster of selfishness, arrogance and dishonor that his son was. It broke his heart, but his eldest son was what he was, a compendium of qualities no leader should possess.

That was what you got, he feared, from a Caelian mother. Barena had been a good woman, he reminded himself, but her brother—well, the less said about her brother, the Caelian king, the better. Blood would tell, he admitted, if just to himself, and Barena's bloodlines had been all bad, inbred as she had been, of brothers who raped their sisters and cousins who married their cousins. But oh, she had been beautiful. . . her sons took after her in that, he had to admit. Or at least, two of them had. He glanced over at Garve`.

"Meric will have his hands full with Nehl, when he gets to Quattar," he allowed. "I fear Nehl will not be happy to be exiled there."

"I don't know why," Garve` objected. "Some would say that Quattar is a more vibrant city than we are. They are noted for their highly spiced food, their fabrics, their music, theater and dancing and their beautiful women. We are noted for long, cold winters and Temple services."

"Some would," Marc allowed. "And in many ways, they would be right.

But the delights you catalog, music and dancing, food and beautiful women— would you say they are the kinds of things that Nehl would appreciate? Nehl has always struck me as an essentially cold character."

"That is a good point," Garve` admitted. "I've never known him to care about women, beautiful or otherwise."

Garve` spoke the truth, and carefully, at that, but he'd buried a sting in the tail of that truth. Nehl did not care about women; he was not the kind of Prince who cared to be charming. He would probably not marry willingly, and might very well not be inclined to sire an heir for the throne.

"What about academia?" his father wanted to know. "I know that according to Margrete, none of you boys had any facility for any intellectual pursuits, but was she right? I've come to question everything she had to say about you boys."

"Well, with the right teacher, and in the right disciplines, Nehl might have taken to the sciences," Garve` found himself confiding. "But Margrete never had any idea who or what the right teacher or discipline might be and she wasn't interested in science herself. I don't suppose she considered it quite a gentlemanly avocation."

"What about friends?" his father inquired. "Are there any friends he might have to keep him occupied or guide his mind and his hand to more beneficial pursuits than he has so far engaged himself in?"

"We had few friends," Garve` admitted. "Bardons and D'Arcys, of course, but ever since he learned that D'Arcy's were involved in the murder of our mother, Nehl has been embittered towards all the D'Arcy's, and while your bringing the elder Hubare and Dellin to justice for her death helped, it did not really ameliorate his feelings towards the younger Hubare or Dellin. He wants them dead."

"But the Bardons?" King Marc persisted.

"Nehl despises them because they do nothing about their people being taken by the Caelian." Garve` shrugged. "He feels the same about the Jidens, hiding behind their Mahdi mercenaries."

"Well, I cannot blame him for that," his father returned. "Bardons are all the same. Hiding out on their lands, never about when anyone is needed to stand up and be counted, never mind fight, and the Jidens worse. And always with the excuses, like their fathers and grandfathers before them."

Marc sneered, making Garve` wonder if his father sneered at him when he was not around. After all, he had been as Bardon, hiding behind his position as the spare heir, never standing up for anything, or anyone, not that he would ever admit as much, even to himself.

"And Jiden?" Garve` continued down the roll call. "Nehl would seem to have a connection there, although Jidens are not wholly of the south."

"Weasels and ferrets, every one of them," King Marc dismissed them.

"Worthless in a fight, but always ready with a knife to stab you in the back. Fitting, that he had those daggers made for his coup. What is a coup but treachery and ambush committed by sneaking traitors?" He shook his head. "Nehl would choose to involve himself with such men."

"It wouldn't surprise me to find that D'Arcys and Bardons have joined them," Garve` mentioned to him thoughtfully.

"D'Arcys!" Marc scoffed. "Sticks up their butts and empty heads," he categorized. "Married nothing but their own cousins and Bardons' for ten generations for snobbery and money and land and every one of 'em thinks they're somehow better than anyone else because of it instead of the imbeciles they are." He frowned. "The current representative of the family stands around and stares into space through every gathering. He's so stupid he suffers boredom acutely, rather than holding an amicable conversation with anyone he considers below himself on the social ladder he and his family made up out of their own arrogance and spite."

"So you don't think they're a part of Jiden's plot?" Garve` demanded.

"They might be," King Marc allowed. "They wanted the throne when they killed your mother. They had it all planned out. Margrete would marry me while I was still grieving and offer to take care of you, then, as soon as I crowned her my queen, her father and brother would kill me and place Margrete on the throne as regent. Then, one by one, you and your brothers would be killed and the D'Arcys would take over the kingdom."

"What happened?" Garve` wanted to know.

"D'Arcys are stupid," his father told him. "And while I might have been stupid enough to marry Margrete to give you boys a mother when I was half crazy with grief, I'm not stupid enough to crown a D'Arcy queen. They pushed, I got stubborn, and then I got smart. End of Hubare and Del." Marc squinted off into the distance thoughtfully. "They'd be the natural choice for accomplice to Jiden," he commented.

"You say the D'Arcys are stupid," Garve` pursued his own thought. "You think we might be able to take advantage of that?"

"We might even do better," his father observed, equally thoughtfully. "They might actually know something." He mused over the thought for long moments. "The current D'Arcy Councilor is both arrogant and stubborn, as well as stupid.

His arrogance keeps him from making friends with those he feels are below him, and his stubbornness keeps him from admitting either his stupidity to himself or his boredom for what it is. We need to figure out a way to use that."

"He speaks to me," Garve` observed.

"Of course he does," his father caught him up on it. "According to his pantheon, you're his better. He'll want to curry favor with you."

"I've never noticed it," Garve` complained.

"No?" King Marc commented. "Well, perhaps he's too stupid to do it well enough for you to notice."

The thought was a revelation to Garve`. He thought back over the man's stilted, awkward speech and considered that his father might very well be right. Huh.

"We'll find a way," King Marc assured him confidently. "Let's have Laren in and have a nice little talk about security."

"Yes," Garve` agreed with him, "I think that's a very good idea. How many men do you think Jiden has working for him?"

"I shouldn't think there could be too many," his father returned thoughtfully. "Secrets are hard to keep for any length of time, and the more people in on the secret, the harder it is for them to keep it."

Huh, Garve` thought, as his father sent for Laren.

"There will be Jiden's household guard—he's been adding to them lately— and D'Arcys and their household guard, at the least," his father calculated, returning to his seat at his desk. "So a hundred men, anyway. Maybe a hundred and fifty, with the men Jiden's been adding on the sly. Who knows how many men he has by now? And there will some of the city guards, the more brutal and sadistic of them will work for a change of administration because they know that in the disorder of the changeover, they'll be able to bully and brutalize at will, at least for a time. And the bullies with half a brain will know that they will be able to get away with a lot more of their sadistic behavior with either a Jiden or a D'Arcy on the throne."

"Throw a few of them in the dungeons?" Garve` proposed.

"Might not be a bad idea," his father praised. He settled back into his seat, thoughtfully. "Might have the city guard captains in to talk to while we're at it," he mused.

"Would that be unusual?"

"Not if we have a good excuse," King Marc told him.

"But what?"

"We could ask them about unrest," his father proposed. "Ask them if they have seen or heard anything." He grinned swiftly. "We could blame it on the Crown Prince."

Garve` laughed at the idea of making such use of his brother's crochets. "He is convinced there's a rebellion brewing somewhere."

King Marc shook his head.

"That's just a smoke screen," he said. "Something he made up to excuse the build-up of Jiden's and D'Arcy's household guards."

Laren paused at the door, a trim, fit man with hair greying at the edges, dressed in well-used fighting leathers he wore like a second skin. One couldn't have pigeon-holed him precisely as handsome, but he came very close. Perhaps if he'd worn a conservative suit and hadn't looked quite so serviceable--

"How did you know about that?" he wanted to know. King Marc swung around in his chair to greet him.

"It's been going on for some time," he added. "Come sit down. I'm sending Nehl and Freddy away whenever a trireme becomes available to transport them, and as soon as they're well enough away to claim plausible deniability, I've no doubt Councilor Jiden, with D'Arcys' help, will be staging a coup."

"You don't say," Laren retorted, sagging a little at the knees as he dropped into a chair. "Who told you?"

"Nehl, in a way," Marc told him. "The boy's not the brightest branch in the fire."

"No," Laren agreed, "well," he frowned, "you have any idea how many men they might have, between them?"

"Figure two hundred," King Marc estimated for him. "At least. We've been considering which men in the guards might have been suborned by their men.

We've room in the dungeons to lock some of them up."

"That's a thought," Laren allowed. He subsided into a brown study. "Anybody in the guards you have in mind?" he wanted to know.

"Who's your worst bully?" Marc asked him.

"Your son," Laren laughed, and then sobered. "Oh," he said slowly, then. "I see what you mean."

"We'll have to work on choke points," King Marc remarked. "And add some security measures."

"Right," Laren agreed.

"Do we have two hundred men?" Garve` asked him.

"We have twice two hundred," Laren assured him. "The problem is not the number of men on each side, it's the number of men on the inside."

"Treachery," Garve` all but growled. He hadn't thought of it that way before. Now he faced it, and the idea raised the hackles at the back of his neck.

"Exactly," Laren agreed with him. "How soon--?"

"At least three weeks, and more likely four," King Marc assured him. "Nehl won't want it to come off until he is safely away on the high seas. My son," he pointed out to Laren, "is an errant coward. He has to have even a young girl chained to a chair so he can torture her with his own hand."

Laren winced.

"Well," he pointed out, in his turn, "most bullies are errant cowards. The one goes with the other."

"I know," King Marc acceded grimly. "So figure two weeks and a couple of days, at most, once they've sailed."

Laren stood up.

"I'll do the best that I can," he assured his king.

"I know you will," Marc returned. He stood up, too. "Bring me the plan, once you've got it made up," he urged. "We'll go over it together."

"Right," Laren said, and took his leave.

# V

# VERE

TO MY ASTONISHMENT, WHEN THE time came, the prince moved me to my new room himself.     He brought me boys' clothing, practical stuff, loose trousers, shirt and tunic, in which to make the trip from the infirmary to a guest room almost directly above it. Nothing above my station, which was apparently that of an indigent urchin, in someone's estimation. No cloak, though, not that I'd need one now in the midst of First Harvest.

Climbing the stairs almost finished me, after more than a month in an infirmary bed, but I understood why they put me up a floor; it would make it more difficult for me to escape. They were careful to keep anything that could be used as a weapon from me as well, which made sense to me. They meant me harm, after all. They wouldn't want me to have anything with which to defend myself. I might hurt one of their grown men. That wouldn't do.

They checked on me daily, tag teaming me. King Marc came to see me in the morning, after I had dressed and eaten, bringing me books to keep me occupied. The ploy was more effective than he knew. I devoured everything he brought me, particularly the histories.

The King struck me as a comfortable man, large, but fit for his age, and even more for his station, his dark hair threaded here and there with a touch of grey, his hazel eyes looking darker from a distance than they did up close. He had an easy manner, not seeming to be given to wearing silks or laces, but comfortable robes over leather trousers and unobtrusive boots. A sword usually hung from his sash, with a poniard to match, and I wondered just how good he might be with them. I feared he would need to be quite good in the very near future.

We went for walks in the Palace's lush gardens, as soon as I was able, and discussed the state of the country, while at the same time avoiding the topic of Jiden's probable plot to take over the monarchy. The people of the Palace city were, for the most part, well to do, with only women and children and the elderly truly poor, making a real rebellion unlikely. The city was both a trade and manufacturing center, with wide streets, numerous shops, open air markets, and homes where cottage industries thrived. Well, like my foster father's smithy.

In the villages and out on the farms, the situation was pretty much the same, with the situations of women and children truly only dire in places where the men in charge failed in their responsibilities to the lowest and the least.

Decent men, honorable men, stopped other men from abusing women and children, inflicting themselves upon them as parasites. Indecent, dishonorable men allowed other men to do whatever they would with impunity.

Unfortunately, there were too many of the latter and too few of the former, but such was life in a patriarchy. As far as other countries went, well, I had little experience of them. What little I had learned of such places, I had been taught by the Temple, but now, given the books the king offered to me to keep me busy, that slight frame of reference had expanded.

Nogaynos had been said to be an idyllic place, both matriarchal and matrilineal in culture, a place where men were not allowed to abuse women and children and where, because of that, only men who chose to be had been poor. King Marc indicated that he thought one of the reasons that the Caelian had decided to go to war against Nogaynos had been that they were patriarchal, and like all fully patriarchal systems, committed to enslaving women and girl children, whatever pretty words they used to cover their villainy. Add that the women of Nogaynos had been strong, particularly magically, and the Caelian's toleration of them would have, of necessity, been limited.

King Marc made me a more than tolerable tutor, in those days, bringing me books in the infirmary, history books, books of historical adventures, and biographies, along with medical treatises, herbologies, geographies and even ancient tales of old. The ploy, to keep me in the palace, to bind me to my recuperation, worked well. I loved the books. I devoured them all, and we 'discussed' them while we walked around the flowerbeds and I gathered strength.

I thought I understood what he was doing. King Marc thought he was 'turning' me to his cause. He had his 'spare' heir dine with me more nights than not, to talk over what was happening in the court and about the history I had learned each day. He was preparing me to 'escape' one way or another, I suspected, so that I would go back to the 'rebel' companions I had and, if I would not spy for him on them, at least I might try to change their minds about the monarchy. He could always have his men bring me back in and batter me again to make me tell them anything I had learned from these imaginary rebel companions during my period of 'freedom'.

I knew that when I left the palace, I had to escape in reality. I had to go on my own terms and in my own time, because I had to be sure I had the strength and the stamina to get entirely away, but I also knew that I had to escape before Jiden's coup. It would be a delicate balancing act, that timing, I knew. The longer I waited, the more fit and able I would be to make a successful escape, but every day carried me closer to the chaos of Councilor Jiden's coup, and I did not want to be here when he struck. I could expect no mercy from Jiden's crew, that had been made very clear to me, and once Jiden had struck, well, King Marc would have no more reason to show me mercy, either. Then again, once men started killing, anyone could fall under the sword. I needed to be well away before the fighting started, and well I knew it.

I wanted to make my way—eventually--to Nogaynos. The histories had helped me to decide that. What I had learned in the geographies would help me to get there, too, I thought, and if I had the good fortune to find a book of maps, well, it would behoove me to copy as many of those as I could. And what I had learned about the Mahdi and Nogaynos would, as well, so I would be well- advised to learn everything I could manage to between now and the night I left.

But for now, I had to make the king think that his strategy was working, that I didn't know that I was just another one of those expendable pieces in that board game he was teaching me. He thought he had important work for me to do. I knew I had important work to do, but I knew it wasn't the same work he had in mind.

For one thing, I knew I wasn't expendable. Well, nobody is expendable to themselves, in their own heart. And sure, I would have willingly died, hanging from that beam, if only to escape the agony those men had so enjoyed inflicting on me. If I was right, if I wasn't deluded because of the agony I was in, and at that last instant of my consciousness, magic had exploded from me in flames, consuming the men who had entertained themselves with my pain, then I was glad. Those men had needed to die for the good of everyone, not just me. The question remained. Did I have magic?

I didn't dare to ask the king for books on magic. But I could read about Nogaynos, the land of magic. And I could make inferences from the references to magic in the stories of Nogaynos. I could think about fire. About how it answered to me at the forge. About how it licked around my hands and sparked towards my face, yet never, somehow, burned me. And I could think about that last moment in the dungeon, when I had seen the flames piercing the bodies of the men who tortured me in that instant before I lost consciousness.

Sometimes, sitting cocooned from the chill of the evening breeze out on the balcony outside my room, reading by lamplight as twilight closed in around the garden, I could hear the king's voice, talking to his middle son. Sometimes I could even hear his son speaking in return. Sometimes they even talked about me, and I listened, of course. Whatever they said, it might be important. If I didn't listen, how would I know?

The one night, I heard the King say, "She is more intelligent than you boys."

This seemed to me to be a curious thing to say, and I wasn't the only one perplexed by this. Garve` seemed to be as bemused by this statement as I.

"Why do you say that, sir?" he wanted to know, his voice carefully respectful, as befit one speaking to his king.

"She has read a dozen books in the last week," the king told his son, sounding as bemused as Garve`. "Books I spent all of one year trying to get you and your brothers to read. And she actually understood them. "

"Well," Garve` returned, sounding thoughtful, "we didn't actually read them."

"I know," the King told him. "But that's the heart of the matter really—she understood why she should read them."

"You like her," Garve` almost accused him.

"Of course I do," the king answered him. "Are you jealous?" He sounded curious over the question.

"No, but Nehl will be," Garve` responded.

I had hardly met Nehl, and I knew Garve` was right. "That may be a problem," the King said, reflectively.

"Oh, no, you are not thinking of having Nehl marry her," Garve` said, aghast.

Well, I could understand his horror at the idea. My cheek and jaw might be straight, but my nose wasn't, any longer, and my face was scarred. I had seen my reflection in the still waters of the garden's pond. King Marc had made sure I had no mirrors in which to assess my new face, but the pond's still waters had shown me enough to guess at the extent of the damage.

I had a nasty burn scar from near the corner of my eye running down the side of my face, barely missing my cheek, to my chin, where the first touch of the hot poker had left a noticeable dent. The scar from a knife blade ran down from just under my ear, missing my jugular by a hair's breadth to head south to my once broken collarbone. Another scar ran from my hairline towards my eye—he'd been aiming at my eye and kept missing—and newly white wings made steaks against the darkness of my hair in several places. And every one of those scars gaped red and angry and raw as they crisscrossed my marred skin.

Those scars, the ones readily seen, were just the tip of the iceberg. My wrists had been ringed with scars, my arms laced with them. My breasts, my belly and my legs had all been marked, even the backs of my hands. Some of the marks were from a blade, and some of those would heal to the point where they would be unobtrusive—in time. Others—particularly those from the tip end of the poker—those would never, truly, be unobtrusive.

Men would never want me. Men wanted young girls, pretty girls, untouched girls, and as those scars told anyone who could see, I was no longer young, I had never been pretty, and I had very thoroughly, been touched. I had ceased to be marriageable the hour and the day that I had entered the dungeon; any hope I might have had of ever living an ordinary life had died the moment those stone shadows had fallen over me. But all that said, the horror I heard in Garve`'s voice at the very idea of his brother's marriage to me blossomed ten-fold in my own heart.

I would kill him or die myself before I would marry the Crown Prince who had put those scars on my body. I would, if necessary, pull the kingdom down around my ears, and set it to flame, first, and I had an idea, born of that instant in the torture chamber, that I might very well be able to learn how to do just that.

"My boy, I would kill your brother with my own hands before I would let him even so much as come near this child again, never mind marry her," the King told him, and he actually sounded as if he meant it, not that I believed him, not even for the merest fraction of a second. Nehl was his son, and I was nothing and no one to him.

He was up to something, but what, I couldn't guess.

"Not that she would ever have him," the King continued. "I know enough of what happened to her to know that your brother was responsible for her condition—and that she knows he is responsible for it. I would not be surprised," the king added heavily, "if that child doesn't know your brother better, at this point, than either one of us ever will."

"I know he gave orders," Garve` told him. "I know he ordered her starved. I know he ordered her to be deprived of food and water. I know he ordered the window opened upon her, and I know he ordered her interrogated."

"Jacob told me as much," the king admitted. He sighed. "You brother does not like women," he said sadly.

"Neither of my brothers likes women," Garve` pointed out practically—and truthfully. "Freddy likes women to use; he doesn't like them as people. That's why he has sent so many of them to their deaths on the Caelian border to supposedly spy for him. They manage to send him a letter or two—before they disappear."

The King sighed again.

"I've been afraid of that," he said. Then he said, meditatively, "But she would make such a good queen."

"Nehl," Garve` pointed out carefully, "is the Crown Prince."

"Yes, of course," the king responded. Then he added, in a complete non-sequitur "You know, doing the right thing, being honorable and decent, is often the best and quickest path to any decent goal."

Philosophically, I thought, his point was interesting but what it had to do with the discussion at hand, I could not, for the life of me, figure out. I had received the impression that Garve`, so very, very carefully, had set himself to undermine his older brother, but what King Marc was getting at, I did not know. I listened, thinking hard, wondering if this conversation meant that I needed to be escaping, and soon. Then the King offered another of his complete non-sequiturs.

"You know we are at war."

He was right, I thought, the raids along the Caelian border coming to mind immediately. I remembered the history I had read. We might not know that they were using poison air at this point, but I suspected that they were, only this time the air didn't kill, it only drugged, making it easier for the Caelian forces to overwhelm each village's resistance without threatening the lives of the invaders. When they had used the poison air to attack Nogaynos, as many Caelian had died of its effects as Mages. In fact, it might very well be that it had killed more Caelian than Mages. Not that anyone knew for certain just what had transpired.

Many of the Mages of Nogaynos, as well as the not-Mages, had fled during the diaspora, and those who had fled didn't know what had happened after they left. From what little we knew, few of those who had fled had returned to their own country, and those who had did not communicate with those who hadn't. Well, they had not the means. They might write letters, but as far as we knew, no one remained to carry them from Nogaynos across the wide plains to Amadea, and if Amadea sent explorers to Nogaynos, few of them came back.

Over the last nearly two hundred years, Nogaynos had faded into obscurity, a mystery to any who remembered it.

Oh, there were legends of course, but no one paid them any mind. No one believed them. They were just stories, fiction, pretend histories of long ago and far away, fit only for the amusement of small children. Nogaynos had existed; that was a fact. Whether it still did—or not—that was conjecture. But right now, to me, that conjecture offered hope, and perhaps a future. One I was inclined, in my desperation, to grab onto with both hands. It was all the hope I had.

"If you had read the history of the war the Caelian made upon Nogaynos, you would understand what is happening now," the King told his son, lessoning him a bit didactically. "This is no time to be creating enemies. We need to be making friends, now, in particular, we need to be showing the Mahdi that we are friends worth having. We need to show them that we are steadfast and true, that we are decent, honorable and trustworthy. Do you think your brother showed any of that in his treatment of the foster sister of his brother's friends?"

"No, sir." Garve''s answer came promptly. He didn't even seem to have to think about it.

"What do you think the Mahdi would feel, if they knew what the Crown Prince had done to her?"

"They might not want to ally with us against the Caelian, sir."

"Oh, they're pretty much over a barrel there," the King told him. "They'd hold their noses and stand with us against the Caelian. They know that if they don't, that sooner or later they will be facing the Caelian all by themselves.

Better to stand with us than to stand alone. The Mahdi know, even better than we, the kind of genocidal murderers the Caelian are. But what do you suppose they will do once the Caelian threat has been put down? Always assuming we are able to do it?"

I didn't think the question rhetorical. I thought there was real curiosity as to what his son might say behind it.

"I don't know, sir." Garve` spoke very carefully. I had the idea he had been presented with concepts he had never considered before, and that he was finding them difficult to comprehend.

"Neither do I, not really," the King told him, "and really, I may be counting our chickens before they hatch. We may not succeed in putting down the Caelian threat, and if they kill us, this conversation may be entirely pointless."

"No," Garve` said slowly, "no, I don't think so."

"Well, and neither do I," the King agreed with him. "Why, do you think, that your brother was so determined to apprehend our innocent young guest?"

"I don't know," Garve` admitted. "I don't believe there is a rebellion. I agree with our friend. But she said Jiden ordered the daggers she was delivering and you confirmed it. So if, as Freddy's informants insisted, those daggers meant something, then it is Jiden who is in the middle of it. Whatever it is."

"But why would the Crown Prince protect Counsellor Jiden?" the king wondered. "If he did not have a use for him? As far as I can see, Nehl has never even seemed to like Counsellor Jiden."

"No..." Prince Garve` drew the word out. "They're up to something, and a coup is the most likely reason they would collude, but it still doesn't make sense to me."

In the gathering darkness, I shivered. Because I could think of only one reason that would cause the Crown Prince to protect a Counsellor he didn't like—and that reason would be if they were planning a palace coup together. And four blades? Well, think about it. One for

King Marc, one for the Crown Prince, one for Garve`, next in line, and one for Freddy, the last of the line.

They'd fit nicely between the ribs when Jiden's men stabbed them in the back. "Now, Nehl doesn't like doing the work of being a king," King Marc

commented. "But he does like the power of the position, the pomp and the status. Look at how he misused it in the case of our guest. Jiden may have promised him the power without the responsibilities."

"I don't understand that," Garve` sounded frustrated. "There was no sense in it!" he protested. "Why her?"

"Oh," the king said, "I think there was. When you stop and think about it, our guest is the polar opposite of the Crown Prince. Orphaned, penniless, dependent upon the good-will of others, she is intelligent, well-educated, even if she had to find a way to educate herself, brave, a skilled, hard worker, everything that the Crown Prince is not. She is nearly ten years his junior, yet she has already made great strides in pulling herself up from nothing. Yet Nehl, who was born with everything, sees himself as hardly better than the nothing from which she has ascended. Can you not imagine the envy in which he drowned, upon finally meeting her and seeing those blades, the fruit of her labor? He must have known the price she could have been paid for them."

It didn't excuse him, I thought. If anything, it but made his depravity and sadism that much fouler. The Crown Prince had been given every advantage. He had no excuse for his choice to be ignorant, no excuse for his foulness, for his laziness and his indisposition for the work of kingship, nor for his indecency and dishonor.

"And you think that excuses him?" Garve` exclaimed, outraged.

"Nothing excuses him," the King told him. "Which is why I have sent him to Quattar to stay and socialize with the D'Arcys and the Bardons with his brother, with instructions to find out what is going on in Caelian themselves, instead of sending more spies in to their deaths in their place."

And he thought they might actually do it? I scoffed to myself, thinking of Freddy's and my foster brothers' shenanigans through the years, the pranks they'd pulled, the times they had spent the money

I had earned on wine, women and song in the taverns. (My adoptive mother had given it to them!)

The Crown Prince might be slightly more serious, but I doubted he had the kind of moral fortitude it would take to keep watch along the River Sanguine through the long nights for the shadows of the Caelian warriors on the water. Any man who got his jollies beating up on a girl ten years his junior, and who had to chain her to a chair to hold her to his abuses so she couldn't defend herself, hadn't any kind of decency or honor, never mind courage.

The Crown Prince struck me as neither more nor better than a craven coward.

# VI

# BALCONY BREEZES

THE CROWN PRINCE WAS, AS everyone in the kingdom knew, twenty-seven.

The spare heir, as we all knew as well, had just turned twenty-four.

And Freddy, the charming scoundrel who played at being a spy, was twenty-two, the same age as the younger of my foster brothers. The older of the pair was twenty

-five, but given Freddy's birth, as the third son of a king, he held, obviously, the lead position in the threesome.

Freddy, when associating with my foster brothers, pretended not to be royal and all the rest of the family pretended right along with him. You could say they knew which side of their bread their butter was on. While I worked, learning the art and the craft of metal working, my older foster brothers played about with their royal buddy, and everyone in the family was good with that but me. But then, I wasn't family, not really. I wasn't blood, as they were fond of telling me.

I just supported them all with my work.

"One more thing, son, before we call it a night," the King mentioned, interrupting my thoughts. "Vere. I've seen those blades she made. She's Nogaynos."

The statement caught me like a blow to the stomach.

"But—" Garve` protested, "How—I thought they were all dead."

"They got some of the women and children out," the King told him. "I ought to know," he added, "my grandmother was one of them. My mother is Nogaynos."

Huh, I thought.

"Some of them made it to Mahdi," the King explained. "Some of them made it to Amadea. Some of them became healers, others artisans. Some of them work with the caravans—what few of them we have left. But the way those blades were made—no one but someone with Nogaynos blood in their veins could do work like that."

"But—But—she let them kill her!" Garve` protested. "Or as near as makes no never mind. Nogaynos were magic."

"So she's only part Nogaynos," King Marc said. "Or she's all Nogaynos but she didn't know it. You don't just use magic, son, you have to learn it, just like anything else, and if there's no one to teach you, even worse, if there's no one to teach you that magic even exists, how could you use it?"

Garve` thought about that.

"So it's like a sword," he finally said, "that you don't know how to use.

Even if you could pick it up, it wouldn't really do you any good. Because you wouldn't know what it was if you saw it and you wouldn't know what it was for."

"More," King Marc told him, "it is as if all the swords you see you don't know as swords and nobody tells you the name of them or what they're for or how to use them. It's as if they don't exist. So you don't really see a sword, even when it's there in front of you because without a name for it, without knowing what it is, how does it exist in your consciousness? You don't know anybody who uses a sword, even, never mind just that no one teaches you how to use it."

Huh. I hadn't thought of it that way. I'd have to get into the King's library and get a couple of books on magic and read them before I left. Somehow. But I knew I'd have to do it soon. I didn't have much longer here. I could feel it.

I thought of working the forge. I'd been working magic all that time, working the fire, and the metal, the bellows and the hammer, never known what I was doing. That was something. It meant I wasn't starting from ground zero. I had, after all, set all those broken bones of mine. And if it had taken hours or even days to set them all, well, I had managed it, after all. And maybe I hadn't really been able to heal them, but I'd sort of managed to splint them, and

considering what bad shape I'd been in at the time, I didn't think what I'd managed to do had been all that shabby. I didn't know enough, though. I needed to know a lot more and I needed to know it quickly.

But how? I didn't think I dared ask King Marc when he visited to take me to his library and let me go free of his books on magic, on healing or for maps of the trails that crossed the plains. I wasn't sure I wanted him to understand that I was interested in magic. I didn't want him suspecting any more than he already did. I didn't know enough magic to protect myself, and I wasn't in good enough shape to have used much of it, I suspected, even if I knew a lot more about it than I did.

King Marc took the matter right out of my hands, however, when he arrived just after breakfast with the request for me to join him in his library while he did some of the paperwork that being a King required. Some of that very selfsame paper-work that his oldest son hated so badly.

"Nobody likes paperwork," he groused to me as I browsed his bookshelves, looking for books on magic, on healing, and for maps, "but it's something that has to be done. If you're going to be a competent King, never mind a good one, you have to do it." He rattled the papers before him. "Take this, for instance.

Some nitwit has proposed a bridge be built over the Sanguine to join Amadea and Caelian."

"No," I said, having found a book with magic in the title. I started trying to wedge it out of the tight press of books on the shelf.

"Exactly," King Marc agreed with me, roundly. "And worst of all, Nehl has gone ahead and signed off on it!" He shook his head. "Fortunately, I got hold of this stack before it went anywhere and burnt it in the fire."

I settled into a chair with my treasure.

"What advantage is it to Councilor Jiden?" I asked him, opening my book. King Marc looked up suddenly. Blinked. Said,

"Well, I'll be damned!" and sprang up to grab a book off the shelves.

I don't know how much later it was when he looked up from his book and demanded, "How did you know that?"

"Everybody knows that Councilor Jiden has business interests along the Sanguine," I told him, barely lifting my head from my book. My blacksmithing foster father would have called Councilor Jiden a 'bent nail'. It was not a matter for debate; it just was. Common knowledge. The book I held seemed, to me, much more interesting than Councilor Jiden.

Power, it told me, came from the elements. From wind, and water, and the earth, from fire and the spirit. I had worked with fire most, so it had been fire which had answered my unconscious call in my extremity—and, of course, the fire on the hearth where my torturer had heated the poker had provided the substance of the flames which had saved me, while the hot poker itself had supplied the spark. My spirit, according to the equation explicated by the book, had provided the purpose, the goal, the aim, the resolution. Which was why, according to the book, when I dropped into unconsciousness, the magic had winked out. Magic, according to it, could only be directed by the mind. No mind, no direction.

King Marc jerked me from my thoughts.

"What do you mean, everybody knows?" he wanted to know.

"His traders deal in potions from the jungle," I told him, blinking as I lifted my eyes from the book. "Everybody who deals with him in the market knows that. Look at the design on the blades—the Sanguine runs right through it, just the way it runs through the heart of his business."

"Could he be behind the raids occurring on our villages?" King Marc demanded.

"Behind?" I blinked at him. "Not behind. Involved in? To his profit? Certainly."

"Right," King Marc said, and started scrabbling among the papers again.

After a while, he leaped up, distracting me from my study again, and scrabbled around the shelves for another book. I left him to it.

The book before me provided plenty of new ideas to keep me busy. Sleep 'spells', for lack of a better word for how to induce deep slumber. Spells to clean clothing, and to mend them and make them like new. Healing 'spells'— boy, did I wish I'd known about them last—month? Where was that anatomy book? I needed an anatomy book. There! Oh, and potions. I'd need something to ground me in potions, as well. I looked up lungs, and then, the book held open with one hand, pulled up potions for the lungs in the other book.

Matching them up, and trying to read both sections at once, I realized I needed a book on herbs, and then, that led to another on gardening. In no time at all I had a semi-circle of books spread out around me so that I could bounce from book to book to bring each piece of information into sync with all the other pieces so that I had a harmonious whole. The problem, of course, was that in a mere three or four days I could not begin to manage to learn everything these books contained, never mind everything I needed to learn. Three or four weeks wouldn't have done it, though three of four years might have at least made a dent in all I needed to learn.

Magic, I realized, wasn't just magic. It had to be backed up by solid knowledge to make it truly effective. Scientific knowledge, a thorough understanding of anatomy, a wide familiarity with herbs and simples, and the expertise to grow them, prepare them, and to use them. It was so much, much more than I had done back in that torture room.

Basically, all I'd done in that room was to gather up fire already available on the hearth and simply explode it everywhere within my limited range. If I'd been stronger, or stayed conscious longer, I would probably have burned down the wooden parts of the dungeon and me along with it. I certainly hadn't had, for instance, the finesse to burn away the bad guys and leave any good guys, had there been any present (which there hadn't, fortunately).

I needed control. Remembering that blink of an eye before unconsciousness, I wondered if I would ever be able to use it when I wasn't in extremity. I had an idea that it would take months, perhaps even years, of study to learn how to control just fire, never mind any of the other disciplines.

What I thought of as a simple 'sleep spell' was actually 'mind' magic. Healing—that took a mastery of both mind and body magic. And power.

Herbs and potions helped to harness the body's own power, which the healer amplified by using the appropriate element to enhance it. The chill of a winter wind could bring down a fever, in extremity, while the heat from the fire could alleviate the chills. Wind could be called to help inflate the lungs, drive the infection from them, even to enhance circulation, along with water. Water could be used to fight dehydration, which apparently could and did escalate a number of conditions, many of which were deleterious to the system.

My conclusion was, from all this, that using magic to augment healing was anything but simple. To do it well, even to do it moderately effectively, the Healer had to know a lot of information. And there was so, so much that could be done through magic, or just enhanced.

Take travel, for instance. There were actually 'travel' 'spells', designed to allow someone to get from one place to another quickly, if not, perhaps, all that easily. Well, they'd take effort and knowledge and skill, which, as far as I could see, all 'magic' did. Huh. 'Travel' spells might be very important to me. They might even be life-saving. Heck, they might even save my life.

Maps. I needed maps. I leaped up and retrieved an atlas full of detailed, fold-out maps and started to study them. What would be the best way, the least traveled way, the quickest way, to get to the forest along the Mahdi border while avoiding people and well trafficked paths?

Lunch arrived, and with it the prince. He looked from his father, sprawled at the center of piles of books and papers, to me, penned in by a similar spread of books, and spoke.

"Am I intruding?" he wondered aloud. "I thought you wanted me to join you for lunch."

"Come in, come in," King Marc welcomed him. "I'd no idea it was time for lunch, I've been so busy."

"So I see," Garve` noted, looking around at the piles of books we'd created. He'd bathed afresh but I could still see the aura of the practice yard around him. "What are you working on?" he asked.

It occurred to me that with war against Caelian on the horizon and a probable coup attempt in the offing, perhaps King Marc ought to start spending a couple of the hours of his day out in the practice yard whanging away at his men with a sword, just in case he needed to defend himself in future. Couldn't hurt. Might save his life. But now wasn't quite the time to point that out.

"I came across a plan put forward by Councilor Jiden to build a bridge over the Sanguine to Caelian," King Marc informed him, "and Vere told me something that I had forgotten about Jiden's business being based on the potions he brings in from Caelian." And he explained what he had learned through his recent study, stuff we both would have known, if we thought about it.

In the past—not the recent past, we had nothing from the recent past on Caelian –the jungle country needed food, primarily grain and beef. They didn't have much of either in their jungle. Chicken and hogs, yes, according to the old books, but it was difficult to keep cattle alive in their jungle, difficult to raise enough fodder for them, and difficult to raise enough grain for people, as well. So, they traded the potions they could make from the leaves of the native trees and flowers and vines they had available, for the grain and the beef they needed.

But even trading for grain and beef, it must be difficult for them to get enough of either to feed their warriors. Warriors, after all, were pretty useless for much of anything but fighting. They didn't raise food and they didn't, in most cases, transport it, either. Thus the need for captives—slaves—to do the work, the problem for the Caelians being that slaves, in order to work, had to be fed.

Amadea was just one of the four countries that occupied our continent, all of them clustered around the interior high plains area which formed a sort of no-man's land set below the northern fields of ice. The great minds (rich dilettantes who spent all their time playing mind games while others—mostly women--fed them, housed them and clothed them) agreed that our world was round, and made up mostly of water. Our continent, which our four countries shared, was believed to be the largest of the continents of our world.     (Maybe it was, maybe it wasn't—couldn't prove it by me.)

Our continent was, in no way, divided equally between the four countries.

The 'western' section of it mostly held the fastness of great mountains, some of them snowy all year around, at least in the north, with deep, hanging valleys and oddly warm beaches—at least by comparison to our eastern beaches--along the western seas. The north-western mountains and valleys were held by the Mahdi. The south-western and central mountains and valleys had been the territory of the Nogaynos people who were mostly all gone, now, after the genocide committed against them by the Caelian people, with their poison air. This western section of the continent ranged around three thousand miles or a bit more from north to south and six hundred fifty miles east to west to maybe eight hundred miles east to west, depending upon where you were in the mountains.

The Caelian had the southern-most area, below the high plains, with its jungles and swamps, from the Lupine River at the base of the southern mountains to the east. The Sanguine river pretty much formed its eastern and northern boundaries of Caelian, from where it emerged from the escarpment of the high plains and split into two branches, to where it emptied into the eastern seacoast at the foot of the eastern coast range, south of Quattar. Amadea occupied the land area above the Sanguine and below the ice fields.

Oh, the eastern coast range was a mere series of hills, in comparison to the western mountains. Thin, long, and curved, this range of almost mountains followed the line of the eastern coast, covering far more than two thousand miles south to north and between three hundred fifty and four hundred fifty miles east to west. Small valleys containing rich farmland nestled into the hills dotted the country and transportation used the ocean as often as the many wagon roads and trails through the coast range. Gentle foothills filled in the area between the coastal mountains and the high plains which lay between the coast range and the western mountains.

The high plains stretched through the interior of the continent.

Rich with tall grasses and rambling herds of large, brown, shaggy bison, it varied from easily two thousand miles from east to west in the far north to far more than three thousand miles east to west in the south. Well over three thousand miles stretched from the ice fields of the north to the line the Sanguine drew at the foot of the escarpment. Dividing the plains from the jungles of Caelian, the river and the escarpment at least a couple of hundred feet above it created two separate worlds.

In the interior, the high plains summers were hot and arid, the winters bitter cold and snowy, alternating between frigid chill and blizzards in which white- out conditions were common. Springs and the occasional man-made well, along with infrequent streams of water that had melted during the short northern summers out of the ice kept the bison and their few predators alive, but it had taken millennia for people to find the water and establish trails all the way across the plains from east to west and back again.

The northernmost route, from Palace City, Amadea's northern capital city, to Mahdi, curved around beneath the ice fields. It held the most water and the least traffic, and was open only from the month of Blossom to the beginning of Apple. Of the two middle routes, only the one to southern Mahdi was still in common use. The lower middle route, that reached from more or less northern Nogaynos to Amadea had fallen out of use since the diaspora, when most of Nogaynos had either succumbed to the poison air the Caelians had sent out over their lands, or left Nogaynos to avoid it. The southern route, from southern Nogaynos across the great escarpment to southern Amadea, was only used in places along the eastern edge by Caelian raiders preying on small Amadean villages and outlying farms.

Most of the population of Amadea lived in the eastern hills and along the eastern ocean, or in the lush ranges of the foothills, reaping the rewards of their rich farmlands. The inland area of the continent got left, pretty much, to the bison and the wolves that preyed on them. There were elk, too, and deer, though their herds were not as numerous as those of the bison. Besides, they seemed to prefer the hills and the mountains, while the bison tended to stay to the plains, at least their larger herds did, though smaller herds had been known, according to the history books, to shelter in the western foothills of Amadea now and again and in the valleys of Mahdi and Nogaynos.

The Amadean people who lived in the coastal hills hunted both, in the fall, to augment their diets. A few hardy Amadean people lived along the fringes of the plains, in stone redoubts from which they ventured forth to hunt, what gardens and fields they had lined in massive stone walls generations in the making, to protect their crops. In the western foothills, it was said that Mahdi and Amadean people had intermarried until you could not tell one from the other, their redoubts built as often of heavy timber walls as stone. Bandits plagued both western and eastern foothills, preying upon both villagers, farms and trade caravans with indiscriminate rapaciousness, eking out a precarious living from their thieveries.

The Caelian might have killed pretty much all the Nogaynos, but they had not managed to take over their territory. However the Nogaynos people had failed, their mountains had not, defeating the Caelians soundly. Now the Nogaynos estates still stood, their towers and palaces of stone still rising cold and alone among their chill mountain peaks overlooking their western ocean— as far as we in Amadea knew.

Scouts from Amadea visited Nogaynos' greatest estates a couple of generations ago and reported them eerie, empty, and forlorn. Scouts who crossed the Sanguine into Caelian—never returned. No one knew what had happened to the Caelian after the death of Nogaynos. Well, no one but the Caelian.

For more than a hundred years after the 'fall' of Nogaynos, the Caelian kept to themselves, hidden deep in their jungles and their swamps among the monsters that lurked there. For whatever reason, the Caelian had not taken over the once richly abundant land of the Nogaynos, with their great central valley, their hanging mountain valleys and their rich coastal pastures. Instead, they cut steps into the cliffs lining the Amadean side of the Sanguine, hung ladders, and raided the rich farms of the small villages in the south of Amadea.

In this way they supplied their needs for grain and meat and slaves, all three in one.

The Amadean army could not seem to stop them. They never saw them coming, they never knew where they would hit next—or when—and they never seemed to be able to catch up with them when they left. Rumor had it that the Caelian would disappear over the side of a cliff somewhere, heading down into the Sanguine, and once they had, neither captives nor goods would ever be heard from again. According to all the histories I had read, this was how the Caelians' war with the Nogaynos had started. I didn't like it.

# VII
# HISTORY LESSONS

**"A**REN'T YOU GOING TO EAT?" Garve` asked me. I looked down at my untouched plate.

"Of course," I said, but instead of taking a bite, I inquired, "Why didn't the Caelians take over the Nogaynos' lands?"

King Marc stopped mid-bite.

"What?" Garve` asked, for him.

"They fought this great war, they produced all that poison air, they murdered every man, woman and child of Nogaynos that they could find, at enormous effort, and some significant loss of their own lives—for why? If they weren't going to try to live on the Nogaynos' lands, in their homes, eat their food, then why go to all that trouble?"

"That," King Marc said thoughtfully, "is a very good question."

"The Caelian don't live in Nogaynos?" Garve` looked from one to the other of us with the question.

"No," King Marc responded, "they don't. Scouts sent to Nogaynos come back, and they tell us that no one lives there now."

"Huh." I tipped back into my chair and regarded him steadily. Garve` looked from one to the other of us.

"The first scouts," King Marc told us, "the ones who traveled to Nogaynos right after the diaspora, reported, when they returned, that there were Caelian bodies lying around everywhere, among the small groups of the Nogaynos' bodies. Hundreds of them in some places. No one had attempted to do anything with them. They were just lying there in piles. Some of them had been killed fighting, according to the scouts, but more of them were just dead, without a mark on them. And this was right after the first reports came to tell us that the Caelian had invaded Nogaynos, some time in my great grandfather's time."

"The poison air," I posited thoughtfully. "Maybe it got caught up in the tree branches, maybe it pooled in low spots in the ground. Before they used it, did the Caelian truly understand how it would work? How long it might take to dissipate? Or did they just not understand the air currents? Then again, the Caelian jungle is very humid, while the western mountains are much drier.

Perhaps in Caelian the humid air and constant rain cleared the air of the poison rapidly, while in the mountains, it hung around until it rained—which could very well take weeks, depending upon when they deployed it. Perhaps when the Caelian invaded, the poison air killed enough of them that it discouraged them from completing their invasion. Perhaps it tainted the crops they stole so that the food they wanted the land for killed them. Or made them sick. Or maybe between the poisoned air and the Nogaynos mages who stayed behind to make a last stand against the Caelian, the Caelian lost enough people so they gave up on the country."

"Wow," Garve` said.

"There is no way of knowing whether you are right, or not," King Marc said, "but I have read the reports of the scouts who investigated, and most of the dead Caelian appeared to be untouched, according to them. Additionally, they recorded that some scouts experienced faintness, but when moved from the areas in which they experienced the symptoms, they recovered, but when other of the scouts tried to succor them where they experienced the faintness, they, too, experienced it. And it is also true that when they tried to eat the fruit and the grain produced in much of the southern area of the country, it made them sick.

Some of them even died."

"Well," Garve` said, "there you are."

"This means," I pointed out, "that the poison air is very dangerous. It would seem, from those reports, that it pools in certain areas and stays there, and that it disperses, when it disperses, only very slowly. I would suggest that, if possible, you find a way to make masks which protect the wearer from the poison air and which provide the wearer with healthy air, and that you provide them to the villages along the border, as well as your soldiers."

"That is more easily said than done," King Marc reminded me, but he made a note of it to himself.

"Also," I observed ruminatively, "I would see about training archers—long- bowmen. To be masked and deployed from hiding, so that when the Caelian forces follow their poisoned air in to decimate the village they're attacking, the bowmen can fire upon them, and decimate them for a change." I snapped the last words out.

I really did not like the Caelian tactics. While war might be all about killing, the Caelian tactics of sending poisonous air out to kill or incapacitate not just the fighters, but the women and children and elders before attacking seemed a good deal like cowardly murder to me. Never mind that they had already committed genocide once.

"Good Lord," King Marc said softly. He stared at me. So did Garve`. "The Caelian warriors wear some kind of hard shell doublet across their chests," he remarked.

"I've heard that, too," I agreed. "But I think, if the arrow shafts are mounted on small, round, sharply pointed steel heads, and the archers pull heavy bows, if the distance is not too great, that the penetrating force might be sufficient to pierce their outer protections." I smiled a bit at him. "This is my bailiwick," I reminded him. "Weapons. And steel."

"Yes," King Marc said, getting excited. "Yes, of course." He made more notes to himself.

"But we cannot get the soldiers to the villages when they are needed in time to do any good," Garve` complained. "The villages are too far apart."

I reached for the atlas, thumbed through the maps rapidly, looking for one I had already studied, found it, spread it out to be examined.

"Put redoubts along the hillsides above the villages, maybe one to each side of each village so that the archers have the high ground.

Station a few of the archers at each redoubt with horses and light cavalry for rapid deployment.

Build lookouts in the trees above every two to three villages, with a powerful lantern shielded so the light can't be seen. As soon as movement towards any of the villages is spotted, the light can be flashed—something like three flashes, pause, three flashes, pause, three flashes pause—"

King Marc's pen flashed as he jotted down my thoughts.

"Someone in the village to keep watch for the flashes, someone to run to the nearest redoubt as soon as the flashes are seen, someone else to run to the nearest village to warn them, and, if necessary, to bring more archers back to defend the village and buy time for the soldiers to get there as well as to cut the numbers of the raiding party. That way, with luck, you might even manage to capture some of the raiders, and even to get some intel from one of them. It won't cost you any more than that idiotic bridge of Lord Jiden's, maybe less."

King Marc wrote as rapidly as his hand could move, and when he had finished, he threw his pen down and, raising his head, said,

"My God, I think I love you. We've made no headway against these raiders for most of the last three years! All we've been doing is chasing shadows all this time. With this strategy--!"

Garve` frowned at me.

"I should have thought of that," he said. King Marc turned to his son.

"I want to adopt her," he said. Turning back to me, he offered, "Can I adopt you?"

I shook my head.

"I've already been adopted once," I pointed out. "It didn't work out too well for me, if you'll remember. Somebody left a king's ransom in gold and diamonds and rubies with my adoptive parents in payment for raising me as their own, and you can see how well that turned out, with my foster brothers and their buddy turning against me and my adoptive parents going along with it, doubtless so that when I disappeared, they could keep the money and the jewels with impunity."

King Marc winced.

"Gold and diamonds and rubies?" Garve` echoed, thoughtfully.

"Well, nobody ever told me about them outright, but I've listened, through the years, and the boys are older than I am, five years and eight years, in fact, and they've let things slip, all of them. I've seen the jewels—my adoptive mother likes to wear them—so I've put things together. That treasure has meant that the boys have not ever had to work, and my adoptive parents have been able to live quite well, even if my adoptive father makes no more than an average wage with his skills. If I am killed in your dungeons, well, then, the hoard is theirs, now, isn't it?"

Garve` winced.

"And Freddy knew this," he more stated than asked.

"Certainly," I assured him.

"So you don't trust adoptive parents, then?" King Marc wanted to know.

"Would you?" I asked him. "My so-called brothers and their buddy betrayed me to the Crown Prince to be tortured to death. Your son, the Crown Prince, chained me to a chair and beat me. He cut me and burned me. He had me thrown into a cell and starved, and he sent his men to hang me from the beams

and torture me again. Even if you did adopt me, I doubt very much," I advised him, "if the Crown Prince would accept me. He'd be more likely to throw me back in that dungeon again the first moment your back was turned, and order his men to finish the job they started on me. And you would refuse to believe he could be so foul, and quite deliberately turn your back upon me to 'prove' to me that he was not as dishonorable as I know him to be. And after I had been tortured to death—again—you would say so sorry. Not that saying sorry would save me one moment of the agony he would be so delighted to visit upon me."

King Marc stared at me for a long moment, and then he looked down at his notes again.

"I see it would not serve," he murmured, just to himself.

"I will hope I have given you enough ideas to go on with," I told him. I glanced down at the spread of books before me. "I think I ought, perhaps, to leave you with your son. If I may, by your leave, take the books with me to study?"

"Of course." He turned to his son. "Garve`, carry the books back to her room for her, will you?"

"Of course," Garve` assured him, and started to help me gather up the books I'd spread out around me. He frowned, as he picked them up. "History, geography, natural science--?"

Fortunately I'd scooped the book on magics up first, and now held it on the bottom of the pile in my arms. King Marc heaved a huge sigh.

"I fear she's learned more this morning on her own than any of you boys learned in a month with your tutors in your school days," he commented.

"But—it's so eclectic a selection," Garve` protested, more to his father than to me. I answered him anyway.

"But it all goes together," I pointed out.

Garve` didn't see it. King Marc almost visibly pricked up his ears.

"The bowmen and the redoubts and the lookouts?" Garve` questioned, skeptically.

"Oh," I told him dismissively. "I know weapons. I design them and I make them. That's the easy part. But you look at the maps, and you match them to the reports King Marc has been going over, and note where Lord Jiden wanted to put his bridge—"

"Did you now!" King Marc exclaimed.

"Of course," I said impatiently. "Look at where the raids are happening—to either side of where he wanted to put the bridge. Then you match up the topography of the area—"

Garve` gasped, and reached out for the map I had left on the table.

"I need you," King Marc said. I ignored him.

"I need to study," I told him, instead of responding to his statement. Or, I suppose, that was a response. Then again, I think he may have thought I was going to study something more or other than what I intended to study.

King Marc flicked his fingers at me. "Go," he said. "Go. Study."

I was happy to obey him.

Garve` followed me, his arms heavy with books.

"You ought to think about staying," he told me, in a shy, serious way.

"Until the Crown Prince gets back from wherever he's gone and throws me in the dungeon again to torture to death? I don't think so." I shuddered at the very thought.

"He wouldn't do that," Garve` assured me seriously.

"So you don't believe that was the Crown Prince who chained me to a chair and tortured me?" I asked him, more rhetorically than otherwise.

"He didn't mean it," Garve` told me earnestly.

Like Hades he didn't, I thought, but did not say. My resolve to get away from the Palace and Amadea itself hardened.

"And anyway," Garve` told me next, "he won't be back for weeks. Maybe even months or years. Father is sending him south to Quattar as soon as the triremes arrive, and Fort Southren, to see what he could do about the Caelian raids. He's supposed to report on them."

I wouldn't bet on it. The kind of coward who chained a young girl up to beat her wasn't the kind of man who would stick around if he came face to face with a Caelian warrior. I would bet that the Crown Prince would take one look at a painted Caelian warrior and run the other way as quickly as a man could run. I didn't say it, however.

Garve` set his stack of books down on my table before the window and stared down at them wonderingly.

"You really mean to study all these?" He wanted to know.

"I really mean to study all these," I assured him. "I know about weapons," I added, for the incredulous expression on his face. "But my education has been very narrow. I know how to work the forge, I know how to hammer out weapons and tools, I know how to fit the shaft of the arrow to the point and how to fletch it. I can season the wood to shape a bow, and set the shafts to a shovel or a rake or a hoe. I can even cut and mold and sew leather."

"You learned that at the forge," Garve` nodded.

"I studied at the Temple, too," I assured him. "I can read and write. I can even draw a little. I studied the Temple's religious texts and sung the days and months and years as the Temple teaches. I was taught law and the history of Amadea, how to cook and sew, spin and weave. I've helped out in my adoptive mother's garden for years. But I know little of Nogaynos' history beyond bed- time stories, and less of Mahdi's or Caelian's."

Garve` shrugged incuriously. "No one does," he pointed out.

"Caelian threatens us, but I know little of the Caelian people beyond that which King Marc's reports describe," I complained. "And then there is the mystery of the Nogaynos. Why did the Caelians kill all of them, if they didn't want the Nogaynos' lands? What was the point of murdering them all? It makes no sense! And what of their poison air? Are we going to face that?"

Very seriously, Garve` told me, "I think we already are."

"Then why aren't we taking samples of it?" I wanted to know. "And finding out what it consists of and what we can do to combat it? Is there an antidote to it? And if there is, what is it? An herb? Perhaps? Or maybe we can use filters against it?"

Transfixed, Garve` stared at me. And then he blinked, and looked down at the books in front of us.

"Study," he told me, and turned to leave the room.

"One more thing," I mentioned, shocked at my own temerity. Garve` turned back to me.

"What?" he wanted to know.

"See if you can get King Marc into the lists for regular sword practice," I suggested to him. "The better able he is to protect and defend himself, and the more strength and stamina he has with which to do it, the better."

He blinked at me again, and then he nodded. "You're right," he said. "I will."

And then he did leave. I latched the door after him, and then spread the books out on the table before me the way I had arranged them before, picking up the magic book again. I had a lot to learn and very little time in which to learn it before I left.

# VIII

## GARVE`

GARVE` FOUND HIS FATHER HEAD down in his books. He shook his head, watching him.

"You're not going to get her to stay," he said. "She's terrified of Nehl." King Marc's head jerked up.

"And well she should be," he averred. "I'll keep him away from the palace and the city as long as I can," he added. "I can always hope that time will help to heal her wounds."

Garve` frowned and shook his head. "I don't think that's going to work."

"She's given me more practical help than the Crown Prince and all my advisors put together, in just a few hours," King Marc said. "I want to keep her around as long as possible." He gestured at the papers in front of him. "Thanks to her, for the first time, we have a workable, even economical, defense plan and even the possibility of gaining some intel on what the Caelians are up to."

Garve` sat down and tipped his head back over the back of the chair.

"I can't believe I let Nehl do that!" he exclaimed, to the ceiling, all while watching his father from the corner of his eye. He would have been a great deal less sanguine about the influence he could see their prisoner exerting over his father if he hadn't been so certain she would refuse to stay with them. This way, she seemed more a curiosity than a threat, and she was showing him the way to gain his father's approbation, as well as the way to exert a little influence of his own in that direction. He felt inclined to regard her with qualified approval.

"Kept our attention away from the coup he and Jiden were planning," his father commented, still working over his plan for the defense of the southern villages.

"You think Nehl was planning a coup? He couldn't have!" Garve` protested, more for show than out of honest incredulity. "He wouldn't have! He's not smart enough. It had to be Jiden."

"Of course he would," his father assured him. "And Jiden's not smart enough, either. Somebody else is involved, somewhere. And he found an easy mark, too. Nehl figures I'm old and stupid and he's young and smart. Also, he needs the power so he can indulge himself in his sadistic tendencies." He shrugged. "I never would have believed it either, before I saw what he did to that child. Now I'd believe anything dishonorable of him."

"I can't—" Garve` broke off, shook his head.

"You saved her life," his father lifted his head to remind him. "Twice-over, if you get right down to it. Once when you cut her down from that beam and a second time when you had her taken from the dungeon to the infirmary. And your loyalty to your brother does you credit, but you need to let go of it. Nehl will only use it against you. He did what he did to that girl because he enjoyed it, but the entire fiasco was engineered so that he could cover up the matter of the coup he and someone else had planned. The cover-up was clumsy because that was all Freddy and Nehl and they're too stupid for something more subtle, never mind more effective." He sighed, and turned his attention back to the papers before him.

"You are doing something about that coup, aren't you?" Garve` demanded of him.

"I've taken precautions," his father assured him. "Not least of them sending Nehl and Freddy to the south to work with the Southern army."

"Yes, but did they really go?" Garve` wanted to know.

"Well, not yet," the King said. "I've received a letter from the commander at South Point that he got my directions regarding your brothers. It will be several days before they reach Quattar, of course. Well, weeks, actually."

"Yes," Garve` wondered, "but how genuine is it?"

"If it isn't genuine," the King told him, "it's a very good forgery—and I don't think Nehl is smart enough to have figured out that he needed a good forgery, because I'd be so familiar with the commander's handwriting. I doubt Nehl would recognize the handwriting of any of his servants, so I doubt he'd imagine that I could recognize the handwriting of any of my generals, never mind my captains."

Garve` considered that. On the whole, he decided, he thought his father might be right about that.

"Freddy?" he questioned.

"Freddy just thinks he's a spymaster," his father said, sneering it a little. "I've notified Laren, Liam and Meric about Jiden's plans, and we've had meetings about it. They know all about the bridge over the Sanguine he and Nehl cooked up."

Carefully, Garve` inquired,

"Do you think Nehl will be able to implement your new plan?"

"Able, yes, would he, probably not. At this point I have to wonder if he is working with the Caelian king as well as Jiden. Bane is his uncle, after all." The king shook his head. "No, I've sent for Meric. I'll go over the plan with him, and then, if he thinks he's up to it, I'll send him down south to take command of the troops there and see the plan implemented."

Garve` frowned.

"Nehl may not like that," he said.

"You think he'll come storming back here?" his father queried. Answered his own question. "Well, he might. And that might just smoke Jiden out. I've got men in place all around the palace, now. The sooner Jiden makes his move, the better. It's difficult to stay on edge all the time. Too long, and that edge gets dulled."

Garve` understood that.

"Vere said you maybe ought to start taking sword practice with the men in the mornings," he commented.

His father grunted.

"She's right," he allowed. "I made a start this morning." He groaned a little, stretching his neck and shoulders. "I had no idea how rusty I was getting."

Garve` nodded, more to himself than to his father. "You and she are well matched," he observed.

"Yes, we are," the King agreed, admitting the truth without demur. "It's too bad I'm almost old enough to be her grandfather, never mind her father. I'd

marry her in a heartbeat." He shook his head. "Not that she'd have me. Not with my track record. Letting my first wife be murdered, and then letting myself be snookered into marrying a rich snob like Margrete D'Arcy. She's too smart for that, and that's before we take Nehl into consideration."

"Nehl would kill her," Garve` said, simple stream of consciousness, and then, shocked, he registered what he had said, and the essential truth of it.

"I know," his father allowed, grimly. "I never, ever, thought that I would have a pair of sons like Freddy and Nehl," he mused, "but I should have, I suppose. Your mother Barena was a good woman, but she was King Bane's sister and her father was a bloody tyrant as well. So, between the blood you got from your mother, and then my allowing Margrete to raise you—well—" He turned to look Garve` in the face. "How did you turn out to be so different?" he wanted to know.

"I don't know," Garve` admitted. Then, quite seriously, he said, "I never liked Margrete."

"Did Nehl?"

"Not really," Garve` answered him thoughtfully. "I don't think Nehl likes any woman."

His father stiffened.

"Is he unnatural?" he wanted to know.

"Not the way you mean," Garve` shook his head, "but as far as I can tell, he's never liked a girl or a woman, and never gotten any real or lasting pleasure from one. Then again, I don't think he really likes any men, either." Thoughtfully, he added, "I don't believe he has any friends among the men, either. Just Freddy and me."

"Cold-natured," his father nodded. "That's the impression I got, too. But, now Freddy—"

"Likes women," Garve` agreed immediately. "Well, pretty women, anyway.

But lightly. Shallowly. He doesn't love them. He takes his pleasure of them and then he leaves them. He's charming."

"But entirely lacking in depth," his father nodded. "Yes," he agreed, "I've seen that too." Palpably, he turned his attention to his middle son. "What about you?" he wondered. "Do you like women?"

"Well enough," Garve` shrugged. And then, with calculation he tried to hide, he added, "I'd have that Vere in a heartbeat, scars and all. Not that she'd have me. I'd guess right about now she has zero use for any man in Amadea."

"Wouldn't surprise me," his father agreed. "Don't give up on her," he advised. "Give her time. You won't find another of her calibre all that easily."

"No," Garve` said. "I know." He didn't mean it the way his father did, but he would marry her if he got the chance, if that was what it took to gain his father's approval. He knew he needed the bulwark of his father to hold between himself and his brother. He knew too, that if Nehl imagined for a moment that he was thinking the way he was, that his elder brother would kill him in a heart- beat.

"Good," his father said. "Who else do you think is involved with Jiden?

Beyond Bardons and D'Arcys?"

The question surprised Garve`, but his mind anchored to one point. "She was delivering four blades," he mentioned.

"Ah," his father nodded. "So, three other members of the group. Freddy and Nehl, do you think? For one? or two?"

"Possibly," Garve` said, not liking that conclusion at all, but unable to argue that it didn't make sense. Unfortunately, it did.

"So who is the fourth?" the King inquired.

Garve` mulled over it. Finally, slowly, he answered, "Not Liam."

"No. . ." his father agreed, equally slowly. "It doesn't seem in character for him."

"Nor Laren, I wouldn't think," Garve` added, still considering.

"We've already talked, and I agree," his father assured him. "Meric seems unlikely."

"He doesn't like either Nehl or Freddy," Garve` reminded him.

"I told him about Nehl's torture of Vere. It--" the king winced a little. "It upset him."

Garve` snorted. He'd already heard Meric's opinion on the subject. As far as the old soldier was concerned torture was something to be reserved for emergency situations and only employed against the most certain of knaves in the most dire of circumstances. It was something never to be employed against women or children no matter what. Nehl's torture of Vere, as far as the old man was concerned, had violated two of those strictures, not just one.

He had never liked Nehl; the old man considered him arrogant, ignorant and now thoroughly dishonorable as well.

"If he thought Nehl was going to be crowned king," Garve` informed his father, "Meric would find a way to take him out and he wouldn't care if he died in the process, as long as he succeeded in eliminating him so he could never become king."

"Yes," his father nodded, seemingly unconcerned by the thought, "I know.

But of the Council, that leaves Bardon and D'Arcy."

"And either one of those two could very well be in on it," Garve` sighed.

"Or both," his father pointed out.

"We don't know that Jiden didn't order more blades, just that Vere had four with her when Freddy and Nehl took her."

"Shall I go ask her?" Garve` inquired.

"Yes," his father concluded, after a moment's thought. "I hate to interrupt her study—I have a feeling the more she figures out, the better for us—but we need to know this much."

"But if it is only the four?"

"Bardon or D'Arcy," his father said, and then sighed, "or Bardon and D'Arcy, if it is not someone outside of the Council—which it could be."

"I'll go ask," Garve` volunteered.

# IX

# VERE

A TAP AT THE DOOR. I raised my head from the book on magic, laid it down on the table, spread open, and dumped another book atop it, also open, effectively disguising it.

"Yes?"

"The Prince Garve` to see you, lady. May he enter?"

Well, that struck me as odd. Lady? I questioned. And then, a prince, asking permission?

"Enter," I called. The door opened a crack, and Garve` crooked his head around it.

"I don't really want to interrupt your studies, my lady," he said, actually sounding apologetic, "but we need to understand about the blades. You were delivering four of them to Councilor Jiden. Were they the only four blades that the Counsellor ordered? Or were there more?"

The importance of my answers struck me immediately. These were questions my torturers had not bothered to ask. Because they knew the answers already?

"My adoptive father was only asked to make the four blades I attempted to deliver to Councilor Jiden," I responded. "That does not mean, however, that additional blades were not ordered from other blacksmiths in order to disguise the number of them to be made. If he had wanted them quickly he might have ordered others from other smiths. It takes time to make blades of that quality— well, any blades, actually.”

“I see,” Garve` said slowly. I wasn’t sure he did.

“You might send a few men around with the blades to ask some of the other smiths if they were asked to make blades to that design, or a similar one.”

“Of course,” Garve` said, coming fully into the room. He eyed the scatter of books spread out around me. “Do you think that Freddy and Nehl are truly co- conspirators with Councilor Jiden?” He asked it of me diffidently.

“Oh, yes,” I assured him.

Perhaps oddly, I felt no compunction about it, no urge to spare his sensibilities. I wouldn’t have guessed he had any, but apparently he did. Surprise!

“The bridge proposal Nehl signed makes it almost certain, and Freddy’s ploy to finger me for the role of ‘rebel’ courier means that he was almost certainly involved as well. Put the two of them together--” I shrugged. He could come to his own conclusions.

He did. I could see him add what I had said to his knowledge of what I had suffered and reach the pretty much inescapable conclusion. Well, as long as you remained honest with yourself. People willing to be dishonest with themselves could always duck any conclusion. Apparently Garve` was at least inclined to be honest with himself in this much. Good for him. Given his position, he might stay alive a little bit longer.

I wondered if he could take in the notion that he might be in just as much danger as his father in the coup. I had the idea that Freddy might just like to be one notch closer to the throne, and I doubted, very, very much, that men who didn’t mind killing their father would mind very much killing one of their brothers, either. Then I wondered if Crown Prince Nehl realized just what his brother’s willingness to kill their father meant for him. Freddy had seen that his oldest brother was a sadistic torturer who didn’t much care whether or not his victims were innocent.

Did Freddy have the intelligence to understand what a monster his brother had become? Or was he mired in the belief that in his brother's pantheon, he was 'different'? If he was, that belief might very well get him killed.

For his part, the Crown Prince had seen that his brother had been willing to betray a girl he had watched grow up, a young girl he might as well have been a brother to. If Freddy would betray his own father, and a young girl raised almost close enough to him to be a sister, what would he do to the Crown Prince in order to ascend the throne? Hum? Or did they think, each of them, that somehow that their relationship with their brother was 'different'? And were they right, at least for now?

I had to get out of here. I really, really didn't want to be here when Jiden pulled off the coup he had planned. I hoped King Marc and Garve` would come out alive, but nothing I knew about guaranteed it. How accurate, for instance, was the King's assessment of the men around him? If he was wrong about many of them, or even about one key individual, that could spell his death. If his own sons could betray him, then anyone could. That recognition gave me a serious case of what my adoptive mother's mother called the 'cauld grue'. I shuddered. I feared I had a very, very limited time to get myself together and get out of here safely, if it could be done at all.

"Freddy and Nehl are heading to South Point," Garve` said, almost as much to himself as to me. "So Jiden might try something any time now, if he intends to do it while Nehl isn't here so he can't be blamed for anything."

I thought he sounded worried. I sighed. I didn't want to point out the obvious again, but his assumption was dangerous.

"Who is to say Councilor Jiden doesn't mean to betray Freddy and the Crown Prince as well as the King?" I asked him. "Anyone who would betray a ruler like King Marc would betray anyone, and even Jiden would know that King Marc is a far more effective administrator than either Freddy or the Crown Prince would or could ever be." I shook my head. "We do not know enough about their plans to make your assumption. And once the Crown Prince and Freddy get more than two thousand miles away from the capital, Jiden, and, or whoever he is working with, would have ample opportunity to dispense with an inconvenient pair of princes."

Garve` grimaced.

"Right," he said. "Well, I'll go tell Father what you said."

"Yes," I agreed, and watched him take his leave of me. Then I looked back at the books in front of me. I needed to go soon.

Too bad, I thought, my eyes lighting on the maps, that I hadn't mastered that 'travel' magic. If I had, it would get me out away from the city and into the forest where I could hide and take the time to learn how to use my magic, at least in a few basic ways, like fighting and healing myself. Perhaps I could try to learn something of it before I left?

I picked up the map to study. The maps showed three major trails to use to get to Nogaynos, which, I knew, was a place I needed to go. Eventually. If I wanted to learn how to use magic, and I did. In fact, I thought I would have to learn, if I wanted to survive.

It had been made very clear to me that I had no place in Amadea. Remaining in the city would be a death sentence, and that death wouldn't be a kind one.

Trying to live in a village somewhere would probably not work out well, either, men being what they were. Well, at least not with my current level of skills.

But if I could learn to harness my magic, beginning with simple spells like sleep and some basic healing, along with some enhanced self-defense skills, I might be able to survive. If I could add some degree of skill with 'travel', I could give myself a fighting chance, and if I could add a few more skills, I might even be able to thrive.

Too bad it was so far to Nogaynos. I needed to go there as soon as I could. What little I knew about the place pretty much assured me that if I could learn how to use my magic effectively, the information I needed to do it was to be found there, in Nogaynos. But getting there wasn't going to be easy.

The shortest route had several disadvantages, one of them being that it was currently the most well-traveled route. That meant it would take me right through the problematical area where bandits raided the caravans crossing the plains. I wasn't at all sure than any small party could get through safely, never mind a single person. Another, much longer route would take me due south along the Amadean foothills. It might be the safest route, generally, but it took me in the direction of the Crown Prince, a frightful consideration under the best of circumstances and I would eventually have to cross the plains, no matter which way I went.

There were not so many roads from village to village that I could guarantee avoiding him, if he should take a notion to travel north, which he very well might. He might very well have planned to come north as soon as Councilor Jiden started his coup.   And the Crown Prince was to be avoided at all costs.

So were the Caelian, and once I left Amadea and turned west, I'd be traveling parallel to Caelian for more than three thousand miles, if I tried to use the southern route. So, I wouldn't be taking that route. It avoided Mahdi, but did I really care about avoiding Mahdi?

That left the middle route, which, from the standpoint of arriving in Nogaynos was probably the shortest. But first, there was the possibility, if not the probability, of meeting the Crown Prince on the six hundred plus miles of the north to south section of trail I'd have to travel before turning west. And second, the trail west had been so little traveled these last hundred and fifty years that I might have difficulty staying on it. And that would make finding water a problem. Would the old springs still be potable, if they were even still there, and not silted up by time? It had been so long. . . .

The northern route, heading north and west into the forests beneath the ice fields before turning south along the Mahdi border, had several advantages, being far less traveled. Far fewer villages appeared along that route, which would make it a good deal easier to avoid them, the Mahdi were seldom a problem, since they rarely, if ever, left their mountain aeries (at least, according to most reports) and I'd have the full expanse of the plains between myself and the Crown Prince. But, I'd have to be careful not to fall afoul of any bandits.

One person alone—well, being taken by bandits would just be another form of slavery, and a dire one, at that. The forests just above the northern foothills on the western side of the plains, if I could reach them safely, would serve to hide me until I could get a handle on some of my magic and could start on the trip south. And, too, it was a good deal shorter than any other route across the plains, since the distance across them narrowed a good deal in the north.

So those were the advantages of that route.

The disadvantage was its sheer distance to Nogaynos. I'd have to travel north before I headed west, I'd have to cross the plains on a little used and very northerly route in late summer, and once I reached the Mahdi foothills I'd have to travel south for at least a thousand miles just to reach the northern borders of Nogaynos. I'd be traveling close to thirty-five hundred miles on this route, and that was a conservative estimate. Even if I could travel twenty miles every day, which was highly unlikely, it would take me at least a hundred and eighty-some days to make the journey, and that would be an optimum outcome, predicated on the idiotic idea that nothing would go wrong. As if any undertaking ever traveled on to its end without something going wrong!

More likely, it would take me around two hundred and twenty days, what with days I couldn't make twenty miles and days I needed to rest—seven months! To make the trip. The best travel season I would get, this far north, would be a hundred and fifty days, and that would mean starting in the month of Bloom, which was, at this point, long past. I wasn't sure exactly what day it was, but I knew we were well into Second Harvest at this point. That meant, I had, at best, ninety days to get across the high plains and get denned up for the winter.

It was late summer now, almost fall, and none of this route could be considered southern. It was, in fact the most northerly route of all those I had considered. No way could I travel twenty miles a day through mountain forests of snow and ice. I'd be lucky to make five miles a day, and what about shelter? And storms?

I'd be lucky to get six weeks travel in before I had to settle in somewhere for the winter, and how was I to carry enough food and gear for five months of winter on my own back? Never mind that I couldn't be considered even close to being in 'good' condition!

No, I'd need a pony to pack my gear, at the very least, and I'd do better with a dog, as well, and not just for company, but to help with the hunting and to serve as a lookout, but a dog and a pony would need to be fed. But even with a pony and a dog, should I be lucky enough to acquire them, the most food I'd be able to carry wouldn't take me much more than thirty days at a stretch. I'd have to stop and hunt meat, and then dry it somehow, as well as gather root

vegetables and greens. The time that would take would mean that I'd have to winter over, at some point in the journey, which would mean building a shelter and laying in supplies for the winter.

Magic could help with all of that—if I could learn to use it well enough.

Some of the skills I had already would help me; I could use a bow and arrows well enough, and I knew how to make bows and arrows. I also knew where there was a pony I could get, if not a dog. And I knew how to build a shelter, and how to do basic stone work.

These things were all valuable, but I'd need a lot more if I was to make it. I reached out and started making a list. Well, lists, actually. Magic skills needed. Sleep, first. Travel, second. Healing, third. Or maybe fighting third and healing fourth. If I could do a better job of fighting, I might not need as much healing. I wanted to have at least some kind of handle on all three before I left—if I could manage that in the five to ten days I hoped to have before I left.

I looked back at the books in front of me. I needed to get to it, then.

# X

# ESCAPE

**"W**E OWE YOU," KING MARC said, "more than mere money can pay. What can we do for you?"

I lifted my head from the book I'd been reading and blinked up at him. Of course he did. I'd wear scars the rest of my life from what his sons had done to me. I noticed he wasn't offering money. I could use money to get away from him.

"You can make sure that this never happens to any man, woman or child in your dungeons ever again," I told him, and gestured towards my scarred face. They hadn't given me a mirror in my rooms but I didn't have to see my face to know what it looked like. I could feel the fresh, new scars in my skin. The gouges and canyons in my face felt dramatic under my fingertips, just sore in some places and outright painful in others.

I knew I had to look a sight. Somehow I'd have to find a way to heal those scars so that they were not so raw, not so dramatic, if I was to have any kind of life to live at all. I couldn't live my life suspended between the bullies who would perceive my scars as proof that I had once been successfully bullied, so, in their view, could obviously be equally successfully bullied again, perhaps even to death, so they would gleefully get to it, and those who would merely shun me because the scars made me look 'different'.

"You're doing it," I told him. "I need books, so I can learn. I need to find a way to minimize my scars, I need to find a way to go forward, I need to find a way to survive."

I needed to learn how to use magic, and where to find Nogaynos and how to get there. I needed to figure out what I was going to need to make the attempt, how long it would take, how much food and supplies I would need, where to get them, and what trails to take. But I didn't say any of that. I didn't think it would be wise.

"Choose a dozen books," King Marc declared expansively. He counted those before me ostentatiously, including the book on magic. Then he went to the shelves and added three more, all on magic and the history of Nogaynos as well, and started signing each book over to me on the flyleaf.

I suspected that he considered books a good anchor to keep me here in the palace with him. Books were heavy, hard to carry, and the more he heaped me with, the greater the likelihood that I would stay. I thought he had a point, but the books wouldn't keep me. I would take some of them with me, and leave others and pray I made the right choices.

To that end, I tried to read every one of the books from start to finish, and to memorize as much of the histories and scouting reports as I could, working in the library with King Marc in the mornings and in my room in the afternoons and evenings. I practiced integrating my magic with my shadow boxing, sword fighting, and knife throwing, and, using the healing manuals, I tried to use my magic to strengthen my muscles and bones and smooth over my skin to repair the damage done to me. I tried to make certain my lungs were clear and that they would work well to serve me when I needed them.

I started winnowing out the books, then, too. I started with the twelve he had given me and worked down from there. I wound up with nine, in three groups of three, but I didn't dare to leave any more of them behind. I might find myself needing them rather desperately, somewhere out on the trail where the cost of leaving them behind might be more than I wanted to pay.

The histories got left out. I would be able to remember most of the information in them. I put the herbology, the gardening book and the big book on agriculture, crops and animal husbandry, in one bag. I put the books on magic into a second bag. The book on martial arts went into the third bag, along with a book on anatomy and the maps.

I was really going to need the forge pony, I thought, just to myself, and the shop come-along with him.

I practiced my sleep spells on my own guards. It would have been too dangerous to have tried them on King Marc, or his guards. They seemed to work just fine, but how could I tell? The poor men were left on duty all night long. They could have fallen asleep on their own at any time without my help. Not that it mattered. I had no intention of going out the door. No, I was going off the balcony, when I left.

Ten nights after King Marc had gifted me with my own library of books, I dropped the bag of books I meant to take with me off the balcony by a line made of braided sheeting. I followed the books down to the garden on the same line.

I eased through the garden carrying the bags on my back until I reached the sea, and then I traveled north along the shore from the palace, using a little bit of 'travel' magic here and there until I left the sea to turn inland towards my adoptive parents' home. It wasn't far inland.

Once there, at the house, I reached out with my mind the way the books had taught me, contacted first my adoptive father's mind, and then my adoptive

mother's, and dropped a sleep spell into each of their minds. My adoptive brothers weren't present, which didn't surprise me—they hardly ever were, these days. I gathered up the food I'd need first, and the cookery gear, pots and pans and utensils, plates and bowls and mugs and the rest, trying to be quiet but taking the bare minimum I thought I could get by with. Then I added my clothing and all the bedding and the money I'd need. I knew where they kept it, the hoard left to pay for my room and board for clothing and my start in life.

Marge` thought I didn't know about it, though how she could cling to that idea when she had forced me to clean her house for her so many times, to wash and iron her clothing and fold her garments and put them away, I couldn't fathom. I took a mere third of what was left—they'd spent precious little of it on me! But I took some of the jewels, the pearls and the opals, works of art that they were, and the strings of sapphires and emeralds Marge` paid so little attention to, as well as all of the loose stones.

Well, those that remained, anyway, a nice little gathering of diamonds, with another of rubies, many of them in 'off' colors, such as those rubies lighter or darker than the classic 'pigeon blood' red and diamonds that were pale blue or even a slightly violet blue. The last would fit nicely with the amethysts the collection contained, just as the sapphires would do well with the blue-ground fire opals.

Most of what jewels and gold were gone had been spent upon Marge`'s adornment, or to make the house larger and more luxurious, or refurbishing the forge, and providing both of them with new and better clothing than they would have had, if they hadn't had my inheritance to spend so. Cassee Smith made a good living, as most competent blacksmiths could, if they applied themselves, but a black-smith's living did not suit Marge`. She wanted more, and better, for herself and her sons, and she had dipped into the store of money supposed to be mine in order to get it. Now she would see me dead, to keep what remained of the fortune left for me.

I left her the diamonds and the rubies she kept in her own jewelry box, hidden inside her book drawer. She wanted them so much she had been willing to connive at murder to have them. Let her keep them to remember her sins by, if she would, which I doubted. Marge` was not the kind of woman who admitted her sins—to herself or anyone else.

I took silver and brass from the money box in the forge as well—I'd earned it! And I packed it down into the space beneath the seams of my back-pack, where the heavy leather would conceal it, leaving only a couple of stones and some silver coin where I could reach them. The brass farthings and a few of the smaller silver coin filled my small purse with a modest fund from which to purchase food, should I have need, a purse and the kind of money that fit with my clothing and gear. I wanted nothing about me to mark me out as a good target for theft.

My throwing knives went into their sheaths along my arms and legs, six in all, with my bow and quiver of arrows atop my backpack and my sword and poniard to my sash along my waist along with another pair of throwing knives.

At least I would go well-armed to face the world. I didn't intend to be an easy mark, if I couldn't avoid becoming a mark at all.

Of course, in some places, simply to have anything at all, including my gender, would mark me as prey, but I could hope to avoid such places.

Certainly I would try. I could not depend upon whatever it was which had removed my torturers happening again. Had it been luck? Had it even originated with me? I didn't know, and I didn't want to test it. I had my swords, my poniard, my throwing knives, and my bow and arrows. Better if I didn't have to use them.

I might be a fair swordsman, I might be a better than fair bowman, and I might be very skilled with my knives, but I was only one person, and one person could always be overcome by numbers, if enough of them came against me. No. Better to avoid conflict whenever possible.

I took tools and some raw ingots of iron and copper I'd formed myself, a small supply of coke, the Smith's spare bellows, stacks of forged steel rods with which to make horseshoes and anything else needing to be shaped out of steel, such as the steel plates which, fit together with the stove bricks, to make the firebox of my stove. Once set up, it would serve as heating stove, cooking surface, baking oven, and forge. The small anvil would have to come with me as well. I'd need it to make the steel frames I'd need for the windows I intended to put in my winter den, and the hinges for the doors I'd have to have to make it through the cold months, and to shape the multiple sets of shoes for the pony I'd need for the trip to Nogaynos.

I checked one item after another off the lists I had pored over in the King's luxurious rooms, one list for the come-along, one for the packs to be loaded on the pony's back, food and bedding, and yet another for the pack to go on my own back. Clothing, more food, and yet more bedding, canvas tarps, a pair of cloaks for me and one for the pony. I wouldn't make it far west before winter closed in; I'd need all the warm clothes and all the warm bedding I could carry to make it through. And as for food, well, I'd never be able to carry enough food to get through the winter, but I'd have to try to pack as much as I could.

Certainly I decimated the stores my adoptive mother had been laying in.

Well, she'd just have to use the money I'd left her to buy more. It wasn't as if she didn't have plenty of it.

Fifty pounds of corn, fifty pounds of oats, and forty pounds of wheat may sound like a lot, particularly when you add twenty-five pounds of dried meat and twenty more of dried beans, but they won't last long through a hard winter, though they are about all one pony can carry. At least I could add that much more to the come-along, with a good fifty pounds in a variety of dried roots, herbs and vegetables, and another supply (five pounds each) to my own back- pack.

The entire time I packed I felt stretched, strained to the limit, my hands shaking with a fine tremor I could feel. I worked as quickly as I could manage. Each minute that passed seemed to tick loudly in my ears.

I didn't dare to take too much—everything I took would have to fit either on my back, the pony's back, or into the small come-along rig the pony could pull—but I feared I might leave behind something I would find I couldn't do without and couldn't manage to make or acquire without risking my life. Of course, I was risking my life now! At least I had my lists—without them, I didn't know if I would have succeeded.

The come-along was so small it could hardly be called a wagon, taller than it was long, narrower at the top than it was at the bottom, without anything that could be designated a seat and completely lacking any kind of cover. Well, unless I wrapped it well in tarps. If I loaded it right with the heaviest weight at the bottom, it wouldn't be top-heavy, it would be stable, stout and durable.

Designed to carry heavy weights, yet still cover difficult terrain without creating a hardship for the pony pulling it, it could carry my anvil, the stove, my supplies and tools, and the bag of books easily, though it wasn't designed to carry a person. Bins for fruit, root vegetables and greens would go on top of the smithing tools, along with the dried meat and beans, cornmeal and wheat to supplement what Nutmeg and I would carry. A supply of sand, lime and soda would give me the ingredients for glass, and the cast iron ingots I included didn't take up much room, tucked around the anvil the way they were, though they were heavy.

The sections of my firebox would fit across the bottom and my stove-pipe could be lashed to the back and filled with more dried beans. The jugs of honey didn't take up too much room along the back. The extra bedding and tarps would go on top to cover everything and help to keep it lashed into place, though both Nutmeg and I would carry tarps and bedding as well as more grain, dried meat and beans and root vegetables. I'd need those tarps for a make shift shelter before I got something more permanent built.

A quick look around the forge didn't bring much of anything more to mind and I didn't have much time to linger, and I knew it. If I hadn't packed enough to get us through the winter, we'd be in trouble, but I didn't see how I could manage any more. The come-along was already heavier than I liked, and I'd put more weight on Nutmeg than I really wanted him carrying. I hadn't exactly shorted my load, either. Whether what I'd packed would see me through the winter and into the spring, I doubted. But I just couldn't see how the pony and I could manage any more weight, or the come-along, either.  If I had left something out, well, I would just have to learn to do without it or figure out something to substitute for it.

I finished hitching the pony up to the come-along, and headed out, the pack on the pony's back even more bulky than the one on mine, for the postern gate in the city wall. I didn't know how I'd manage 'travel' with the pony, but I knew I'd need to figure it out. It couldn't be much more than four hours to dawn, and I had to be well out of sight of the city's walls by then, if not into the forest itself.

The 'travel' spell I'd learned from my books had been problematical in the city, even with just me, and if it hadn't been dark, with few people out and around, I don't know if I could have managed it, but using it, I had gotten the distance from the palace to the forge, which generally took about an hour, on foot, at a walk, in ten minutes. It couldn't, I figured, be any more difficult out on the road, even in the dark, but how I was to manage it with the pony and the come-along, I couldn't guess. I'd have to try though, more, I'd have to make it work. Somehow.

At the postern gate, the 'sleep' spell worked again, most effectively. And once the guards were deeply asleep, the pony and I slipped out through the gate, the latch balanced to drop back into its housing and lock again behind us. Then we were away, the road north and west stretching out before us. I started down it, leading the pony, and at the same time, I started to work at the 'travel' spell to include the pony, chanting the spell in rhythm with my steps.

Nutmeg wasn't a small pony, he was almost—but not quite—big enough to be considered a horse. I could ride him well enough, and so had my adoptive brothers when they were younger. He had a nice little shifty single-foot pace that fit into the travel spell much more easily than I had expected it to or had even dared to hope it would. And, with the road stretching out before us in the spare light of a waning moon, a good many of the problems I'd faced in the city disappeared. We moved along smoothly, and, in something like three or four hours' time, we had managed to get a distance that would usually take a full day of travel and more besides, away from the city's walls.

I felt tired, and Nutmeg looked as if he had traveled a full day, and a long one, at that, but we still had a little time before dawn and I knew we, each of us, still had several miles' travel left in us. I figured we ought to get off the road and into the trees now, and head north as well as west for a while, until we could find a sheltered place to make camp.

More 'travel' spell gave us a bit of a boost, and as soon as we got well into the trees, I tied Nutmeg to one and left him to rest, returning to the road to obliterate any sign of where we'd left the road as best I could. I had no idea just how far we had come, but I knew we'd come a lot farther than a person could normally come in three or four hours. I could take some comfort in knowing that we'd managed to get a lot farther away from the city than anyone could reasonably expect.

No one would be looking for us this far out away from the city. Here, Nutmeg's unshod hoofprints would elicit little attention, if any, but the marks the wide wheels left, under their heavy load, would bring me all kinds of unwanted attention, if anyone noticed them. If at all possible, I didn't want anyone to know we'd passed this way.

I doubted we'd run into outlaws this close to the city, knowing, as I did, how well patrolled the trade routes were. Northern Amadea tended to be pretty free of outlawry in general, with more of it to be found inside the city than the country-side, but that didn't mean I wouldn't run into bad luck out here beyond all help. I could fight, but I'd rather not, if I didn't have to. There was entirely too much chance that I would lose.

In under the trees I couldn't use 'travel' much and didn't even try, really.

We struggled from tree to tree for what seemed like an eternity, with the moon down, now, and the shadows under the trees making it difficult to see. The trackless, uneven ground made the come-along hang up here and there, and I wished I'd thought to learn a 'see in the dark' spell. By the time we stopped under cover, to hide from the lightening sky, the road seemed far away, though it probably wasn't, really, and I unhitched Nutmeg from the come-along and unloaded his packs, pegging him to a tree by his front foot so he could graze.

I didn't really make 'camp', I just cobbled together a bedroll out of the tarps and bedding I'd packed, snugging it back into a small copse of large-leaved saplings with a tarp over it to help hide it. Then I curled up into it to sleep as the first light of the coming dawn illuminated the leaves and branches of the trees all around us. As soon as we'd both gotten some rest, and a little something to eat, I thought, as I drifted off, we'd head farther into the woods, bearing west, until we found a good place to settle for the winter. I could always hope we could make it to the Mahdi side of the plains before we had to stop and den up through the seasons of snow, but I wouldn't be counting on it. I suspected I would have to spend two seasons of travel and two winters denned up through the cold and the snow to make my way to Nogaynos.

I thought it a very good thing I had that book of maps King Marc had given me.

# XI

## GARVE`

**"S**HE'S GONE."

King Marc looked up from the work he had spread out in front of him. He had been at work for hours, barely aware of the people who brought the reports in to him to read, never mind anyone else.

"She can't be," he returned. "She had all those books. She couldn't possibly carry all of them."

"There were three books left on the table in her room," Garve` informed him. "She took what few clothes we gave her."

"Weapons?" King Marc demanded.

"She had none," Garve` reported.

His father blanched.

"Defenseless . . ." he murmured, more to himself than to his son. His gaze bored a hole in the wall as he stared, appalled at his thoughts.

"She went out the balcony," Garve` told him matter-of-factly. "She tied sheeting together and used it."

Garve` didn't exactly consider it good riddance to bad rubbish, but neither did he comprehend his father's concern. The girl was, after all, just another common member of the hoi polloi and she had freed him from the need for courting her. Huge relief rolled over him at that thought, though he tried to hide his sigh.

She should not have been abused, of course, that had been entirely wrong, but he did not understand his father's feelings about her. That she had left barely rated a shrug from him. At least now, he thought, with some relief, he would not have to marry her in order to inherit the kingdom. He felt rather grateful for that, more to the cosmos than to Vere.

"Her guards?" His father demanded.

"Never heard a thing," Garve` assured him.

"I don't like it," King Marc told him.

"Nobody likes it," Garve` pointed out calmly.

"Have you sent to her adoptive parents?"

"I've got men on their way."

"They'd better not lay a hand on her!" King Marc snarled. "Did you make that clear to them?"

"Of course I did," Garve` assured him, completely mendaciously. How, he wondered, careful not to let his thoughts show on his face, were they to force the girl back here if she didn't want to come, if they didn't lay a hand on her?

"Better look in the dungeons," King Marc advised him. And then, "No," he decided abruptly, turning on his heel, "I'll do it."

In the dungeons both Garve` and the more than apologetic dungeon-master followed him about as the king forced every cell to be thrown open, every interrogation room to be exposed in its entirety.

"I would never," the dungeon-master all but whined, from King Marc's heels. "If anyone had tried to bring that girl back down here, I would have hidden her in my own rooms and sent for you!"

King Marc swung around on his heel and eyed the anxious man narrowly. "According to you, both the Crown Prince and another man took her out of the cell you'd put her in and took her to a room and tortured her, on two different occasions, all without your knowledge." He said it heavily.

"I did know it when Prince Nehl took her," the man returned, shame-faced. "I had no idea what he'd do to her, but I did know he took her. But I thought he just meant to ask her some questions. I never dreamed he'd lay a hand on her, or allow any other man to hit her! We don't torture girls down here! We don't torture anybody. Not like that! I didn't know about the second man. I swear.

I never even saw him." Garve` winced for him.

"Yet you didn't have her taken to the infirmary immediately upon realizing that she had been tortured, either time," King Marc accused him.

"No, sir," the dungeon-master admitted, "and that was wrong, and I knew it. But the Crown Prince--!"

"From now on out, the Crown Prince gives no orders in this dungeon and lays no hands upon any prisoner. And should that particular lady reappear in your world—or any girl! Any girl at all! You will notify me immediately! And I will stipulate whatever alternative care is to be instituted. No one else!" The king almost roared it. "And," he snaked his head threateningly at the hand wringing dungeon-master, "you will order immediate medical care for any girl who shows any sign—any sign! That she has been harmed in any way! Is that clear!"

"Yessir, that's clear," the dungeon-master assured him, bobbing his head dutifully. "And I swear to you, I would have called in the healer right away, if the Crown Prince hadn't ordered otherwise! I swear it!"

"In fact," King Marc continued, to Garve`'s shock, looking around himself thoughtfully, "you may find yourself housing the Crown Prince here himself, one of these days, if he ever repeats this behavior of his."

"Sir? Your Majesty?" The dungeon-master blanched at the very idea.

"Help the Crown Prince to torture one more young girl," King Marc informed him, staring him right in the eye, now, "and you may find yourself in a cell with him. We'll see how well you like it when he lays hands on you the way he did on that young girl!"

The dungeon-master dropped to his knees, his face etched in horror, proving that he knew exactly what had been done to Vere.

"No, your majesty," he gulped.

"We," King Marc lessoned him, "do not torture women or young girls in this country! We do not starve prisoners, we do not torture them, we do not open windows on them, and we do not leave them to lie upon bare stone floors!" His voice increased over every word until it reached a dull roar.

"No, your majesty," the dungeon-master nodded, dutifully, from his knees. "I didn't know," he moaned, excusing himself.

"You had to know!" The king roared it. Then, catching himself, he took a deep breath and managed to lower his voice to something approaching reasonable. "We house prisoners here until they can be tried for their crimes, if they did, indeed, commit crimes," he continued his lesson. "We keep convicted felons here who are serving out their sentences, men who have been proven guilty. We do not even put men who have not yet been found guilty in with those who have. How, on God's green earth, could you have ever imagined that it was all right to torture a child?!"

"Please, sir," the gaoler begged. "I never did, sir. Never, I swear it!"

"He broke her nose," King Marc told him dangerously. "He broke her cheek- bone. He broke her jaw. She was taken from the interrogation room unconscious. You are the dungeon-master. You had to know!" He shouted the last words.

"The Crown Prince?" the dungeon-master sounded horrified over the question. "He swore she was all right," he insisted. "That she was just shamming it, that he hadn't hurt her. He swore!" the man insisted.

"The Crown Prince," King Marc repeated. Firmly. "My son," he mourned. "A dishonorable monster who beat an innocent young girl for nothing more nor better than his own enjoyment of doing it! And then lied about it! And your job—which you failed to do! Was to check on her condition YOURSELF! To make certain of it!"

The dungeon-master swallowed hard.

"I didn't know," he said again, dully, this time. King Marc snaked his head again.

"Not much of a dungeon-master, are you?" he more stated than asked. "Never," the dungeon-master promised him. "Never again."

"You are here," King Marc informed him, "precisely to made certain that such things don't happen."

"Yes, your majesty," the dungeon-master agreed, humbly. He stayed on his knees as King Marc swung about on his heel and left the dungeon. He did not even attempt to stagger upright, despite the chill of the stone on his knees, until he heard the last of the three doors between the dungeons and the upper reaches of the Castle clang to

a close. Then, slowly and carefully, he lurched to his feet as Garve`
watched him with silent curiosity, from the shadows.

"Got him fooled, she has," a coarse voice declared, and the
dungeon-master turned in the direction of the voice, his jaw jutting
forward as he regarded the heavy, harsh features of the man now in
front of him. He raised his voice.

"Guards!" he called. To the man, he said only, "You knew." He
breathed it out. Repeated it more loudly. "You knew!"

"'Course I knew," the man informed him loftily. "I was there when
the Crown Prince beat her, now wasn't I?" he bragged. "Helped him
to chain her down to the chair myself, I did."

When the guards came, and the dungeon-master ordered them
to take him, he acted like he couldn't believe it, that he couldn't
understand, yanking at his arms as the guards anchored him by them.

"What do you mean by this?" he demanded. "I'm the Prince's
man, I am, and you've got no right to do this! No right!"

Garve` watched, and he listened, as they mured him up in a
cell. So Nehl had men in place, brutes like that one. How many,
he wondered, as he followed thoughtfully along the way his father
had taken before him, did his brother have among the guards? Had
he suborned men along the palace walls, as well? Did he have men
among the city guards? Men like that brute, men with a taste for
sadistic pleasures? Bully boys, the corrupt, like Jiden, criminals who
wanted a change, the better to be able to ply their brutal, torturing,
murdering, thieving trades?

He reached the stairs, taking the steps two at a time as he mulled
it over. And what of Freddy? He asked himself. He knew whatever
Nehl was up to, the two of them were in it together. Had Freddy been
in that room with Nehl when he was beating on the young girl that
Freddy had known since childhood? Had Freddy acquiesced in that?
Had he stood there and watched? Or had he taken part in the beating?
Had he put his share of bruises on her body? Cracked her ribs and
broken them with his own fists?

He thought he could never, would never, feel the kind of horror
he felt then, knowing the truthful answers to at least some of those

questions would be in the affirmative. But the one fact he knew for certain made his blood run icy cold in his veins—that the two of them had been in it together. Because if they had been in it together, and if they would do what they had done to a young girl that Freddy had known, and known so well, what did that mean for him? How did he figure in their plans? Hum?

He knew he didn't matter to Nehl. He never had. Nehl didn't like girls because his nature was too cold to allow him to 'like' anyone. Once Nehl had managed to kill their father, Garve` realized, with a chill that shook his entire body, he'd be coming for Garve` next. He had to wonder, would Nehl have him chained to a chair so he could beat him, the way he'd beaten a helpless girl? So he could enjoy breaking his bones the way he'd enjoyed breaking her bones?

Garve` shuddered at the very thought, because he believed, right down into the depths of his heart, that Nehl would do it, if he could. King Marc wasn't the only one who needed to make the best use of his time out in the yard. Vere's advice applied to him just as much as it did to his father, and, Garve` realized, he could learn to beat his brother on the field of battle. He was bigger, he was taller, he was more muscular, and he was faster and stronger than his brother.

Than either of his brothers, actually. If he applied himself to his exercises, he could make himself into a formidable swordsman.

Nehl was not an outright bad swordsman, but neither was he an outstandingly good one, even if he did think he was. Mostly, he was just mediocre with his blades, not that anyone would tell him so.

Well, of course, he was the Crown Prince, and Margrete had brought him up to believe himself better than anyone else. His masters had to cozen him into learning anything, to coax and sweeten everything they tried to teach him with a coating of sugar. No one ever told him anything more critical than that his foot- work needed practice, or that he needed to keep his blade up. Margrete hadn't allowed it and the Crown Prince had grown up believing that he was a good deal better at just about everything than he was.

As long as he never had to fight for his life, this misapprehension was only dangerous to the men around him. But if he ever had to really fight—well, Margrete's insistence on such unwarranted praise might cost him his life.

It had made Nehl lazy. Mentally lazy, mostly, but physically lazy as well. He didn't train as hard as he could because he believed he was already better than anyone else. Such thinking would not serve him well on the field of battle, where his opponents wouldn't care overmuch that he was the Crown Prince, except that, if they could kill him, they could count themselves the victors.

Garve` wondered if that opponent would be his father, or if it just might turn out to be he, himself. Would Nehl force them to the battle? Or would he and Freddy sidle around like the cowardly snakes they were, getting others to fight their battles for them? He thought of Jiden. And Vere. Nehl had to have her chained to a chair in order to feel safe enough to beat her. So yes, Freddy and Nehl would sidle about behind them and get others to fight their battles for them.

Garve` wondered if his father realized that.

# XII

# VERE

IAWAKENED TO FULL SUNLIGHT AND a snoozing pony. Nutmeg had eaten his fill and now I had to find water for him. I packed him up, added the harness to the little come-along, and then hefted my own pack. Then, with a last look at my map, I started out, leading Nutmeg behind me and chewing on a stick of dried meat. I had water for myself, but felt a little ashamed to be drinking it when Nutmeg hadn't had any water.

We were lucky. We found a small stream in not much more than a mile and Nutmeg drank his fill while I ate a corn cake. It was chewy, but filling, and made, with the water and the dried meat, a fairly good meal. I gave Nutmeg an oat cake of his own, and then, finishing with a few slices of dried apple, I started out again, but this time Nutmeg and I followed the stream up into the hills. It seemed to me to be as good a direction as any, considering that the stream flowed both north and west at the same time and the going was easy enough so I could engage my 'travel' spell.

Far behind us, much farther than I had anticipated we had come, only the tallest spires of the city remained visible from the high ground and they looked small and distant below us. As we moved through the day, it became apparent to me that we had come a good eighty miles in the night, meaning that the 'travel' spell had worked a good deal better than I had hoped it would, probably due to Nutmeg's measured, rhythmic strides. The realization brought an optimism to me that I hadn't felt for a long time. If the 'travel' spell worked that well, it would provide me a real advantage in being able to get a safe distance from the city before having to hole up for the coming winter.

Somewhere along the line, we were going to have to turn to the west to head for the Mahdi border, and we had better do it well before we hit the ice fields, but I figured we had fifty or sixty miles to go before we did that, if not more, so I wasn't worried. Yet. When the stream started to lean to the west, I felt quite pleased, and we kept on following it. I couldn't say it was easy going.

The stream flowed along the bottom of a long draw, and where it was wide enough for the little cart, that was fine, but most of the time we had to cut along the sides of one hill or another, crossing back and forth over the stream to whichever side of it provided the easiest going. The little come-along was relatively heavy, and that didn't help. There certainly wasn't any possibility of using 'travel', or at least, not beyond the barest hint of it. Instead, I had to find a way to use levitation on the side hills to keep the little come-along balanced, so it wouldn't tip over.

We made slow time. In one sunny little swale, we came across a handful of small apple trees, all of them heavily loaded down with fruit. I picked every apple I could reach that was anything close to ripe, harvesting a rich supply of them, but the early ripening of the apples only made me remember all the more how little the time I had left to travel before we would have to den up for the winter. I made stopgap bags of my tarps and loaded them down with as many apples as I could carry, managing enough so that I began to feel bad for Nutmeg, what with all the cornmeal, oats and wheat he had already been carrying. I added as many as I could to my own pack, and tried to see that the little carry-all took the worst of the weight before heading out again.

Now I tried to use 'travel' while balancing the little come-along with levitation and helping Nutmeg out with it as well, to lighten the load he carried. Once I got the hang of that, I added lightening my back-pack a little, to take the strain off my feet and ankles. We started to get along a little better, then, though managing the spells took a lot of my attention and more than a little of my energy.

I doubted we covered more than four miles an hour on our own, and if I was able to double that with 'travel' I would have been surprised to learn it but we did manage to keep going. We traveled for more than eight hours, leaving the city so far behind I could not only not see the tallest spires, I lost even the sense of its existence. The fastness of the forest seemed to close in around us, sheltering us as we traveled in a hushed quiet that wasn't—quite--silence.

Finding a bit of a flat along the stream, we settled there for the night and made a small camp just a few yards up the hill from the stream where Nutmeg could get some grass.

I even dared to have a bit of a fire, in some rocks I dug out of the stream.

The dried pieces of branches I found here and there made a nice little fire, and I managed to cook a hot meal for dinner. After breakfast the next morning, seeing as the stream was heading the right direction (slightly north but mostly west) and not too steep, we just kept following it along. Three weeks later, we were still doing the same thing, having located a small orchard of orange trees and loaded up on them, as well.

I'd loaded easily another ten or fifteen pounds of them into my own pack, given the depredations I'd made on the victuals in it. It didn't seem like much, considering how much extra weight I'd loaded on poor Nutmeg and the over-

flowing bags and bins in the come-along. I'd loaded even more on it, which was now, between the oranges and the apples, so top heavy I feared it would turn over on every side hill without the levitation.

But we still managed to keep going, though sometimes it seemed that the stream we followed got shallower and narrower every day. At least it dipped almost as much south as it did west, these days. Given how early we started each morning, I figured we would have made about twenty miles or even a little more each day without any 'travel' help, and quite possibly twice that with what 'travel' help I was able to summon. Some days—the good days—maybe we even made three times twenty. I hoped.

The entire time the stream faithfully guided us mostly to the west, but stayed well into the forest, climbing all the while in a gradual, subtle grade. I think we'd managed to get something over eight, or maybe even nine hundred miles from the city without seeing any signs of human habitation anywhere by the time we arrived at the area where the stream originated.

We hadn't gotten all the way across the plains, I didn't think, but I could at least suspect that we'd managed to drift well enough south to leave the bitterest of the cold to come behind us. I had hoped to get to Mahdi before winter set in, but I thought that was now a vain hope. I doubted we'd gotten anywhere near the Mahdi border, which I had hoped to at least reach before we stopped for the winter, but I suspected this was the best place we were going to find to winter over, so we'd best dig in and make the best of it.

The spring from which the stream issued forth was a small one, burbling out of the rocks at the base of a rounded hillside where a scattering of aspen among the evergreens made a nice little copse to hide our den. I took a long look at the place and didn't have any trouble visualizing how I could make that little U- shaped area into a shelter that would keep us through the winter very nicely.

If I was right, I'd managed to make eighty or even ninety miles the first night, with all the 'travel' I'd used, and maybe forty or even fifty miles the next day. Estimating something over forty each day since, with the possibility that we had managed to make even more meant a minimum estimate of nine hundred miles and a strong possibility we'd come even farther. That meant I was far enough from the city to hunker down and dig in for the winter, if I wanted to.

I tried to figure the distances we'd come as conservatively as I could; I limited how much I factored in my use of 'travel' and tried to allow for the winding of the stream. If I'd underestimated how much advantage the 'travel' spell had conferred upon us, we might even have come a thousand miles or more, though I figured nine hundred would be more accurate. I admit I hadn't factored in how the levitation and 'travel' spells might have interacted, or imagined that they might have amplified each other.   Frankly, if nine hundred miles was all we had managed, I was a happy camper.

I tried pinpointing my position on the map without a great deal of success. If I judged by the terrain I saw around us, by the types of trees and brush, and by what little I could see from the high ground we'd occasionally crossed, I'd estimate we had come closer to fifteen hundred miles than a thousand, but that couldn't be right, could it? The 'travel' spells couldn't have made that much difference, could they? I just didn't know. I had no experience with the magic to go by. All I knew was how tired using the spells together continuously made me.

I did know how many days I'd been traveling at this point—twenty-four.

Those I could count and record in my little travel journal, and I had, along with descriptions of the trails I'd followed—when there had been trails—and the camp sites I'd spent my nights at. I studied my maps in the firelight of my evening campfire thoughtfully. If someone had told me that I had followed the stream not merely to the borders of Mahdi, but well inside them, I would have been astonished. If they'd added that I'd even managed to get about a hundred miles south of Amadea's Palace City's position, I would have been beyond astonished.

Oh, I knew that following the stream had kept me focused on its meanderings, and I had known I had been traveling vaguely south as well as west, navigating the side hills of the draws the stream traveled along had absorbed all my attention. Just keeping the come-along upright had required concentration. That I had crossed over a pass through the mountains via long, gradual climbs I realized without really comprehending it. Oh, I was elated—a little—but I didn't truly understand what I had managed.

I might have paused an hour or two here and there to gather up some wild rice in sheltered swale, some oats from a sunny slope, some wheat from another sweep of ground, and red beans to dry from a veil of creepers hanging from a network of branches, but I hadn't spent long at it. What I had gathered mounded the come-along in a hill of its own, two or three large sacks from each unexpected gift of nature's bounty, a surety that, with the addition of a little meat, I would make it handily through the winter. I was deeply grateful, but none of those gifts made for any kind of useable landmark, and all of them distracted me from the acknowledgement of the extent of the sheer distance I traveled.

Amadea's Palace City was an anomaly. Set a couple of hundred miles below the ice fields, it stretched from a deep inlet that created a quiet bay in which ships could safely drop anchor, across several miles just above the sea to the forested foothills under the ice fields. It had sprung up where it was because it had both access to the sea and to the northern-most trade route from Mahdi, and through the centuries it had sprawled out between the two trade hubs. Goods that came in from Mahdi could be transported through the city, loaded on huge galleys, and then transported south to the cities along the coast to the south, fetching up in Quattar.

Or at least, they had before the northern route had been closed by the encroaching ice some nearly three hundred years ago. By then Amadea's Palace City had been well established and the closing of the northern sea route hadn't seriously impacted the city's markets. It hadn't hurt that the northern route across the plains was far and away the shortest route to Mahdi. Never mind that it wasn't open until the end of the month of Bloom and sometimes even the start of First Harvest, and started closing down by the end of Apple. With a Nogaynos Mage who had good command of their travel spells, not much of a problem. Without?

Well, since the diaspora when finding a good Nogaynos 'travel' Mage started to get difficult to do, not much travel came over the northern route. Too hard to get from one end to the other before winter closed in and whichever end you got stuck on you stayed through the winter and started back the other way come spring. I'd been lucky so far.

The maps showed clearly where the Amadean border stood along the northern route, some three hundred and fifty miles from the Palace City. By the landmarks, I knew I had passed that boundary and left it far behind long before the end of the first week I'd been on the trail. Unfortunately, traveling through the hills the way I had been, seldom staying on established trails any length of time at all, additional landmarks had not appeared often. If I were to go by the number of trails I had either followed or merely crossed, I would have estimated that I had come more than twelve hundred miles since leaving the Amadean border behind.

I thought that far too optimistic an assessment of the distance I'd come, but I wasn't sure it mattered. I'd started late in the summer and traveled deep into Third Harvest. Apple now looked me in the eye, and Blood, with the first freeze, when the pigs were slaughtered and made into sausage and deer hunted for their meat, would arrive hard on Apple's heels. Snow would soon follow, Bitter and Ice scurrying along on its heels. Thaw would be a long time coming, with a not-so-sweet Mud resulting from Thaw.

This far north, winter came quickly and would remain for long. We were reaching the end of Harvest, now. Better, I thought, to get settled for the winter, here, than go on and get caught out in the first blizzard, trying to build some kind of shelter while fighting the wind and driving snow. And then next Spring, we could start west again, maybe shifting a bit to the south as soon as we could catch sight of the plains.

I didn't want to get caught out on the plains—there would be little cover there, and no place to hide, either from the wind, the snow, or the King's men, never mind bandits. I wanted to stay in the woods, but well outside the Mahdi border, go as far as we could before the end of summer, and then find a good place to winter over again, if we hadn't made it to Nogaynos by then. There, we'd build another shelter and lay in more supplies for the winter.

We could start traveling all over again in the spring, assuming I'd managed to lay in enough supplies to do it. If I hadn't, I'd get a late start, if I got any start at all. If I was really lucky, I'd reach Nogaynos two autumns from now, hopefully early enough to lay in winter supplies. Or at least, that was the plan.

That, and to spend the winters studying magic. I had the books King Marc had given me and I meant to practice, beginning with building my stove out of rock and the metal sections of the old forge

I'd brought. I'd already picked up some rocks out of the stream that I could use; I had recognized copper and iron easily enough—rocks with copper in them had streaked green in places, where the copper had been exposed to air and oxidized.

Copper, I knew, was always useful, and if I could harvest both rock and iron from the stream, I would do very well indeed, and for more than one reason— the metal and rock would be good practice materials for my magic. I knew how to forge metals already—adding magic might not be easy, but it ought, at least, to be a natural progression. Finding the stream, I told myself, as I laid myself down not far from it, that night, had been a real blessing.

I spent most of the next day cutting grass to dry for Nutmeg for the winter and mapping out the footprint of the winter shelter I intended to build. The stove, I thought, would fit nicely in the middle of the space, a few feet to the far side of where the spring came out of the rocks. With a little ingenuity, I could pipe some of the water from the spring to the far side of the shelter to where I could, I suspected, form a small water trough for Nutmeg. Some of the chill water could be warmed in a small reservoir at the back of the stove for bathing and washing dishes. I could form a small sink in the rock just beyond the spring, while still channeling the majority of the water into the stream.

I enjoyed the work of building the shelter. None of the problems it entailed seemed insoluble, and the days remained long enough for me to make headway on cutting enough of the grass growing along the stream's swale to dry a goodly stack of hay to feed Nutmeg through the winter as well as to work at raising the walls of my shelter and spend an hour or two an evening studying my books. I found plenty of local stone to use, a good bit of it coming out of the stream bed, some of which even provided me with cooper or iron ores to use in my forge.

Because I didn't want to make it obvious that anyone lived in my winter camp—or even that it was a winter camp—I took the rocks I needed from well down-stream, and took out what trees I needed from a goodly distance away. I used levitation and 'travel' to get both timber and rocks back to my camp. It was a good practice, and using my magic felt exhilarating. It was so very helpful.

With it, I could take down trees, denude them of their branches, split them, lift them, transport them, all things that, without my magic, would have been, if not impossible, at least difficult, labor intensive, time-consuming and which would have created a trail right back to my door. With the magic of levitation and 'travel', I was able to transport sections of the trees back to use in the shelter without leaving so much as a leaf out of place, never mind a trail.

By the end of a week, the outline of Nutmeg's shelter had taken shape, along with the extension to the rockfall over and in front of the spring, and I'd managed to almost half fill the back corner of the haymow I was building. I had already decided that I'd put my larder behind the spring, into a nook in the rock. According to the book of magics, I would be able to bespell either meat or vegetables or almost anything non-living to keep fresh for practically ever. One simply bespelled whatever meat or milk or eggs or fruit or greens one wanted kept fresh, and then sealed it inside glass containers which could be square or round or just about any other shape at all, as long as the glass was then sealed and kept sealed until the food inside was wanted. So far, it seemed to work.

I practiced with the couple of spare glass jars I had, and the spell seemed both simple and easy to use. Uncooked rabbit meat I had sealed inside the jar had emerged after five full days as fresh as the moment I had sealed it up and ready to prepare, and so did the greens. That didn't mean much. But—if I could make the spell work for any real length of time, it would allow me to keep food fresh all through the winter.

Everything the geography told me indicated that I was still far enough north that I would see freezing temperatures throughout the winter, and that winter would come comparatively early here, and stay throughout most of Mud month. I needed to stock up on roots, greens, fruit and meat, as well as any squash or additional grains I could find, and I needed to do it soon. Right now, I was already making trips to lower elevations to gather fruit and greens that were even now ripening, or in many cases, already ripened. Soon, I would have to start catching more than rabbits.

I knew how to make glass. My adoptive father had taught me how to make it in the forge. It had been one of the first things I'd learned to make. A smith had a furnace in order to make iron into steel. It worked just as well for glass, particularly if you weren't too finicky about how transparent it was, how thin, or how free of flaws.

I didn't have my adoptive father's furnace, and without it, glassmaking would be a lot more difficult, so before I could make glass, I needed to get my stove fully installed so it could serve as my furnace. I had the cast iron plates I'd brought with me on the little come-along, and they would make the back, the top and the front plates of the stove-furnace. I could use the additional ingots I had made to make the reservoir to hold the heated water. Once the stone sides and floor of the stove-furnace had been made, I could assemble the rest and start burning the wood I had left over from my building projects. I could use the shavings to get the fire going, and after that, it would just be getting things done in order.

I started my day cutting hay and laying it down to cure up where it could dry well. Then I took Nutmeg and we went down stream to where we could gather fruit and greens and edible roots to carry back to camp. Once the fruit had been cached in my evolving pantry, where at least, for now, I could keep it cool and retard its spoilage, I would check my snares and hope I had scored at least a rabbit or two. If I had been fortunate enough to catch one, I skinned it, pegged the skin out to dry, so it could be tanned with the magic spell I'd found, and then dumped the rest of the rabbit into the stew pot.

What daylight I had left, at that point, I would use in building the furnace, or once it had been finished, the rest of the shelter. The idea was to make it look as if it wasn't any kind of habitation at all, but just a continuation of the hill itself, mostly rock outcrop with a little bit of dirt and grass and more than a few shrubs to disguise what it actually was.

The door, which opened into the hay and feed room section of Nutmeg's space, I secreted behind a scatter of trees and rocks that masked the indentation in the hill that formed the stable. I even disguised the fence that bounded Nutmeg's paddock as patches of brambles punctuated by trees, both living and dead, and piles of branches. The wild roses didn't hurt, I could use their branches to twine everything together, and their hips would make me a lovely

tea to drink through the winter. At least, I reminded myself, I would have plenty of honey to sweeten it with, given all I'd packed. (Poor Nutmeg!)

The paddock covered about a third of an acre and though I had cut the grass inside of it first, it had already achieved some re-growth. With a little bit of grain, it kept Nutmeg well-fleshed and more than content, despite the trees dotted about through it.

The area to what I thought of as the front of the shelter, and the side, where the stream meandered away, comprised an additional something like three quarters of an acre. As I got each area's grass cut and set out to dry, I would peg Nutmeg out to graze over it in the evening, as soon as we had brought in the day's gleanings in fruit and greens and roots. I had the oats, wheat, and corn I had brought with me from the city warded and stored safely with the roots I'd gathered, but I needed to get the glass containers made for all the additional vegetables and grain I'd gathered.

Deer were just about as fat as they were going to get, at this point, so I needed to do some hunting. With what I had now, one good-sized deer or two smallish deer would just about keep me for the winter, providing me with both meat for eating and fat for candlelight. I just needed the glass to store the meat. Well, and the pots and pans to cook with, but I had four I'd brought with me from the city, and the ingots I'd loaded in the come-along would make me more as soon as I'd got the higher priority items made.

Sand I was able to easily get enough out of the stream bed, and some of it even contained iron. I'd brought soda and lime with me, albeit not in large quantities. Well, I'd been limited in the weight I could carry, the weight Nutmeg could carry, and what would fit into the come-along, which wasn't large. With four three inch wide wheels on steel spokes and double axles, the come-along could carry a lot of weight, so I'd loaded it with all the really heavy stuff, the anvil, the pots, the copper and iron ingots, the cast iron stove plates, the brick lining for the stove, most of the extra apples and oranges, and the additional oats and cornmeal, that sort of thing. And, of course, the soda and lime and the rest of the things I'd need to make my special, unbreakable glass. (I'd known I'd need glass for long-term food storage.)

Then I got busy.

# XIII

# FREDDY AND NEHL

FREDDY BOWED OVER THE OLDEST D'Arcy girl's hand and pretended to kiss it and she simpered up at him from under her fake eyelashes. Freddy smirked at her and pretended he cared. In fact, he was bored. All three D'Arcy girls, and both Bardon girls were all stupid, malicious, spiteful and conceited. Every one of them thought they ought to be able to marry a prince, never mind that there were five of them and only three princes. Apparently, along with everything else, they couldn't do simple math. Freddy despised them. He'd rather have been haunting the docks at home with Liard and Siward.

Keeping his sigh silent, he led the girl out onto the dance floor, glancing over at Nehl to see what his brother was up to. Nehl worried him a little these days. Since he had chained Liard and Siward's foster sister to a chair in the dungeon and beaten her with his own fist, Nehl had become erratic; Freddy never knew quite what he would do next. The sound of the girl's bones breaking, her gasps of pain, her truncated screams, her palpable agony, all had released something in Freddy's brother that disturbed him. Twice, since then, Nehl had sought out unprotected girls from poor families, taken them to ugly places, and beaten them to death.

Now, Freddy didn't care that what his brother was doing was wrong. He didn't care about the injuries or the suffering the girls had endured. He didn't care that his brother had tortured the one girl and murdered two others. He had no moral aversion to what his brother was doing; he had no moral feeling about it at all. He did care that his brother might no longer be completely sane. And he did, very much, care that his brother might one day decide that beating young girls to death wasn't good enough and that he might start on men.

This bothered Freddy, for several reasons. Nehl might one day pick on the wrong man and get more than he bargained for. Nehl, as Freddy dimly realized, just wasn't all that great a fighter. He had good reasons to want his victims tied down before he started beating on them; he didn't intend for them to be able to hurt him in return.

No, as far as Nehl was concerned, he intended to make certain that his abuses of his victims all ran one way. That wasn't what bothered Freddy. What bothered Freddy was the thought that, if Nehl once started to enjoy the brutalization of men, what was to stop him from moving on to Freddy? And enjoying the sport of brutalizing him?

Freddy no longer had any illusions about his older brother. Nehl cared about no one but himself, and he would not hesitate so much as a split second to harm any one of his own family. And as to that, Freddy knew all about his brother's machinations with Privy Councilman Jiden to kill his father. In fact, Freddy knew for a fact that after Nehl got rid of their father, that he intended to turn on their brother Garve` and get rid of him, too. Just in case Garve` might ever get the notion that he wanted to sit on the throne.   If Nehl ever, for even one moment, thought that Freddy wanted the throne, then he would murder him right then and there, and nothing that Freddy could say or do would stop him and Freddy knew it.

And if Nehl started killing men, even if he chose old men, and men already maimed by time and life, Freddy would know that he was starting to come unhinged. If he started murdering men, people would notice, and once they noticed, they wouldn't take long to realize just who was doing the murders.

People didn't much care about the murder of women and young girls. Rape or murder or both young girls and women and people would turn their heads away and let you. Or at least men would, and since men controlled the law, Nehl could rape, torture and murder all the girls and women he wanted to for as long as he lived and nobody would do anything about it.

It also meant no one would do anything about Freddy, which meant, to Freddy, that as long as Nehl stuck to murdering girls and women (particularly the poor ones) he, Freddy, would be all right. Because Nehl made him help.

Made him help to find them, made him help to charm them into coming along with them, and made him help to tie them up so that Nehl could beat them to death without fear of their managing to do anything to harm him. And Nehl made him help to dispose of their bodies.

When girls and women went missing, the men in whom the responsibility of enforcing the laws had been entrusted would refuse to look for them. They'd call them runaways and prostitutes and ignore their suffering and deaths. When their bodies were found, if they were found, months and years later, they'd refuse to do the work to identify them. And, as long as they could deny that they knew who they were, they would refuse to investigate their murders. They would even deny, any chance they could, that they had been murdered, all of which made Nehl's sadistic little murder hobby safe.

But men didn't feel the same way about tortured and murdered men. After all, they were men, too, and sooner or later, they'd get old. They'd feel sympathy for men who'd been maimed by life, empathy for the elderly victims. They'd investigate, and they'd do it right now. Men were larger than most young girls and the small women Nehl felt secure enough to brutalize. Their bodies were heavier in most cases, and more difficult to dispose of without someone seeing something they shouldn't. Those lawmen would find out who the men were, they'd trace their last movements, and once they did that, they'd find Freddy and Nehl.

Nehl, Freddy thought, might be able to get away with it. He was the Crown Prince, after all, and if he made a real effort, which Freddy was sure he would make, he might even be able to blame everything on Freddy. Freddy was the youngest prince. Third in line for the throne. He wasn't, strictly speaking, needed, not with Nehl the heir, and Garve` the spare. He would hang.

Freddy wondered, was that why Nehl wanted to sit on the throne? Because being a king would give him the impunity to do whatever he wanted to whomever he wanted to do it to? And plenty of sycophants to help him do it? Nehl certainly hadn't spent months engineering this coup with Councilor Jiden because he wanted to do the work of being a king. Nehl hated the Council meetings, the long hours of listening to boring people drone on about their problems in the audience chamber, the legal briefs he was supposed to read, the reports from the outlying districts, and even the social events. He hated the making and the writing out of well-reasoned decisions. He hated all of it; it bored him. Yet Freddy knew, for a certainty, that Nehl wanted his father dead.

That brought him around the Councilman Jiden and his coup. Now they had left the city, and arrived in Quattar, would Jiden spring the trap as he was supposed to?

# XIV

# THE COUP

SOMETHING AWAKENED HIM. HE DIDN'T know what. Then it came again, the faraway ringing of steel upon steel. Marc threw the covers away from his body, jammed his legs over the side of his bed and grabbed for his fighting leathers in the dim light from his evening fire. Working his fingers rapidly, he pulled on the quilted trousers and shirt, then his leathers and finally his chainse. He moved quickly. By the time he had gotten his head inside his mail shirt, he thought the ringing of steel had come perhaps a yard closer. By the time he had his coif in place, he knew the sound was closer. He jerked on his over-robe, dark grey, to make it more difficult to see him, added his sword and his knives, jamming his feet into his boots.

By the time he had made it half-way to the door, he'd secured them to his feet. Jerking open the door, he peered at his guards, mere shadows against the corridor walls. Wall sconces, widely spaced, provided just enough light to see them by, and not one glimmer more. Both of them wore the same dark sort of over-armor robe he had donned, and both had their swords out, holding them at the ready. Marc nodded at them.

"Let's go," he directed. "Prince Garve`'s rooms. They'll strike there soon, if they're not there already." And once they had Garve` and his guards with them, they'd have a larger group with which to fight off the attackers.

They heard the clashing sound of steel on steel well before they reached Garve`'s apartments. Slipping up on the combatants, they found half a dozen men attacking Garve` and his two guards. The guards were armored as well as armed, of course, but Garve` had not had time to don his chainse.

Marc shoved his knife into the back of the man in front of him. It took a good deal of force to breach the armor the mercenary was wearing, but he was able to breach it, telling him that the armor wasn't of the best. He twisted the knife to make certain of the man's death, and turned to see that his guards had done the same for the men in front of them. That left six defenders facing three, odds not to the attackers' liking.

Garve`'s guards closed ranks in front of him, then, and they finished the men left with some dispatch. Marc looked at his son, assessing his condition thoughtfully. Garve`'s guards both showed minor wounds, despite their armor, but his son had not a mark upon him. He nodded.

"Get your armor," Marc advised his son, turned to the guards. "How bad?" he demanded.

"Nothing to mention," one of the guards retorted. "The blood's mostly theirs."

Marc eyed him sharply.

"Truth?" he challenged. "There are bound to be more of the mercenaries in the house and we'll be set to hard fighting for the rest of the night."

"Truth," the first guard assured him.

The second guard looked doubtful. Marc nodded at him.

"Get you to the infirmary," he ordered. Then bethought himself. "Can you get there on your own?" he wondered.

"I will manage," the man assured him. He put up his sword and stepped away from the group, beginning his journey through the palace corridors. Marc saw that he limped as he moved.

Good, he thought, knowing he'd done right to send the man to the infirmary. He would have held them up, and as fighting exacerbated the injury, sooner or later the man's leg would have buckled out from under him, with the result of certain devastation for him, and quite possibly equally devastating results for those depending on the strength of his sword. This way he'd not be a weak link for the group, and at any rate, Marc knew he could not afford to lose a loyal man if he did not have to. He needed all the loyal fighters he had. This way, in a day, or perhaps two, the man would bel ready to take the place of other men who had wearied of the battle, or been injured themselves.

The sound of a soft step on the carpet caught at his attention and he turned again, only to see Laren arrive with a pair of guards of his own. Laren looked relieved to see him. Marc raised his eyebrows in question as the head of his Palace Guard approached.

"They slipped through the gate," Laren reported. "Jiden opened it for them. Jahn D'Arcy is with them, and the younger Dellin, with Matias Bardon. That we know," he qualified. "We've got the gate closed for now, but there's fighting in the inner bailey and we don't know how many got through before we discovered them." He raised his own eyebrows in question of his own.

Marc shook his head at him.

"The sound of the swordplay here by Garve`'s room woke me," he said. "I armed and brought relief down here. Shall we visit my rooms and see if Jiden's men have reached them yet?"

Laren toed the dead men to their backs, regarding them enigmatically. He gestured at one of them.

"That one's a D'Arcy household guard," he commented. "The others are mercenaries."

"What I thought," Marc nodded. "Patchwork armor," he added, in explanation.

Laren eyed the dead men again, nodded.

"Armor's not much better on the D'Arcy man," he observed.

"Let us hope that the rest of them are no better," Garve` said, from the door, now armed and helmed, another of the dark grey over-robes hiding his mail.

Marc nodded, headed back down the corridor to his apartment. Laren caught him up, and then he and two of the guards took the lead, while the last guard covered their rear. Marc paid little attention to them. Already, he could hear the sounds of men pounding on his door, trying to get in. He shared a small smile with Laren, and then they had reached the men.

Taking them from the rear, surprise gave them a considerable advantage in the dim glow of the mage-lights in the wall sconces that sort of illuminated the palace corridors. Eight men had been sent to collect King Marc, a Bardon

guard, a D'Arcy guard and a Jiden guard leading them. Marc, Laren, Garve` and one of the guards all had their first men down before the rest even became aware of their presence. After that, it was a slaughter, with five against four and every one of the five better armed and armored. Laren was particularly deadly, and Marc's two guards were hardly less so.

"Fourteen," Laren muttered as they headed to the throne room. He sounded grim. Fourteen men had made it through his blockade at the inner bailey gate, and the thought did not please him.

They came up with a group on the stair, and this time they had little surprise to aid them and there were no less than ten men in the group. Even so, Laren had two down before the fighting could begin in earnest, and the two men assigned to Marc as guards had two more down before Marc could blink, not that he did, since he had engaged a man of his own. Garve` and the guard behind him did not get into the fray until they had fought the men down to the first landing. Even there, the men found scarce enough room for two men to engage, never mind more.

Marc managed to get his man down, and then, suddenly, he looked up to realize that the last man was being dispatched while he looked on. He glanced over towards Laren.

"More of Jiden's men," his arms-man informed him. He toed one of the dead men. "Fat and out of shape." He all but sneered it. Marc counted in his head.

"Twenty-two," he said. "Where are the other two?"

"Ran," Garve` told him.

Laren shook his head.

"Not good," he frowned.

"Ran where?" Marc wanted to know.

"Towards the throne room," one of the guards answered. Laren grimaced.

"Forward," he suggested.

But before they could get there, they got caught up in the fighting in the hallway. The fact that they were five against twenty didn't seem to matter much in the narrow space between walls, especially not when the larger force was caught between a valiant few in front of them and the five of them in the rear.

Before long, the invaders had been reduced to four men fighting back to back, and losing. They tried surrendering—one of them was Jahn D'Arcy—but they were given no quarter.

"Clean up," Garve` muttered mostly to himself, as they returned to their progress towards the throne room, gathering up their own guards on the way, "is going to be a bitch."

"We'll put the losers to it as soon as we've decimated their numbers a little more," Laren told him.

"Forty-two," Marc informed him. "I'd like to know where those two ran off to and who they are," he added.

"In time," Laren promised him, with a grim smile. "In time."

Jiden himself, with one of the Bardons and the other D'Arcy milled about the throne room with, at a guess, another twenty men. Marc heard Jiden whine,

"Where are they? They ought to be here by now."

"We're right here, Councilor," Marc advised him, and lunged towards him.

He didn't reach the man, of course, one of his guards interposed his body between them, but Marc was just getting warmed up and he dispatched the man quickly. Laren had already cut through his first opponent, and engaged his second by then, with Garve` and Marc's two guards finishing up with their men. Marc caught a glimpse of the shock on Jiden's face at the speed with which his men went down. He hadn't expected the skill level of the Palace Guard, or their superior arms, which had been stupid of him.

Penny proud, pound foolish, Marc thought, slamming his way through a second opponent. What, he wondered, as the man went down, had Jiden been thinking? These men hadn't been properly trained for this action. They hadn't been armed appropriately for it, or in any way adequately prepared for the kind of close fighting they should have anticipated. At every juncture, they seemed to be catching the men unawares. They shouldn't have been able to do that, not that Marc was complaining, mind you, but still--

He hammered his way through the second man just in time to catch the sword of a third. Jiden was running, damn it! And he couldn't get there in time to stop the bastard! He heaved the man in front of him away from himself, but Jiden had already reached the audience chamber door.

His inattention cost him, as his opponent got in a sharp blow under his guard.

His armor held, but he knew he would have a nasty bruise there tomorrow in spite of the padding under the steel. It brought his attention back to the man in front of him, which, very soon, he was able to make the man regret, as he managed to jam the tip of his sword into the underarm joint of the man's sub-standard armor to devastating effect. The man's arm dropped, useless, allowing Marc to pound him into the floor without hindrance. He was too late. Jiden pulled the door open.

A dozen palace guards poured into the room then, sweeping Jiden up on the way, just as Laren shoved the last of Jiden's men before him. None of them wore Councilor Jiden's livery, but even Marc recognized some of the faces.

Sixty men dead, and all to pander to this man's pride, as he sought to gain a place in his world that he did not deserve and wasn't competent to occupy. Marc looked down at his blood-soaked robe and then back up at the cowering weasel of a man being dragged towards him.

He snarled, staring at the flawless armor worn by the man in front of him. Crafted by someone highly skilled at such work, Marc could not spot a single imperfection in the chainse that would allow his blade passage. So he rammed his poniard directly into the little weasel's face, smashing the bridge of the weasel's nose on his cross-guard, the force of his blow sending the point of the blade through the back of the traitor's skull. Wrenching his arm back, his poniard came free with a sucking sound that sickened him.

Cleaning his blade on Jiden's spotless robe—the men's hands on the former Councilor's arms, holding him in place, made the body's collapse slow—he slammed it home in its sheath just as the men released their hold and let the body slump to the floor. Undoubtedly shocked by his actions—well, the time it had taken them to let go of the Councilor's arms gave evidence of that—they yet did not display it on their faces. Some of them might even, perhaps, have felt satisfaction. How many of his men had died this night? How many of them would languish, tomorrow and tomorrow and tomorrow, in the infirmary?

"What about the rest of them?" he asked, point blank. "The other D'Arcy-- Dellin--and Matias Bardon? What about Hubare D'Arcy? And how many men have we lost?"

"The gate's closed," the guard who had led the men to the throne room reported. "We've lost a dozen men at the least, and no less than two dozen more will have to be taken to the infirmary. At least fifty got through the inner bailey gate and how many Jiden brought through before we engaged them, we don't know."

"We'll start a sweep," Marc assured him. He turned to Laren. "Sixty-four," Laren told him. "So far. Counting Jiden."

Marc raised one eyebrow towards him.

"So how many can there be left?" he wondered aloud.

Laren curled a lip in a tight smile back to him.

"Not enough," he said.

"So," Marc told the head of the group of guards before him. "You go east, we'll go west. Start on the ground floor and work up." He didn't tell them to kill any of the mercenaries or household guards who didn't belong that they found. He didn't have to. The guards bowed and headed off to start their canvas to the east.

He let Laren take the lead to the west, hefting his sword again. The bloody front of his robe flapped around his legs as he walked, reminding him of the death he had waded through this night. And, he thought, with an inner sigh, the night was not over yet. Dammit.

# XV

# THE DEER HUNT

DEER HUNTING ISN'T AS EASY as all those hunting enthusiasts like to make it sound. First, you have to find your deer. Then you have to get close enough to the animal to shoot him, and then, assuming you succeed in hitting him, you have to hope you also manage to kill him. And afterwards, if you've accomplished all of that, comes the worst part of all—you have to actually butcher the animal. Gah!

After three days of hunting deer and never seeing a single doe, never mind a buck, I buckled down with my magic books and figured out how to use a tracking spell to find one. Then, after every deer I managed to track got away before I could get close enough to use my bow, I spent another couple of days learning how to use my magic to get close enough to use my bow, and another couple of days after that figuring out how to use my magic to make sure I killed the deer. The anatomy part in the animal husbandry section of the agriculture book gave me adequate information to allow me to butcher out my poor victim. Then it took me two more days to put the meat up so it would keep and to purify the deer fat into tallow I could use to make candles.

First, I filled the storage cupboards I'd built in the front corner of the enclosed combination front porch and stable that shielded the rest of my shelter. The bottom two shelves held two and a half gallon jars of grain, corn, wheat and oats, mostly, with dried beans and rose hips, and the roughly made bins of apples and oranges. The next shelf up held a crock of honey, some sugar, yeast, soda, some of the most common spices, salt, some pepper, baking powder, and dried eggs and milk, on one side, and more fruit and roots on the other. It wasn't a lot of food to carry me through five months, particularly when I'd need to share the corn and oats with Nutmeg, but I did have more stored in the cupboard in the feed room.

It still wouldn't be enough. I'd need a decent amount of meat to add to what I had in the way of fruit, roots and grain in order to make it, and I'd be happier if I had a comfortable margin to allow for bad weather or worse luck.

So far, the upper shelves in the kitchen pantry held the glass cases of meat, mostly the thick cuts from the shoulders, back and hind-quarters. Each reinforced section of shelf held fifty pounds and each side of the storage closet held five sections of shelves. The single young buck I'd killed hardly filled two shelves. I still had three more of the glass cases in just those three shelves to be filled. Never mind the other three shelves on the other side of the storage closet waiting to be loaded down with provisions. The ribs I barbequed over a pit-fire, but as I did it, I brooded over the stores I had so far. I needed more meat, more fruit, and more root vegetables. I hadn't even made a start, so far, on filling the smaller pantry in the shelter.

So far, my hunting expeditions had produced more fruit, greens and roots than they had meat. I needed to bring in another small buck, if at all possible, before resting on my laurels and more fruit, greens and roots wouldn't hurt. I didn't have much time to do it. Autumn was wearing on, and I needed to make more glass and finish enclosing my shelter.

I felt seriously behind schedule. The roof wasn't any better than a couple of tarps spread over the roof tree, and the front walls had yet to be fully sealed, and that wouldn't do when it snowed. Snow is heavy. I wanted more glass to use to seal both roof and walls, but making glass took time and I needed to get the food in now, while it was still out there to forage. Worse, it wouldn't be long before the deer started finding the foraging growing slender for them, as well.

Better to bring in a fat young spike now, than wait until he had lost thirty pounds.

So, I went hunting again. The first four days I brought home more fruit, greens and roots than I did meat, though I did managed to scrounge a few rabbits. Better than nothing. The fifth day I lucked out and brought down a young spike. I don't think I got more than eighty pounds of meat out of him, and he only filled up the one side of the big cupboard in the enclosed 'porch', but I found that good enough to allow myself to concentrate on finishing the house.

The green tint the iron imparted to my glass suited me. Set into wood casings that joined the branch wood I used for my roof, it allowed sunlight into the nearly windowless shelter below while preserving the illusion that the roof was not a roof at all but a network of branches belonging to the copse of trees that surrounded the shelter and disguised it. A little magic picked out of my magic books added to the recipe meant that while the glass let light into the space, and it let the person inside the space look out, anyone outside couldn't look in. All they'd see reflected back to them would be more forest, more shadow, and more bark and branches.

The addition of more of the small panes of one way glass set into the unpeeled upright outer sections of logs stuck into the ground outside the lower walls of rock and dirt only enhanced the illusion. Set between planks covered by more of the unpeeled upright sections of logs, by allowing the viewer to seem to see into the copse of trees, it made it almost impossible to perceive the 'house' they masked.

It wasn't much of a house, not really. It wasn't square, and it wasn't round.

The area to the right of the stove at the center of the construct formed a rough semi-circle maybe ten feet at its deepest point, and probably something like eight feet at each 'end' while maybe twenty feet deep, at best. The 'front' section was more of an inverted V than a semi-circle, and it fit into an area that could only be considered another semi-circle by stretching that term a great deal out of shape.

Stone pillars I'd cobbled together with a combination of mortar and magic supported the whole, along with walls made up of more stone, more dirt, and some sections of split trees with the branches and bark still attached. Magic rooted each section of tree and kept it alive, allowing the evergreens to stay green, while the sections of oak and maple lost at least some of their leaves, if not all of them. More magic prevented any sparks from making it up and out of the glass and metal lined chimney.

Building the place had taught me a lot, and the repeated use of the same spells had allowed me to hone them to better serve me and to fix them in my memory. Too, the more magic I used, and the more I fit my use of it into the natural world around me, the deeper the well of magic seemed to reach into the fiber of my being. I felt the magic of earth, air, water and fire taking root inside me the way the branches I used took root in the earth I set them in.

This progression, according to the books I studied, corresponded to the natural order of things. If those accounts were to be believed, I was merely finding which magics suited my talents best. So far, I had shown a proclivity for fire (the forge), earth (my stone-work and the work I had done with wood and growing things), and air (one element of making glass, the others being fire and earth), and also a necessary component of the 'travel' spell, as well as a key element in levitation.

When I piped the water from the spring to the ante-chamber for Nutmeg, routing it through the hot water reservoir and the water-closet behind the stove, and from the spring the other way, under the rock and out to supply the stream the way it always had, I was supposedly channeling the element of water. Well, at least somewhat. So far, so good.

My winter home, such as it was, held the spring and the cupboard behind it, sunk into the rock, with a sink in the outer wall and work spaces smoothed into the stone to either side of it, for something that might, if the utmost in generosity was employed, be called a kitchen. Beyond the 'kitchen', to the 'front' of it, I'd put together a rough—very rough—trestle table and a couple of equally rough stools to eat at. The space to the front of the stove comprised my forge, with a 'sitting' area beyond it, then the reinforced door to the ante-chamber, and beyond it, I'd built a half-partition screened across the upper section by the deerskin, with the second hide hung long ways to make a kind of door.

My bed, such as it was, a mound of dry leaves piled up inside a rough branch-wood plank bed-box and tucked inside a tarp, with my blankets set out atop that, had been bracketed at the head by a second plank box. It contained shelves for my clothes in the bottom and more shelves for my books on top of that, with an additional plank that folded down to give me a place to read and study. This one I'd smoothed a bit to write on, if I wanted to take notes.

Four wrought-iron candle-stands, each holding five of my tallow candles, lightened the place, though I'd made four additional glass lamps to hold single tallow candles which could be carried about to add illumination to any particular area where it was wanted. The kitchen and sleeping areas would be pretty dark, without them.

The sleeping area butted up against the hill in the back and the ante-chamber on the side, with the water closet and the stove on the end opposite the head of my bed, and so had no light at all other than the little that filtered down from the roof. The kitchen was nearly as dark, with the end burrowing into the tumble of rock beyond the spring, the side consisting of more of the rock, and the other side the stone of the chimney and the stove. Only the front area opened to any particular light other than that filtering down from the small skylights in the roof.

The floor consisted mostly of smoothed stone, except in the sleeping area, where I'd used smoothed planks over the leveled dirt of the hillside, or the kitchen where I'd used more of the smoothed planks to make a level area over the jut of the rocks around the spring. The area around the stove and underneath my forge consisted of stone, of course, as less likely to catch fire from a spark, and the sitting area off to the side of the forge sported more of the smoothed stone. It wasn't the pristine painted and papered, carpeted and tiled modernity of an Amadean house. It was rustic, dark, lacking even the softening of a hide rug, and the sitting area, such as it was, held no furnishings in which to sit, never mind lounge.

But even with the first icy fall of snow sifting down, it was warm. I had a half a cord of wood and more, stacked to either side of the stove in neat squares, and another cord of wood layered along Nutmeg's partition, literally from wall to wall. A teakettle hummed on the back of the stove, filled with water keeping hot, while a pot of soup simmered gently on the back of the stove on the other side of the chimney. A short cloak put together all of rabbit skins made a warm cape to fit over my longer, woolen cloak to help me keep warm out in the snow that awaited me, with a deer-hide vest to go under both, made from the hide off the legs of the deer I had already killed.

For trousers, I wore denim under my woolens, with deer-hide laced around my lower legs from the tops of my boots to my knees. My woolen tunic and silk undershirt stretched easily to just above my knees, and the deer-hide vest I'd made covered all but the hems of both shirt and tunic. With my cloak and cape over the top of that, and my knapsack on my back, I'd be warm enough, I told myself, and another deer would be welcome, for the meat, of course, but also for the hide. My deer-hide greaves above my boots were a boon. A deer-hide tunic to wear over my silks and woolens would be even more welcome. Too, the larger portion of a full hide would make a curtain to section off the water-closet better, make it more private, while still allowing for the circulation of warm air.

Primitive, I would have allowed, but still utilitarian. And, after all, I didn't mean to remain here in this shelter beyond this winter. Doors would stay behind, but the deer hides would go with me, like the rabbit hide cape and the deer hide greaves and vest, rolled up into lightweight, easily packed padding. I had to look forward to another winter in the mountains before I reached my destination. The more portable, lightweight hides I could take with me to use next winter, the better.

Besides, I assured myself, I'd be able to gather some herbs while I was out. They'd show up nicely against the dusting of snow that powdered the ground. I marked several pages in my herbology book, memorized their contents, and thus fortified, took myself out to hunt down a deer and collect a few herbs to add to my store while I was at it.

The day I chose to make my foray dawned clear and crisp. I decided to head as much west as I could manage, and maybe south a bit as well. I reasoned that the snow and chill wind would drive the deer down, towards lower elevations and warmer weather. I didn't intend to go too far, because I'd have to get the deer back, if I found one, and even if I chose a smaller buck, I'd still have to nearly halve the carcass. I'd be lucky to be able to carry the hide and more than half the carcass back. More likely I'd have to bring Nutmeg back to pack whatever I couldn't carry back to the shelter.

So, taking up bow and quiver of arrows, strapping on my sword and daggers, and adding a staff for additional stability in the snow and ice, I started out, carrying my field kit, my knapsack and just-in-case supplies, first aid kit, tarp and basic bed-roll. I didn't intend to remain out overnight, but one never knew. I was all alone out here. Best to be prepared for all contingencies.

By mid-morning, I'd found several herbs to harvest, and I did so, careful to make certain I didn't damage the plants, but simply helped myself to leaves or roots they could spare without taking harm. The result didn't amount to much, but even small amounts of these herbs could be important, according to my herbology book. I was glad to get them. I meandered here and there for a while, looking for more herbs before giving up and activating the tracking spell I'd devised for hunting deer.

It took me until mid-afternoon to come up with a small group of deer that included a moderately sized young buck. Slipping downwind in a stalking crouch, I eased closer to the deer, using magic to cloak my approach until I could bring my bow to bear. I nocked my arrow as silently as possible, drew the string until the arrow fit right where it belonged, and let fly, using magic to guide it true. The buck went down, settling slowly into the snow while the rest of the small group fled. I approached my kill deliberately, crunching through the snow carefully, making certain the buck was dead.

Now came the struggle to hang the buck from his hind legs to bleed out, my next to least liked of the chores ahead. Sweating and swearing, I managed to get the buck's hind legs attached to my pulley, and once there, into a tree to be field- dressed. The work that followed was unpleasant, but necessary. This was about survival, not entertainment.

By the time I finished, late afternoon hovered around me, the air chilling on my skin, the sky beginning to darken. Night came quickly this time of year, so I bent to the tasks that remained grimly. I needed to get as much of the meat as I could back to the den as quickly as I could.

I had started the work of separating the deer into quarters to carry when I first heard the howling. It sounded faint, eerie, and even distressed, not the sound of a hunting wolf, but the sound of a wolf calling for help. I didn't really want to deal with a wolf, distressed or otherwise, but something drew me towards the sound.

I fashioned another tracking spell, modifying it to lead me to the source of the eerie call, and started out following it, carrying my pack but leaving all but a couple of dozen of the strips of the deer meat behind, hanging high in the trees. I hoped that the deer meat might persuade the wolf, if I found him, to regard me with more good-will than he might otherwise. A hungry wolf would likely be crotchety, while a wolf with a filled belly might regard me with more equanimity. Then again, I had probably crossed the border into the land of Mahdi in my hunt for deer. The wolf howling into the night in search of help might just as well be Mahdi as a wild wolf, not that I'd ever seen one. I had no idea what a Mahdi might look like.

I didn't at all expect what I found at the end of my tracking spell.

# XVI

## A WOLF IN A TRAP

AS I FOLLOWED THE LIGHT thread of my tracking spell, I called out, trying to send out a friendly greeting ahead of me. I got back a questioning, almost hopeful 'a- roo?' and sent back 'I'm coming!' The 'a-roo' turned excited, even sounding pleased. So, I thought, a dog, not a wolf, and somehow in trouble. I tried to move faster.

The dog would call an 'a-roo!' and I would answer that I was coming, and two breaths later, the dog would 'a-roo' again. What began to worry me was that once the excitement waned, the dog's 'ar-roos' began to grow weaker. I didn't dare to go much faster—the light was failing now, but neither did I tarry. I now felt certain that the dog was in trouble, and that it was unable to move from wherever it had gotten stuck. I hoped I would be able to get it unstuck, but I feared, stuck or unstuck, I would have to stay out over night with it. I doubted the dog would be strong enough to make it back to the shelter with me. It certainly didn't sound strong enough for the journey.

Thus thinking, I almost overshot him. If he hadn't lurched upwards, I might have. I sat down abruptly and shrugged off my pack and assessed the problem. The pup was a big dog, but young, I doubted as much as a year old, and he might look like a wolf, but his eyes were intelligent, if pain-filled, his attitude anything but feral. He tried to throw his upper body into my arms, greeting me with a relieved 'roo-a-roo-roo!' as I wrapped my arms around him. He threw his head back onto my shoulder and tried to lick my face.

One of his hind legs had been caught in a trap, an old one with corroded hinges and a rusty step plate. It had been covered with leaves and dirt and had obviously been there a long time. I suspected that the smell of metal had been long ago attenuated by leaves and soil and the weathering of years. It had lain here, just waiting for this adolescent pup to come frolicking by and put a foot in it. Poor baby.

He was far too thin and he'd clearly been here without food or water for some time. How long I had no idea. I grabbed my bowl and my water and poured him some and while he drank that and ate the strips of venison I put down for him, I got my small copper and glass lantern set up, lighting the three small tallow candles in it and then looking around for a tree to hang it in. I used my staff to probe about thoroughly before taking a step away from the pup, just in case there might be another trap hanging around, but I made it to the nearest tree without difficulty, hung my lamp, and then, by its light, returned to inspect the trap more carefully.

The thing was a big bastard. I looked over at the pup, who now, with his thirst and hunger sated, at least for the moment, lay quiet, his head wobbling with his fatigue and what lingering pain my spell hadn't been able to completely obliterate. I gave his butt a light pat.

"Stay awake, now," I advised him. "I'm going to need you to pull your leg out of the trap in a minute here."

The big pup blinked at me and forced his forelegs to stiffen.

"Right," I said, and jammed the tip end of my staff into the trap, shoving it against the trip plate. The trap creaked, and the teeth opened a couple of inches. Gritting his teeth, the pup lurched out of it, jarring the trap. My staff slipped in the ice, and the trap snapped back closed again, this time on my staff. The pup gasped a

'Ruff!' but he was clear.

My staff wasn't coming back out of that trap, which gave me a greater appreciation of the condition the pup's leg was likely to be in. I grabbed my bow and used it to make my way back to the tree and recover my lantern so I could get a closer look at the pup's leg. A glance over at the pup showed me that he had used all his remaining strength to get clear. His head had dropped, and he looked to be about half way to unconsciousness. I grabbed my bed roll and my first aid kit from my pack and moved to take a closer look at the poor pup's leg.

It wasn't good. The trap had broken the bone and torn up both muscle and ligaments and tendons, and the pup had chewed on what hadn't been torn up by the trap. By the light of the lantern, I set about cleaning out the wound and alternately sewing the damaged tendons and ligaments back together and healing them back together with magic. I straightened the bone, and with a combination of splints I carved, bandages from my kit, and more healing magic, I brought what I could of the bone and skin back together and then wrapped it all up in an attempt to immobilize his leg as best I could.

Getting a tarp and blanket under his heavy body when he was sodden with a combination of relief from fear, relief from the worst of his pain, and the healing I had done, was difficult, but he managed to tip his shoulders up a little for me. Doing anything with his hindquarters was beyond him, but I managed to lift him enough, using the last ounce of my magic, to get the blanket and tarp under his rear end as well. After that, I pulled my pack to my head, the tarp and blanket over my back and side, and curving my body around the pup's body—I suspected he outweighed me! I spread my cloaks over him, first the heavy woolen length and then the rabbit fur before I fell into sleep myself.

I'd pretty much poured out my magic, such as I had, with profligacy that day, using it to track the deer, using it to kill the deer, using it to get the deer into the tree, and then using it to track the pup, find him, ease his pain and heal him—no wonder I as much passed out as slept. It wasn't safe, but we lucked out and nothing disturbed us during the night.

I awakened at first light to the big pup licking my face and whining excitedly.

I gave him more water and the last of the strips of venison, washed my fingers and ate a corn cake myself, and then checked his leg. In the daylight, it looked cleaner than I could possibly have expected, and when I helped the pup to get to his feet, he wobbled, and then tottered to a tree. I turned my face away and busied myself with shaking out blanket and tarp and rolling everything up and packing it away. I helped myself to more water from my almost empty water bottle, and ate another corn cake, trying to decide the best way home.

The pup staggered over to me and, in trying to lie down, pretty much pitched himself into my lap. I hugged him, helped him to sort himself out, and then reached for my magic, almost surprised to find it. Using what I found, I did what healing I could, concentrating on his leg, mostly, but working some with his general condition as well. Then, with his shoulders and front legs in my lap, his head tucked under my chin, I did a finding on my shelter, honing my 'sight' in on the terrain between us and my shelter.

"Ok," I told the pup, "let's go home."

I helped him up onto his feet, shrugged into my pack and my weapons, and headed out, moving slowly, so the pup could follow. He moved better on three legs than I expected, but I didn't know if he could hold out all the way to the shelter, even if the distance was more like the third leg of a triangle than anything else. I stopped so he could rest at mid-morning, and shared a strip of dried venison with him. The pup snuggled in to my side and fell asleep with his head on my thigh. I let him sleep. I even dozed a bit myself, and when we both awakened, about an hour later, I tried healing him a little more.

We managed to walk two more hours before we had to stop and rest again, but this time after no more than half an hour and another half strip of dried venison, he was ready to go on. On our next rest, I was able to see the configuration of the land of my sanctuary ahead of us. By now, the pup was lagging, but I used the last of my magic to heal him again, and then coaxed and insisted upon his following me until I'd managed to get him to the shelter.

Once I'd managed to coax him inside, into what was left of the warmth. I settled him before the stove, built the fire up again, and then I went back out to gather up all the tiny, soft bits of ever-green twigs and dry leaves I could find and carry inside. Adding a sheaf of Nutmeg's dried grass, I whip stitched the edges of a tarp to each other, stuffed the rectangle of cloth it made with the leaves and twigs and dried grass, covered it with the blanket and then coaxed the pup to get up long enough to collapse onto it. I stuck another strip of dried meat into the pup's mouth, put a bowl of water beside the bed, and then took myself into the kitchen to prepare a meal for myself. After eating, I took myself to my bed and fell into it and into sleep.

Sometime in the night, the pup awakened me with his whimpering. Unable to stand it, I got up, lit one of my small candle-lamps, and went to the middle of the room where the big pup sat, crying in his sleep. I put more wood on the fire, pulled my warm cloak tight around me, and then sat down on the bed beside the pup, waking him. He curled every bit of himself that he could get into my lap, wrapping a big paw around my arm, and dropped off back to sleep.

In the morning, after I'd fed us both, I sat down on the bed with him and had a little heart to heart with him. I explained about the deer I'd left hanging in the tree, and how we needed the meat, and that he couldn't come with me to get it because it was too far. I took him outside to relieve himself, and then made sure he had plenty of food and water, and then I took Nutmeg and went to get the deer. The pup curled himself up on his bed and sighed a very put-up sigh—but he let me go.

The round trip took all day, even with Nutmeg, and by the time I got back the pup was desperate to get out again, but he was rested enough, and alert enough, to appreciate the deer I'd brought back. The deer, barely short of frozen, still had to be hacked up, preserved, and stored away in the glass containers. The pup watched me work with interest that looked very close to acute to me. When I put a couple of half-frozen strips of meat into a sizzling pan for us, he looked from me to the pan with lip licking anticipation.

We ate when the food was ready, and then he laid down again on his bed and dozed while I finished hacking up the venison and packing it away. After I finished, I took a shower, cleaned myself off, dressed again to let the pup out, built up the fire, and, the pup back in, I guided him over to my bed. By that point, I was so tired, I didn't care if he gave me fleas. If he had 'em, I'd already been exposed, so to speak. I helped him up onto the end of the bed, threw his blanket over him, and then snuggled down into it myself. This time the pup didn't wake me up in the middle of the night.

In the morning I felt good enough to try to do a little more healing on the pup's leg, working, as best I could, to strengthen the bone and do a little more work on the small blood vessels and nerves. My efforts were cautious, and certainly tentative—after all, I didn't know what I was doing, despite the healing manual, but I had to try. If I kept at it persistently enough, maybe I could get him moving better, and ease his pain somewhat.

After breakfast, I started work purifying the deer fat so I could use it to make candles. The pup watched me, fascinated. I thought he looked to be moving better now, dropping a toe to touch the ground every now and again, though not putting any weight on his leg. Clearly on the mend, he was eating everything I put down and begging for more food whenever he thought he could con me out of it, but otherwise, his manners were impeccable. Someone had raised him well.

The weather worsened again, with snow first threatening, and then delivering on its threats. I started work on the deer hide. We needed it.

I could not have asked for better behavior out of the pup. He yipped to go out, hopped out on three legs and then returned, watching everything I did with earnest eyes and an intent expression, sometimes patting my hand with a paw, as if to ask me to explain something. I generally did. I found him good company, warm in the bed at my side and feet, and an unfussy eater. Anything I put in the bowl before him, he ate, no questions asked, and licked the bowl afterwards.

Pretty soon I just started giving him a ladle full of the stew in the pot. Because he was so thin, I filled his bowl at least four times a day, and fed him little bits of corn cake at odd intervals as I worked.

Since he was eating out of my bowl, I perforce, made another for myself, this one mostly of copper, because that was what I had. Then I got the idea of making glass bowls, and tried that. The bowls came out rather heavy, and somewhat green, but they worked well, easy to wash and dry. Their only drawback was that if you dropped one on the stone floor, it would shatter. I couldn't have that. Broken glass was dangerous. So I cracked my books and experimented with magic to make an unbreakable glass bowl.

The result came out a rather deep blue-green, but even when thrown at a Rock (outside) it merely bounced, instead of breaking. I was quite pleased with it, and made more of them, and then added glass mugs to my repertoire. The pup watched me, seemingly fascinated, as I made a set of them, and then

additional eating utensils to go along with them. I don't know why I did it, except that now I was no longer alone, it just seemed the thing to do, and anyway, I enjoyed doing it, enjoyed learning how to mix magic with the act of making glass.

Then, I think it was the fifth morning since I'd brought the pup home, I heard more of his characteristic 'a-roo! A-roo!' outside the shelter. I hurried to the door, but the pup beat me to it, already answering. The sound echoed inside the structure, until, as I got the outer door open, the pup burst out, running on three legs and sending out his own happy, excited 'A-roo! A-roo!' out ahead of himself. I had no doubt at all that his family had come for him.

The wolves burst across the small meadow at the front of the shelter, big grey wolf-dogs, two males, both of them nearly half again as large as the pup, and two females, about the same size as he. Well, one was a little larger. Maybe the other was about the same amount smaller? I watched them come from the hidden outer door in the enclosed porch wall. Each of them carried a bedroll and a pair of not so small packs on their shoulders, secured by a surcingle around their girths and across their chests.

The packs didn't seem to slow them down as they surrounded the pup, nosing him and inspecting him from stem to stern, taking particular note of his broken and bandaged leg with its carved splints. I had 'healed' it a little each day and it could have been far worse than it was, but given all the damage he'd done to it trying to get out of the trap, he was doing well to be able to touch his toe to the ground. The two females stood to either side of him, shoulder to shoulder with him, shoring him up, while the two males shrugged out of their packs.

I wasn't prepared for what happened next. To my utter

astonishment, the biggest male stood up on his hind legs and turned into a man, right before my eyes. The Nogaynos book had mentioned Mahdi wolves in passing, but it hadn't elaborated, and I had never expected anything like this! I might have doubted my eyes, but the second male, almost as big as the first, stood up and changed as well. Both of them immediately pulled trousers, shirts, vests and cloaks out of their bedrolls and jerked them on rapidly. I didn't blame them, it was cold outside, and the snow was still coming down.

The larger of the two men started towards me, with the pup staggering along behind him on three legs at the best speed he could make, yipping and ruffing at the man as he came. I went to meet him before the pup fell down and injured his leg again.

# XVII

## FAMILY REUNION

**"S**LOW DOWN!" I CALLED TO him as I approached. "He can't keep up with you! It's slippery out here!"

The man glanced back at the pup and then slowed, as if just then realizing that the pup hadn't stayed with the others. The pup took that moment to try to dash past him and I dropped to one knee to field him, closing my arms around him to hold him to his feet.

"Easy!" I advised, "Easy! I don't want to have to heal your leg again today! There's only so much healing I can do in one day!"

The pup whined at me, crowding close and growling at the man. I stood up. "You know better than that," the man admonished the pup. He held out his hand to me. "I'm Wraith," he told me. "This is Shade. Reve and Shadow will be with us in a minute, as soon as they get their clothes on. It's cold out here." To the pup, he asked, "Where's your pack?"

The pup sneezed at him.

"Why don't you change?" the man asked him next.

"N'yea, I think he's better off on three feet than one in all this snow and ice," I reminded him.

The man winced.

"Might have something there," he allowed.

The others joined us. The second male handed the first his pack. I could see the family resemblance—they were both big shouldered, tall and powerful, with thick thatches of dark grey hair threaded through with black, and dark grey eyes to go with it. Strong-featured, you couldn't call either of them handsome, but striking would cover it. They looked from my scarred face to the pup and back as if something wasn't quite right.

"Why don't you change?" the girl asked the pup, repeating the man's question. At a guess, she was about my age, but taller, and more lithe, with an unscarred face. I think she might have been described as statuesque.

"Clothes?" I commented. "It's cold, and he doesn't have any."

"Another good reason not to change," the man agreed.

"Come in," I suggested. "I don't have much in the way of furniture, I just got the place built and I haven't had time to add them—or much in the way of materials, either, come to that, but at least it's warm inside.

I had the candles lighted, because the day was so dark, but the fire was going, and as soon as we got the doors closed behind us the place started to warm up.

They all looked around with wide eyes.

"Wow!" Reve said, if I had the names right. "You just built this?"

"I couldn't stay in the city after I got the scars," I told her. Shrugged. "So I came out here to stay, for a while."

She nodded as if that made perfect sense. The other man came forward, held his hand out.

"I'm Fort," he said in greeting. "Shade's older brother."

"Vere," I told him, allowing him to take my hand.

The pup growled at him and shifted closer to me, leaning heavily into my legs. I got the impression he might be telling his big brother to back off. At a guess, big brother wasn't much older than twenty. I'd guess Shadow at something like eighteen, and I imagined the pup—Shade—might be something like fourteen or fifteen.

Reve grinned at the pup as if he amused her. "I think my son has a crush on you," she said.

I smiled down at Shade and rubbed the back of his neck. "He's all right," I said.

"What happened to his leg?" Shadow wanted to know.

"I found him in a trap," I told her. "A rusty old monster of a thing.

I managed to get him out of it, fixed up his leg as best I could, and then got him back here. It will probably be a while before he can travel."

They all nodded.

"We found the trap and your staff," Wraith said. "We didn't find Shade's pack." He frowned at his son. "I'm thinking you're very, very lucky to be alive," he told him.

Shade nodded and sneezed.

"Food," I said. "And tea. I'm sorry I don't have chairs for everyone, but there are two stools and the dog bed." I moved to the cupboard as I spoke, fetching bowls and spoons to set out on the table. I brought one of the bowls to the stove and ladled it full of stew and handed it to Reve. The next bowl went to Wraith, and then Shadow and Fort. Then I set the tea on to steep before I sat down with my own bowl and Shade's on the dog bed. The rest of them sat on their packs, except Shadow, who squeezed in next to Shade on the dog bed, not as careful as I would have liked to see not to impinge on his broken leg.

"So—" Shadow started, just before spooning her mouth full. She chewed and then looked down at her bowl. "This is good!" she exclaimed.

"Don't talk with your mouth full," her mother admonished her.

"I don't know how long Shade had been there in the trap before I found him," I admitted. "A couple of days, I fear."

Shade looked up from his bowl and nodded. I reached over his shoulders and gave him a rub. Shade finished his food, licked his muzzle clean, and then snuggled his head into my lap.

"You must be a dog person," Shadow remarked. "Most people would have been too scared to help Shade."

"I always wanted a dog," I admitted. "My adoptive mother would never let me have one. My foster brothers had one, but--" I lifted my shoulders in a shrug.

"You're Nogaynos," Fort said, matter-of-factly. "What was she? Amadean?"

"I don't know what I am," I admitted. "I have managed to help Shade with his leg, and I have tried to 'heal' it, but I don't know how much help I've been with it."

"If you hadn't 'healed' his leg, he would have lost it by now," Fort said, "or at least be well on his way to losing it. We all saw that trap, and if he was in it for two days--" he shrugged.

"He is very, very lucky you came along," Reve told me.

Shade looked up at me and snuggled closer. I wrapped my arm around him and hugged a little.

"I was alone," I said. "I've appreciated the company."

Wraith blinked and looked out what passed for windows. Then he looked back at the stove and the piles of wood around it.

"This," he said thoughtfully, "is a very good den."

Then he looked down into his bowl. "We are going to need to go hunting, as soon as the snow lifts," he concluded.

He was right. I had nowhere near enough meat in to feed this crew for the next six weeks, never mind the winter, even with the third buck I'd just killed, and Shade was not going to be ready to travel anywhere for at least six weeks and probably eight, if then.

"Best wait until the snow lets up," I suggested. "Besides, I'm going to have to make a pair of snowshoes so I can travel around out there."

They all turned to look at me as if I was crazy. Practically, I pointed out, "I have a bow. It would be best if you tracked and located the deer. Since I have the bow, all you have to do is to get me close. You'd have to run it down. I don't. I'll kill the deer and then you can clean it, skin it, butcher it out and get it home."

Not that it would work that easily. Nothing ever did.

"It's not that we have nothing to do in the meantime," I pointed out. "We need more furniture. Chairs for the table, a couple of sofa beds you can sleep on, maybe even, when we've brought down a few more deer, we'd have a couple of extra hides we could use for rugs on the floor."

I couldn't help but think that we'd need to bring down at least one more deer for each of them, with another for the pot.

"Bear would be better for that," Reve commented thoughtfully, looking about herself thoughtfully.

"I like this," Shadow informed us. She meant the dog bed. I winced.

"We've going to need more dry leaves and twigs for tonight," I observed. "Shadow can share a bed with Fort, Shade shares with me, and if Wraith and Reve take the shape of their wolves, they should be able to fit on the floor bed--" was it insulting to call it a 'dog' bed? I wondered. "But we'll have to fix something up this afternoon for Fort and Shadow."

"We've got supplies we can offer," Reve informed me. "We always travel with three sets of clothing, two blankets and two tarps apiece. And we have food." She got up from the stool she sat on and started rifling through their packs.

"I've got enough meat to keep us going for a few days," I assured her. "You might as well keep what you've got in your packs—"

"No," she assured me, as she started to set the packs of dried venison out on the table, "Let me make sure it's still dry."

"Ah," I pointed to the racks to either side of the stove. "Set the meat out there, and when you're sure any moisture it's picked up has evaporated, we can seal it up again."

Fort came to help her immediately. I noted that Shadow had already made herself to home by invading my sleeping space. Reappearing, she almost accused, "Books. You have books."

"A few," I agreed. I looked towards what I had intended to be my sitting area. "Let's go harvest what we can from the trees for bedding material and see what lumber we can make of the trees I've got down," I suggested.

"You've got something cooking on the back of the stove," Reve commented, peering into the big cauldron simmering there.

"Applesauce," I told her. "The apple drops aren't going to last much longer, so I thought I'd sauce them and see how much juice I could get off them."

"It smells wonderful," Reve told me, taking deep breaths over the cauldron.

"Apples, honey, cinnamon, nutmeg, and a touch, just a touch, of cloves," I told her.

"When you can smell them cooking all over the house, then they're done."

Shade huffed from his bed in the middle of the floor under the windows.

Another bed, first, I was thinking, as we dressed to head back out into the cold, and then stools for the table. I took my knapsack to gather the bits of leaves into, and once we'd filled it, we carried it in and laid the bits and pieces out on blankets before the stove to dry.

We had to fill my knapsack four times to have enough for one bed.

Reve sacrificed one of her tarps to make the mattress cover, and I whip-stitched the ends together and then enough of the long side to keep the packing in. Making the bed boxes took longer, requiring that the planks we used be cut to match and holes carved in the planks with plugs to match to hold them together, but they went together speedily by comparison with the stools. Those had to be carved by hand, each and every piece, from the seat to the rungs that held the legs together, and the legs themselves.

Wraith watched me carve one seat, and then he seized another piece of planking the right size and started to carve it. By the time I had reached the legs, Fort had figured out what needed to be done, and he had started carving appropriate branches into legs.

By dinner time we had a stool for everybody, even Shade, who wouldn't be using one for some time, and a place setting in front of it. I cut big hunks of venison for everyone, slapped them into a pan on the stove to cook, mixed up a pan of corn cake to stick into the oven, and dipped off several ladles of apple juice to add to a pot of boiling water with some cinnamon and nutmeg for apple tea. Everybody went outside before dinner, and when they came back in, Shade changed with them, dressed in too big clothing belonging to his older brother, got his leg inspected and tied up again, and then, hopping on one leg while suspended between his father and brother, got brought to the table to eat. I served everyone a chunk of venison, added a piece of corn cake, slathered both with applesauce, and then filled each mug with apple tea.

"I would never have thought of the apples," Reve remarked, her voice hushed as she inhaled the aroma of her tea, which she held almost reverently before her, with both hands.

"Stretches the meat," I pointed out.

"Enhances the flavor, too," Fort commented.

"Good," Shade closed the discussion. He ate avidly.

His father eyed him speculatively. If possible, the boy looked even thinner in his human form than he had in his wolf persona. His bones stuck through the loose shirt and tunic he wore almost aggressively, and it would have been clear to the most casual observer that he needed every bite in front of him. Halfway through the meal, I transferred a hunk of my meat and a piece of my corn cake to his. He flashed me a brief glance and said a polite 'thanks' before demolishing the food.

"Be careful," Reve told me gently. "Feeding a man from your dish is a courting gesture."

I stared at her, stunned. When I found my tongue, I managed,

"I am not courting a boy," I told her, trying to keep my voice down but saying it definitely. "He has gone without food and is still growing. He is in desperate need. I do not need the extra food. He does."

"Ah," Reve nodded, as if in satisfaction. "Nurturing."

Everybody seemed to stop and think about that. Shade said, as if he merely stated a fact, "She is a Nogaynos queen." Shadow frowned at him.

"How do you figure that?" she wanted to know. "Nogaynos, yes, I can see that. Anybody can. But a queen?"

"She heals," the boy told her. "She hunts. She talks to animals. She makes things."

His father considered that, and then concluded, "He has a point."

I said, a little impatiently,

"I was raised Amadean. I know only very little of Nogaynos."

"But you have a book on Nogaynos," Shadow pointed out in her turn.

"A book which was," I informed her, "written, as far as I can tell, before the genocide."

"Well, it would just about have to be," Reve reminded. "I do not think the Nogaynos are writing many books now."

She spoke as if there still were a Nogaynos. I turned my attention to her.

Wraith distracted me.

"Was there a book on Mahdi?" he asked his daughter.

"No."

"Then you won't know anything of Mahdi," he said.

"Hearsay only, and not much of that," I admitted. "I had heard of Mahdi wolves, but I had no idea--"

"No one does," Fort said, with some satisfaction.

"Does it tell you in the book that Nogaynos women choose their men?" Wraith wanted to know.

"Not in very much detail," I admitted. "I can't say I understood it."

Reve winced.

"Mahdi men follow the same customs," Wraith told me. "It is permissible for a Mahdi male to attempt to bring himself to a particular female's attention, but he may not claim her until she claims him." He frowned at his son. "Shade has been telling me and his brother that you are his." His frown deepened. "I understand his feelings, but that is not correct behavior."

I glanced at Shade and he was blushing. I wanted to pat his head, knew I couldn't. So, instead, I tried a misdirection.

"What are you doing out here in the snow?" I asked instead. "However did Shade get out here all by himself?"

# XVIII

## SMOKE WOLVES

**"W**E ARE SMOKE WOLVES," REVE answered me. "We claim a long history of being closely allied with Nogaynos people."

"We even carry Nogaynos blood!" Shade told me proudly.

"We do," Reve agreed with him. "In fact," she continued, "our matriarch's grand-mother came from Nogaynos in the diaspora and both Wraith and I carry Nogaynos blood in our veins, as well."

I nodded. That made sense to me.

"Some of the Nogaynos people were clairvoyant," Reve said next.

'What's clairvoyant?' I asked myself, but did not say aloud. I wanted to hear the story. I could ask about clairvoyance later. Or look it up.

"And they, knowing that something bad was coming, got their children out to Mahdi before the genocide. Others got their families out when people first started dying, knowing something was wrong, but not what."

"Mahdi wolves welcomed them," Wraith took up the tale. "Nogaynos blood, mixed with Mahdi blood, made us stronger."

"Grandmother says we were getting too inbred," Shadow commented. Reve frowned.

"Cousins mating cousins is always bad, but it does happen," she observed. "But there's no gainsaying that Mahdi and Nogaynos blood together made us

better." She huffed a sigh. "Not that everybody admits it. In the north, some of the packs don't treat the Nogaynos children as well as they ought."

I nodded. That sounded more likely, to me.

"The Smoke pack is one of the stronger packs," Reve told me. "Well, most of the stronger packs carry Nogaynos blood. Some of them always have, even before the diaspora. The Smoke pack is one of them."

O . . . kay, I thought. I found that interesting.

"Recently," she added, "my younger sister claimed a male from the Negri pack. They are a very survival of the fittest pack--"

"Let me guess," I said. "They're a pure Mahdi pack and proud of it."

"Exactly," she agreed with me.

"They look Caelian to me," Shade said.

"How do Caelian look?" I inquired, curious.

"Like the Crown Prince of Amadea," Wraith answered me. When I looked surprised, he added, "Didn't you know that the Crown Prince's—and all the other princes'—mother was Caelian?"

"No," I shook my head. "It is never spoken about. She was murdered by one of the noble families, which one is certainly not common knowledge, but since the king married into one of the noble families afterwards, her life and death are never spoken about."

"Hypocrites," Fort scoffed the single word. I was inclined to agree with him.

"Well, anyway, the Crown Prince looks as though he might be pure blooded Caelian, and the youngest boy, what's-his-name?"

"Freddy," I supplied.

"Freddy," Wraith nodded, "looks clearly half-blood, at the very least, and he could be taken for a pure blood, if you didn't know any better."

"Interesting," I said aloud. It certainly was.

"Well, anyway, Rade looks as if he could have some Caelian blood himself," Reve commented.

"The male your sister married?" I clarified.

"Claimed, not married," Shadow corrected.

"M'yea, I'd expect the females in his pack to have something to say about that, if they're all these 'pure Mahdi' types and he's all that good looking," I pointed out.

"They might've," Reve admitted, and then added, "well, I know they did.

But they were all so closely related to him, cousins and aunts and nieces and no one any less closely related in the pack. Their matriarch said that she was all for 'pure Mahdi' but not for insanity. And his going to any one of them would be incest and that was insanity. So Rene got him, and she's already pregnant, and Rade's over the moon and so is his Matriarch, because they've been having all kinds of trouble with sterility and birth defects and the like because they're already too inbred."

Well, I thought, that made sense. "But?" I left it hanging.

"But it's traditional for the male to come to live in the female's pack, or to start a new one," Wraith explained.

"And anyway, if Rene went to Rade's pack, they'd kill her," Reve admitted, unhappily. "Rade's pack isn't—" she paused, "right."

"The new Matriarch tries," Shadow defended her.

"Yes, she does," Reve agreed. "But she hasn't been Matriarch very long, and she's not nearly as inbred as the others in the pack. She even took her mate from another pack, a male with some Nogaynos blood at that, but if she couldn't whip half the female portion of the pack at a time, and if her mate couldn't

easily do for half the males, she wouldn't have made it. They'd have killed her by now. As it is, either she's going to have to kill some of them, or they're going to have to leave and set up their own pack sooner or later, or the entire pack is going to explode."

"Getting rid of Rade was a good move on her part," Wraith commented. Reve's expression soured.

"I'd agree, if only he hadn't come to our pack," she said.

"Rene is young and very pretty," Fort commented. "She made herself a favorite of the Matriarch's quite deliberately."

"Rade's a bully," Shade said. "Fort," he bragged, "could take him down with one hand tied behind his back."

"Yes," Fort agreed, in his matter-of-fact way, "but it would not be well received. Better we take on the quest to make contact with Nogaynos and give things time to settle out."

If they would.

"Yes," I allowed, "but why would any of the Nogaynos wish to contact a pack in which 'pure Mahdi' is the guiding principle, or a pack in the process of being torn apart by a bully?"

"Good point," Wraith returned.

Reve looked around the shelter thoughtfully, then back at me.

"I'm thinking, when we get to Nogaynos, if we can find a place we like, why not form our own pack?"

"Three females?" Wraith wondered aloud, as if asking if three would be enough to establish a pack. Or maybe, I considered, as if three females would be too many. Depended on the females, I supposed.

"And one of them a Nogaynos queen," Reve reminded him. "She may be young, but that is all to the good," she added. "Given all that she is doing now, if she will study, and the books she carried with her promise that she will, there is no telling what magic she will come into in her time."

I had to allow that she might have something there.

"It has," I thought aloud, "only been a matter of months since I learned that I had magic. I used it in the forge in small ways growing up, but I did not know what I was doing. Not really."

"How many elements?" Reve wanted to know.

"Fire," Shade told her. "And earth."

I thought of my tracking spell and the magic I used to guide my arrows. And air, I decided.

"Communication with animals is of the spirit," Reve pointed out.

"Umm," I objected, "I don't know that I communicate."

"You do," Shade assured me. "Not telepathy, but you do communicate."

"What about water?" Wraith wondered.

I shrugged. I had done the plumbing from the spring, but was that magic?

Or merely technology?

"I can swim," I said.

"It's more than that," Reve said, dissatisfied.

"If she has fire, earth, air and spirit," Fort summed up, "and she is just at her beginning, then she is a queen."

"Yes, but how strong?" I demanded, depreciatingly. "Outside of the forge, how much can I do? Shoot an arrow accurately?" I scoffed. "Plenty of people can do that much without magic, and if a mastery of fire—if you can call it that—makes working the forge easier, well, still, plenty of people who have no magic can master a forge well enough."

"Are you sure?" Wraith asked me. "You say that you worked the forge for years without any idea that you were using magic to manipulate it. Could not the same be said of any artisan? Or of any marksman as well? Maybe they have magic too. A touch of air magic. A little bit of fire. Who's to say they don't?"

I looked at him and thought he might have something.

"In the old days, before the genocide," Wraith continued, "Nogaynos people moved freely through all the kingdoms. Nogaynos women took men to them who pleased them wherever they found them. Some even stayed with them.

You may find, in Amadea, a village here and there which thrives and prospers though the matriarch from whom their gifts descend may have been long forgotten. Well, that is patriarchy. Patriarchal men will never credit a woman with success, or indeed, with value in any way at all, and they will not allow a strong woman, a foundation woman, to be remembered. But still, her blood and bone and her gifts will live on after her for many generations. The patriarchy will always seek to stamp out the memory of her legacy, because patriarchal men can never tolerate a woman's legacy, and they will, of course, eventually succeed, but that does not mean that she did not live, that she did not have value, or that she did not leave a legacy."

He had a point.

"We need a place to winter over before we start for Nogaynos in the spring,"

Reve said. "You should come with us. You will be safer than you would be alone."

Well, I knew she was right about that. I watched, surprised, as

Fort and his father started to pick the bowls and eating utensils up from the table to ferry over to the sink.

"Hot water in the reservoir behind the stove," I pointed out, and soon they had a steaming pot of it in the sink, all filled with shaved bits of soap from their stores. Wraith washed, Fort rinsed and Shadow dried. Reve rested her attention on Shade.

"Where did you lose your pack, son?" she wanted to know.

"I'd got caught in the trap, and I shrugged out of my pack to see if I could find something in it to help and a man came, a man who looked Caelian, and he snatched it away from me when I was changed to human so I could use my hands to open the trap. I needed a staff like Vere's to get it open and I didn't have one, so I had to change back to a wolf to keep warm."

"He saw you in human form and he still left you in the trap and took your pack," Reve repeated, just to make certain, I thought, that she understood him correctly.

"I think perhaps we ought to go back there and do a little tracking before we start hunting deer," I said, meeting her eyes.

"Oh, yes," Reve almost purred. We shared a smile. "What did this man look like?" she asked Shade.

"Biggish, blonde, bearded, blue eyes, old," Shade told her. "He had that Caelian nose."

"Huh," Reve said. She nodded. Looked at her son. "About time for you to change back?" she wondered.

"Let me try doing a little healing in each form," I offered. "See whether that works better."

"Now," Reve returned, sounding intrigued, "that's an idea."

We each took an arm and got Shade back to the dog bed, where I shoved the overlarge trouser leg up and ran my hand over the break lightly, numbing the remaining pain and healing it. When I finished, I sat back on my heels.

"All right," I said, "while I round up the splints and the clean wraps, you can get out of those clothes and change. I'll do a little more healing and then wrap your leg up again and we'll hope you can get around a little better." I fixed my eyes on him sternly. "Do not try putting any weight on that leg yet."

Shade gulped.

"No ma'am," he said.

Ma'am. I'd just barely turned seventeen, I thought. But I forced a smile and left him with his mother. Dipping out some hot water to wash my hands, I set out some of my newly made glass jars to sterilize, and then pulled the cauldron off the stove to transfer to the table. It was heavy. Wraith said, "Here, let me get that," and then yipped at the heat of it. I eased it to the table and showed him my hand covers.

"Pot holders," I told him. He was waving his hands around in the air. I said "Here, let me see," and healed them. They weren't much burned. He'd jerked back before they'd gotten hot enough to blister. Tapping the ears sticking out from the side of the pot, with their enameled insulation, I explained, "Only touch the pots on their handles when they've been on the stove, and only with potholders."

I picked up a silver spoon out of the water in the sterile bath by its tip end and waved them around in the air to cool. Then I plunked it down into the glass jar, did the same again and again until each jar had a long-handled silver spoon in it. Then I picked up the ladle and started pressing down the apples until I got a pool of clear juice separated from them. Dipping it out of the cauldron slowly, I managed to fill two quart jars with the juice before I could no longer separate enough juice to even half fill the ladle. Even then I stuck to it until I could fill one of the pint jars. After that, I gave up and started filling the rest of the quart jars with the sauce.

Both Reve and Wraith watched me carefully, bringing the stools back to the table and sitting to watch me. For the intent stares with which they watched me fill the jars, I offered,

"Tomorrow morning, after breakfast, you can help me to slice up the rest of the drops and get them started to simmering."

"You have more?" Reve sounded startled.

"There's a bit of an orchard, oh, maybe half a mile or so below us here," I told her. "I picked all of the apples I could carry and then I gathered up the drops and started making applesauce with them. Apples make a good addition to oatmeal, and they're good on bread, and with this preservation spell, it'll keep a long time." I put a bit of wax into a pan on the stove just long enough to melt, and then started to paint it around the threads on the mouth of each of the glass jars.

It was simple, wax the jar, say the incantation, push the magic into it, and then seal the lid down onto the jar tightly. Wax the next jar, repeat incantation, push more magic, and so on. I left the jars out on the table to cool. Wraith already had the cauldron and the ladle washed and set out to dry. I emptied the water-bath pan into the sink and set it out as well.

"All that, for what?" Reve wanted to know. "Six meals?"

"Probably twelve, not counting the apple tea," I nodded. "But bread or oatmeal sweetened with a little applesauce is a lot better than oatmeal or bread without it."

"There is that," Reve allowed.

"I'll put them away in the morning when they've cooled," I told her. "Time now to do a little studying before bed." I eyed them sternly. "If you go out in the night, close the doors after yourselves, and when you come back in, make sure they're latched securely." And then I remembered. "Oh," I told them, "and don't try to go out Nutmeg's door. It may look open, but it's warded. Nutmeg can go in and out, and I can, but no one else can."

"Wards," Reve repeated, almost reverently.

My wards were pretty rudimentary—I'd made them reading out of the book—but they worked, and that was all I cared about. I took one of the candles off the shelf and carried it with me into my sleeping area. My bed wasn't quite as primitive as the rest of the mattresses in the house. I'd brought my mattress from my former home, along with my brothers' and my sheets and blankets, and all the lush, cotton batting stuffed comforters not being used by my adoptive parents at the time I was leaving. I'd brought all the spare pillows as well as mine, too. Compared to the food and the tools and metals I'd brought, they were nearly weightless, if bulky.

They made a warm nest for me, the pillows tucked up around my back, the candle set into its candleholder above the fold-down bit of desk that extended over the head of my bed. I folded it down now, laid the book on Nogaynos out on it, and prepared to begin my before bed hour or two of study.

# XIX

# A DOMINANT BITCH

I HAD NO MORE THAN GOTTEN absorbed in my book than Shadow let herself into the space as if by right and plopped herself down on my bed.

"That's a very old book," she said.

"Yes, I realize that," I told her, frowning.

"Oh," she said brightly, "wasn't I supposed to come in here?"

"Not without an explicit invitation," I returned. "This is my private space."

"Then what's HE doing here?" Shadow wanted to know, hooking her finger at her younger brother, who had already sacked out at the foot of the bed, having managed to ruck up the end of the comforter so that it covered his now furry back. I reached out and straightened it out a little to cover him more completely.

"He had an explicit invitation," I returned shortly.

"That was before you knew he could be human, too. You thought he was just a dog," she said, cheekily.

Well, that might be true, but he was just a pup. She was older and she was being obnoxious, and furthermore, she knew it and was pulling dominance games on me.

"HE is not interrupting my study," I told her. "You are. And furthermore, you are fully aware that you are interrupting and equally fully aware that you are unwelcome. Leave." I did not intend to play her games. They might be common-place among the Mahdi, but I wasn't having any of them. These wolves could either behave courteously or leave. I had magic and I had a sword and a dagger and thanks be, I could use all of them, if I had to.

"Just think of me as a chaperon," Shadow told me, making herself at home on my bed and no move to leave.

"This is my home and you are a guest in it," I informed her, biting off each world. "And this is my private space and you are intruding in it. Get out." I raised my hand. Magic crackled from my fingers as I bared my teeth at her, ready to fight. I set the book aside.

All right, all right," she said, and started to back out. Behind her, a hand grabbed her by the scruff of the neck and she whisked out of my sight. I stared at the deer hide curtain waving back and forth for long moments and wondered if I was going to have to spend my day tomorrow while the apples stewed making a door and putting it in. Feared I had better do it, and make it a high priority, too. Dammit. That would include hinges, too. Dammit.

I shoved the Nogaynos book back onto the shelf and took down the magic book that included magic martial arts. My skills in that department were still woefully inadequate. Time I started working on that, too.

Shade poked his head up around the comforter and whined softly.

"I'm not angry at you," I assured him, and he turned and crawled up the bed until he could snuggle his head into my lap. I rubbed his ears as I opened the book and started studying the first basic moves the book prescribed for self- defense and he whined a little in response and then dropped back into sleep. I didn't blame him. He'd had a big day.

So had I. I hadn't any more than covered the first three positions than I heard the door close, quietly, and the latch set. The candles were blown out, and I heard the sound of dogs curling around in their beds before silence descended.

In the quiet that followed, I started to nod. By the time I reached the fifth position, I realized that I was not assimilating anything. I gave it up, put the book up, snuffed the light, and delved down into the bed.

I started the next morning stoking the fire up and selecting the bits and pieces I had to make the hinge straps I'd need for my door.

Once I got them set out to cool, I'd get something for breakfast, and after that, I'd get the apples on, and as soon as they started stewing, I'd get started on the door. It didn't take me long to pick up on the wolves diffidence—they were keeping a very low profile, especially when I started swinging my hammer. Shade three-legged it out the door behind his big brother, and once he'd made it back in, he went immediately into my sleeping space and settled there. Reve and Wraith took Shadow out of the shelter and kept her out. I wasn't sure just what Fort was up to.

The snow hadn't let up, and that meant I'd need to make snowshoes, as well.

Wonderful, I thought, punching holes in the hinges for the wooden plugs I'd carve. And that was another thing, I growled to myself. I needed to make more wood glue.

By the time I had the door finished, and ready to hang, the wolves were back.

Fort and Wraith changed and dressed and came to hold the door while I set the hinges. No one said anything about my not needing a door.

Once the door was set and latched, Shade limped out of the room on three legs and made his way outside for a brief foray, and then came back into the house again. I followed him as far as the corner cupboard, picking the worst of the apples out of the boxes to bring in to stew. By the time I had filled my pot, Shade was ready to come in with me. Wraith took the pot away from me and set it on the table for me, while I carted the now cooled jars to the pantry and stacked them on the shelves there.

Reve followed me, looking at the sealed glass tubs of venison stacked there on the cold side. She gasped at the sight of the meat stored there, and then glanced back at her daughter admonishingly. I doubted it meant much. I got a knife and started coring the apples. Shade watched for a moment, and then he limped back to the sitting area, gathered up his borrowed clothes and changed. Using a stool as a walker, he made his way back to the table and then sat to help with the apples. I gave him my knife and got another, and pretty soon

Reve and Wraith had joined me with knives of their own. After that, it didn't take long for us to fill the cauldron with sliced apples.

I added honey and spices, and some water to the mix, and then we settled the cauldron to the back of the stove, which had burned down to a nice set of coals, by that point. No one had eaten anything, as far as I could tell. I brought out some dried venison and set it out on a plate in the middle of the table, and then threw some oats in another pot, added hot water, and put it on to simmer. The

apple cores went out into Nutmeg's feed bin, to his delight, and then I pottered about through the few planks I had left until I found one too short to be much of any use. I brought it in to work with, just in time to dish up the oatmeal. A few slices of the half-cooked apples in the bottom of the pan added flavor, and then I sat down to eat. Shade and I commandeered the stools.

Clearly, Shade was not happy with his parents; he wasn't speaking to Shadow at all. I had no idea what was going on there, but I kept an eye on Shadow myself. I didn't trust her.

While Fort and Wraith took care of clean-up, I started cutting squares out of the plank, and once I'd got as many hunks out of it as I was going to, I started to carve off the corners, the excess pieces of wood going into the stove.    Fort got the idea of what I was doing first. He disappeared out the door, coming back with appropriate branch wood with which to make rungs and legs. Next thing I knew, Wraith had arrived with an armload of more branch-wood to use in making backs for the stools. More dried venison provided a quick lunch, and by the time the pot roast had been seared and loaded into a pot to slow-roast with roots and greens, we had half a dozen 'chairs' ready to allow us a sit-down dinner.

Shade had stayed in his human incarnation so he could help with the carving and gluing. Many hands, as the old saying goes, make light work. I could never had made four chairs so quickly, but then again, without them, I would never have needed so many chairs. So, that was a wash.

"I had a thought," Wraith said, as we sat down to dinner. Reve looked up at him questioningly.

"As soon as the storm breaks, we see if we can bring down another deer," he offered, in response to her expression, "and we have a look around to see if we

can find Shade's gear. Then we take Shadow back to Rene and her grandmother and the pack. We'll leave her there, and head back here for the rest of the winter. With any luck, we can pick up some corn-meal or oats, or maybe both, on the way back."

I thought it an excellent idea. However long they would be gone would save on my stores. Fort and Wraith were big eaters, and neither Reve nor Shadow were exactly shy about their trenchers, either. Three deer were not going to last long with them around. I'd need at least six to even have a hope of making it until spring with the four of them around, and I couldn't say I'd miss Shadow and her dominance games. I knew if she stuck around long that sooner or later she'd be trying to pull another one on me.

I knew they'd be back. They'd seen the promise of a comfortable winter den here, away from their combative relations, warm and well-fed and protected.

Nor could I say I much minded. I thought heading south with them in the spring sounded like a very good idea. Better than going alone. But they had to stay well fed. So far, they'd behaved with perfect circumspection around Nutmeg, but I didn't trust them to keep to it if they got hungry. I doubted hungry wolves could be trusted.

Shade seemed to agree with me. That didn't surprise me. Fort's agreement did. He drew up his elbows, planting them on the table beside his empty bowl and addressed his sister seriously.

"Grandmother did not want you coming with us," he reminded her. "She didn't care if we left on this wild goose chase, as she called it, but she didn't think you should go. She said it was a waste, and you know you've always been her favorite."

"Except for Aunt Rene," Shadow said.

"Aunt Rene," Fort pointed out, with unruffled serenity, "is an older generation."

This observation seemed to strike Shadow forcibly.

"Aunt Rene," she reminded him weakly, "is mother's much younger sister."

"Who may very well find herself taking over her mate's pack," Fort returned, "if their matriarch doesn't stay, and she might very well not."

"There is that," Shadow returned, thoughtfully.

I noticed that Wraith and Reve stayed very quiet during this exchange.

Shade's eyes moved quickly from one to the other of his parents, flickering a little, and I got the feeling there was something wrong there, but I didn't mention it. I couldn't help but think it would be a good thing if he was in better physical shape when whatever it was came out.

Wraith, Reve and Fort cleaned up after dinner, while Shade changed and went outside. By the time he had gotten back, I had the jars set out in the sterilizing pan with their lids, the ladle and the silver spoons and the wax on to melt. I had gotten two quarts and a pint of the condensed spiced apple juice off the sauce when Reve joined me.

"I've been meaning to ask," she said. "What are the spoons for?"

"Keep's the glass from cracking from the heat," I told her. "The silver absorbs the heat and radiates it up and out."

"So why not cool the applesauce before you put it in the jars?" she wanted to know.

"The spell to keep the sauce fresh works better if its sealed into the jars hot," I told her. "It doesn't take much magic," I added depreciatingly. "It's a good beginning spell to get my feet wet with."

"You had plenty of magic last night," she mentioned.

"I was angry last night," I pointed out.

"Yes, I got that impression," she allowed.

"I have more magic when I'm angry," I decided to admit. "I need to study very badly," I amplified my admission, "but I have very little time to do it.

Shade's advent, and more, yours, means a lot more work for me, and a lot more hunting, and perforce, much less time to study. And your daughter came waltzing into MY space as if it was hers and interrupted my study time—as if that was hers as well."

"Disrespectful, offensive, disruptive and insulting," Reve nodded.

"Simple dominance games," I spit out, angry all over again.

Reve winced.

"I don't mind Shade," I said. "He was in that trap, all alone, for days, in hideous pain, and he could have been killed at any time. That man came and stole his gear and left him there to die. He had no food, he had no water—" I waved a hand. "He is not deliberately disruptive, he is not disrespectful—" I broke off again. Gathered myself. "And yesterday, after you came, he was utterly exhausted. He needed rest, and Shadow came in and disturbed him just as much as she disturbed me. To play her nasty dominance games." I looked at her searchingly. "Weren't any of you the least little bit worried about him?" I wondered.

"Three days and nights," Shade surprised me by saying. He was standing next to the table, leaning on a primitive crutch either his father or his brother had made for him from a couple of stout branches. He dropped into a chair. "I called and called," he accused, "but you didn't come." Reve winced.

"Did you even know I was missing?" He asked it plaintively. His father sighed.

"Not right away."

"Not damn soon enough," Fort added. He cast a grim glance towards Shadow.

"Well, how was I to know he'd go and get himself caught in a trap?" she wanted to know.

"You didn't have to lie about him!" Fort snarled at her.

"I didn't lie!" Shadow disagreed with him. "I just thought he'd gone off on his own to scout ahead."

"I had," Shade said flatly. "Doesn't mean you shouldn't have come looking for me a lot sooner than three days when I didn't come back."

"You're a big boy," Shadow told him lightly.

I knew how he felt. I remembered how I had felt when Freddy had betrayed me and I had languished in that dungeon, and no one had come looking for me.

"Enough," I said. "I know how Shade feels. I've been where he was, and no one from what was supposed to have been my family came for me, so I do understand. I'll be frank. If I hadn't found him when I did, you'd have lost him. So think on that, for a change." And I got up and cleaned up after my sauce- making, and then headed for my space and my books.

I found Shade there before me, curled up at the foot of the bed in his furry form. As soon as I had nestled down into my comforter at the head of the bed with my book of magics, he crawled around to snuggle up against me.

"No more going off on your own," I told him. "Alone is bad. I've been alone because I had no choice about it. You've got a choice."

He pushed himself closer to me and snuggled. I rubbed his ears until he did the wolf version of purring, and studied. I managed a good hour of study before my eyelids grew too heavy to prop up and I scooted down into the bed to sleep. One thing about a big pup-dog in the bed, I thought, as I drifted off, it was a lot warmer.

# XX

# QUATTAR

FREDDY LOOKED DOWN AT THE bloody corpse of the young girl Nehl had just finished beating to death. His brother had made a stinking mess of it. They'd have to take her body, bed-covers and all, and pay for them, too. He frowned. The last body they'd thrown off the headlands had washed up in the harbor.

Something about the ocean currents. Freddy didn't understand ocean currents. He didn't want to understand ocean currents, but he didn't think people would much like the body of another young girl who had been beaten to death washing up in the same place.

Men didn't intend to do anything about the murdered girls, but neither did they like having their noses rubbed in their own utter lack of decency and honor. If they shoved this body off the headlands in the same place it meant that she would likely wash ashore in the same place. They couldn't have that.

They'd have to find a different place to dump her body. Somewhere that didn't just wash her on down to the harbor for everyone to see. Bother it! Freddy cursed to himself. Thanks to those ocean currents the whole thing was going to be a giant pain in the BE-hind.

He looked over at Nehl. His brother had checked out in a way that Freddy was beginning to learn, was the usual result of one of his murderous sessions. He rocked in his chair, humming to himself and occasionally addressing the body as if she were still alive and could answer him. His face wore the expression of a man who had just enjoyed a good, vigorous romp in bed with a prostitute, relaxed, contented, even satiated.

Freddy had learned that during this period, Nehl did not want to hear anything from him. He did not want to be interrupted, he did not want to be distracted, he did not want food, or drink, or anything, really. The best thing that Freddy could do, for the next ten or twelve hours, was just to leave him alone. Eventually he would dump the body on the floor and then take a nap on the bed. The blood wouldn't bother him in the slightest, nor would any other bodily substances that didn't follow the body to the floor.

When he woke up, he'd want a meal, and then, sooner or later, Nehl would pull himself together and help get rid of the girl's body. It would be Freddy's job to see that there was water for him to use to wash, clean clothing for him to put on, and a plan to dispose of the body. And, for the next three or four weeks, his brother would be—well, not fine, but at least his usual self. Until the next time.

The next best thing Freddy could do now was to find a new dump site.

Tomorrow would be soon enough to find the horse and cart they'd used to get rid of the other body. He considered. No point in remaining here while Nehl relived the pleasure of hearing the girl's bones snap under his fists, the delightful feel of her body under his hands. Personally, Freddy didn't 'get' it, but then, he supposed he had his own vices, albeit much more plebian ones. He might as well head back to Bardons' mansion for now. It would be easier to find a new dump site in day-light.

The security at the Bardons country seat was laughable. Freddy got in the front door without a single challenge, and he didn't even try to sneak in. The problem with the Bardons, he thought, as he made his way towards the inner chambers, was that they were arrogant. They'd had all their own way for far too many generations and now they thought they ought to be kings.

He sneered internally at the thought. As if. He knew that they thought that taking part in the coup would give them a leg up towards the crown they sought. The truth was that if the coup managed to get rid of all three princes, as Freddy suspected the architects of the coup intended, as well as the king, the country would degenerate into civil war among at least three of the so-called 'noble' houses in very short order. It might, he considered, be a good time for he and Nehl to decamp to the fort at Southren. If Garve` and his father were taken out by the coup, being surrounded by protective military might be the best place for them.

The more Freddy considered this, the more he thought it was the right thing to do. He didn't like the idea of being here in Bardon-D'Arcy territory after the coup. What was to stop the Bardons or the D'Arcys from deciding that getting rid of all of the princes between themselves and the throne would be a capital idea—and acting on it? Nothing, as far as he could tell. But in Southren, at the fort, surrounded by all those military types sworn to the throne—well, Freddy calculated, that was the safest place they were going to find.

It would put a damper on Nehl's hobby, however. Dourly, Freddy admitted that his brother wouldn't be happy about that. Ought he to leave Nehl here and take himself off to the fort by himself? It would leave Nehl vulnerable, but did he really care? Nehl was getting to be a real pain in the butt with his need to kill young girls. It seemed almost like a drug he had to take, to Freddy. Would he go without killing for a couple of months? Could he go without killing that long? Would he even believe he ought to?

Bardons weren't the only arrogant people about—Nehl would never believe that the aristos would turn on him. More fool him. And he was truly enjoying his indulgences here as he could never have enjoyed them under his father's nose. King Marc would never have stood for Nehl's activities--if he ever became aware of them. And he might, if Nehl didn't start behaving with more discretion.

Taking himself to Southren would serve to disengage himself from all activities connected to Nehl, and that, in and of itself, might be beneficial. As long as his brother limited himself to beating young girls to death for his entertainment, no one was going to do anything about it, that was certainly true. But. That didn't at all mean that if—or the way Nehl was going, when—people realized who was killing those young girls, and how, that a sort of hushed miasma wouldn't find its way to his name.

What was that old canard? 'Murder will out'? Right. Bodies bore a sort of silent witness, and what Nehl did to his victims a veritable blind man could see. People might not 'do' anything about Nehl's crimes, they might never put him in a dungeon, or hang him, but decent, honorable people would avoid him if they could, and they'd soon be putting some effort into doing it. The doors of their homes wouldn't be open to him, the better innkeepers, the kind beyond bribes, who would secure their safety, would be less welcoming, some of Nehl's guards would be less conscientious, and only sycophants would volunteer to befriend them.

Then again, so what? Honorable, decent people were not thick upon the ground, and innkeepers who could not be bribed were equally few. And some of their guards were less than conscientious now, if for more personal reasons. Nehl would probably not even notice the difference, and why should he?

Besides, in a few days, after the coup, he would be the king, and he could order the palace servants to bring him appropriate victims for his entertainment, and then it would be their problem to get rid of the bodies. A murderous king wouldn't be liked, but what could they do? Nothing, that's what.

Still, Freddy concluded, heading for his rooms, going to Southren right about now might be a very good idea. In fact, the more he thought about it, the better he liked it.

Movement at one of the ante chamber doors caught his attention. A page hurried up to him, proffering the kind of envelope he recognized instantly.

Palace stationary. His mind leaped to the conclusion immediately. The coup.

"For his highness," the page intoned, handing it to him. Freddy saw his name on it under Nehl's, and accepted it. Theoretically, since his name was on it, it was his right to open it, but he knew that Nehl wouldn't like it. And so what?

He thought, sending the page on his way, unrewarded. Giving

the boy a tip never even occurred to Freddy. He had already forgotten about him. His entire attention had fixed itself to the envelope he held. Freddy knew very well how to have his cake and eat it too. He had to know what had happened.

He let himself into his rooms, looked the door and settled at his desk, lit the candles, and then set his letter opener to the flame. Wiping the soot off with his handkerchief, he carefully slipped the blade under the wax seal, and then under the gummed flap to either side of the seal. The flap came up. He eased the folded letter out—he counted two pages! And then unfolded the sheets. His father's handwriting leaped off the page to his eyes and he closed them in disappointment. His father was still alive then. That meant the coup had failed.

The story the letter told seemed anticlimactic after the simple knowledge that the coup had failed. Freddy folded the pages back together and then, still careful, eased them back into the envelope. A little more heat applied to the wax of the seal saw the envelope pristinely closed again, the gummed flap pressed firmly back together as if never opened. Freddy remained in the chair for a long moment, considering.

He and Nehl were here, a thousand miles or more to the south, unconnected to the coup. His father had seen to the death of the aristos involved—Jahn and Dellin D'Arcy and Matias Bardon--he said he had killed Councilor Jiden with his own hand. He had also said that the household guards and mercenaries involved in the coup, about a hundred and fifty men in all, had been killed as well, so there was no one left alive to bear witness to his and Nehl's connection to Jiden. Well, other than the debacle of the girl he and Nehl had apprehended delivering those blades to Jiden.

Anyone with half a brain who knew about that piece of idiocy could put two and two together, and Freddy now knew that his father had. A force of that many men slipping into the palace at night—if his father hadn't been warned and ready for them, they would have succeeded. Then his mind seized on the names his father had sent. Jiden, Matias Bardon, and Jahn and Dellin D'Arcy. His hand closed into a fist. Four men, four daggers. Jiden had never intended for Nehl to take the throne. His thoughts stuttered with that conclusion. They had to get out of here and get to the fort at Southren and they had to do it now!

Freddy tucked the envelope inside his shirt, and then he started moving, quickly, deliberately, setting out his bags and packing his clothing and bedroll. They'd get food on the way out, he told himself as he packed Nehl's kit. And, he added, just to himself, as he slipped down the front stairs—nobody would be about in this part of the house at this hour of the night—if Nehl wouldn't come away with him to the fort at Southern, then he could just stay here and take his chances with the Bardons and the D'Arcys.

Nehl was still asleep when he reached the run-down warehouse and it took Freddy a good five minutes to wake him. Nehl didn't want to awaken. He flailed out with a bloody arm in Freddy's direction. Freddy ducked.

"Go away," Nehl groaned.

"Be glad to," Freddy assured him, and at this point, he meant it. His patience with his brother was just about exhausted. "Just as soon as you get up, wash up and read the letter from the palace."

Nehl lifted his head, fighting for alertness.

"The coup?" he wondered.

"You need to read it," Freddy insisted.

Moving slowly, but no longer reluctant, Nehl forced himself out of the bloody bedding and sat up. He stared at Freddy. Freddy pointed at the bucket of water and the basin he'd laid out with soap and towels. Nehl staggered over to the bucket, looking, for all the world, as if he was fighting a huge hangover, pulled off his bloody, ripped shirt, and started to wash.

Silently, Freddy brought him fresh clothing. Nehl finished washing, dried himself, and put on the clothing Freddy had brought. He did not thank his brother for his care; in fact he didn't even notice it. He took it all for granted. Instead, he asked,

"What are we going to do with her?" He tipped his head towards the body without, quite, looking at her. Freddy shrugged.

"Nothing. She can stay here. Better than washing up the same place the other girl did," he pointed out. "With any luck, no one will bother poking around here anytime soon, and if she does start smelling--" she already had "well, the whole area smells bad, so what's one more bad smell?"

He handed his brother the envelope.

"It's from the palace," Nehl said blankly, staring at it.

"Open it," Freddy urged him.

Nehl did. He read the first page with one sweep of his eyes, his knees buckling. Freddy shored him up. Nehl looked up, his hands shaking.

"The coup failed," he said faintly, as if such an outcome had gone beyond disbelief.

Freddy took the letter from him and pretended to read it. Looking up, he told Nehl,

"Those four blades, they were for Jiden, Matias Bardon, and Jahn and Dellin D'Arcy." His lips twisted with memory. "Not for us."

"Father was ready," Nehl concluded.

"He had to have been," Freddy agreed. He folded the letter up and put it back into the envelope.

"But how--?" Nehl questioned.

"That's not the point," Freddy told him. "The point is that they tried to kill Father and Garve` both, and that they had a contingent in the throne room. Why were they in the throne room, if they weren't going to crown a new king?" he wanted to know. "And they had household guards with them from Jiden, Bardons and D'Arcys. Who were they going to crown?" he demanded of his brother. "Jiden? Matias Bardon? Or Jahn D'Arcy?" He shook his head.

"We've got to get out of here."

Nehl shook his head like a maddened bull, but then his eyes snapped into focus and he regarded Freddy with a functioning brain behind them. Finally.

"You think Bardons and D'Arcys will be after us?" he wanted to know.

"I don't know," Freddy told him honestly. "I do not intend to chance it. I'm leaving for Fort Southren now. I packed up your kit and brought it with me. I'll buy supplies on the way. You can come with me, or you can stay here. Up to you. I've brought your horse."

His horse, Freddy thought. What a crock. Nehl didn't own a horse, he didn't ride well at all, and he, in fact, disliked the beasts rather a good deal.

"You think they'd harm us?" Nehl demanded, outraged by the very thought. "Us?"

"They intended to murder Father. And Garve`. What makes you think they don't intend to murder us?" Freddy asked him. "And anyway, I don't intend to find out."

He started for the front of the warehouse. Nehl followed him hesitantly. "You're just going to leave her?" he bleated at Freddy.

Freddy shrugged.

"She's dead," he said callously, and kept on walking. "She won't mind." Nehl glanced back rather blankly.

"But you're always so careful about not being found out," he complained.

"But this time, when they do, if they do, we'll be long gone," Freddy assured him. "They won't even think of us."

Nehl thought about it. He did it slowly, and with difficulty.

"I see," he said finally. He gathered his horse's reins and mounted with his usual awkwardness. All the riding lessons in the world by some of the best instructors the D'Arcys had, could not manage to make Nehl into any kind of rider.

He was probably frightened of the horse, Freddy thought, ungenerously, although why he might be, Freddy couldn't imagine. He'd never even fallen off, for cat's sake. He gathered up his own horse's reins and mounted easily.

Freddy was no one's athlete, but he could manage to ride a horse with a fair degree of efficiency. And he could find the road west, as well. He headed the horse out of the warehouse district as the sun burst through the clouds to show him the way. He shook his head slightly to himself. He'd rather have left the city at night, but he had no intention of sticking around that long. The sooner he got out of Quattar, he thought, the better.

# XXI

## COOPERATIVE EFFORTS

IT STOPPED SNOWING THE NEXT day and we worked at making snowshoes for all of us. The day after that, we started out at first light, leaving Fort to watch over Shade. Neither Wraith nor Reve was entirely happy about that, but no way was Shadow staying at the shelter without me there to guard my books. I knew they'd be the first targets for her malicious dominance games. Reve had tried to tell me that she was just being a teenager, but I'd let my anger spark from my fingers and that had been the end of the argument—for now. I didn't trust any of them.

We cut sign of Shade's gear, first. The bastard who had stolen his packs had shredded his shirts and tunics, and tried to shred his trousers, without much success. His heavy cloak, blankets and tarps had just been strewn about and now languished under eight-nine inches of new snow, icy in some places and wet in in others. We dug them out, shook them off and rolled them up again.

The bastard hadn't even attempted to do much with the leather packs. He'd just left them lying, empty, having taken all the food Shade had been carrying and left the rest. We dug things up, emptied out any snow or ice they'd collected, shook everything out and then packed it all up again. I'd see if I could do anything with the torn shirts and pants. Maybe I could mend them with magic. Anyway, I could at least try.

Reve shifted, we packed her things up in her son's packs, and

170

started out again. She cut the scent of deer quickly, and we followed it carefully. None of us were moving quickly. The snow hadn't drifted much but travel was still slow, though Reve ran a little ahead of us, since according to Wraith, she had the most talented nose of the family. I used a touch of 'travel' here and there to keep up, and when she stopped, Wraith snarled slightly.

"I'll never be able to change in time to get close enough," he groused softly. "No problem," I assured him, barely breathing it. I had already unlimbered the bow and strung it. Now, as slowly and silently as I could move, I raised it, nocked my arrow, set the magic, and let fly. The arrow struck true, the young buck leaped straight up, and then came down, crumpling into a heap. Wraith leaped forward himself, but Reve had beaten him to it.

"Huh," Shadow said, looking from me to the buck. "Lucky shot," she concluded.

I didn't bother to respond.

Wraith got the buck into a tree, bled and gutted it, and then all three of them changed, and ate their fill of the spoil while I started the skinning. When they'd all sated themselves, they changed back, dressed, and we cut the deer into quarters, with the ribs on the side. Wraith and Reve each took a rear quarter, and a portion of the ribs, while Shadow and I each took a forequarter with a smaller section of ribs, and I took the hide. We left what remained of the head.

We got back to the shelter just before twilight, finding the boys had spent the day reading my book on Nogaynos. They seemed excited about it, and Shade became even more excited when he saw that we had his pack, but then when he saw what had been done with his clothes, his excitement turned to ashes.

"I might be able to fix them," I offered, as I started a roast to searing over the fire in the stove the boys had kept going. "First I need to take care of the meat, and then I'll need to clean up, but after that, I'll use a cleaning spell and then darn them together as best I can and then see what we can do with magic."

This prospect intrigued both boys, and Reve, as well. They got Shade's clothes out and laid them out on the table, working at fitting the pieces together, which would save me a good bit of work, so I didn't complain about it. Wraith cut the meat carefully, so I could fit the most pieces into each of the glass containers they could hold, but we still had to lay a good bit of it out onto the drying racks. The rest of the meat just fit into the cold case. Lined with snow, it would keep the meat until it could either be eaten or dried, whichever came first. With this crowd, I didn't think there would be much left to dry. Wraith went out to collect more wood to bring in to dry for the fire, and I washed up at the sink with Reve.

Tomorrow, I thought, as I went to get my sewing kit, I'd have to go to work on the hide. At least, I told myself, as I did it, I could 'tan' the hide with magic instead of the usual noxious substances used to do it.

"You ought to read the book on Nogaynos Vere has," Shade told his mother, as I worked. "We figured out from the introduction that it was written at least a full generation before the diaspora."

"According to the book, the men and women worked in teams," Fort added. "The men couldn't do much magic, but men descended from certain women were more likely to have daughters with strong magic, and when their daughters married men from other strong women, they got even more magic."

"But they had to go out, every third generation, at least, to keep the magic strong," Shade added.

"So no inbreeding," I nodded.

"Apparently, if the parents are first or second or even third cousins, the magic cancels itself out," Shade paraphrased what he had learned, "but if a person mates with another person from a magical family and they're not related, the person gets both kinds of magic their parents have. So, Vere has to have ancestors from earth, air, fire and spirit families, in order to be able to use each of those talents."

Reve nodded to this.

"One thing I can tell you," she informed both her sons. "She's a dead shot.

We'd never have brought that buck down on our own."

"Yes," I qualified, "but you could turn that around the other way--I'd never have found that buck on my own."

I'd found the closest color of thread in my kit and started to add a running stitch along both sides of each tear in the shirt I was working on. If I'd had the fabric, I'd have mended the tears, but I didn't, so I had to attempt to darn the tears in the hope that once they were all darned, that I could find a spell to bind the threads and make the fabric a hopefully even stronger whole.

"Let me do that," Reve suggested. "You get your book and see what you can find in the way of a spell that will fix this."

Fort had lighted the candles in the candle-holders, which reminded me that I needed to start the fat from the buck to the purification process in the morning. City living, I thought, was, in some sense, easier, since things like candles were purchased instead of made, and so were most clothes. And the candle-makers didn't make them from 'scratch' in a sense, because they purchased the tallow already purified to work with, and the wicks, as well. Any more than the clothes were made 'from scratch', since the shirt-makers and the pants makers all bought the fabric pre-made and dyed. Somebody spun the thread, and somebody else loomed the cloth, which somebody else dyed in colors they had created from plants and roots or perhaps even insects.

Well, I couldn't speak to wicks. I'd brought a ball of wick-twine with me when I'd come. It was something that didn't take up a lot of room or weigh much. But out here, if we wanted cloth, we had to find and harvest the flax or the cotton or the wool, clean and prepare it, spin it to thread, and then set the thread to the loom and weave it ourselves. Dying the cloth was an extra half dozen steps most people didn't bother with; they were simply too much work. They took too much time and energy people didn't have to spare, so that most cloth came out some variation on beige or brown, natural shades of the undyed fabric.

I'd thought of that when I'd brought half my adoptive mother's sheets with me when I'd come out here. (One could argue that they were my sheets, since the money given to my adoptive parents to pay for my care had been spent on them, instead of on me, while I was working the forge and bringing in yet even more money for my adoptive mother to spend. So I suppose you could say that they were doubly mine!)

I got my book on practical magic and then added a couple of my spare candle-lights to the table so both Reve and I had additional light by which to work. Mending magic, according to the book, was earth magic, and that gave me a good feeling. I had found that I liked the feel of earth magic. I liked trees and plants and dirt, and fabric, when you thought about it, came from the earth, sometimes directly, sometimes indirectly. Flax and cotton were plant fibers, after all, and sheep ate grass, which came from the earth and which then grew their fleece through the mechanism of their animal bodies.

I tried a bit of the mending spell on a section of torn hem along the bottom of one trouser leg, and it worked so well I tried it on the darned fabric of Shade's shirt. It worked like, well, magic! I couldn't say it made the shirt look like new, but I had an idea it strengthened the fabric of the shirt and lessened some of the wear and tear I had no doubt Shade had subjected the shirt to. Reve's darns were a lot more basic than the darn I'd put in, but they did the job of knitting the rents in the fabric together for the spell to work on them, and they didn't take nearly as much time as my darn had, so that was all to the better.

By the time I headed to bed with my book, I had repeated the same spell often enough that I would remember it, and Shade now had two shirts and a tunic he could wear, as well as a pair of pants. Poor Shade was ecstatic at the idea that he could now have enough clothing so he didn't have to stay in wolf- dog form all the time or wear his brother's borrowed clothing. I think his brother appreciated it as well, since he didn't have much in the way of clothing to wear, himself.

The next day I pretty much guilted the wolves into going out with me to bring down another deer. The fourth deer didn't mean that I had enough to feed Shade through the winter, and if the rest of them did return (and I wasn't going to hold my breath over it) they wouldn't be able to carry enough meat to make any meaningful difference between what I had and what we needed. The meat from the deer they'd brought down had disappeared rapidly, between the large roasts they demolished and the meat that had to be dried for them to take with them. Almost nothing of it would remain for me and for Shade by the time they left.

We needed another, and the sooner we brought one down, the better, while the deer still had plenty of flesh and a goodly bit of fat on them. If we waited until the wolves got back, the deer would have been pulled down by cold and slim pickin's, maybe as much as twenty-five pounds down, and if not that much at least by twenty. Twenty pounds was a lot of meat for just the two of us.

Reve's nose was good, I'd give her that. She cut scent almost immediately, leading the rest of us to a small herd of deer. This time I didn't take the smaller buck. I wanted as much meat as I could get. The big buck was too big to pack back to the shelter. The spike didn't have enough meat on him. If this was to be the last hunt for a while, I'd take the middling buck. With luck, he'd dress out somewhere between a hundred and twenty-five and a hundred and forty pounds. The closer to the latter, I thought, as I brought him down, the better.

Shadow ate her share of the spoil, but when it came to carrying the meat back to the shelter, she managed to get by with something like twenty-twenty-five pounds worth, and mostly those were ribs. I know I carried at least forty pounds, and so did Reve and from the looks of the hindquarter Wraith had strapped on his back, he was carrying close to fifty, at least, and maybe as much as sixty. I wasn't inclined to quibble. A lot of what we carried would be waste bone, but I figured the wolves would enjoy nibbling on it between meals.

This time the butchering went smoothly. Most of the meat had to go into the cold cases until I could get enough of the glass cases done to hold all of it, but in the meantime the drying racks could be filled again, and I could put another roast in the pot. Nobody in this crowd minded eating pot roast, and you could never have enough dried venison on hand. Not that I couldn't throw a preservation spell or two on the meat to keep it fresh while I was getting the glass containers ready.

"We'll be leaving first thing in the morning to take Shadow back to the pack," Reve told me, as the last of the deer went into the cold case. She said it as if she expected objections from me.

I just shrugged. The sooner Shadow departed, the better. I watched Wraith clean up the last of the mess thoughtfully. He and Fort did a good job. I didn't understand why both of them had hunched their shoulders like they felt guilty about something.

"Fort's going with us," Reve said, as if she was saying something shameful.

I shrugged again. No skin off my nose, I thought. I figured families always had favorites and it didn't surprise me that Shadow was this family's favorite. I'd already realized that Shadow had been the reason they'd left Shade in that trap to die. I thought he probably occupied a position somewhat like King Marc's son Garve` as the spare heir. They had Fort for an heir, Shadow as the family favorite, and Shade, well, he was just extraneous.

"Well, then," I nodded to them, "I guess we'd all better turn in early after dinner." But I rested my hand on Shade's shoulder when I eased by his chair to check on the roast. I knew it would have meant a lot to him to have Fort stay to make sure he was going to be all right. To Shade, I said, "I've got to make glass tomorrow, but you might as well read the book on Nogaynos while I work.

Maybe you could read it aloud to me?"

Shade's solemn face lit up at that, and I smiled back at him. I'd never had a friend before, or a companion. I was sorry Shade's family didn't appreciate him more, but I couldn't help thinking, their loss, my gain.

Relief filled Reve's eyes at that, but I turned my face away from her. While I didn't think Shadow should be asked to return to their pack all on her own— well, I wouldn't have trusted her to go! I thought having both her mother and father with her ought to be sufficient. Shade was younger than Shadow, and he needed his family too, particularly after the experience he'd just had, but apparently they couldn't see it, or if they did, Reve, at least, wanted me to stand in for them. I wanted to tell her that if she kept doing that, the ties that bound their family would wear away over time until they couldn't hold any longer. I knew. I'd learned my lessons about family ties the hard way.

But I didn't say anything. After dinner I left Wraith and Fort to the clean-up, Reve packing their gear, and Shadow pouting, and took to my room to study.

Shade fell asleep pressed tight against my side. I left him there when I finally closed my book and blew out the candle-lights. And that was another thing, I thought, as I drifted off to sleep. I needed to start the fat from the deer purifying tomorrow after I finished with the glass. I'd have to ration my sand and lime out carefully—I didn't have a lot of either left.

Oh, by spring, I could get more sand, but by then I wouldn't need it. And wasn't that always the way? I thought, as I let go of all thoughts. Getting sand out of the stream-bed now would be difficult, dangerous and uncomfortable, not something I wanted to do if I didn't have to. So, I'd just have to make what I had last.

# XXII

## FORT SOUTHREN

THE COLONEL TURNED THE LETTER over in his fingers unhappily. "I don't like it," he said.

Freddy lifted a shoulder. The room he stood in looked shabby and worn, the furnishings barely one step up from primitive, the chairs featuring animal skin upholstery, the desk scarred, the bare plank floor dirty. Books stood about on unfinished lumber shelving and the only window the room possessed had been set up high in the wall. Composed of small, diamond shaped panes, the glass held a distinctly green cast that filtered the light coming into the room through it oddly. The hearth in the back wall was small, with a cast iron section of stove set inside it to maximize the heat.

He imagined that keeping the room warm in winter would be a good deal easier than cooling it in the summer. Place would be an oven, he concluded.

It had been a long ride from Quattar, by his lights, and Nehl had complained what seemed like every step of the way. He hadn't liked sleeping on the ground, he hadn't liked eating jerky and corn cakes, and he hadn't liked cooking over a fire any better. Mornings were too cold, mid-days were too hot, riding was uncomfortable, he didn't like wearing a hat, and the trail was dusty. Now, the sight of Fort Southren filled him with foreboding. Nothing suited him.

Freddy had to admit that the fort looked raw and primitive, for all that it had been here nearly a hundred years, the buildings shabby combinations of stone and timber, what glass they had in the windows small and badly tinted with the green of the local iron. What sidewalks it had—and it didn't have many—had been crafted from raw lumber. Shrinkage, cracking and general wear and tear had made it treacherous underfoot, but still better than the mud liberally sprinkled with gravel in some places and sand in others with the occasional clump of weeds to make it interesting.

The town of Southren had grown up all around the fort in a sort of haphazard sprawl that left the stockade front of the fort to face the road. Thanks to the periodic raids of Caelian warriors, the town had quickly become known for a surly lack of hospitality and a general all around crankiness. Southren folks had quaint little sayings like 'the only good Caelian is a dead Caelian' and others of the same ilk. They believed strongly in 'killing your own snakes' and their use for the mostly ineffective soldiers supposedly stationed here to protect them had long ago become as sharply limited as the protection the soldiers afforded them.

For their parts, the soldiers avoided their mandate to seek out and kill the Caelian raiding parties as much as they could get by with, earning them heaping helpings of the locals' despite, which they returned in kind. Freddy suspected that neither the D'Arcys nor the Bardons would be inclined to look for them here, or even believe they'd come here. That was the point.

He didn't expect luxury. He did expect that when he and Nehl were ready to go home that they could requisition an escort from the fort to take them there.

In the meantime, they'd just have to be patient and tolerate the place until they could manage to make their way back to the capital. Not, Freddy admitted, just to himself, that Nehl would be able to endure a place like this long. If he would just keep his mouth shut for a few days--!

At present, Nehl was staring about himself with a sort of horrified wonder, as if he couldn't believe what his eyes saw. Freddy crimped his lips at the corners to keep from laughing at him and forced his eyes back to the Colonel's face. He wondered what the poor man had done to get himself exiled to this godforsaken place. The unfortunate commander of the fort's forces regarded the letter Freddy had given him rather as he might have regarded a snake handed to him, and a poisonous one, at that. His eyes had widened on the first page in such a way that Freddy suspected the man recognized the king's own handwriting.

Good, he thought. We won't have to argue back and forth as to whether the letter is genuine. It'll save on time and people's tempers. Nehl's was variable at the best of times. Freddy worried that at the moment it would tend towards real volatility. Freddy concentrated on the Colonel. At present, Nehl looked too shocked and horrified to say or do much of anything.

Not a large man, and certainly well past his prime, the Colonel had traveled far enough through the process of losing his hair to be labelled 'bald' though he had trimmed his hair back so tightly to his head that you couldn't tell where the bald began and the hair ended, which was doubtless the point. He hadn't bothered to keep in shape, his little round tummy made it clear he was perhaps fonder of his after dinner claret than he probably ought to be, and that he kept and enjoyed a good cook. His uniform, on the other hand, look frayed at the cuff and his boots could use a good re-soling.

The same couldn't be said of his weapons. His knives and his sword looked well-used and well-kept, both belt and sheaths well-worn. Freddy wondered how the Colonel could wear the weapons of a fighter and still look as soft as he did, as reluctant to fight.

"A coup," he repeated, meditatively.

"Father crushed it, of course," Freddy reminded him, "but you'll notice who he names as having been involved in it. Jahn and Dellin D'Arcy. Matias

Bardon. We were staying with Bardons. I didn't think it would be all that safe a place to remain, under the circumstances."

"We haven't heard anything about it," the Colonel protested feebly.

"You think my father's going to publish something like that?" Freddy asked him curiously. "Particularly knowing where his sons are staying?"

"No, of course not," the Colonel replied, more confidently. "He's going to want to find out who was involved with them."

"Oh," Freddy told him, "I rather imagine Father's taken care of the plotters already." He shrugged. "Well, he makes that pretty clear in the letter, but he'll make sure of it before he sends for me and for Nehl to come home."

"Oh," the Colonel nodded, as if that made sense to him, "of course." He gestured towards the door. "I'll have one of the men take you to a set of rooms. We always have several spare." His expression turned morose. "We need more men," he said. "We have space for almost twice the men we have. And we could use more horses, too."

"Well, you can use Nehl's, while he's here," Freddy volunteered. "Nehl won't have any use for him."

Nehl turned his attention to them at the sound of his name. "Hunh?" he wanted to know.

"We're going to our rooms," Freddy told him, knowing that his brother had sunk too far into misery to be taking much of anything in. The trip west from Quattar had not been easy on him.

"I'm never going to let you talk me into anything like that again," Nehl told him now. "They'd better bring a carriage to take me home," he added, grumbling it.

Freddy ignored him.

"Our bags are in the stable," he informed the Colonel.

He plucked his father's letter from the Colonel's fingers, folded it up again and tucked it into the envelope. "I'll be writing an answer to father's letter as soon as we get settled," he added. "Do you have a man we can send home with it?"

"Huh?" his question roused the Colonel from a brown study of his own. "Yes, yes, of course."

"Anything you'd like me to add?" Freddy asked him.

"Oh?" the Colonel questioned, suddenly alert. "Oh, yes, of course. We need more men, particularly more archers, and more horses. And as soon as we can get them." His expression lightened. He looked at Freddy with more attention and Freddy knew that it had occurred to him that Freddy might make a valuable conduit to the King for him.

"I'll be sure and tell him," Freddy assured him.

The Colonel brightened. He moved to the door and opened it, calling for a man to come and take them to their rooms, telling him to have someone go to the stables to get their bags. He didn't introduce them, and the man, when he showed them up the rather rickety stairs, didn't give them his name, either.

The rooms, when they reached them, didn't amount to much. None were overlarge, and if they had been granted a sitting room, well, that was about the best you could say of it. At least there was a rug on the raw plank floor. A pair of windows in the outer walls looked down over the back garden, what could be seen of it through the small, green-tinted panes, and there was a hearth on the side wall. The sleeping area had been partitioned away from the sitting area by a screen that reached no more than the length of a bed, the remainder of the room open to the heat from the hearth fire. Freddy suspected they'd appreciate that, soon enough.

He found a pedestal desk behind the door, in the near corner of the room, complete with envelopes and paper in the drawers. Puling the chair out from under the center drawer, he sat down, drew out a paper and pen, and started to write. The sooner, he considered, that he could get this letter off to his father, the better. He made certain to include the Colonel's request for more men and horses.

It would never have occurred to Nehl to curry a little favor, but Freddy didn't mind doing it. The more secure he could make his position here with the Colonel, the better. Besides, if the Caelian were active in the Southren area, more men would help to keep him secure, not to mention Nehl.

While he wrote, Nehl ranged around the rooms, which consisted of one large chamber partitioned into two, attached to a large bathing chamber which included a water closet. One end of this chamber had been partitioned into a dressing room. The walls had been painted at one time, a long time ago, but time and wear had faded them to a pale, dingy grey. Even the plain wood partitions had been battered and worn to scarred, nearly colorless boards in which the wood grain had all but disappeared.

Nehl reappeared in front of him. "This is a dump," he declared.

"We're safe," Freddy reminded him.

"They expect us to share a room," Nehl sounded horrified. Freddy shrugged.

"We've each got a bed," he pointed out practically. He set out his seal, warmed some wax, dripped it on the flap of the envelope, and, mindful of how easily he had opened his father's missive, dribbled it in waves to each side of the flap. Adding a larger blob at the apex of the flap, he applied his seal to the

center of the wax, and then withdrew it to allow it to cool. "I'm going to take this down to the Colonel to send to Father, and then I'm going to arrange for someone to do our laundry, take a bath, and put on my last clean shirt."

"But we're going to be stuck here all winter!" Nehl protested. Freddy shrugged.

"You can leave," he said. He wouldn't give Nehl much chance of getting anywhere alive, once the Bardons found him, but given Nehl's proclivities, Freddy wasn't sure that would be all bad. All he knew was that he wasn't going with him. He could already see ways to make his stay here more pleasant.

"And go where?" Nehl wanted to know.

"Home?" Freddy asked him lightly.

"I wish," Nehl mourned. "I'd have to ride a horse to get there, though."

"Well, then," Freddy shrugged. "Why don't you make the best of it?"

"Best of this?" Nehl scoffed. "There isn't any best of this."

"Sure there is. I intend to cultivate the Colonel, find out everything he knows about the Caelian situation, and then when Father calls us home, I can impress him with everything I've learned."

Nehl narrowed his eyes at him.

"And cut me out?" he demanded.

"Not at all," Freddy assured him. "Play along with me, and I'll make you look so good he'll forget all about the fiasco of the girl."

Not that he would, though Nehl would never realize it. Nehl had beaten the girl and laying a hand on a female was a good way to permanently wind up on his father's blacklist. Freddy wouldn't have put it past his father to have cut Nehl out of the succession, once he found out what Nehl had done to the girl, and if their father ever found out about Nehl's proclivities, Nehl would not only be cut out of the succession, he'd find himself a permanent resident of the palace dungeon.

But he didn't mention any of that to Nehl. His brother wouldn't appreciate it, and he wouldn't really accept the truth of it. He'd just think Freddy was trying to put one over on him, and once Nehl got that idea, Freddy knew his days would be numbered. Nehl might not have the nerve to kill Freddy himself, but he would find a way to make it happen. Freddy knew his brother.

Fortunately, he thought, he was a lot more intelligent than Nehl was. He would need to keep his wits about him at all times in future. Nehl was dangerous. Nehl was capable of hitting him over the back of the head and tying him to a bed and beating him to death the way he killed his girls. He was capable of drugging his food to do the same thing. If he could lay hands on a poison, he could be counted upon to use it. Nehl might even pay a couple of men to knock him out and tie him up for him. Nothing could be put beyond him.

He stood up.

"I'll be taking my letter down to the Colonel, now," he said to Nehl. "Anything you want?"

Nehl had slumped down to a seat before the fire. He shook his head despondently.

"Winter," he murmured, just to himself, despondently. "Here." Freddy left him to mope.

# XXIII

## WINTERING OVER

THE WOLVES LEFT AT FIRST light, each of them loaded up with thirty pounds of my venison, a good bit more than a single deer would provide, all told, when they'd eaten as much of my meat as they had while they'd been here. Shade saw them off mournfully, keeping a stiff upper lip and all that but his eyes showed that his heart had shattered. If only they'd left Fort with him—but they hadn't, and I couldn't do anything about it. I wasn't his family. I hadn't chosen someone else over him—someone able-bodied while he was hobbled by an injured leg—and I knew it wasn't the first time they'd done it.

Maybe the first time hadn't been when they'd failed to come after him and find him before he'd spent three days and nights in a trap, maybe it had been the thirtieth time. It still hurt. And it would hurt the next time they failed him.

I wondered if they'd just not bother to show up again. I couldn't say I'd be all that surprised if they didn't. Families that failed their kids, in my experience, always had plenty of excuses to do it. Those excuses might change a bit, here and there, but they'd still be excuses, and the only time they failed their kids just once, were the times their kids died from that failure. Shade had come very close to being one of them. Well, I'd saved Shade, but that only gave his family another chance to fail him and more excuse to do it.

I got my molds ready while the fire heated, and then I got started on my glass making. I already had more containers than I could carry with me when I left, I thought, irritably, wishing I didn't have to leave them behind. I'd have to gather up sand and lime and soda and the rest to have with me when I built the new shelter, wherever I spent next winter. And I'd have to put the stove together

again, and cut more wood to burn in it, and then I'd need to make more glass, whenever I got where I could winter over, and all the glass here would go to waste. Drat it.

One thing I could say about it, by the time I got done, the shelter would not only stay warm for the rest of the day and half the night, the stove would also dry a lot of meat and do a good job of roasting the venison I'd thrown into the pot. We'd eat well—at least until the food ran out.

After a while, Shade got out the book on Nogaynos and started reading aloud to me. The information was almost too engrossing. I had to stop him a couple of times so I could concentrate on what I was doing with my glass. I needed to get several quart jars out of these last measures of sand and lime, as well as the glass cases I needed for the venison. I had to balance what I had with what I needed to make carefully, in order to manage it all, and then there were the spells to make the glass unbreakable. But at last it was all finished, both bespelled and annealed, and I could start the fat purifying for candle tallow and sit and talk over what Shade had read with him.

We almost missed lunch.

Shade, I found, in the following days, was very good company. Learning how to use magic, and how to form spells, through going over them with him, talking about the magic, asking questions, trying to figure out the whys of things, and the hows, helped to make them stick. We refined the healing on his leg, which meant that he healed more quickly and more completely and had a lot less discomfort. He started to gain a little weight, too, which, after his ordeal, he'd needed. He wanted to get out hunting. I knew he was right, but it was too soon for his leg.

I bought time by making and fitting skis to the come-along, so we could use it to drag the meat back, if we managed to find any. I could have used more magic than I did, but that would have meant it was ready too quickly. This way, Shade got to help me fix it and it took more time, allowing his leg to heal more. When we finally did go out to hunt, Shade came along in wolf form and did the tracking, running along on three legs and just touching the toe of his broken leg in the snow now and again, more balancing with it than putting weight on it. I thought it good exercise.

His tracking nose worked a lot better than my spell and took a lot less out of me, which was a good thing, because I was going to have to skin and dress out the deer, cut it into quarters and get it back to the shelter in the come-along.

Shade was understandably chuffed at being able to find deer so quickly, and he absolutely gorged himself on entrails. He took a nap while I did the hard work, which didn't surprise me, because he hadn't been out in a while and he had to be tired. I doubt he'd have been able to make it back without the rest. He was certainly dragging by the time we got back to the shelter, although he wasn't the only one dragging by that time.

Still, I managed to get the deer butchered out into hunks of meat that would fit neatly into the glass cases, bespell them and then seal them and tuck them away into the pantry before completely collapsing. While I was doing that, tired or not, Shade managed to build up the fire in the stove, sear a hunk of meat on both sides, and then plop it into a roasting pan with a few edible roots and get the whole affair cooking. I washed and then fixed apple tea for us.

We might have dropped into bed after dinner too tired to study, for once, but I felt better. We'd harvested about ninety pounds more meat and that meant twenty more days of food—assuming the oranges, applesauce, roots and cornmeal and oats held out. I thought about putting out more snares for rabbits.

I'd let them go for a while, because it wasn't a good idea to trap all the rabbits in the area out, but I could set out a few more snares, and rabbits would be a nice change from venison now and again. And besides, enough additional pelts to add another row around my rabbit fur cape would be more than welcome in the cold and Shade needed more warm clothing when he was well enough to spend more time in his human form. Maybe a long rabbit-skin vest to wear under his cloak?

I had never had a real companion before and Shade made a good one. He never let the pining I could feel in him make him mean. I knew he missed his family keenly. I knew it, but I knew I didn't really 'get' it.

Oh, yes, I'd had adoptive brothers, foster brothers, whatever you wanted to call them, as long as you didn't call them blood—they'd told me often enough that blood was thicker than water and they were blood and I was water. And, too, they were years older than I, so we'd had nothing in common. They'd never worked the forge, and I had. They'd been their mother's darling boys, and I hadn't been her darling anything, just her drudge.

Even as dour, disapproving and borderline abusive as my adoptive father was with his 'teaching', working with him at the forge had been better than with her in the house. Not that she ever worked with me—she simply dropped a list of labors she wanted done by the time she returned into my lap the moment my eyes opened in the morning, whenever that might be, and then disappeared for a day of gossip, needlework and shopping. I'd wondered where she'd gotten the money until one night I'd over-heard an argument between my adoptive parents about the jewels and the money left with them to see to my upbringing.

My adoptive father had been having a fit about how much of it she had spent and informing her that I had paid for my room and board with my work at the forge, never mind whatever I did for her in the house. Not that he noticed what I had been doing in the house in the way of work, he just knew I did something.

My adoptive mother told him to mind his own business.

My adoptive father said it was his business; he'd given his word of honor. The money had to be kept for me for a dowry. My adoptive mother told him that no one was ever going to marry me to claim it, and my adoptive father had told her that if so, then the money was mine to do with as I pleased, not hers.

And so on around they went, to no purpose, when it came down to it.

My adoptive mother went right on stealing and spending my money, and my adoptive father would do nothing about it but stew in silence.

But I understood, however vaguely, that Shade felt tied to his family by ties of blood, and now was suffering from the double betrayal of those ties, first, that his family had not gone looking for him promptly when he had been caught in that trap, and secondly when they had all left for the winter with his sister, and not even Fort had stayed here with him, to make sure he was all right. I felt for him, but in a sneaking way I was glad that they hadn't stayed. With the wolves gone, we had just enough cornmeal, oats, and wheat, with the fruit and the roots I'd gathered, to eke out the winter, with the meat we had. If they'd stayed, we'd have wound up finishing the winter with meat and nothing else to go with it.

The wolves might not have minded being limited to meat alone; I would have.

Now, with just Shade, the two of us could study my books together, pore over maps and plot out the trails we hoped to follow in the spring, marking villages that might be able to provide us with grain or fresh greens and fruit, and possible areas that might do to winter over in. I had been surprised to find that I had reached the central borders of Mahdi, and even penetrated inside of them, if not very far inside. I had gotten a good deal farther than I had estimated. The 'travel' spell, combined with levitation, had apparently worked a good deal better than I had thought they would.

I found that interesting. I wondered if I could include Shade in the spell the way that I had Nutmeg. Being able to use 'travel' effectively would clearly make a mote of difference in how far we would be able to get over the next travel season. If the 'travel' spell worked well enough, we might even be able to make Nogaynos before winter, though I suspected that might be wishful thinking, given how little we knew of the trails ahead.

It would all depend upon how far we were able to get over the summer. We hoped for two thousand miles, but that was probably pie in the sky, given how far north we were. We certainly wouldn't be able to get an early start, given how late Thaw, Mud and Bud would arrive here in the north, especially this high up into the mountains. Probably, we'd be lucky to get fifteen or sixteen hundred miles before we were forced to den up for winter again.

I was pretty sure that with just Shade and Nutmeg, that I could include us all into my 'travel' spells, and if I could do that, then we could get much closer to Nogaynos before having to settle in for the winter. If I had to 'carry' Fort, Wraith and Reve with my 'travel' spells, I wasn't at all sure how far we could get before having to dig in for the winter.

I doubted, this first summer, if we'd be able to travel far enough to worry about which side of the Lupine we were on, but sooner or later, we'd have to cross either some of the tributaries of the Lupine or the Lupine, itself. The two great rivers, the Lupine and the Sanguine, bracketed Amadea's southern plains, the east and the west. The Sanguine drained the eastern section of the plains, carrying the water from the low, coastal range, its high and hugely dramatic waterfall forming the corner boundary between Amadea and Caelian. The tributaries of the Lupine drained the east side of the western mountains of Mahdi and Nogaynos.

At some time in the far distant past, some great upheaval had either raised the tectonic plate that formed the Amadean plains or lowered the plate holding what became the Caelian jungles. Or maybe both. According to the geography book, the Sanguine River's cliffs rose six hundred feet over the water at the falls. The river, at that point both wide and deep, crashed into a great rock formation at the bottom of the falls which divided the river into two streams.

One of the Sanguine's streams flowed to the east and the south until it poured into the sea, while the other flowed to the west, gathering up more water from the streams flowing off the escarpment that formed the plains until it joined the Lupine, which flowed almost due north-south. The western arm of the Sanguine crashed into the southern Lupine, the two rivers joining together in a great whirlpool which had carved out another huge hole—on the Caelian side—before flowing down to the sea. Thus, the two rivers formed three sides of the boundary that almost literally walled Caelian off from the rest of the continent.

The southern branch of the Sanguine, and the southern branch of the combined Sanguine and Lupine cut Caelian off from Amadea in the east and Nogaynos in the west.

The east-west branch of the Sanguine formed the northern border of Caelian and separated it from the escarpment of the central plains. The country's southern border dropped away into the southern sea, providing more than three thousand miles of low coast-line. To the north and the west of the Lupine, Nogaynos rose in a mountainous rain forest quite different from Caelian's low- lying jungle. In the east, the same could be said for Amadea's southern tip.

How the Caelians had ever managed to cross either river, I had no idea, but I supposed it was possible. Getting up the cliffs to either Amadea or Nogaynos, on the other hand, seemed entirely unimaginable. The pictures showed what looked to be unclimbable cliffs on the Amadean and Nogaynos sides looking down on low lying lands, deeply green, the layered canopies of trees stretching out as far as the eye could see. I shivered, just looking at those pictures.

Somehow, I told myself, we had to stay to the west of the Lupine, even if that meant we had to cross each of its numerous tributaries.

Sometimes, when Shade read things out to me from the Nogaynos book, it would dove-tail with something I was reading or had read in one of the magic books, or in the geography. We'd try to reconcile the information into as coherent a whole as we could then, talking it out in a way that made learning it, at least for me, much easier. Other times it was the geography book we'd be comparing to the Nogaynos book, trying to tease out more information that would tell us the best route to take to reach our mythical destination. It never really did, and what information we found on the villages we might come upon in our way we had to admit might be a good deal out of date. We just had to hope we managed to choose our route wisely.

We also tried experimenting with all sorts of magic together, in an attempt to expand my repertoire, things I might not have tried if I had been here in the shelter all alone. We tried to decide which things might be most useful, what defenses would serve us best, and whether we could manage to use them well enough to keep us safe. We certainly always had plenty to do.

We maintained a number of snares throughout the rabbit pathways through the 'fence' that enclosed Nutmeg's paddock, and through the trees beyond the meadow. Those snares caught enough rabbits to vary our diet nicely. We made Shade a rabbit-skin vest, and used deerskin to devise an outer cape over his old wool cloak to keep him warm. We experimented with wards, and I learned how to weave fire and ice, earth and air, spirit and identity altogether.

Nutmeg now had his own 'personal' wards, as did Shade, and as I did. The shelter had all kinds of protective wards, from look-away wards, through no-see- um wards, to do-not-touch wards, and do-not-pass wards. I'd improved on my basic 'sleep' spell, and spent hours with my herbology and anatomy books to widen and deepen my healing skills.

I think Shade shot up a good two inches, and he hadn't been short to begin, but the growth made him clumsy, sometimes, and occasionally awkward, the way his arms and legs kept changing lengths on him. So, we put the comforters and several blankets down on the floor as wrestling mats, and practiced the

martial arts we found in the books as best we could, though I can't say we became all that proficient at much of anything. We did a lot of fencing, too, and I know we expanded our skills there, but we had a long way to go before we got really good. At least our coordination improved.

The magic book had a combination recipe and spell for a straw-man sparring partner we could, supposedly, learn from, but I didn't trust myself to get everything just right. If we were going to give the thing a sword, I wanted to be sure the automaton would be properly programmed to teach us, and not hurt us. So we floundered around on our own. If nothing else, it was good exercise, not that snowshoeing around in two feet of snow and ice wasn't.

We still had a decent amount of meat left by the time spring started to wear away at the icy snow winter had left and green started to perk its way up through the warming soil. The deer were quick to snap up each green blade—I identified the herbs I'd want later and surrounded them with wards designed to keep both the deer and rabbits from denuding them before they could reach a decent degree of growth. In some cases I'd make infusions from their roots, in others, I'd use their dried leaves. I tried not to ward them all; the rabbits and the deer who'd kept us through the winter now needed sustenance, themselves, after existing through the winter on leaves and twigs.

I needed to scrape up what I had left in the way of lime and soda and the rest, and mine a little sand out of the stream bed so I could make some small vials for the tinctures and infusions they'd make. I had the half dozen I'd brought from home in my pack, but with all that I'd learned from my books, both of herbs and magic, and all the new herbs I'd found here in the meadows and the wood, I'd need at least a half a dozen more for the medicinals they'd make. I knew from the old herb woman back in the city for whom I'd made potion vials over the years—you could never have too many potions on hand. She had warned me over and over that whatever potion she'd left home, it always turned out to be the one she needed.

We would be heading out on a long journey in a few weeks. I needed to carry all the herbs, infusions and potions I could find the ingredients for before we left. We'd never know when we might need them.

# XXIV
# REUNION

A S THE DAYS OF WINTER turned into weeks, and the weeks turned into months, Shade's pining turned to muted despair and finally into a hopeful kind of buried, unadmitted anticipation. I knew he was thinking that surely, surely, his family would come now.

I didn't know what to say to him, how to comfort him.

Hope along with him? But he wasn't admitting he hoped.

So while I did hope along with him, I didn't do it aloud. What to say? I could only think back to what my years with my adoptive parents had been like, and what it had been like in that dungeon, hoping that someone would come for me, get me out of there, and no one ever coming.

This wasn't quite the same. The day came when we should have left the shelter and started south. I made excuses, I put it off. We took down a young spike buck so we'd have fresh venison, and more dried venison. We packed and re-packed our gear so we could fit in more glass cases of preserved venison and more jars, some of them still holding applesauce. I found more herbs, collected and dried more herbs, made more infusions, more potions, more tinctures. And then one day, when we were returning from yet another foraging expedition, we found the fire going in the stove and Wraith, Reve and Fort butchering out the quarters of a young spike buck.

Shade, who had been in wolf form, charged them without bothering to change to his human form or even shrug out of his packs. I just closed the door after us and smiled in heartfelt relief as I shrugged out of my own pack. I wanted to demand what had taken them so long, but I didn't say anything. I just put some water on to boil for tea and swiped a hunk of the venison to roast.

They chattered on about staying on for the birth of Rene's baby, a healthy boy. They seemed greatly pleased about it, though Fort had the grace to look ashamed of their leaving Shade here waiting for them. At least they'd brought some dry beans and cornmeal with them, enough to give us a good start. We still had a little bit of the applesauce left, and a few oranges. (Shade hadn't much of a taste for oranges.) There were even a few apples. (Those preservation spells worked a treat.)

"So," Reve wanted to know, as soon as we settled at the table. "When do we leave for Nogaynos?"

"As soon as we can get that meat all dried," I told her. "We'll need plenty of dried meat to take with us, a decent supply of herbs, and grain for ourselves and Nutmeg." I looked around the room, thinking of all the things we'd already packed. The plates for the stove would have to go, of course, and as many of the glass containers as we could fill. "Most likely we'll have to winter over a second year on the way."

"Most likely," Wraith returned, readily enough. Sighed. "The furnishings won't go, however." And he looked at the table and the chairs wistfully.

"The mattresses aren't heavy," I observed. "Nutmeg can take two atop his regular gear, and the last one will go over the top of the come-along. We've got the tanned deer hides, I'll get that last hide tanned before we leave, and, of course, our tarps. We ought to pick up more grain—cornmeal and oats, at least, and more dry beans, if we can get them—at our first opportunity, but I'd like to keep the weight on Nutmeg down under one-eighty whenever possible. One- sixty'd be better. Within reason, the come-along can take the heavy stuff."

They all nodded solemnly, at that. Reve glanced towards the stove, where the venison was drying. She looked thoughtful.

"Nutmeg," she said, as if just discovering it, "is important. We won't have to keep stopping to hunt as often because of him."

"Or risk buying supplies as often," I advised her. "Remember that. And remember, too, that the heavy stuff on the come-along he pulls will get us set up for next winter."

"Yes," Wraith looked at the stove thoughtfully. "We couldn't carry all that cast iron."

Fort turned his attention to the stove as well. Without the least lead in, he blurted,

"I should have stayed."

"Yes," I agreed, without making any excuses for them, "you should have.

Your mother and father with Shadow, of course. But Shade had weeks to go before he'd be fully ambulatory, so you should have stayed with him. He might very well have needed more help than I could give him." I almost added, for

heaven's sake! He's your youngest. Just a kid! But I didn't.

Reve blinked at me.

"You wouldn't have minded?" she wondered. "Fort, I mean."

"I didn't have the feeling that Fort was dangerous to me," I allowed.

"I wasn't," Fort hurried to say. "I mean, I'm not."

"I didn't think of that," Reve said, a little blankly.

She didn't think of what? I wondered. That her son had still been, at best, three-legged then? All but helpless in a fight? Or that I hadn't been afraid of Fort?

"We are Smoke wolves," Wraith said thoughtfully. "We have served Nogaynos queens for a thousand years. Leaving Shade with you, in your care, would be, for us, the most natural thing in the world to do. Had you indicated that Fort would be welcome to stay, he would have stayed, without question. That is how it works, for Smoke wolves."

"Oh—" I started to say he wasn't putting their abandonment of Shade on me, drawing myself up and back, when Reve interrupted me.

"It is my fault," she said. "You were raised in Amadea. You're young. We are Shade's parents. You would not have been raised to question our decisions. Nor would you understand that Fort and Wraith were not raised to question my decisions. All Mahdi wolves are matriarchal and matrilineal to a large extent and Smoke wolves are to an even stronger extent because of our history of serving Nogaynos queens. We see that Shade is yours now, that he has bonded to you. How that bond will mature as the two of you get older, we don't know, but we do know that it exists. I didn't realize that you would believe that Fort should stay with Shade. I didn't realize that you would accept Fort for Shade."

I glanced quickly over at Shade, to see that he looked very intent, very conscious of things I doubted I even understood.

"We keep expecting you to think like a Nogaynos queen but you don't," Fort said slowly.

I waved an impatient hand.

"I care about Shade!" I informed them all unhappily. "If you'd left him for a mere three weeks or so, that would have been one thing. Not good, but within reason. But you didn't. If you were going to be gone that long, you definitely should have left Fort with him!"

"Ah," Reve sat back in her chair. "You're quite right, of course," she returned ruefully. "I am not a matriarch, nor am I a dominant. That's the very reason I was chosen to make this trip. Well," she corrected herself, "I and mine. In my reasoning, I considered first what I thought you would prefer and secondarily what my daughter needed. It never occurred to me to split the family group beyond that Shade was not able to travel with us." She sighed.

"We should not have stayed to see the baby born."

"If you had left Fort, that would not have been a problem," I pointed out.

"You are a very strong alpha," Wraith commented meditatively. "You seek to see everyone cared for."

"I will swear to you," Fort assured me almost anxiously, as if that would make peace.

"Swear to your brother!" I burst out, an eyelash from losing my temper. "He is your brother! Your younger brother! Pay to him at least a little of the loyalty you owe your bond of blood with him!"

Why I would imagine his purported loyalty to me would be worth anything when he hadn't any for Shade escaped me. Shade circled me with an arm. I couldn't tell whether he was pleased, or just wanted me to shut up. Wraith kicked back in his chair and shared a significant glance with Reve.

"Loyalty is important to you, then."

"Of course it is, as one who has never received it!"

Reve, Wraith and Fort all sat there, as if I had said something important. They exchanged glances and then, almost as one, they nodded. They looked pleased. So, when I dared to look at Shade, did he. I didn't understand it.

Shade patted my shoulder and stood up.

"Let me get the map," he deferred to me, "and explain our thinking."

Three days later we packed up and left. In a way, I regretted leaving, but though I could have cultivated a garden and maybe even grown a little corn, I couldn't have managed to grow enough to get through the winters comfortably, and I'd already decimated the rabbit population. To stay, I'd have needed to find a way to get oats and wheat, cheese and eggs. Well, I could maybe have developed a population of chickens, with enough care, but there wasn't enough grass for both Nutmeg and a cow, especially with a calf, as well, and the deer population wouldn't hold up long to the amount of hunting we'd been doing.

Goats, maybe, I considered, might have been the answer. You could get milk and cheese from goats, and the male kids could be butchered out for meat. Add a decent garden, some chickens, do a little trading, rabbit and deer hides for oats and wheat . . . but it wouldn't support a family of wolves, I didn't think. The kids wouldn't supply enough meat, and even raising rabbits and chickens, I didn't think it would suffice, even gleaning the orchards in the vicinity.

Of course, a couple of deer every fall to supplement the rabbits and chickens might make the difference, but then again, they might not. The growing season here, this far in the north, was pretty short. Hard to tell. I didn't intend to try.

The idea, I reminded myself, was to get to Nogaynos, find a place there, where we could settle down, try to make contact with some native Nogaynos, if we could find any.

Big if, I concluded, and concentrated on pulling everyone together so that I could work the 'travel' spell. Collecting up Nutmeg and Shade came easily, the spell allowing me to increase our speed enough to keep the wolves pushing to keep up. This system allowed me to get us well over a hundred miles in no more than three days, and get us to the first village Shade and I had marked on our map. I looked around it carefully as we walked towards the small inn almost blocking the entry into the village.

The place wasn't large, and from the appearance of it, didn't exactly welcome strangers. We'd sat up on the hill for several hours before deciding to actually visit, and seen that all the inhabitants at least looked to be human.

According to Wraith several of the 'people' he saw were Mahdi, but he thought it appeared that they chose to pass as human, at least whenever they expected to be where they could be seen, so he and Reve and Fort and Shade all presented themselves in their human form. It was not impossible that the human contingent in the village below did not welcome wolves.

The inn itself had been sized to fit the village. I'd have guessed it had room for half a dozen over-night guests and not much more, though the main common-room would have easily hosted a dozen and the stables easily that many horses. So maybe it formed a gathering place for people heading out on the trail?

I asked the innkeeper for a night's lodging and where we might be able to purchase some grain and even some fruit or vegetables, if any were available. He didn't seem to think we'd be able to buy much, but pointed us towards what I would have called a 'general' store. People gawked at us curiously as we made our way to it along a board side-walk, as if strangers did not frequently visit the village, but weren't outright unfriendly, not that they were friendly, either. The store, when we reached it, hadn't a lot to sell. There wasn't much left of anything.

The shopkeeper was at least as interested in our deer-hides as he was my copper and silver coin. We wound up trading both for dried milk, eggs, cheese, cornmeal and oats, as well as some ground wheat. Twenty pounds of each, with no more than a dozen eggs didn't sound like much, and wasn't, of course, but it would make a great deal of difference to us. I was glad to settle for it, and we packed everything up, with a spell on the eggs to keep them from breaking and another to keep them fresh, with wards over everything else before settling down to an inn supper.

The inn's beds were clean and free of bugs, which said a lot, but the beds themselves were actually less comfortable than our dog bed mattresses and the blankets had been worn threadbare. We had to add our own in order to sleep comfortably through the night. At least we got breakfast and dinner with our beds. We packed up and headed out right after breakfast.

"Would you say that was typical of the villages in these hills?" I queried of Wraith and Reve, as we settled to the trail.

"At a guess," Reve nodded. "Not that we've had much experience with them."

"Bandits," Wraith commented. "They mostly raid the caravans gathering in the foothills—well, the groups heading out of the hills to join the caravans," he clarified, "but they hit the villages in the fall to gather supplies to make it through the winters."

"Most likely after harvest and in the spring, when they're going short," I thought aloud. Too bad, I thought, that small groups of fighters couldn't be spread about through the areas between villages—they could help with harvest and with an alarm system they could catch and exterminate the bandits as well as help with the harvest—always assuming they would. The problem with fighting men was that they would undoubtedly merely replace the bandits in preying upon the villagers. I sighed at the acknowledgement.

"The Mahdi wolves and Nogaynos queens used to work together to keep the bandits down," Reve mused aloud. "The villages through here were very prosperous, then. They sent fine woolens to the city, and medicines and even supplied food for the caravans to travel on. They provided guides, and mages, to protect the caravans."

I stared back at the village we'd left. They certainly had come down in the world since then, I thought. No one could have called them prosperous, now.

"When the Nogaynos mages came to them and asked them for

succor from the Caelian, the villagers sent them on," Reve continued. "They were afraid of the Caelian, afraid they'd send their poison air against them. Instead," she concluded dispassionately, "the plague of bandits came to stay."

"I'm going to make a guess that the Caelian couldn't have deployed their poison air this far north," I offered. "Air—dissipates--any concentration fairly rapidly, and that the Caelian died from the poison air in such large numbers when they invaded Nogaynos argues that they lacked anything resembling expertise in deploying it."

"It is said that a great many of them died," Reve allowed thoughtfully.

"Perhaps even more of them than Nogaynos people, since most of them left—or hid. But not everybody chose to leave Nogaynos when the Caelian came. Some chose to stay and take their chances, according to the old stories, especially those in the high mountains, and in the north."

I thought that made sense. How well would the Caelian people, from their low-lying jungles, adapt to Nogaynos' high mountains, their crisp coolness and long, frigid winters? Mountains which probably contained all kinds of secret places in which the natives of Nogaynos could hide out and watch the invaders stumble around helplessly—or at least nearly helplessly.

"Which would argue that Vere is right that they were not very expert with their poison air," Fort added.

"I don't understand why people didn't go back to Nogaynos, afterwards," I complained. "Surely the poison air dissipated within a few days, weeks at most. And the reports King Marc had indicated that the poison air didn't get very far north at all."

"Oh, I think many of them did," Reve assured me. "Nogaynos is huge," she reminded me. "You could hide ten thousand people in those mountains, and no one would ever know it."

"But with the invasion, they would have returned quietly," Wraith pointed out. "Poison air might have accounted for the diaspora, and it might even have accounted for some of the deaths of the Caelian, but I doubt, I doubt very much, that it accounted for the deaths of practically all of the invasion force."

"Ah," I nodded, catching on to what he was intimating. "Children sent out of the battle zone. Resistance fighters slipping back in once they were all safely away, perhaps trapping the poison air and the Caelian warriors in shielded areas so the Caelian commanders would believe that the poison air hung around longer than they had predicted. Making the Caelian believe that they had so poisoned the ground and the air and the water that the land wasn't worth having. Perhaps? And then living in their land in hiding to make it seem as if the Caelian had killed all the Nogaynos, but the land wasn't worth the having?"

"But then, why still hide?" Reve wanted to know.

"Because they knew that the Caelian would build their forces up again?" I hazarded a guess. "Because they had identified a pattern of Caelian behavior through the years? And they didn't want to have to keep fighting the same war over and over again?"

"Likely," Wraith agreed dourly. Then concluded, "We would like to find out."

"Given the increasing frequency of their raids against the southern villages in Amadea," I told him thoughtfully, "it seems likely that the Caelians are ramping up again. Only this time, their target appears to be Amadea."

# XXV

## NEHL

"DISPATCH," THE MAN SAID, WITH a salute, and dropped the sealed scroll on the table in front of Nehl and Freddy. Nehl snatched it up, grabbed his knife and peeled up the seal.

The private dining room looked raw, primitive and rustic, by palace standards, but it held three roughly rounded tables which half a dozen chairs circled, and two small rectangular tables, at one of which the two princes sat, atop a rough plank floor. The room held a hearth, and not much else. One door led into the kitchens from which the aroma of searing meat issued, while the other led to the outer environs of the fortifications. A pair of guards flanked it, standing ready. For what, no one specified.

None of the walls were finished, never mind painted, and the room, being an inner space, had no windows, adding to the room's security. While functional, the room couldn't have been called comfortable, beyond its basic warmth from the fire laid on the hearth.

"What does it say?" Freddy demanded, looking up from his trencher, not that his brother had even managed to get it unrolled, as yet. His brother ignored him. He peeled the scroll open, and perused it with a single glance. He raised his eyes to the waiting courier and flicked his fingers at him.

"Go," he said, with scant ceremony and no respect. The man turned on his heel and exited the room, already well aware that no tip would be forthcoming from Nehl or his brother. Neither Freddy nor the

Crown Prince saw the commiserating expression on the guard's face as the courier passed through the door. They wouldn't have cared if they had seen it. They might not have even understood it.

"So," Freddy said, now having read the scroll. "We get to go home." A broad grin began to stretch across his face. Freddy had not enjoyed his current sojourn in the 'land of the lost' as he called it. Freddy was a staunch adherent of soft beds, rich food, elegant dinners and fawning flatterers. Rough soldiers and rougher quarters did not suit him, though he had at least attempted to make the best of his exile. It was better than being assassinated by the Bardons. Just.

"Yes, but what did Jiden tell him before he died?" Nehl wanted to know, his eyes searching the far wall as if it held answers. It didn't.

"It doesn't sound as if the old man asked him anything," Freddy observed.

He let the scroll drop to the table beside his mug of ale.

"So what does the old man know?" the Crown Prince demanded, suspiciously.

Nehl never thought about the luxury in which he had been cocooned since infancy. He would never have said he liked it, never mind required it, but if possible, he disliked the rough living in this hastily constructed frontier fort even more than his brother did. The Caelian had attempted to burn the Amadean forces out of it repeatedly, and it was therefore in a constant state of being rebuilt or renovated so that the outer walls were stone, and not timber.    Even some of the inner walls had been pulled down to accommodate being re-built in fire-resistant stone.

"Everything," Freddy shrugged unconcernedly. "Why do you think he sent us here?" Freddy never even considered the idea that his father would do something to his sons in the way of punishment for their disloyalty. Or, call it what it was, treason.

Nehl frowned, but it made sense.

"It's taken him this long to get rid of Jiden's people?" he only half asked his brother, ignoring the food in front of him.

"He did it unobtrusively," Freddy pointed out to him, using his knife for emphasis. "Unobtrusive takes time."

The Crown Prince considered this. Clearly, Freddy possessed the more facile brain, of the two of them.

"Or Meric did it," Nehl offered.

"More likely Laren," Freddy retorted. "He's there," he reminded. "The old devil's here, and he wouldn't leave that to someone else to do. He'd want to do it with his own hand."

Nehl nodded. That made sense to him. He frowned.

"It won't be so easy, getting rid of Laren," he observed, almost as much to himself as to his brother.

"Forget about that," Freddy advised him.

Nehl raised his head and turned towards his brother, his frown deepening. "What?" he wanted to know.

"We've got bigger problems," Freddy informed him.

"We have?" Nehl had no idea what he was talking about.

"The Caelian are up to something," Freddy told him. "They're escalating." Nehl shrugged.

"So?"

"I think they're softening us up for something," Freddy told him. "Like an invasion." He frowned. "They already got rid of the Nogaynos," he pointed out, "but it cost them more people than they could afford. They poisoned the air and the poison they put in the air poisoned the ground, and it got them, too, when they tried to invade. Rumor has it that a lot of the ground in Nogaynos is still poisoned, and the maps indicate that the entire country is mountainous.

Popular opinion says that the Caelian aren't much interested in coping with mountains."

"So?" Nehl repeated.

"So that leaves us," Freddy reminded him. "Mahdi is on the other side of Nogaynos, and the Mahdi are fighters. All the old tales say so. There's a reason they call them Mahdi wolves." So saying, Freddy proved that he had not wasted the winter in the southern fort.

Nehl studied his brother's words, trying to make some kind of sense of them.

He didn't do it easily.

"But what about the poison air?" he wondered.

"That won't work twice," Freddy told him. "I don't think. The Mahdi were allies to the Nogaynos. They took in as many as managed to escape the genocide, mostly kids, but maybe some of the old people made it. Probably some of the old people made it. They probably got out with the kids. A hundred and fifty years?" he asked rhetorically. "They'll have some way to combat it by now. Bet on it."

"So you think the Caelian are coming after us, because we're the easier targets," he finally concluded. "Why?"

"Good question," Freddy allowed. "What do they take now?" His question was rhetorical, not meant to be answered, but he got one, anyway.

"Women and grain, meat and fruit," a third voice replied for him. "And a few men to carry the supplies."

The voice belonged to General Meric. His white hair declared him well past his prime, and so did the spare lines of his aging body, but he still stood straight, so that while no more than average height, he seemed tall. With more sheer presence than both the princes had put together and more to spare left over he dominated the room effortlessly.

The guards at the door straightened, interest brightening their eyes, respect changing their features from bored resignation to alert commitment to their duty. General Meric doffed his heavy woolen cloak with a swirl just missing flamboyant, hooked it to the cloak rack, followed it with his hat, and then came forward into the officers' mess, claiming a table near the hearth where he could sit with his back to hearth fire and the wall, and where he could command both entrances to the room. He didn't even seem to think about what he did.

"What does that tell you?" he demanded of the princes, as if lessoning them. "They want women?" Freddy returned the question, waggling his eyebrows facetiously, obviously not taking the lesson seriously.

"They want food," Nehl returned, more heavily, without the question. He sat back into his chair, sticking his legs out in front of him, his feet crossed at the ankle. He regarded the general narrowly. He didn't look precisely interested, but he had clearly settled in to hear whatever the general had to say.

"Exactly," the General caught him up on it. "What does that tell us?" he demanded.

Women streamed from the kitchen, in answer to the sound of the general's voice. One bore table settings on a tray, another bore a tureen of a rich and aromatic soup, while another carried bread and cheese and yet a fourth a pitcher of something hot and steaming aromatically into the air. Clearly, had either of the princes noted it, the general was a favorite with the kitchen staff, but neither Freddy nor Nehl bothered to pay any attention to this display of favoritism.

They simply didn't notice it.

"They want food," Nehl shrugged, repeating himself. He didn't care what the Caelian wanted, and he couldn't have made his disinterest more clear if he had tried. The Caelian were not his problem, as far as he was concerned. He cared nothing at all about the young Amadeans the Caelians were kidnapping, and not a bit more about those they killed.

"Each raid manages to get away with about six hundred pounds of food," the general lessoned them. "They use the women and the men to carry it, and they always take more girls and women than men and the captives they take are always young. They like them no younger than sixteen, and no older than twenty-two or three. Old enough to carry a good bit of weight, but young enough to still be relatively easily cowed."

"You can't tell me that they took the girls just for carrying stuff," Freddy objected, caught up, almost against his will, in the conundrum.

"No," the general admitted heavily. He didn't pursue the topic. Instead, he returned to the matter of supplies. "The Caelian have always raided along the Sanguine. How they get up and down the cliffs we don't know, but they do.

They always have. There is no other way they could get here, unless they're coming across country after rowing up the coastline. It used to be they just raided in the Fall, after harvest. Now they've been raiding all the year around, taking more people and more food. Why?"

"Because they need the food?" Freddy asked in return, lightly.

"Yes," the general returned, not altogether patiently, "but why now? Why do they need more food than they needed before?"

Freddy and Nehl looked from one to the other and back again and shook their heads.

"Does it matter?" Freddy wanted to know.

"Could it be," the general offered, as if hoping against hope that they would finally start using their minds for something other than plotting coups against their father, "that they need more food now because they have more people?"

He looked from one to the other of them as if hoping they'd get his point.

They didn't.

"Women do the work," he pointed out. "They raise the gardens, work the fields, spin and weave the fabric and make the clothes. They cook and clean and bear the children, tend to the sick and the aged and raise the children. The slaves work the fields and take care of whatever animals they have.  The warriors sit around on their butts and drink the ale the women make, eat the food the women cook, wear the clothing the women make—and fight. Occasionally they hunt, but hunters stop well short of providing fifty percent of any group's food. Usually, hunters provide somewhere from ten percent of a group's food to twenty-five percent of it. Too many hunters taking too much game means that in short order, there is no game. So, in order to feed those warriors, you have to start stealing food from people who don't keep a large group of warriors around. Now what happens when you start keeping a bunch of warriors around?"

Freddy and Nehl both shook their heads, clearly making no sense of the lessons the general was so generously (and patiently) providing them.

"Food starts to get really scarce for women and children. Women who are starving die in childbirth. Babies whose mothers die seldom survive them in such a climate—first because having been born of a starving, overworked

mother, they aren't healthy to begin with. Men who have fewer women to rape, start raping the young girls, who, between being starved and raped, bear children much younger. Then, as a result, they die all the more rapidly and all of a sudden the female population includes only a few wily old women and some very young girls and not much in between."

"And so the warriors start to steal more women," Freddy concluded.

"Who in their turn will be worked, starved and raped to death." The general nodded. "So first we have an increase in raids, but as they loot and burn all the villages close to the Sanguine, and the survivors, if there are any, gather up whatever they can find and move inland, the Caelian warriors will have to travel farther and farther afield to find them to raid. Sooner or later that will require Caelian bases on this side of the Sanguine, and once those are established, war will inevitably follow."

Having brought the princes step by step to understanding of the process they found themselves in the midst of, the general turned his attention back to his food, now cool enough to eat. He watched, imperturbably, eating his meal, as the two princes discussed this, rather hotly, by all appearances.

At last, Nehl turned from his argument with his brother, and addressed the general.

"We're going home," he announced belligerently, as if he expected another argument.

The general merely nodded.

"I'll give you four men," he allowed. Freddy looked startled.

"That's all?" he demanded.

"That's all I can spare," the general told them. Then he grimaced.

"Actually," he pointed out, "I can hardly spare them. I could use a hundred more men." Growling it, he added, in frustration, "We have yet to find where they're crossing the Sanguine, or how they're getting up the cliffs."

# XXVI

## GENERAL MERIC

WHAT HE NEEDED, MERIC THOUGHT, but did not say, was a Mahdi wolf. He'd put it into his dispatch to the king, but he knew the likelihood that he would get one was just about nil. He had to ask, though. Just in case it wasn't a total impossibility. Once upon a time, and within his memory, too, the Amadean King had been able to request a couple of Mahdi wolves when they needed them, and get them, but he feared those days long over. He sighed, just to himself.

He couldn't entrust his dispatches to the princes, he thought. He knew the two of them well enough to know that they'd open any dispatches with which they were entrusted, read them, and then destroy them, just to do it, if nothing else. He'd learned entirely too much about the princes since they'd been sent to him to gather intelligence to trust them with anything, no matter how innocuous, never mind something sensitive like the information he was sending back to the King.

Intelligence, he scoffed to himself. As if either of these two young popinjays had any! The thought of either one of these idiots ascending to the throne of Amadea horrified him. He didn't doubt that if he took these two out into the darkness of one of the ruined buildings in one of the villages that had been attacked and slit their arrogant, useless throats, he'd be doing his country the most and greatest service of his long and—if he said it himself—distinguished career, but he couldn't do it. He didn't murder men.

Order a man executed, he'd done that, yes, but always for abhorrent crimes against women and children, and occasionally other men. It didn't bother him to do that. It never would. Some men just needed to die for the good of everyone, and as a simple matter of justice.

The princes—they disgusted him. They were stupid, arrogant, they had no commonsense, no decency, no honor, and their malice and spitefulness appalled him. The men set over them to guard them despised them, and the serving women loathed them. They were thoughtless, careless, inconsiderate—he'd had to hold himself back from flogging them over and over again—one didn't flog princes, unfortunately.

He could have. Physically, thanks to their arrogance, even as old as he was, he could best either one of them, fighting them one at a time. If he was willing to kill them, he could have killed either one of them, and almost effortlessly. It would have taken some effort from him, but he could kill both of them, even if they came at him together—and they were the sort of nasty cowards who would—but for the same reason, they didn't have the skills necessary to take him. All of their instructors had been forced to praise them for levels of effort he wouldn't have accepted from a raw recruit, and many of their raw recruits arrived with as many skills as they had. But, he reminded himself, what could you expect from a triad of boys raised by the D'Arcy clan?

King Marc, he repeated to himself, should never have married Margrete D'Arcy in the first place. Making it a marriage without consummation or even living together and pretending to be married, a marriage where he'd never allowed her to be addressed as so much as 'princess' never mind crowned her queen, had amounted to adding insult to injury. Making her nothing more nor less than a glorified nanny for his sons had been insane.

The D'Arcys had been insulted, but the men understood—he blamed them for his Caelian wife's murder. Margrete didn't care; she just hated his guts, and divorcing her for doing such a rotten job of raising his sons hadn't improved matters any.

Meric wondered if the middle boy was any better than these two.

If he'd been certain that the boy was an improvement, he might have done King and country a favor and gotten rid of this precious pair. But what if the middle boy was just more of the same?

"We'll leave in the morning," Freddy volunteered.

Meric nodded. He'd see them off, just to make certain that they did leave.

He wouldn't put anything past them. He just watched them get up and head for the interior room they inhabited. The guards crossed the room, checked out the interior space, and then turned to the mess. Meric waited to speak to them until the princes had left the room.

"Any man touches a woman on this trip I want to hear about it," Meric told both guards. "Other than that, I'm taking volunteers to go with them. Just remind them that I'll be following along in a week or two, so if they get off on abusing girls and women—or letting the princes get off on doing it—I'll find out about it."

Meric smiled at the man. It wasn't a nice smile. The guard flinched. "And if they don't know what I'll do about it," he continued conversationally, "then they're too stupid to live." The guard ducked his head.

"We'll pass the word," he said.

"Going home would be nice," the second guard muttered, "but going with those two? I'll pass."

And so much for the princes, Meric thought, just to himself. If a man would turn down a pass to go home and get away from the miserable task of chasing the will o' the wisp that the Caelian raiders were, just to keep away from the more miserable wretches that the princes were, how could either of them expect to lead the country? In order to be able to reign effectively, a King had to have the military behind him. Meric shook his head to himself.

He doubted that a single man of the units he had with him here in the south would follow Crown Prince Nehl willingly. The prince was an arrogant bastard, and they all knew it, knew, too, that he was an errant coward. He'd left them to fight the raiders off without his help too many times and too many men had seen him do it. Seen him turn tail and run! From the enemy, instead of staying and fighting against men who were beating the young girls and boys and murdering the men, the old and infirm, and children—just to do it. And his brother Freddy had run with him.

That wasn't something the men would forget. Ever. The princes were young and strong, they were well-fed and well-armed, they weren't exhausted from back-breaking labor. The villagers the Caelian murdered couldn't say any of those things. If Freddy and Nehl had attacked one of them together, working as a pair, even mediocre swordsmen that they were, they might have been able to kill or at least wound one of the Caelian.

They didn't even try. Freddy and Nehl didn't care about anyone but themselves, not their country, not their fellow soldiers, not the young girls, the children or the elderly of their country. Bloody murder, even the bloody murder of babies and children didn't bother them as long as the Caelian didn't aim a sword or javelin their direction, and they displayed their lack of care for every- one to see over and over again.

Meric couldn't imagine that King Marc would enjoy having them back home again, but he had lifted the terms of their exile and they'd be skittering home as quickly as their cowardly boots could carry them. Meric smiled a little snidely, just to himself. And their boots would be carrying them, too. He wasn't giving them any horses to ride. He had few enough as it was—the Caelian killed their horses whenever they got the chance.

They seemed to understand that the horses were the only thing that allowed his men to have any chance of effectively following them. Archers on horseback had even allowed them their rare, few victories over the raiders, forcing them to leave their captives and the stores they'd loaded on them and run away with only the supplies on their own backs.

Meric thought of the strategy they'd used—half of the archers to keep after the Caelians and their captives while the other half stopped and nocked their arrows and let fly. Then they'd mount up and continue the pursuit while the forward group stopped and nocked their arrows and let fly, and then around again. Sooner or later the Caelians would cut their losses and leave the overburdened captives behind. Archers were very effective against the Caelian, Meric considered, kicking back into his chair and allowing the pictures to form behind his eyes.

The girl's ideas had been brilliant. They worked, and, with a few tweaks here and there, he thought he could make them even more effective. But he needed more foot-soldiers and more horses to follow up the archers and hold the Caelian captives safe while the archers continued the pursuit. If they could just press the damned Caelians hard enough--!

Meric pulled himself out of his ruminations and took himself off to his desk to write up his letters to King Marc and Laren and the under-generals charged with providing him with the men and materiel he needed to get the Caelians on the run and keep them there. Once there, he called for three men to ready themselves and three horses to take them north in the morning. He'd send them out at dawn, Meric thought with a smile, just for himself, before the princes were even awake. They'd never know they'd been bypassed as couriers.

Bastards.

Not that the princes were bastards in the technical sense, he thought. And he couldn't fault the monarchy's practice of keeping the bloodline open. King Marc's mother had been Nogaynos, and his grandfather's mother had been Mahdi and the results of those infusions of blood had been highly successful, both Marc and his father had been healthy, reasonably intelligent and better yet, reasonable, even-tempered, even-handed men who had grown into strong, measured kings who reigned well. Marc's father had even had the good sense to go into retirement and allow his son to take over the administration of the kingdom while he was still young enough and strong enough for it—while he still wanted it, but before he turned bitter with waiting, and perhaps twisted, less reasonable, less even-handed in his approach to his people.

King Marc had cut his administrative teeth on his father's personal estate, learned his lessons in a smaller venue where his mistakes wouldn't do harm to the entire nation. Then, when his father and grandfather deemed him ready, he had been moved into position to take over the kingship. For King Marc, for his father and his grandfather, this arrangement had worked wonderfully well. But for Marc's sons? Meric wondered if their grandfather had brought them to his estate to teach the skills of proper administration only to be balked of his purpose by their stupidity and innate viciousness.

Rumor had it that Freddy and the Crown Prince had abducted a young girl from the streets, secreted her in the palace dungeon and tortured her for their own entertainment. Rumor had it that King Marc had somehow found out about their crimes and saved the girl when she'd been on the point of death. That he'd kept her in the palace under his own wing until she'd recovered, and he could learn the right of whatever had happened. Meric hadn't believed the rumors until King Marc had sent Freddy and Nehl to him, asking him to do what he could with them to mend matters.

Mend matters! Meric scoffed to himself. As if he could make decent men out of a pair of rotters like these two. They were too old to change, now, too set in their ways, beyond any help of his. Maybe if he'd gotten them younger, before their habits were shaped and their minds poisoned by D'Arcy arrogance, maybe he could have salvaged something of them, tempered that something rotten in them.

Now, after months and months of dealing with the pair, he had no doubt at all that the rumors regarding the princes were true and the truth probably even more lurid than the rumors. He could believe any calumny of the princes. In his opinion, there was something basically wrong with them, wrong from their very cores, something born into their very blood, something which, once exposed to the D'Arcy arrogance, had festered and spread until it had rotted the two of them from the marrow of their bones out. Bad blood.

Marc's marriage to the young Caelian princess had just seemed more of the same practice of keeping the lines open when he had done it. It had seemed perfectly reasonable, and it had to be admitted that the girl had made an acceptable queen. She'd been pretty and young and made herself amiable to the nobles. Best of all, from their point of view, she hadn't meddled in affairs of state the way Marc's mother and grandmother had. It had taken years to realize that she wasn't very intelligent, because she had been so personable, and few of the nobles had ever come to realize it.

But it had to be admitted that she came from the Caelian aristocracy that had plotted and accomplished the Nogaynos genocide. However pretty and personable the girl had been herself, she had come from people—from men, at any rate—who were simply evil. Her people had been mass murderers, and however pretty her face, King Marc should have taken note of that and turned his face away from her. Well, he hadn't, and now he was reaping the reward for choosing a pretty face over a warm and steadfast heart. What was worse, if any of the Caelian's sons came to succeed him, the entire country would be paying for his mistake.

Maybe, Meric told himself with a sinking heart, it would come down to slitting a couple of throats in the dark. He wouldn't like doing it, he wasn't a murderer by nature, but if his country needed him to do it—well, he'd never shirked his duty in his life, and he wasn't going to start now.

Neither Crown Prince Nehl, nor his brother Freddy, could ever be allowed to take the Amadean throne. All Meric could do was to pray that the second boy, Garve`, bettered his brothers.

# XXVII

## BANDITS

IT IS SAID THAT TRAVEL is broadening. I don't know about that. We didn't seem to really see a lot but narrow trails and small villages, most of them pretty poor, if you judged by the lack of things they had to sell. Occasionally we stopped at small farm-holds to buy some eggs or some root vegetables and greens, or the occasional bag of grain. People didn't much like seeing us, and they didn't have much to spare to sell. We certainly weren't welcomed. Apparently bandits outnumbered the travelers around here.

Somehow, we managed to get enough in the way of provisions to keep going. I didn't really know how. We didn't look prosperous, I knew. We looked about the same as they did. Maybe a little better because of the magic I'd used to refurbish our clothing, or because in any village we found clothing we could wear, we snapped it up, even if it was secondhand and often as not stained as well. I'd been able to find a little gold in the creeks here, a little silver in a couple of streams there, enough so we had a little money to buy supplies with, which was more than some people had, if not enough to mark us out as rich. It kept us eating.

I managed to get proficient enough with 'travel' magic so that we could get something like forty miles or so a day, most days, and every fifth or sixth day we'd rest and do a little gathering of our own. We'd make camp somewhere there was water and grass enough for Nutmeg, set some rabbit snares, and then scrounge around to see what we could find in the way of greens and edible root vegetables to collect. If we were far enough away from one of the villages and any farm-holds, we could usually scare up a buck or two.

In this way we made a couple of hundred miles every ten days or so, making our way mostly south and a little to the west as we could. Sooner or later we were going to have to find one of the mountain passes on my map, and head west into the mountains for fair, but in the meantime, we just kept traveling, heading mostly south through the foothills before finally starting up into the

mountains. We'd got started late, in the beginning of Blossom, and as the days rolled on, we traveled through Bloom, First Harvest, aka 'Hay' month, Second Harvest, aka 'Corn' month, and finally reached the headwaters of the Lupine. We looked down at it, a narrow ribbon of silver in the faraway distance, winding its way south, skirting the base of this mountain and then that, widening out a little here and there where the ground leveled out for a bit, before it got caught between slopes again and started falling over rocks.

"We need supplies," Reve fretted. I agreed with her, but—"I didn't like the looks of that last town," Wraith mentioned, unhappily.

"Yes, but we're getting up into the mountains now," Reve objected. "Will we even find another town where we can buy supplies?"

"The last two villages the map showed weren't even there any longer," Fort shook his head disconsolately.

His caveat had merit. The question, would the next village the map showed be there? Nagged at me. At all of us, really. Our map was an old one, a hundred and fifty years old at least. Maybe even two hundred. We hadn't been able to find a newer map to use to update it, and no one seemed to know much of anything about anywhere more than fifty-sixty miles away. I would have questioned whether all of them were telling the truth when they denied knowing anything, but challenging them wasn't going to get us anything in the way of helpful information and would simply shove them farther towards becoming our enemies. And Reve was right. We needed supplies.

Oh, we'd managed to keep going on rabbits and the roots and greens we'd managed to glean here and there as we traveled, but we needed grain and dried beans. We were heading into Third Harvest as well as the mountains and we needed to lay in the supplies we'd need to den up for the winter, because that was exactly what we were going to need to do, and soon. 'Winter' here was likely to be five months long, or close to it, and we'd have to have some food to travel on, when Spring came around again.   I figured three and a half pounds a day each for five people times a hundred and fifty days, or a rock bottom minimum of twenty-six hundred pounds of provisions. And yes, ok, we could bring in a few deer here and there, and a rabbit now and again, but we needed a lot more than deer and rabbits and we all knew it.

"Do we want to head back to that village?" Fort wanted to know.

The answer to that was no, I didn't. I looked out around us. I figured we'd gotten something like four thousand feet in elevation into the mountains. The types of trees around us indicated that, and so did the plants at their feet. I shrugged out of my pack, pulled the geography book with the maps out of it, sat down on it and opened the book. Everybody else gathered around me.

"I doubt," Wraith observed, "that village would have the supplies we need even if they would sell them to us—which I also doubt."

I thought he had a point. Shade nodded at the book. "What do the maps say?" he wanted to know.

"Not much," I frowned. He knew as well as I did that the maps in the book were all of a hundred and fifty years out of date, if not more. "No other villages within twenty miles in any direction but a half a dozen farms and ranches in a span of fifty, sixty miles. Maybe we could get supplies at one of the farms?"

"There's a thought," Wraith concurred.

"What about finding a high place?" Shade wanted to know. "Somewhere we could maybe look around?"

Sounded like a good idea to me. I studied the elevations on the topographical map of the area the book provided. Looked around us to try to orient myself to where we'd be on the map.      Out of the corner of my eye I saw Nutmeg throw his head up. I dumped the book into my pack and crouched, pulling knives from the sheaths on my calves and sticking them into the ground in front of me.

Nutmeg stomped a foot and following his gaze, I saw the first of the men breaking from the trees. Dressed to blend in, the men didn't stand out, and they'd gotten entirely too close to us while we communed with the maps. They rushed us now, swords and knives in hand, meaning to over-run us.

"Bandits!" Fort exclaimed.

"Circle!" Wraith directed. "Backs to backs!"

I pulled up a knife and sent it out on a thread of magic, didn't watch to see it sink home between the bandit's eyes. I had already sent the second knife out on a second thread while I pulled a thigh knife to send after it. The second thigh knife followed it, and it, in turn, was followed by the pair at my waist. After that, they had made it too close for throwing knives. Somewhere, at the back of my mind, as I met one sword with my own sword, the other with my poniard, I repeated the count. Twelve of them. Twelve bandits against five of us!

I didn't bother to stop and think that I had already cut them down to six. I didn't have time to think about it. I was too busy parrying the one sword with my poniard while I slapped the other swordsman away from me and tripping him so that he crossed in front of the other man giving me the necessary split second to bury my poniard under his sternum. He dropped away from me, taking my poniard with him, but giving me the opportunity to deal with the second of the men. Fencing with him left handed, I had to do some ducking and diving to stay within his reach while at the same time not allowing him to bring his greater strength of arm and longer reach to bear against me, my only advantages my quickness and superior skills.

He hacked at me almost clumsily, his blade heavy and ill-made. I didn't have time to test myself against him, given the numbers of the bandits who had attacked us, I knew it was imperative that I finish him quickly and go to the aid of any of the rest of our party finding himself or herself fighting against odds. I could hear my adoptive father's harsh voice in my ears as I parried, ducked and twisted.

'The object is not to duel your opponent' he snarled in my mind, 'it's to survive—and to make sure your companions stay alive, not to score points! Kill your opponent! Kill him quickly! Make sure he's dead and then go on to the next one!'

The blade dropped from my arm to my hand and I flipped it into the bandit's face on a thread of magic, right between his eyes while my left hand kept his blade engaged with my sword. Spinning, I flipped the sword to my right hand and dropped the blade in my left arm sheath to my left hand, ready to throw it, only to see the dead men at Reve's and Wraith's feet. Even as I watched, Fort dropped his opponent. Shade's adversary was still on his feet; I flicked the blade into his face, burying it between his eyes almost casually. Looked around.

They were all down, all twelve bandits, spread out around us in a circle, the men I'd killed with my throwing knives farther out away from us, those killed by our swords closer to us. Wraith and Reve walked among them, taking care to make certain each and every one of them was dead. I frowned at them. Fort put my misgivings into words.

"They're not carrying much in the way of packs," he commented. "They must have a camp close by."

Wraith nodded. To me, he said, "Gather up your knives."

I'd already started. I noticed that Reve had pulled one of their knapsacks open and begun to paw through it.

"Get any food they're carrying, and any spare clothing," she advised, as she jerked those items free. They didn't look to me as if they had much.

I yanked my knife back and started to clean it on the dead man's shirt. I didn't actually feel much in the way of regret that they'd died. Mostly what I felt was relief. They'd meant to kill us. Well, at least Wraith and the boys. I suspected that what they'd meant for Reve and for me would have been worse than death. I'd learned the hard way, back in that Amadean dungeon, that there were things worse than death.

By rote, I just kept retrieving my knives, cleaning them meticulously, and then sheathing them again. I might have been a little shocky. I'd never intentionally killed a man before.

"Let's finish this and get to high ground and start looking for those farms," Wraith suggested. "I don't know but what I suspect these men were based in that village we passed."

"You think they targeted us and tracked us down to attack us?" Fort wanted to know. "Surely we don't look all that prosperous."

"Compared to these men, we do," Reve told him. She started tossing the clothing she'd recovered into one stack on the come-along, and the food—some grain, some dried venison—into one of the bins.

Wraith turned to me.

"Can you erase any sign of us?" he wanted to know. I looked around us.

"Wounds?" I wanted to know.

"A couple of cuts," Fort admitted, reluctantly.

Shade looked down at his torn sleeve and the blood on his arm. "Just a scratch," he said.

I threw a quick clean spell his way, along with a stop bleeding and a general heal everything and turned to Fort. He needed pretty much the same attention; both Wraith and Reve appeared untouched. I turned back to help Reve finish up with the inventory. We didn't live under the kind of circumstances that allowed us to turn our noses up at warm clothing or food. Either might make the difference between life or death for us, and well I knew it. The food these men carried might not mean more than two good meals for each of us, but two good meals were not to be derided.

"We'll eat well tonight," Reve assured me, as I turned out the last knapsack, throwing a couple of the best of them into the come-along to hold our finds. I swallowed, looking back at the dead men.

Twelve of them, I thought. They'd come against us twelve to five! And just as I thought it, Wraith clapped me on the shoulder.

"We've got you to thank that we're alive," he said. "You and those knives cut those numbers down so we could fight our way out of it."

I nodded jerkily. What would have happened, I wondered, if there had been even one more of them? Would we be the bodies being stripped of everything?

"Let's get to that high ground and see what we can find," Reve advised, yanking my mind away from the dark questions. There hadn't been thirteen of them. There had only been twelve, and we'd managed.

High ground, I repeated to myself, and forced myself to start erasing every sign that we had ever been here. After a moment, Reve led out, with Fort and then Shade, and Wraith bringing up the rear, with me on his heels, obliterating every sign of our passing as we slipped away from the scattering of dead men. Somebody would find them, I supposed. Sooner or later.

# XXVIII

# THE FARM

**"WELL,"** I ASKED BOTH WRAITH and Reve, as we looked down on the farm below us. We couldn't see much of it from here, but we could identify the apple trees easily enough.

I've since heard the kind of decision we faced then 'time to fish or cut bait'.

With third Harvest coming up quickly, we needed to find a decent place to winter over and get our stores of food in for Nutmeg and ourselves. That meant we needed decide whether to follow the Lupine south, or to head more to the west—and into the mountains. According to our map and the notes I'd been able to glean from the locals along our way, if we turned west and headed for the closest mountain pass, we'd have to do all our own gathering for food and supplies, because heading west meant villages and farm-holds would become even more scarce than they already were. If we kept going south, we would actually find more villages and farm-holds, like the one below, as they tended to gather close to the river.

I wasn't at all sure I wanted to visit more villages or farms. None of those we had so far visited had welcomed us—the people had all been cold and borderline hostile. Even our small store of gold and silver hadn't warmed them up much, and to be truthful, they hadn't had much in the way of supplies to share. I knew from living in the city that river towns would incline to roughness more often than not, probably reminiscent of the docks and the warehouses in Palace City in Amadea. None of us wanted to deal with that, especially knowing that the likelihood was that we'd be considered little better than marks for the rougher element, and any representatives of anything that passed for law and order would be more apt to support the locals than they would transients.

We numbered only the five of us, two men, if you stretched the point a little, two kids and one woman wouldn't intimidate anyone. And all right, Fort, Shade, Wraith, Reve and I had all practiced enough with our blades to be considered competent, and I could throw my knives pretty accurately, and use my bow just as well if not a little better, but still, a small group like ours could be easily out-numbered, as our recent set-to with bandits had made only too evident. We'd been extremely lucky to get out of that little contretemps alive and well, magic or no magic.

And all right, maybe I'd used a bit of magic to make certain my knives flew true, but when you got right down to it, I only had so many knives, and once the would-be killers closed with us, throwing knives couldn't be depended upon for much of any help. I didn't have much more. What little work I'd managed to do with my books, I'd done on ward crafting for protection, refining my 'travel' spells, and some levitation for the come-along and Nutmeg, to help with the weight on both of them.

Wards had a lot of handy-dandy uses, but fighting hordes of thugs wasn't one of them, as far as I could tell. Well, other than as defenses. Too, strangers, as we would be, wouldn't be allowed the privilege of self-defense in any of these little villages we had encountered. Push back against anyone of theirs, and they'd all come against us, like stirring a hornet's nest with a stick. Better to avoid them, if possible.

At best guess, we'd come close to two thousand miles so far and were maybe only three or four hundred miles or so from the Nogaynos border. None of us expected much to change in the people's attitude—if we found any—once we got to Nogaynos. Since the diaspora, Nogaynos people had become notably reclusive. They remained secluded in homes no one seemed to know anything about—or at least no one seemed willing to talk about.

So, when it came to collecting supplies, we were pretty much on our own.

Things could have been worse. I needed lime and soda and sand if I was going to make more glass, but it looked to me as if I could find plenty of sand along the river. So that was one down. Where I'd get the lime or the soda I didn't know, but I rather thought I'd manage somehow. Metal, well, the elements for metal could be called from the earth. I'd done it before, I could do it again. All I had to do was to find a place in the earth where the elements could be found. I already had some of what I needed.

"We could fish," Fort pointed out.

We were by no means out of food, but fishing sounded good to me. A little variety in our meals wouldn't hurt, and I might be able to find some roots and greens above the river to add to our stores, not to mention a rabbit or two. This late in the season, we might even be able to add a bird or two to the mix. A plump partridge would roast up rather nicely, I couldn't help but think. I looked up the hill into the brush hopefully.

"Let's get away from the river," Reve suggested. "We can come back down during the day to fish, but it just seems a bit too open right here--"

I looked around. She was right. It was open.

"We'll find a better place to fish," Shade assured her, as we climbed back up the hill.

"Farther upstream, maybe," Fort added. The wrong direction, of course.

"Let's find another vantage point and see if we can see more of the farm that way. And maybe a tributary coming down to the river," I suggested. "We ought to be able to find a more secluded area upstream."

"And in the right direction," Shade added. "Point," his father allowed.

So we climbed to the highest point we could find and looked all around. And what do you know, there was a creek off to the west heading down to the river. It was hard to see, because it flowed down an area where two hills came together and there was a lot of brush, so that you had to more infer that a creek was there, than actually see it, but if we were where the map insinuated we were, that was a creek. Bush creek, to be exact, and a very good name for it Bush Creek was, too.

When we got to it, it turned out to be a good deal wider and deeper than I'd expected from the look of it, and we found a place to camp uphill of it. One of those little sort-of flats that seem to crop up here and there among the hills, it had some lush grass, a few herbs and wildflowers, and even a few things that grew edible roots, altogether a very nice little camping place. We unloaded Nutmeg and pegged him out to graze right away, with enough rope so he could drink from the narrow little stream that cut across the grassy spot and joined the creek a way down the hill.

Shade and Fort got busy with their fishing lines, I scrambled around to find enough rocks for a fire pit, and Reve and Wraith started fitting a couple of small lean-tos back into the trees. I added some wards to contain any sparks the fire might throw off, and then began to ward the entire campsite more seriously. By the time Fort and Shade had returned with their fish, I'd found some herbs and greens, dug up some roots, and put together a rather nice baked potage, with corn-cake atop the rest and had it baking in the coals. The boys had cleaned their fish and removed their heads, so I rubbed them with salt, added some of the herbs I'd found and some lemon slices, and set them to roast. It all made a very satisfactory dinner, with enough left over for tomorrow, and the day after that, if we stayed that long.

Everybody went to bed pleased, and the next day we decided, once the boys had caught more fish, to head west along the creek towards the orchard we'd seen from the hill. While they fished, Reve and I worked our way up and down the creek gathering all the herbs and roots we could find. Oh, we were careful not to take everything—we left enough so that this time next year there would be just as many roots and herbs for travelers to find, after all, we weren't starving so we didn't need to be greedy. That night I filled one of our empty glass cases with filets of fish and spelled it to keep the fish as fresh as the moment they'd been caught before packing it away in the little come-along. Nutmeg, having demolished about half the grass in the tiny hill meadow, took to the trail the next morning with equanimity. I suspected that he realized the little sort-of flat did not contain any kind of sufficiency of grass for the winter. Not that we'd be stopping for the winter just yet. We figured to get in at least ten more days before we started looking for a place.

Two days later we stumbled into what once had been a rather nice little farm, complete with a couple of acres of apple orchard, a rich, if weedy, garden, a small field of corn, another of oats, and yet a third of quite nice hay, despite the weeds, which, this high in the hills, had yet to mature too far beyond its best cutting. Unfortunately, someone had burned the small farmhouse to the ground, the bones of the people who had died inside well weathered. I suspected it had been a couple of years since the place had burned, and from the looks of the bodies, they'd been put to the sword, first, before the house burned. Our bandits, probably, or another group just like them. The barn, such as it was, had taken some damage as well.

Before we'd been there long enough to make sense of what we saw, we heard a frantic baby whinny coming from the battered barn, and, before we could do much but stare, a colt erupted through the door, attempting to run towards us— well, towards Nutmeg, really--on three legs. Nutmeg nickered back to him and both of us moved towards the colt. Once we reached him, the colt, spent, nestled into Nutmeg and subsided, head down. His left foreleg was swollen all the way to his knee and I eased up to him, using Nutmeg on the other side of him to keep him quiet, and eased a hand down it, easing the pain as best I could as I stroked him.

A nondescript bay, with no discernable markings, the colt looked to be maybe six or seven months old at best, but the lines of his legs and body told me he'd been well bred. Old enough to wean, but a little pot-bellied, if not in really poor condition, he'd have brought a pretty penny if someone had shaped him up a little and he hadn't had that swollen leg. Someone had put a lot of time and effort and hard-won knowledge into breeding him only to have him stolen with his mother. I wondered who they were and where they were. Or if they were any longer. Had they ended up the way the people at this farm had?

A bit of frayed rope dangled from his neck with the remnants of a rope-burn showing me where he'd been left tied somewhere and worked himself loose.

Maybe when he'd been separated from his mother? But how had he gotten here, then? He'd been managing to pick up enough feed about the place to get by, but he didn't look well. The swelling in his leg looked like a major problem. He'd been handled at some time, though, and not too roughly. He let me lift his foot to look at, and stood quiet while I did it.

Reve eased up to him and put a hand to his neck and he didn't flinch. She rubbed a little, and he seemed to like it. I let his foot down carefully.

"I think he's got some glass in there," I told them. "Let's get Nutmeg unloaded, and I'll see what I can do about it. I'll need some water to flush it out—I think he's got an abscess--and then once I've got it opened up and drained, I'll clean it out and pack it and then see what I can find to put a shoe on that foot. If I can pad it up a little, he might even be able to walk on it a bit, once I've been able to heal it a little."

"You can put a shoe on?" Shade was inclined to be impressed.

"My adoptive father was a smith," I reminded him. "He did just about anything to keep the money coming in, including shoeing horses." Which he hadn't been very good at, not because he didn't understand proper shoeing techniques, but because he had no affinity for animals in general or horses in particular. A really good shoer had not only a good command of shoeing techniques, but a definite way with horses.

"I'm not sure I like it here," Reve advised me as I collected the gear I was going to need.

"We won't stay here," I assured her. "We'll find a place somewhere above the orchard to camp tonight. Then we'll gather whatever we can pack away and head on up the mountain for another twenty miles or so. Or maybe thirty. I'd rather not winter too close to this place."

"Why not?" Fort wanted to know.

"Because someone murdered everyone on the place and then burned the house over their bodies," I pointed out. "And who knows how far from here they might be."

"But maybe we already took care of them," Fort argued. I shook my head.

"The colt's presence argues for the existence of another group," I reminded him. "Somebody left him here to make it on his own, and no decent, honest group of men would have done that—they wouldn't have needed to. And

besides, this colt is valuable. No," I persisted, "they stole the colt and his mother, and when he was lamed, they left him here to make it on his own or die because they couldn't afford to stop running long enough to take care of him.

They cut their losses, took the mare and split. That doesn't mean they won't be back after they've sold the mare for whatever they can get for her."

Wraith returned from inspecting the buildings that remained.

"Whoever it was, the house was burned and the farmers killed at least a couple of years ago," he assured me, as I got to work on the colt's foot. "The gardens and the fields are just volunteering each spring." He shook his head. "Must have been a really nice place, once upon a time," he commented.

"Some people are just mean," Reve observed. She had the right of that.

"Doesn't mean it wasn't the same group that left the colt here," I observed.

"They may be using this place as one of their hide-outs. Not regularly, from the looks of things, but just now and again, whenever convenient for them."

"Not entirely unlikely," Wraith, reluctantly, agreed with me.

The abscess opened, and pus poured out, taking little particles of glass with it. I ran my fingers down the colt's tendons, gently pushing the infection before them. The colt heaved a huge sigh and sagged against Nutmeg's body. I kept working my fingers over his leg, careful not to hurt him, driving the infection and any glass out with it and the colt let me. When I had done that as best I could, I flushed the wound in the bottom of his foot with disinfectant, packed it, and then tied a cloth around it. Holding his foot up, I urged Nutmeg to take a few steps forward and to the side so the colt would move with him. That way, Fort and Wraith could clean up the area I'd pushed the glass out into.

"We'll dig that spot up and tuck it away," Wraith volunteered.

"Be careful while you do it," I warned. "The colt picked up that glass somewhere, most likely around here."

# XXIX

## JAGR

I LEFT THE COLT STANDING CONTENTEDLY with Nutmeg while Reve fed him handfuls of oats, and reconnoitered the barn. A place such as this one had once been would have had shoeing supplies. And sure enough, at the near end of the barn, I found a room with the remnants of tack that hadn't been stolen, shoeing supplies, and medicinals. None of the medicinals remaining would be useable, unfortunately, but the shoeing supplies, though dusty, were exactly what I needed. I cleaned everything up and carted the box off to where Nutmeg and the colt waited, but not before I had found where the colt had been tied and barricaded into what remained of a box stall.

Whoever had tied the colt there had not intended for him to survive. They had left neither food nor water in the stall for the colt—they hadn't even left a bucket for him! and once I got a chance to inspect the knot in the rope around his neck I could see they had intended for him to choke himself out, fighting it. The clever colt had fooled them. He had rubbed at the rope until it had frayed and torn apart. I'd have to remember that, that he was intelligent.

"They meant to kill him!" Shade told me, as I worked over the colt's foot. "They stole his mother somewhere," I told him, putting it together in my mind as I leveled up the colt's foot with the rasp. "And along the way, maybe when they were stealing her, he got some glass in his foot. By the time they got this far he would have been limping badly, and the mare was probably balking at leaving him. So they

232

brought them here, tied him in the stall and barricaded him in, and then they rode the mare away."

"That's not good," Reve, who was holding the colt steady, remarked, at the same time Shade wanted to know,

"How long ago?"

"At least a week, and it's bad," I agreed with Reve. "How can you tell?" Fort wanted to know.

"And why is that bad, if they've been gone a week?" Shade demanded.

"It took that long, at least, for that abscess to develop to that point," I said to Fort, and then, to Shade, I said, "Because it means that this place is known to the outlaw element in this area."

Having cleaned, re-packed the abscess, and added a leather pad, I started to setting the first nail.

"You two need to find us a camp site well above the orchard, some place hidden, tucked back into the trees, just in case, while we clean out as much of the garden and the fields as we can."

As soon as I got the second toe-nail set, I let the colt put his foot down and rest for a moment. Wraith appeared in my peripheral vision.

"There's a small field of wheat in back of the garden," he told me. "About the time we manage to gather up the rest of the harvest and get it to wherever we're going to winter, the wheat ought to be ready."

"Excellent," I replied, easing the colt's foot to the front of my leg so that I could nip the tips of the nails off and clinch them. The colt had very respectable hoof walls, and he seemed almost pleased to have me working on his foot. Of course, the fact that I kept pulsing a little low level pain relief and healing into his foot and leg along as I worked couldn't have hurt. I let his foot down to rest his leg a bit, and then eased it back up so I could set another couple of nails.

"That," Wraith commented, as I worked, "is a very well-bred colt."

"And one who was well started," I pointed out.

I didn't believe I would get more than five nails into his baby foot and I didn't much care. I didn't intend for the shoe to be on it all that long.

"Good lines, good temperament—his mother would have been well worth stealing."

Wraith frowned. I finished clinching my nails and set the colt's foot down gently. Stroking him, I encouraged him to put his toe down and balance on it for a moment to see how it felt. Painful, I observed, but not excruciating.

"Let's get them watered and then see if we can get them over to the orchard. There's plenty of grass there for now."

When presented with a bucket of water, the colt drank thirstily. I intuited that he'd found it difficult and painful to make it as far as the farm's stream and had been forced to choose between the stream and the grass until he'd started to feel so bad he didn't care much about either. Now, he put down two buckets- full of water and then walked beside Nutmeg, using three legs and his toe, to the orchard to graze. As soon as he reached the orchard, he dropped his head and started to grab at the grass scattered around under the apple trees.

I found that a good sign. A horse that could eat was a horse that could mend.

A bucket of water tied to the fence provided him a nice sense of security—he had people taking care of him again—and after he had grazed for a couple of hours, he laid down on the ground and curled up to sleep. Nutmeg stood over him as his mother might have, earning himself another couple of hands-full of oats, just because.

In general, Nutmeg was both gregarious and good-natured. He liked people in general and most girls specifically. Particularly little girls. He was also a clever little horse and I knew he got bored back home in the stable behind the forge. He seemed to enjoy traveling, as long as I didn't pack him too heavily or try to go too far all at once. He liked his creature comforts, which made him approve whole-heartedly of wintering over somewhere he had a warm stall and plenty to eat. Now he seemed to be indicating that he found the colt's company a welcome addition to our little group, and that he was fully aware that the colt was a mere baby, and a distressed one at that, in need of cosseting and comfort.

People, I thought, too often gave animals too little credit for their perceptions. Then again, I'd come across more than a few human-type people that Nutmeg could have given lessons to in general understanding. Some people, I supposed, were smarter than some animals, but I very much doubted that all people were. Just because people could talk with words didn't mean animals didn't have a language they could communicate with. Maybe we were the stupid ones because we were too dumb to admit it. (Or too arrogant?) Oh, well.

Shade and I headed up the hill with our packs, looking for a place out of sight of the farm where we could tuck ourselves back into a copse of trees and hide while we stripped the farm of as much as we could carry. That wouldn't be anywhere near as much as I would like.

"There'll be pigs about," Shade mentioned, as we walked. "I saw stys in the back of the barn, there."

They'd be half wild by now, and pigs could be dangerous. I smiled.

"Ham for the winter," I said. "Unfortunately, the bandits that murdered the householders probably took the cow."

"They might have had a couple," Shade pointed out.

"Would be nice if they were still around," I agreed. We shared a smile. A yearling or two year old steer (or young bull) would provide a LOT of meat. Depending on how big, maybe enough for the entire winter, particularly if we could supplement it with a ham or two. I liked beef a lot better than I liked venison.

"They had sheep, too," Shade pointed out. Yes, but would any of them still be alive?

"Predators?" I questioned, knowing Shade's nose was a lot better than mine and picked up on that sort of thing.

"Not close," he told me. "I get the feeling the main predators around here are men."

He was probably right. I stopped and turned around to look back the way we had come. Not far enough, I thought, as I gauged how far we'd walked. And this area would be visible from the farm. Still too open. We'd need to go farther, get higher. I looked back at the stream that threaded its way through the farm. The headwaters ought to be somewhere up here. I turned around to survey the forest.

"What about up there?" Shade asked me.

I looked the direction he pointed out. "Let's see," I proposed.

We headed up. I wanted to find a place where we could camouflage a couple of small lean-tos, stash our gear, and cache supplies from the farm inside protective wards until we could find another well-hidden spot to site our den for the winter. The problem was that I foresaw difficulties getting everything we'd need for the winter from the farm. Harvesting everything there would take considerable time and effort. I didn't mind the effort, but I did mind the time. Not so much because winter was closing in on us, as because I didn't want to linger around a place obviously visited by bandit elements.

The plain fact of the matter was that the farm had enough food, that, with a little work and supplemented by a few rabbits and some deer, it would support a dozen men all winter long. Bandits, however, were not the kind of men to put in a day's work if they could avoid it. They would let women and children starve before they would lift a finger to feed them, if they couldn't do it by theft and murder. From what I had seen, admittedly, just at a glance, the gardens had all the root vegetables, beans, greens and squash we could handle. Add the orchard, the corn, wheat, oats, and hay, and we could spend a month harvesting everything the place had. I didn't want to stick around the place for a month.

Corollary—Nutmeg couldn't carry all that. Neither could the little come- along. If we added, each of us, forty pounds to each of our packs, and if I packed two hundred pounds on Nutmeg (which I had no intention of doing) and added another two hundred pounds to the come-along (which I might, just barely be able to do, if I packed it just right) we might be able to get a grand total of six hundred pounds of supplies in to our winter quarters. We needed four times that. The farm could provide it. But—how to get what the farm provided to winter quarters thirty or forty miles away? Because I didn't want to be any closer than thirty miles to a place bandits frequented.

Obviously we would have to make more than one trip. It would take three, most likely, or even four or five.   How did we make three trips over the same or similar ground without leaving any trace for venal bandits to follow? Humm?

Relays? I asked myself. Get everything to a relay point, a cache, and then move it on from there? After warding it six ways over, of course. Then go back after everything has been moved to the new relay point and erase all trace of our travel or of having been there?

Might work, I considered, turning it over in my mind. With a copious use of magic. Travel and levitation, I supposed, and perhaps wards? I could do travel and wards. Levitation, well, I'd been levitating the come-along for nearly four thousand miles, at this point. But how else were we to get over the land without leaving a trace of our passing? Then I wondered, could the bandits track magic use? Huh. Good question.

# XXX

# NEHL AND FREDDY

"WALK?" NEHL SQUAWKED. "WE HAVE to walk?"

"I can't spare the horses," Meric reminded him. He smiled slightly. "Have a nice trip," he said. "It shouldn't take you more than twenty days."

"Twenty days!" Nehl complained. "It took us almost that long to ride the distance!"

"Really?" General Meric didn't sound very interested. "How odd." But they didn't have his attention any longer. He had opened a folder and started to read the report it contained. "Well," he commented, "there will be a trireme in port in Quattar in twenty days, or thereabout, and you can take passage on it back to Palace City, if you can get to Quattar before they offload and take on their provisions for the return trip."

"What about our stuff?" Nehl wanted to know. General Meric barely looked up from his report.

"Anything you can't carry, you can pack up and we'll send your bags on with the supply wagon when we send it on to Quattar." He glanced up quickly to make brief eye contact. "And be sure you draw enough supplies for the trip," he added. "With any luck the men going with you will be able to add some roots and a rabbit or two to your meals now and again, but you'll need to take enough food for twenty days, at least. Good thing there's water on the trail," he concluded. "At least you won't have to carry that. Well, not more than enough for a couple of days, anyway."

"How much food will we have to carry?" Freddy asked, wincing internally. "Oh, about sixty pounds, I'd say," General Meric offered, without taking his eyes from his reports.

Freddy reeled. Sixty pounds!

"We'll just have the men carry it," Nehl shrugged.

"That won't work," General Meric informed him. "They have to carry their own food. Of course," he glanced up briefly, again, "I can send you back without any men to go with you. After all, you managed to get here." He tipped his head thoughtfully. "Either one of you know how to set snares for rabbits?" he wondered, a bit curiously.

The answer was no. Faintly, Freddy urged, "Come on, let's get packed."

"I'm not leaving all my things here," Nehl declared. "And I'm not carrying sixty pounds of food on my back!"

Again, General Meric glanced up.

"Oh, then you're staying?" he inquired mildly. "No, we are not!" Nehl returned stoutly.

General Meric looked up from his report and actually regarded him for a long moment.

"Huh," he said. He tipped his head, as if he inspected a two-headed calf or something of the like. "Well," he shrugged, "good luck."

Nehl sat down.

"Give us horses," he said. He sounded to Freddy, very like he had in the nursery. He wondered if his brother would descend to throwing himself onto the floor and kicking his heels. He didn't think it would have the same effect on the general that it had on Nanny. He looked at his brother, and then he left Nehl with the General to work things out.

It had been a long winter, he thought, as he headed up to their rooms. Spring had passed in a blink, and now summer was dragging on interminably. It was deadly, and given the depredations of the Caelian raiders, in more than one way. He wanted to go home. If he managed things carefully enough, he could take ship on the trireme without Bardons or D'Arcys ever realizing he had returned to Quattar. They couldn't kill him if they didn't know he was there, he told himself, with an inner sneer towards the nobles who had tried and failed to kill his father. Nehl, he reminded himself with exasperation, would involve himself with them, no matter how well the both of them knew that all three 'noble' families were incompetent.

He'd told Nehl they'd botch the affair, and that he ought not to take up with them. Don't have anything to do with them, he'd warned. You know they're too inbred and arrogant to be able to do anything successfully, particularly not something as difficult to pull off as a coup, he'd said. But had Nehl paid any attention to him? Of course not.

He'd gone and tied himself in with them anyway, and now what did they want to do? Get rid of him, that's what. And worse than that, they wanted to get rid of Freddy, too. And if Nehl thought he was going to cool his heels around the fort, here, while Nehl threw one temper tantrum after another, until he forced General Meric to throw him into the brig, being bored out of his mind, then Nehl could just think again.

Winter had been one thing, but once Nehl had started killing his girls again, that was just too much.

Fort Southren was far too small a place for girls to go missing in. One he'd gotten away with. Two, well, the jury was still out on the second one. If Nehl was stupid enough to try for three, General Meric might just decide that the world would be a better place to live in without a certain Crown Prince in it, and if he thought Freddy knew what Nehl was up to and didn't do anything about it, or worse, helped him, well, Freddy knew that he might just join his brother in an early grave.

He had no intention of dying in a dark alley with his throat slit, but the general was just the man to do it if he ever figured out what Nehl was up to. General Meric might be the only man in the entire country who would put an end to Nehl's little murder games, and permanently. The old man had more honor in his little finger than all the men in Quattar, and Palace City, too, like as not, and well Freddy knew it. Fort Southren wasn't Quattar. It wasn't ruled by the Bardons and the D'Arcys. If it had a population of much over a thousand people over and above the military contingent, Freddy didn't know it.

Here in Fort Southren, everybody knew everybody else. And they didn't just know their names and their faces, they knew their parents and their business, their friends and their enemies. One girl maybe got taken off by Caelians. Well, the Caelians had continued to raid off and on through the winter, and they'd even hit a couple of places in Mud and Bud. But questions were already being asked about the second girl, and he didn't want to be around when somebody started to figure out the answers.

If Nehl was arrogant enough, and stupid enough to stick around and try for three, well, he'd deserve whatever the general did to him. Freddy wasn't going to stick around to be tarred with the same brush.

Obviously, he considered, as he climbed the stairs, he'd have to choose the clothing he brought with him carefully. He had a feeling Nehl was going to be obstinate about things. Nehl, he thought ruefully, didn't always think things through very well. He had a feeling his brother had met the one man he couldn't bully into buckling under to his demands. It would be interesting to stick around to watch the clash of titans, but it wasn't worth his life. He was out of here. Just as soon as he could make arrangements for whatever of his belongings to be shipped on later he needed to make arrangements for, and as soon as he could pack his bags, make arrangements for supplies and a guide, he'd be heading home. Nehl could follow along as he pleased. If he pleased.

By the time he had the things he meant to take with him packed up, and the rest of his things boxed up, Nehl had still not appeared. Nonchalantly, Freddy hefted his pack and trundled down the stairs to request men to carry his boxes down to be loaded on the supply wagon whenever the next supply run occurred. He glanced into the general's office, but neither Nehl nor the general was still there. Huh.

He rousted out one of the more competent of the sergeants and asked him who he would recommend as a guide/companion for a trip on foot to Quattar. The name the man offered rocked him a little, since he knew him as the brother of the first girl Nehl had killed. But, he pinched his lips and went in search of the man. Well, boy.

Finding him, Freddy had a moment's second thought. Raggedy, scrawny, unkempt—he'd never seen such a scarecrow. But, the sergeant had been certain, and, when he asked the boy for a list of the supplies they'd need to make the trip, the boy came up with a list so promptly and so easily that Freddy was impressed against his will. He hauled the boy to the sutler's and outfitted them both for the trip, the boy from the skin out. It was an expensive business, but he was able to manage it so that the boy never saw the money changing hands.

Well, better safe than sorry. Call it part of his fee for guiding Freddy back to Quattar.

They didn't wait for morning. Freddy didn't want to chance the contretemps he knew would occur if he ran into Nehl before he got away. He had no intention of carrying Nehl's pack for him, or getting half-way to Quattar and finding that they were out of food. The sergeant had told him that the boy could hunt for them on the way, so they wouldn't have to carry quite as much food as the general had recommended, but Freddy had no intention of going hungry.

The boy got him about eight miles down the trail before they stopped for the night, but there was enough daylight when they set up camp that he was able to roll his bed out on a nice, cushy nest of leaves and grass. They made ten miles the next day, and maybe another ten the third day, the boy breaking him in to the trail in easy increments. The fourth day they made twelve miles, and twelve again the fifth day. He brought in a rabbit that night, and the next day they left the trail to take a little short-cut of the boy's devising, coming out on the trail again the eighth day well over forty miles on from where they'd left it. Freddy began to consider the kid a very good deal.

Sixteen days later he walked into Quattar to see the trireme just arriving in port, paid the kid off, and moved his gear on board. He figured he could camp out on board until the galley had laid in their provisions and was ready to leave. It amused him to pretend to fit in with the rowers, and he even took an oar to help to shift the galley from one dock to another for loading.

After sixteen days on the trail, he had sun-browned, his already blonde hair bleached out to something very close to white. He had grown lean and hard, and worn his clothing enough so that it didn't look anything like the sort of clothing a prince would wear. His boots had been scuffed and scraped to a fare-thee-well in ways that could not be faked, and his beard looked as white as his hair. He didn't bother to shave it off. Oh, he'd trimmed it, but he wanted the disguise it afforded him. No one would believe that the scruffy, trail-hardened backwoodsman could be the young, handsome Prince Freddy now!

Nehl arrived ten days after he had, with an entourage of four men and a wagon full of his boxes, and Freddy's as well. He looked sour. He didn't bother to supervise their loading onto the trireme, he just told the men to put his gear on board and stalked over to the captain of the ship to inform him that he was coming aboard. On the way, he walked right by Freddy and didn't even give him the first look, never mind a second. He certainly didn't recognize him. Freddy grinned to himself and did not bring himself to his brother's attention.

He wondered how long it would take for his brother to recognize him, laid an internal wager with himself. With any luck, he reminded himself, he'd be back at the palace before Nehl paid him any attention.

He settled into the stern of the ship, behind the rudder, and pulled his faded cloak up around his ears. (The breeze was brisk out here on the water, even tied to the docks.) Nehl stomped into the raised cabin (of sorts) and didn't reappear until supper, by which time all his boxes had been loaded, stacked, and tied down for the coming journey, and the men and wagon had gone.

Freddy collected his supper, took it to his sheltered little nook in the stern of the ship, hunkered down and ate his meal. A man came by and collected his bowl, and Freddy pulled the heavy woolen canvas of a spare sail up around his shoulders over his cloak, settled more deeply into his nest against the stem of the ship, and rested, well hidden from the rest of the passengers.

Resting, he slept, waking only with the turn of the tide and the sound of the oars, taking them out of the harbor. He yawned, listening to the splashing of the oars in the water until the rhythm sent him back to sleep.

# XXXI

## THIRD HARVEST

**"WHAT ABOUT THERE?" SHADE WANTED** to know.

I looked up the hill where he was pointing and considered. The copse of trees looked as if they'd nestled into a dimple in the side of the hill with a skirt of elderberry bushes gathered about their legs and a petticoat of gooseberries, frilly and sprawling, underneath them. I wandered closer. The copse of trees traveled back along the side of the hill for some little distance, wider at the front and narrowing behind until they fetched up in little more than a trailing line. If we brought in some more elderberries from other places, and stuck them into the side hill with a little magic to keep them green, we could tuck the lean-tos under them and even put up a bit of a shelter for the horses.

Nutmeg would like that. Not that it was cold or anything; it might be late summer but the nights were still comfortable, if a bit cool here in the mid-range slopes of the mountains. I didn't think, however, that temperature had anything to do with his penchant for shelters. I thought he had another, perhaps more significant matter in mind-- predators. A shelter, however ephemeral, tended to make a statement to predators that whatever prey animals had been provided with it had real protection as well. In real terms, of course, the wards I put up would have more impact on predation than a strip of canvas strung in a tree, but the canvas was visible. It informed the predators that they might face something more than mere canvas to contend with in order to catch their meal.

A hungry predator might be willing to take the chance, but this time of year, most predators were not going hungry. Nutmeg didn't care; he was wise enough to take any advantage he could get and I was inclined to agree with him.

Predators were like bandits—the less we had to do with either of them, the better.

We spent the next three days at the farm, harvesting everything that was ripe that we could scrounge and packing it up to our first cache in the come-along (mostly hay and grain) leaving Nutmeg to rest and eat in the orchard with the colt. I got to practice my wards, levitation and travel magic over and over again, the repetition allowing me to refine it and make it a lot easier to combine.

I threaded wards all around the farm, first look-away stuff, nothing's here, and then go-away spells and finally mind muddling spells so that even if they got past the first two sets of wards, the third set wouldn't allow them to know where they'd finally gotten when, or if, they got there. I couldn't help thinking that we might need them if we remained here as long as I thought it likely to take to gather all the hay and grain we needed, never mind the contents of the garden and the orchard.

Shade and I scouted out a second cache about five miles up the mountain from the first cache, and then Fort, Shade and I ferried the contents of our first cache to the second, using the little come-along and a lot of levitation to get it done. Three more days saw the first cache filled up again. I couldn't say Nutmeg grew fat on the orchard grass while we did it, but he certainly did gain weight. So did the colt.

He'd developed into an inveterate beggar, and not just for hand-outs. He wanted to be rubbed, scratched, and most of all he wanted his leg stroked. He acquired the habit of holding his leg out to me whenever I approached, wanting me to run my hands over it, to pick it up and check it out. It amused me to indulge him.

In a week he started managing to make the trip to the first cache in the evening (with a lot of help from levitation) to spend the night and then back to the farm to graze the orchard in the morning. Traveling the short distance—about a mile and a half as the trail winds, not that there was a trail, there wasn't, and I was taking very great care that there shouldn't be—was good for him.

At the end of the second week, Shade and I left Fort, Wraith and Reve sorting out the new arrivals at second cache and headed out to find another area to use as a cache. About seven miles on, we found another copse of trees set into a hillside much like first cache.

"Winter here?" Shade wanted to know as we investigated it.

"Not enough space," I returned. "It'll make a good hide, but we'd need at least double the room for the horses, and I wouldn't mind being farther from the old farm. I don't like being this close."

"Close?" Shade echoed. "Heck, we're at least twelve miles away, if not more."

"More like thirteen," I agreed. "That's still too close for me. I don't like sticking around even now, but we have to if we want to get enough hay to see the horses through the winter, never mind have enough food for us."

And winter, this high in the mountains, was likely to come in early and leave late. We'd have to have enough food not only to withstand that long winter but to travel on come spring. Places to get food would be few and far between. In that sense, at least, the farm was a godsend. Between the gardens and the orchards and the fields we'd be set, both for winter and for spring and maybe even for a good bit of summer as well, if we were careful.

But there was more than one way of being careful. We set up the lean-tos, tucking them well back into the hillside under cover, taking care not to mark the land or the trees and brush while we did it, bringing the brush we cut to use from far enough away to avoid marking this area. Then we spent the next two days moving our supplies from the second cache to the third and then from the first to the second.

By the time we'd gotten all the hay and corn in, we'd set up a fourth cache another six or seven miles on, and day by day we ferried a load of supplies from each nearer cache to one farther on. I mended some old gunny sacks we found in the barn and cleaned them, and they helped enormously in getting things from one cache to another. A canvas dump we found at the back of the barn turned out to be useful as well. Torn, stained, worn through in places, dirty, they'd been relegated to a pile probably deemed useless. I cleaned them, mended them, and we made more sacks from some of them while retaining the rest of them for use on our lean-tos.

Small sacks of soda and lime, a row of used horseshoes, a couple of rusty pipes with equally rusty fittings and several useful tools traveled from cache to cache in the little come-along with the rest of my hoard. The anvil and the stove awaited final transfer at the fourth cache, but I kept my toolbox with me on the off chance I might need it. I scavenged metal fittings from the burnt out farmhouse, as well as a nice sink. It never ceased to amaze me that men so enjoyed destroying women's homes.

I glanced towards the scorched bones with the thought. I'd have liked to gather them all up and bury them in a nice little marked plot, but we didn't dare to do it, at least not until we'd transferred all the supplies we needed to our

caches. The bandits intermittently using the place might not notice that we'd harvested everything, especially if they came through a month to six weeks from now, but they would notice if the bones were no longer among the ashes and they'd certainly notice new graves. So, giving the remains a decent burial would have to be the last thing we did before we left for the last time.

Threshing the grain seemed to me to take forever. The work was slow, boring and repetitious. We packed up the grain as soon as it was cleaned, filling the huge old crock and the big gallon jars we'd found in the barn that I'd cleaned out and mended, with the wheat, and poured the oats into the canvas sacks we made and sewed closed, once they were filled. Once all our packs were filled, we took a break and carted everything we had up to our fourth cache. Third Harvest was drawing to a close by the time we had managed to get all the wheat and oats harvested and carted up to our fourth cache. Our third cache was full, as well, and our second cache overflowed with straw from the oats and the wheat. We still had the squash and apples to come ripe yet.

It was time for us to find a place to put our winter den.

# XXXII

## LAST CACHE

HUH, I THOUGHT. WE'D FOUND it. Perfect. A good forty miles from the farm- hold, the small hanging meadow contained plenty of grass for the horses, a lovely copse of trees to screen the den skirted it. The den itself could be dug into the shoulder of the hill easily enough—a bit of a start had already been made. A spring, in the exact place I would have put it to be able to direct water to the kitchen, the horses, and the meadow.

Let's see, the storage cabinets would go there—Shade, Fort and Wraith had Nutmeg unloaded by the time I'd finished the first set of ruminations. They pegged Nutmeg and the colt out at the edge of the meadow while Reve and I got busy marking out the den and getting the stove set up. The guys had lean-tos put up for us near the horses by the time I had the piping started, and once the stove was up, Reve fired it up and started cooking. Shade came to help set up the pantry—the sooner we got it up and filled, the sooner we could start getting the third cache cleared out.

I built this den the same way I built the first, with a roof of stone and iron and glass with some wood beams and sheathing here and there and walls of stone with some wooden framework at strategic points. The glass was tinted slightly green, which was all to the good, and only allowed those inside to look out, not those outside to look in. It reflected the branches of the trees back to the observer, making the small copse of trees look a lot bigger and more dense than it actually was. And it was unbreakable, of course.

I made the walls thick, a layer of stone, a layer of packed earth, and then a second layer of stone. The dirt showed through the rough stone here and there and the outer stone work I made to look natural, so that anyone coming into the small meadow would simply see more of the shoulder of the slope than was actually there. The windows were high and narrow and added to the illusion that the outside observer was looking into the copse of pine and oak, disguising the den quite effectively. Then, too, the den wasn't shaped like a house, but more like the side of a hill.

The place wasn't really round, it was more wide than deep, somewhere between six and eight feet behind the stove for the bath and maybe a little over twenty feet from the back of the stove to the front wall. The kitchen area stretched somewhere between eight and ten feet to one side of the stove, and my sleeping alcove on the other side didn't quite make eight, while the area before the stove fanned out in a semi-circle containing the dining space, the gathering area, and two sleeping areas, one for Fort and the other for Wraith and Reve. A door between the bed alcoves opened to a small 'cold' room six feet at the widest point and maybe three feet at the narrowest for additional meat storage.

The stable area, on the other side of the outer wall of my sleeping alcove spanned the area from the 'cold' room to well back into the hill. Nutmeg had the larger space at the back, at something like ten by twelve, while the colt had the smaller loose box in front, at something like ten by eight. By spring I suspected he would be as big as Nutmeg, but it would do for now.

Both Nutmeg and the colt had their own, well-warded, doors, so they could go in and out of their loose boxes at will. I'd set the wards to keep out both predators and the cold, though they had only limited effectiveness at doing the latter. A door in the exterior wall faced the door that opened between my sleeping and study area and the foot of Fort's bed. You could slip out of the house through the pantry behind the kitchen, too, but I hadn't put anything that looked remotely like a door there and it would be a real squeeze to get through the trees, though I supposed that would be all the better since the trees would hide us if we had to slip out.

Hay and straw storage occupied most of the rest of the sheltered area, and I'd used the refurbished pipes to pipe water in for the horses. I calculated that we had just short of about two ton of hay for each of the horses, along with a couple of hundred pounds of oats apiece. Barely enough, but we could peg the horses out in the grass for another month, at least, and maybe, if we were lucky, for the better part of two months.

The farm-hold had been small; maybe a third of an acre of corn, at least a half of an acre of oats, and probably not much over another half of an acre of wheat and all volunteer, at that. And if there had been much over two acres of hay, I would be surprised. Well, if we needed to, we could probably add a little bit of corn to the oats for the horses along through the winter.

The fences I put up, such as they were, consisted of the branches of bushes I wove together, with some dried branches added artistically where breaks in the barrier needed to be blocked. I augmented the bushes and the branches with wards. It wasn't a straight fence, or a square one, or a round one. Regarded as a fence, it look hap-hazard, but then, I wanted it that way. I wanted anyone looking at it not to recognize it as a fence at all. I didn't even want them realizing that it formed a barrier all the way around the meadow. The more people thought it was 'just brush' or 'just a dead branch or two' the better.

Animals, of course, would know it was a barrier and instinct would tell them not to try to cross it. But then, in a lot of ways, animals were smarter than people. I wanted to keep both animals and people out, especially predators, whether they had two legs, or four.

I wound up having to add more storage behind the kitchen, we had so much squash, and we had beans drying just about everywhere, red beans, pinto beans and even black beans. We didn't do too badly in root vegetables, either, and the herbs, greens and garden stuff made for wonderful meals. Give Reve something to cook with besides venison and a few root vegetables, and she could put on soups and stews fit for a king. Or at least for King Marc. He ate soup and stew. I knew, because I'd seen him. I wasn't all that bad a cook, either, when you got right down to it, and even the boys could manage a meal in a pinch, though a little help wouldn't hurt, in their case.

The apples and the squash finished up just about the same time. The boys set up rabbit snares around our various caches every time we made a trip down or back, so I had to start putting together more glass jars and meat containers.

Wraith and I set out frames for the rabbit furs so I could tan the hides for vests and cloaks. A half a dozen rabbits from each cache site added up to a lot of hides, quickly.

Fort found some of the farm-hold's sheep. The poor things hadn't been sheared for a couple of years and they were badly in need of it. Their fleece had all sorts of things caught in it and it was dirty and not very fine, but there certainly was a lot of it.

We sheared them, taking care not to take them down too close to the skin, leaving them a thick layer of fleece, given that winter was coming, and I dug around in my books until I found a spell for cleaning wool. It wasn't very different from the spell I used in cleaning clothes, so I tried it and it worked a

treat. A lot better than trying to pick everything out and then wash the wool as well. It still had to be carded, of course, but Wraith knew how to make a spinning wheel and Reve knew how to use one. Before long, I had applesauce stewing on the back of the stove and a good couple of hours to study every day. Luxury.

Blood month came and we had to hunt. We still had some meat, and of course, there were the rabbits, but five people? Rabbits would run out, even running snares at each of our emptied caches. The rabbits we caught in the snares made a nice change from venison and good stews, but would never provide enough meat for the winter. We'd managed to lay in two nice bucks and had their hides tanning, when we found the little group of cattle.

There weren't many of them, an old bull, two old milk cows, one quite old, from the look of her, and two heifers, a two year old and a calf. A yearling bull calf and a two year old bull completed the family group. The two year old, a big adolescent, kept trying to push the old bull into a fight and the others weren't happy about it, the old cow and what looked like her daughter lowing uneasily and pushing the younger stock away from the combatants. The old bull tried blocking the youngster away, but it was obvious that though he was bigger and stronger, the younger bull was quicker. In a knock-down, drag-out fight, the old bull would probably win in the end, but not before the younger bull got in some pretty good licks and did some real damage to the old bull. It was possible both of them would wind up dead and probable that both would be seriously injured.

We didn't need that much meat, but oh, well. We could always dry it to carry as travel rations for spring. I knelt behind a tree, and before the youngster could gore the old man, I put an arrow behind his elbow. The youngster made a huffing sound, and dropped to his knees. The old bull stepped back, his eyes bright. Lifting his head and bellowing his success, he trotted proudly over to his girls and led them away. The cows looked a lot happier at this point, and they meandered along with him in what looked to be contentment.

The young bull watched them start to leave and tried to get up. I shot him again. This time in the eye. Wraith and Fort and Shade leaped into action, cutting his throat to bleed him out, pulling out my arrows and returning them to me to clean. I eyed the young bull thoughtfully, and turned to Reve.

"That's going to be a lot of meat," I told her. She grinned at me.

"Yes, isn't it?"

# XXXIII

## PALACE CITY

FREDDY WATCHED THE SPIRES OF the city draw closer thoughtfully and wondered if he would be able to get home safely. He knew he didn't look much like Prince Freddy right now and the four full weeks it had taken the trireme to reach the capital city in sun and wind and salt spray had burnished his skin and further whitened his blonde hair and beard. Plus, offering to take a turn at the oars every day had put some muscle in his arms and legs. Not much—it would take more than four weeks to put real muscle on him, but the act of rowing had, as he had known it would, made him invisible to Nehl. He grinned a little to himself as he thought it.

Four weeks on a ninety-six foot trireme, and his brother had never even noticed him, never mind recognized him. The fact that he had managed such a feat amused him. He never intended to inform his brother of his accomplishment, but he could hug it to himself now and again in future to give him a warm little niggle of satisfaction. But Nehl was a blockhead, he told himself as he gathered his gear.

Inserting himself into the ranks of the oarsmen hadn't been difficult. Every oarsman had been a hireling, signed on for the trip, some of them for the round trip, some of them for one way. They'd been more than happy to take a break for a couple of hours and perfectly willing to teach him how to effectively pull an oar and it hadn't taken him long to catch the rhythm of it. Spending three hours at an oar each day had kept the trip from being unutterably boring. He didn't know how Nehl had stood it, just sitting around all day staring at nothing, but then, he supposed that Nehl would have had the same—or an even worse!

Reaction to the idea of spending time at the oars.

The trireme consisted of three banks of oars on each side, two of them before the mast, and one behind the mast and in front of the cuddy where many of their provisions had been stored. A single mast with sail situated well behind the middle of the ship and well before the cuddy provided most of the trireme's motive power, but an interaction between the wind and the oars gave the ship a surprising—at least to Freddy—amount of speed. In the old days, the galleys had carried Nogaynos mages who had called up the wind, according to the legends, allowing the long-ships to make two hundred miles a day.

Well, Freddy thought, with an internal shake of his head, try finding a Nogaynos mage now. The history books might swear up and down that they had existed, but for all of him, they might as well be a myth or a legend. He'd never heard of one, never mind met one.

But still, the galley had made the trip in far less time than it would have taken on foot or on horseback. The trade caravans took a hundred and twenty days of travel time to get from Quattar to the Palace City, and that did not allow for the stop time in the various small towns and settlements along the way where they traded spices and fabric for furs, hides and handcrafted leatherwork to sell in the capital city's markets as well as provisions to get there. The galleys could make six round trips from Quattar to Palace City and back again in the time a caravan could make one round trip.

Freddy wasn't sure how many people each would require. Twenty riders, at least, for a caravan, to guard the pack horses and lead them, with maybe a couple more to scout and lead. He knew the trireme took something like sixty people to manage. Two sets of oarsmen, just to begin, each shift rowing for three hours, then resting and eating for another three while the second shift rowed, and then taking up the oars again. Each man rowed two shifts each day. Freddy knew about that. Then six men to see to the sail and the ropes and the rigging, with two more to spell each other at the rudder and four cooks to keep everybody fed.

The triremes delivered mail, tools, and things too heavy or too awkward to pack on a horse along with the occasional passenger. Space aboard a galley came at a premium. The cuddy provided primitive bunks for four people, and hammocks for four more and that was it (which was why Freddy had tucked himself up inside what amounted to an oiled canvas bag in the small curved space along the stem at the stern of the ship). Storage along the sides of the ship between the ranks of oars was limited. Anything particularly heavy had to be fit somewhere into the middle of the ship to keep it stable in the water, while more fragile or water-sensitive cargo had to go into the cuddy.

Bulky things got stacked in front of and in back of the cuddy, to either side of its doors. Freddy's backpack had fit nicely in his nest in the nook made by the stem of the ship in the stern. What clothing he had brought, and his bedroll served as padding between his body and the bare planking. How his brother had managed the passage, Freddy didn't know (or much care).

Shipping anything on board one of the long-ships was expensive. Speed—all those oarsmen—had to be paid for. Only the wealthy could afford to have goods shipped to them via galley. The mail—well, the government underwrote a portion of the expenses for half a dozen galleys for the right to ship government dispatches on them, with the proviso that the galleys carry a certain amount of regular mail for people for a reasonable fee each trip. It worked to allow the country to remain in contact, as the galleys put in to a select group of small port cities all along their routes.

Of course, neither long-ships nor caravans ran during the winter months of bad weather. Caravans tended to winter in the south, as did most of the long- ship crews. It lengthened the travel season for them.

Before making this trip south, Freddy might have had a cursory knowledge of these facts; now he had a visceral understanding of them.

Big difference. He wondered if Nehl had learned anything at all during their sojourn in the south, doubted it. Nehl, as far as he could see, after watching him brood for the last two weeks, had learned nothing in the last few months.

He wondered what his brother would get up to now. Well, it wasn't his problem, he told himself, as he hefted his backpack in preparation to disembark from the galley. He intended to find a good, mid-range inn, get a hot bath, shave his face, buy himself a new set of clothes, and then present himself at the palace. See what his father had to say about the coup.

And, a mere twenty-four hours later, having followed this agenda, he found himself facing his father in the ante-chamber outside his father's library, drinking tea.

"Your trip seems to have done you good," his father commented, sipping his own tea. "Have you seen your brother?"

"We came up on the same trireme," Freddy told him. "Not that Nehl would acknowledge me. I spent the days taking a shift at the oars. He spent them staring at the horizon."

"So where is he now?" his father inquired.

"Unknown," Freddy admitted. "I cleaned up, brought myself a new set of clothes, and came home. Nehl disappeared." Probably to hunt down a new victim upon which to work off his ill-humors on, Freddy thought, but did not say.

His father nodded.

"We were staying at Bardons' place when your letter came about the coup. I decided that we ought to get ourselves to Southren and surround ourselves with the military contingent. Nehl wasn't too happy about that, and when we left Southren, General Meric saw to it that we had to hire our own guides and horses to make our way back to Quattar. I found a guide and we walked. I carried a single backpack, and left the rest of my boxes for the general to send back whenever it was convenient for him. Nehl hired men and horses and a wagon and brought all of his clobber. It may have taken him some time to get it all unloaded, and then to find someone to get it to the palace."

"Ah," his father said. "The difference between a spy and a Crown Prince, in action." He nodded to himself. "What can you tell me about Bardons?" he wanted to know.

"They didn't yet know that the coup had failed when I left," Freddy pointed out to him, "and I didn't linger long enough in Quattar to learn much on the return trip —I meant to avoid them if at all possible. But I would say that when I left, they were much as usual—mostly arrogant and somewhat stupid."

"You think the failure of the coup would change that much?" his father wanted to know.

"I doubt it," Freddy told him honestly. "Nor do I think it will change D'Arcys much, either. I think they are what they are."

"D'Arcys lost both Dellin and Jahn," his father stated, thoughtfully. "As far as we could tell, Hubare the Younger wasn't with them." He shrugged. "Maybe they were holding him back for some reason, or maybe he got away." He frowned at the thought, not best pleased by it.

"So what are you going to do about them?" Freddy asked him curiously.

"I don't know," his father returned. "I've dissolved the Council for now. I'll continue meeting with Lord Liam, Laren, and General Meric as I consider appropriate, but the rest of them--" he shrugged. "It would be better if I didn't have to see them for a while."

Freddy just nodded. His father leaned forward.

"Can you tell me anything about the Caelian situation?" he wanted to know.

"Meric's frustrated," Freddy told him, thinking back for every detail he could remember. "The archers, supported by cavalry, are effective against the Caelian raiders, but only in the most limited of manners. Too often they're too far from where he needs them when he needs them. He needs more horses—more cavalry. The reason I had to walk out, and that Nehl had to hire both horses and men for the trip to Quattar from outside the fort was because Meric really can't spare them for frivolous travel. He doesn't have enough of either. You want to make him a happy man? Send him a hundred more archers and a hundred more horses."

"Will they be enough?" his father demanded.

"No," Freddy told him frankly, "but they'll put a dent in what he needs."

"Good," his father said. "I'll talk to Laren." He smiled briefly. "Are you up to a court dinner?"

Freddy straightened his shoulders. "Of course."

"Your funeral," his father retorted, with a wry smile. "I'll see you at dinner." Freddy forced himself to smile back.

"I'll look forward to it," he assured his father, mendaciously.

"Good man," his father told him, standing. He clapped Freddy on the shoulder and returned to his library.

Freddy took it as the dismissal it was, relieved to have gotten through it so well. He'd managed, he considered, sitting down again and helping himself to another cookie, to separate himself from his brother in his father's mind, and even to make a few points for himself. Good. Now to take himself back to his rooms and see if he could get himself together for tonight. Not that he expected a large company. Not with Bardons, Jidens, and D'Arcys missing. Oh, well, he thought, not regretting that they wouldn't be present one bit. At least it would be a quiet gathering.

He took himself off to his rooms to see what he could put together in the way of evening dress. He must have something left in his closets that would do.

# XXXIV

# CROWN PRINCE

NEHL AWAKENED. HE HAD NODDED off after the explosive violence of his release after so many days and weeks of frustration. He'd held himself to no more than three girls in Southren, and he'd not managed to indulge himself with his 'hobby' since leaving Southren. Oh, the men he'd hired to see him to

Quattar would have allowed him to rape any unprotected female he'd found between Southren and Quattar, but they wouldn't have allowed him to beat her to death, not that he'd found any females to batter on the trip.

He'd managed to find one in Quattar—well, like any city, Quattar had people held in poverty created by the abuses of the wealthy, making unprotected children and girls easy to find—and satisfy his urges before going aboard ship, but he hadn't had time for any more than one. Unfortunately. After his time in Southren and the trip from Southren to Quattar, he'd had a lot of frustration built up. Now, he raised his head and looked around the stinking corner of the abandoned warehouse in which he'd taken refuge with his last victim. Dingy, dark, filled with shadows, and reeking of fish and refuse, it offended his sensibilities, if the very idea that he had sensibilities, after what he had done to the girl lying in the dirt not six feet away from him didn't comprise an absurdity beyond comprehension.

He pushed himself up on hands that ached. His skinned knuckles were bloody; he thought perhaps he'd broken a bone or two in his fingers. He shrugged to himself, and pushed farther upright. He'd make a visit to the palace infirmary and get his hands fixed up when he had cleaned up and gotten himself better dressed into something befitting a prince.

He pushed himself all the way to his feet, and ignoring the blood on his hands and his shirt, walked out of the warehouse into broad daylight. He'd sent all but a basic duffle up to the palace. Collecting his duffle now, he took himself off to the nearest inn, neither noticing or caring that it fell onto the lower rungs of its kind, and ordered a bath and a meal. The water of the bath was tepid, at best, and not particularly clean, but he didn't notice. Lassitude dragged at him, and by the time he had finished his meal, he was ready for a nap. He made no particular attempt to barricade the door, though he had quite a bit of money on him, and no one tried to break in to get it. Perhaps the blood put them off (more fool them). Or maybe the devil takes care of his own. (More likely.)

In the morning, he got up, washed his face, slicked back his hair, dressed in his best remaining clothing, and took himself to the palace and the infirmary there. It took but a matter of moments to see his hands healed, since he could command the best of the healers to his service, and he headed back into the palace again. Finding his boxes had already arrived, he changed clothing— again! and went in search of—what, he didn't quite know. (Or care.)

Finding Laren in the yard, he allowed himself to be chivied into a bout of arms, which his sparring partner allowed him to win, despite his mediocre skills. Well, after all, he was the Crown Prince.

Appearing (uninvited) at dinner, he was not surprised to sit down to his regular place, set and ready for him. He had not sufficient understanding to realize what had gone into that feat by the staff, the rumors on the grapevine that he had returned, the rushing around to gather and prepare a few of his favorite dishes to welcome him home, the extra work for the servants in preparing his room and laying out his clothing. He wouldn't have cared if he had realized it. He wasn't even surprised when his father greeted him as if he'd been at dinner every night for the last month and he had nothing of substance to say to his father when King Marc inquired about his stay in the south.

He complained, instead. General Meric, he informed his father, was insolent and insubordinate, his men were dirty, slovenly, and rude, and none of them had paid him the proper respect. As far as he was concerned, they were nothing but a bunch of swaggering fools. The Caelian, he said, were no more than vermin, and ought to be exterminated. How this was to be accomplished, he did not elaborate. That was for somebody else to figure out. And do.

He had nothing to say about either Bardons or D'Arcys, dismissing them out of hand as in-bred imbeciles. Quattar society he found boring, the city itself undistinguished, and the ocean views insipid. He shrugged at the notion that the women of Quattar were generally found to be particularly beautiful and the sport fishing for which the city was renowned, deadly.

"So," his father summed up, "you pretty much have nothing good to say about anybody or anything."

Nehl bridled. He wanted to take offense at that; he intuited that his father's summation found him wanting, but he couldn't figure out how. When his father asked him if there was anything at all in which he took an interest, Nehl actually considered the question. The honest answer, that the only thing that quickened his blood was the thought of hunting down another young girl and beating her to death, he was smart enough to know wouldn't find any favor with his father.

Barring that, he couldn't think of anything.

So he just frowned. His father regarded him thoughtfully, noting the scarred knuckles with their fresh abrasions and the bandages on his fingers.

"I wonder what would happen if you were to be taken out into the middle of the high plains with a knife and a bow and a knapsack with some supplies and left to find your own way?" he mused aloud.

Nehl stared at him, aghast. "What?" he gaped.

"Would you make it back out? Do you think?" his father challenged him. Nehl didn't even consider it.

"You wouldn't!" he protested.

"The very fact that I formulated the question means I have considered it," his father informed him.

"But—but—bu--" Nehl burbled.

"You haven't asked after your brother," his father pointed out next, shifting his grounds.

"He's fine," Nehl assured him, with a shrug.

"How do you know that?" his father asked him.

"He's always fine," Nehl tossed off.

"You think so?" his father asked. "Where is he now?"

Nehl looked around himself, as if he would be able to see his brother at the table. And, in fact, there he was, seated with Lord Liam's family, chatting amiably with the Lord's older, horse-faced daughter.

He gestured. "He's right there," he said.

"Did you know it before you looked?" his father inquired of him.

Well, the honest answer was, no, he had not. But instead of admitting that, he said,

"Of course." Freddy always did fall on his feet, he thought, resentfully. He knew that Freddy was making points with his father by his engagement with Lord Liam's family. Damn him. He turned his head to regard Garve`, sitting stolidly to the other side of Freddy, silent and stoic. At least Garve` was not cutting him out with his father. He almost sneered at the sight of him. Not that Garve` could, useless bump on a log that he was.

King Marc regarded him a long moment in silence, as if he intuited that his son was lying to him, but then he let it go. Nehl felt his collar tighten around the base of his neck. He refrained from sticking a finger under it to pull it loose. He knew he'd lost his father's approbation, not that he realized he'd never had it.

Instead, he told himself that it all went back to that pestilent girl. If his father had never found out about her, he'd still be King Marc's fair-haired boy, but now he could not think of any way to get back into his father's good graces.

Too bad, he couldn't help but think, that he hadn't managed to kill the girl. Dead girls, he had discovered, told no tales. If he'd killed her, and quietly had her body disposed of, there wouldn't ever have been any contretemps to begin with. Though why his father cared about a little whore—all women and girls were whores as far as Nehl was concerned, no matter how unspotted their innocence—he would never know.

"It's a good thing you weren't here during the coup," his father commented then, apropos of nothing, as far as Nehl could see. "Jiden's men made a try for Garve`, but he and his guards managed to hold them off until we could get there to help. No doubt if you and Freddy had been here he would have sent men to see you both off as well."

Nehl considered that. He wasn't sure just what his father was saying. Was he glad that Nehl hadn't been in danger? Did he think that Nehl might have been a target? What?

"I would rather have been fighting with you," Nehl finally responded, carefully. Maybe, he thought, with a touch of resentment, if he had been there, with his sword, Jiden's men might have managed to kill his father. Maybe with one more sword, it would have tipped the balance.

The idea that he had either skill or fortitude enough to have made a difference, on either side of the conflict, was ludicrous, but Nehl would never understand that.

"Fighting beside me, do you mean?" his father wanted to know, with a lift of one eyebrow, "or against me?"

"Beside you, of course," Nehl assured him. King Marc nodded to him.

"We were pretty well prepared," he returned. As if to say, 'your sword wasn't needed'. "But the conspirators had hired around a hundred mercenaries to fill out their household guards, and if it hadn't been for the choke-points we'd arranged, we would have had a much harder time with them."

"Choke points?" Nehl heard himself echoing.

"Positions where physical barriers allowed a few of our men to control which and how many of their men could get into the palace," his father explained, as if Nehl shouldn't have learned all about choke-points in his lessons years before.

Nehl nodded as if he understood. It was still about as clear as mud to him, but he didn't dare to say so. He understood enough to know that continuing to ask for clarification made him look stupid. Not that he believed he was stupid; he didn't. He just hadn't bothered to remember trivial things like 'choke- points'. That didn't make him stupid, he told himself. Just selective in what he bothered to think about. That was all.

"There was actual fighting?" he faltered, remembering Jiden's promises that no one would be killed but his father. Not that he had cared, really, but it had sounded good.

"Oh, yes," his father assured him easily. "Quite a bit of it, actually." He frowned in remembrance. "It was really a perfect example of penny proud, pound foolish. There were more of them, but our people were much better armed and armored. If their men had been outfitted with better armor, just one case in point, we would have had a much more difficult time with them. We

could strike through their armor and they couldn't strike through ours, which made holding the choke points a good deal easier, not that a few of them didn't get through some of the private back entrances. Well," he concluded, more to himself than to Nehl, "we've shored those up. Nobody's getting through them now."

He was attempting to warn his son away from making another try for the throne, but from Nehl's expression, that warning completely missed him. He appeared wholly oblivious to his father's intent. Instead, he returned to the beginning of the story.

"They went after Garve`?" he wondered.

"And me," King Marc nodded to him, marking the question with internal interest. Had Nehl not meant them to take out Garve`? "We had to take them down in the throne room where they came together. I don't know though," he commented, "whether they'd merely have fought among themselves if we

hadn't been there to take them all down. They might have. They didn't seem to have figured out which one of them ought to occupy the throne. Jahn D'Arcy apparently thought it was to be him, while Matias Bardon had planned to take the throne for himself and his family. Jiden got there first, of course, intending to claim it for himself."

"Huh," Nehl grunted. "Then Freddy was right."

"About what?" King Marc wanted to know.

"Getting us out of Bardons' place before they found out about the coup. He insisted we get to Southren, where the military could protect us." He appeared to consider this. "I thought it was a crock," he observed, "but he might have saved both our lives."

"He probably did," King Marc retorted.

Bastards, Nehl thought viciously. They never did intend to put him on the throne. No wonder his father had sent them away from court.

"You ought to hang them," he advised.

"We did," his father assured him. "We got them all, every one of them who was involved in the conspiracy."

"And their families," Nehl insisted.

"Well, now, that might be a different story," King Marc objected. "Who is to say that any one of the women had anything to do with the coup? Why, they might have tried to talk their stubborn relations out of it and been ignored. And as for the children, well, they didn't have anything to do with it, either. No," he concluded, "we got the main troublemakers, and while some of the men left at home might have harbored ill-intentions towards you and Freddy while you were there, they may have learned the error of their ways by now."

"I don't know," Nehl equivocated unhappily. Unfortunately, he didn't have any difficulty believing that either D'Arcys or Bardons had intended to put one of their own on the throne instead of him. (It was what he would have done in their place!)

"If you find out anybody else in those three families up to no good, you let me know," his father advised him. He didn't say what he'd do about whatever suspicions his son had, but Nehl didn't notice that, nor the limits that his father put on his advice by stipulating 'those three families'. He just nodded, and settled back into a brown study.

Maybe, the thought drifted through his mind briefly, as he attempted to grasp the problems inherent in the information his father had given him, he would go out and find himself another girl to entertain him tonight. The pressure eased from his shoulders at the very thought. Yes, he told himself, he'd do that. It would take his mind off things.

He didn't specify what things. He just settled back in his chair and checked out mentally. It would never have occurred to him to attempt graciousness, to make himself amusing to the people around him, and even if it had, he wouldn't have known how or had any idea why he ought to do it. Tasked with such a question, he would have said it was their duty to amuse him, not his to entertain them, but as it was, no one bothered him and he was able to sink into his own reverie, in which the sound of a young girl's muted agony and the feel of her bones breaking under his fists occupied all his attention. He registered his father turning away from him to speak to Lord Liam, but he didn't care about the elderly (from his standpoint) lord, and he ignored it. Within an hour he had taken himself off to his bed, bored and stupid with it, his movements lethargic.

Finding his bed, he dropped into sleep, forgetting to remind himself to get up in the night to find another victim. It didn't matter to him. Tomorrow was another day. He could go hunting then, if he felt like it.

# XXXV

## SECOND WINTER

S O WE WERE SET. WE had enough wool so that we could all have new woolen sweaters and trousers and new blankets, once we got the wool spun to thread and a loom to weave it into fabric on. We had all the meat we'd need, with plenty to dry to have to take with us when we headed out in the spring. We had ample apples, and plenty of dried berries to make pemmican with, as well as to eat over the winter. I could rest.

Wraith, Fort and Shade made a table and chairs, and bed-frames to hold our freshly filled mattresses. I had my little combination chest, desk, and book- shelf. We spent some time during the evenings trying to figure out where we could be found on the map I had. Once we'd satisfied ourselves that we had our position located accurately—well, within a few miles here or there—we had been able to find one of the old mountain passes into Nogaynos and the best way to reach it.

If the map was accurate. It might not be. It was an old map, and things changed in a hundred years or more. Trees grew. Landslides happened.

Streams even changed course sometimes. Occasionally the two were even connected. But, even with all that considered, a pass still ought to remain a pass, of sorts, at least, and this pass appeared to travel generally southwest, so if we angled over the shoulder of our mountain, we ought to be able to drop down onto it readily enough, though we might have to either back-track or go around a bit in order to join it.

The colt should be ready to go by spring. He had almost lost his limp already. He just favored his leg a little now and again. Give it another week and I'd pull that shoe, trim his feet up a bit and let him go barefoot again. I'd cut the pad out and his foot looked to be healing nicely. The swelling had gone down within a few days of my opening the abscess and draining it, so it shouldn't take long to finish healing.

I named the colt Jagr, just because, really. He seemed quite happy with having landed in our midst. He had Nutmeg for an equine companion, he had plenty of food and water and people to wait on him. He got brushed every day, he could be in or out, as the spirit moved him, so he could get just as much exercise as he wanted and he didn't seem to have any trouble identifying the Mahdi wolves with the people he knew. Shade was Shade to him, regardless of whether he was two-legged or four, and the same for Reve, Fort and Wraith.

They might have been dogs for all the attention he paid their four-legged personas. Perhaps he had learned his nonchalance from Nutmeg. He certainly copied enough of Nutmeg's other mannerisms. Good thing Nutmeg was such a good role model.

We had a good, hard freeze, long before Blood month was over, and nothing would have it but that we added a pig to the larder, since we knew that there were pigs in the area. Somewhere. Wraith wanted bacon and Reve mentioned ham, and both Shade and Fort reminded everyone of sausage, mentioning that with all the apples we had, surely we could have apple sausage?

It took the boys three days to cut the scent, but once they did, they were off.

I couldn't keep up. Reve stayed back with me and the boys managed to herd the pigs in a circle. I brought down one of them, a hefty youngster that probably wouldn't dress out at too much more than two hundred pounds. Reve and I went back to the den for Nutmeg and the come-along, with Jagr following along for the fun of it.

Once we got the pig home, we spent the next three days dealing with it, but Fort and Shade got their apple sausages—good thing Reve knew how to make them, because I didn't—and we cured hams and bacon and ate barbequed ribs and everybody was pleased. The honey we had from the farm's bees allowed us to honey cure the hams, pleasing Reve, and the rest of us, too, when we roasted one.

After that, we passed an idyllic winter. I took the colt's shoe off, trimmed up all four feet, and within a week he was running around the meadow without a hint of a limp. I had ample time to study and to update my travel journal and the maps I worked over so assiduously, updating the old maps in the map-book, when it seemed appropriate, making new ones when only new maps would do, annotating both with modern information. The old book I had dated from the era before the diaspora, more than a hundred and fifty years ago. I had to expect it to be out of date. The information in my journal, and the new maps I was drawing would bring that older data up to date.

When I wasn't studying, I was either making more arrows or practicing martial arts with Shade and Fort. Reve and Wraith tried to teach us as much as they knew about sword-work, and we practiced whanging at each other pretty much every day, though Reve made us blunt the tips of our blades. Mostly we practiced with shields we made by hand, but sometimes we sparred with swords and knives, and other times just swords. Each of us spent some time each day cutting wood, as well, which built muscle and stamina. So did snow-shoeing, after it started snowing, which it did in the middle of Blood month.

The stove was a good one, providing both a cooking surface and heat, with a small oven for roasting and baking, but it still required wood to burn. I estimated we'd go through two cords before the winter was through, so we took the little come-along out and gathered up all the dried branches and dead trees we could find to cut up for firewood and dragged the sectioned branch-wood back to the den. I got plenty of practice in using levitation and 'travel' together to keep from laying any trails that might lead to our den. I hoped we were too far away from the farm and the bandits to have to worry about them, but better safe than sorry. If they couldn't find a trail leading to us, I thought it far less likely they would actually find us.

The month of Snow lived up to its name. By old Nick's night, we had nearly a foot of snow on the ground, and it stayed through Bitter and Ice and well into Thaw. High in the mountains where we had wintered, the snow had packed up to eight feet in some places, and ten in others already, and it was not in any hurry to melt. Long before Spring, it had reached the gargantuan height of twenty feet.

While below us the season was shifting towards Mud, our environs were still encased in ice. Thaw came late to the mountains and when it finally did come, it shifted through Mud to Bud so quickly we almost missed Mud altogether.

We shifted packs around through the month of Bud, rearranging what to carry over and over, getting ready to leave. Impatient to get on the trail, we took off long before all the snow and ice had gone. Patches of it lingered in the shadows under the trees when we started out for the pass and the air still held a distinct chill. But we were antsy. We wanted to get going. No more den winters for us! We meant to spend the next winter in Nogaynos in a real house and we might need all the time we could squeeze into the travel season to fix up one of the old Mages' ruins.

So, one fine, crisp, breezy spring day along towards the end of Bud, we started out, carrying all the provisions we had remaining, making a fine little procession as we started out onto a trail still packed with snow in the high places, Fort in the lead. Shade followed with me and the come-along, followed in their turn by Nutmeg and Jagr. Reve and Wraith brought up the rear.

Nobody bothered to lead either of the horses, they didn't need to be led, and leaving them free meant that they could snatch a bite to eat along the way wherever one became available. Nutmeg certainly wasn't going to try to push the come-along, and Jagr was more than willing to keep to his place behind Nutmeg. He, after all, was still a baby.

At first we were able to pretty much just follow our noses southwest, but when we reached the spine of the mountain, we realized that we were going to have to backtrack a little to reach the pass. Ahead of us, as far as we could see, the shale sides of mountains dropped too sharply to the trail to be negotiated safely, so back we went, along the side of the mountain as best we could, trying to keep the pass in sight, at least now and again, even as we traveled the wrong way. We had no trail to follow, we just slipped and slid along as best we could, adjusting our rate of travel and our formation as it seemed to suit us and the terrain we traveled best, hoping we'd reach a point where we could drop onto the trail sooner rather than later.

We formed an interesting little convoy as we trundled along the side hills, the Mahdi wolves spread out in front of me, threading through the trees. Then I would follow with my bulky pack sticking up over my head and the come-along trundling along behind me, heavily loaded, with high sides and big, hefty wheels on its narrow chassis, levitation holding it steady and 'travel' keeping it moving. After the come-along, Nutmeg minced over the ground, his multiple packs bulging out on each side and above as well, making it difficult for him to go between some trees, so that he was always having to duck back and find a wider way.

It wasn't a heavy pack, really, but the bed bags, though not heavy, stuck out all over, bulky and awkward. Last of all, behind Nutmeg, and almost obscured by Nutmeg's ridiculous bed-bag mountain of pack, came Jagr, wide-eyed, looking everywhere and throwing dance steps into his stride every now and again out of pure excitement.

It took us a day and a half to reach a place where we could slide down through the pine needles and shale to the trail that would lead us through the mountains. 'Travel' was out of the question in that tricky going. But once we got onto the trail, there, I could activate the 'travel' spell and I did, at once, though I can't say it did us much good. The trail was old, and looked as if it hadn't been used for at least a generation, possibly two. Then again, maybe I was being conservative again. Overgrown in some places, most of the rest of the path was rocky and if you'd told me it had been four generations since anyone had walked this ground, I could have believed it. We had to stop for the night where the trail allowed us, other-wise, we'd have to stop in the middle of the trail, which was not always very wide. In fact most of it wasn't very wide.

In some places, the trail followed the stream that followed the ravine created by two mountains coming together, while in other places it climbed up above the stream, curving around the side of the mountain in a narrow ribbon. Some of the slopes were forested, some were mostly shale with the occasional pocket of wild-flowers. Many of them were rather steep, and on all of them, the footing was slippery and treacherous.

As the days went by and more of the snow melted above us, the stream ran higher and faster and I feared for the trail we were following. If the stream flooded it, all we'd be able to do was to either go up, or go back. I wasn't at all sure that we'd be able to do either, once we confronted water across the trail.

We might even find ourselves trying to do both. We tried to arrange it so that we camped at night in the higher areas, just watering ourselves thoroughly in the areas where the water was easy to reach and filling our canteens for the sections of trail where we traveled far above it.

I didn't expect to find people on this apparently little used mountain pass and we didn't meet anyone. Neither did we see sign that anyone lived in this rugged wilderness. If there were any villages in these mountains, they had been well hidden. Hey, if there were even any homes around about, we didn't find them. We didn't even see any sign of habitation despite periodically, whenever it was feasible, climbing to a high point above the trail and surveying the path ahead.

We tried to see where it was eventually taking us but failed. Too many mountains surrounded us for us to see very far. We tried to spot smoke from a hearth-fire (or even a camp fire) but saw nothing. We looked for the peak of a roof, signs of a fence, or a stable, sheep or cattle and found nothing. No walls, no trails (other than the pass we followed, if you could call it a trail, at this point) nothing that could, by the greatest stretch of the imagination, indicate a village, farm, or ranch.

About the only positive we could say was that though we could see the winding snake of what passed for a trail through the mountains for miles ahead of us, the water never overtook it, though here and there it came a bit close. The supplies we'd saved from the farm, the variety of meat, venison, beef, pork, the squash and the root vegetables all stood us in good stead, though we laid snares for rabbits where we could and gathered more herbs and roots wherever we found the plants that provided them.

Occasionally, when the trail didn't widen out enough for camping, we climbed out of the ravine and camped in the first flat area we could find large enough for all of us. Sometimes we had to do it to find enough grass for the horses. Our supplies of oats and corn grew thin, and I developed the habit of counting out the pounds of meat remaining to us, as well as celebrating every rabbit we caught.

# XXXVI

## MOUNTAIN SPRING

THE MAP, WHEN CONSULTED, ADVISED us that the pass would take us just about three hundred miles into the interior, and that it tended to the west and the south in about equal degrees, although it wound about a good bit doing it. Given the mountains all around us, I didn't imagine we would find an easier route, or a straighter one. At forty miles a day, or more likely thirty, three hundred miles wouldn't seem like much, but at the rate we were traveling, twenty miles a day seemed a lot more accurate. At one point we reached, rather high on the side of the mountain, half the trail had washed out, leaving little more than a thread no more than a foot wide indented into the shale both above and below it. We all stopped and regarded it unhappily.

The wolves could get over in on four legs, if it didn't slide out from under-neath them, and admittedly, it was less likely to do it under them than anyone else, given that their weight would be spread out over their four legs. I could probably make it over it. Maybe. Under the proviso that I was lighter than anyone other than possibly Shade. Maybe even Jagr could make it, though I considered that less likely, since he outweighed me by several hundred-weight, but Nutmeg would never get the packs over it, and the come-along was out of the question. So was leaving our supplies. So, we could either back up until we could find a place to climb the slope and try to go around, or we could back up until we could find a place to turn around and go all the way back the way we had come.

Last of all, and this still meant backing up a considerable way, we could back up until we were completely clear of the slide area, all the way back to where we had camped the night before, and I could pull out my books and see if I could find a way to cut back the side of the mountain and make new trail. I wasn't much in favor of that one. I didn't like the idea of the responsibility falling all on my shoulders. What if I couldn't do it?

Well, we didn't have to make the decision right away. The first thing we had to do was to back up. This didn't mean much for me and the wolves. All we had to do was to turn around and face back. Nutmeg and the colt didn't have room to do that. Reve gave Wraith and Fort her saddle-bag packs, changed into her wolf, scrambled around Nutmeg, me and the come-along, slipping and sliding through the shale until my heart took up lodging in my throat, and finally managed to come out on the trail in front of Jagr.

I'll give the colt credit. He stood quietly, regarding her patiently as she changed back to two legs, dressed (it was too chilly not to) and took hold of his head with one hand, putting her other hand on his chest. Gently, she coaxed him to back up, which the colt did, obediently, and again patiently, feeling for each step, for no less than a hundred yards, before the trail widened out enough for him to turn. She led him back, then, until there was room for Nutmeg to back into the area and then turn himself. Then she kept hold of both the horses while I went back for the come-along, which, with levitation and 'travel', I managed to get back to where she was holding the horses. Wraith passed me on the way, jumping over the come-along with his wife's pack in his mouth—it was still a bit chilly, this high in the mountains, even though it had to be the beginning of Bloom by then—and then Fort and Shade did the same just because they could.

Wraith sent the two of them scrambling up the side of the mountain from there, to see if going over the top was going to be a possibility. The two of them came back shaking their heads, which was not good news. Going around, they did not think, was going to be a possibility, unless we went a lot farther than they had in the time they had taken.

"What about a place to camp?" I wondered.

"Not the best, but not the worst, either," Fort allowed, which I did not find encouraging; we'd camped some pretty poor places on this section of our trip. One memorable camp had been so steep we started sliding down hill whenever we fell asleep, and that had included the horses.

"There's a semi-flat place up-hill a ways," Shade added, "with some grass for the horses and I smelled rabbits."

Good enough for me. We packed up and, with Shade and Fort leading, headed up to this 'flat place'. That Shade, I thought, as I used both levitation and 'travel' to get the come-along up the hill behind the horses, always good for an under-statement. 'Up-hill a ways'. Ri-i-ght.

But he was right about the grass, and, if we snuggled up close, even an area level enough for all of us to sleep without having to be afraid we'd start sliding down the hill. I got started unpacking Nutmeg. Reve started putting together the camp, with Wraith's help. Fort and Shade set out rabbit snares. Once I got Nutmeg unpacked, I dumped my own pack and got the fire started for Reve.

Then I went to the highest point I could see from camp and looked out over the trail, looking for landmarks.

The plain fact of the matter was, I had no idea how to safely undercut that hillside so that we could widen the trail to something safe, and still shore it up so it wouldn't slide out from under our feet at the same time, and I didn't think a few hours cramming in my books was going to do the trick. I had a feeling we were going to have to go up and over and then down again, and we might have to go quite a way before we found a safe way to get back down to the trail again. However, I went and got the book of maps and started trying to find where we were on the trail and what the maps said about the topography we might have to travel over. I hoped we might even be able to cut across country to a different trail that would take us the way we needed to go. Why not? I thought. This had once been an inhabited land, even if rather sparsely.

At least I had a few hours of daylight left to pore over my maps. We were still too short of food to be able to waste good travel time trying to figure out a route, even if Shade's and Fort's snares turned up a rabbit in time for breakfast. I thought of stories I'd read as a kid about people moving places by wagon and having to tie wagons to trees and winch them down mountain sides from tree to tree. I didn't want to have to do that, but I didn't think my levitation skills were equal to getting Nutmeg or Jagr safely down that cliff side, never mind the come-along. Although, now I considered it, the come-along might be easier. I wasn't sure. For it, I'd have to use 'travel' and levitation, but then again, I'd been pairing the two of them to get the thing down the trail for days, now.

I thought about trying to get Jagr and Nutmeg down the slide on the other side of the narrow section of trail again, using 'travel' and levitation. I might have been willing to attempt it, if the section of trail I'd be landing them on would be more than maybe two feet wide at the most. And I had to wonder, too, how solid the footing would be once I got them there, always assuming I did, which might be assuming much too much. So no, I really didn't like that option and if the option of widening the trail was out as well, and I really thought it was, that left only heading out across the mountain if we were to go on. I wasn't real fond of that one, either.

Still stewing over the maps when twilight deepened to the point where I couldn't see any longer, I still hadn't found anything solution to our problem. I made myself stop and put the book of maps away. Shade bumped shoulders with me as we headed to our bedrolls.

"We'll head out in the morning and do some scouting, just the two of us," he offered. "We'll find a way, and then you can 'travel' us back to get everyone else."

He was right. With just the two of us, we could travel faster, even without 'travel' to aid us, then the whole group could go together. Here there was grass for the horses, and a rest for Nutmeg wouldn't hurt, since he was carrying the heaviest pack. Well, except for the come-along. But it didn't get leg-weary.

And, with any luck, Fort could come up with a few more rabbits while we were gone.

"If we can go by the map, if we can get about thirty miles or so across country, we can cut another trail that will take us almost due south," I told him, as I prepared to roll down into my sleeping blankets. "The question is, can we get across that thirty miles."

Shade considered that.

"We'd better tell the folks to give us three days," he concluded.

"At least," I agreed.

We lucked out. In the morning there were two rabbits in the snares, so we had a good breakfast before taking off.

It took us four days to work our way through to the alternate pass to the south, and then get back to the group, and even then, the best we'd been able to find would be an eight foot slide on shale to the trail. We'd be lucky if Nutmeg didn't scrape his legs up on it on the way down, and I'd need to use every bit of my skill and my magic so that he could make it safely, unless we unloaded him at the top of the slide and then sent him down without his load. The come- along—well, we could winch that down from a tree at the top, and we could do the same thing with Nutmeg's packs. It would take us all day, or maybe even two days, to get everything down onto the trail, but I wasn't sure I cared about that.

The trail itself wasn't particularly narrow at that point, nor very high up the hillside. If the horses came down a little sideways, they would be able to jump themselves up the trail easily enough when they landed, and there they'd be.

Too, about three miles on, the trail widened out to a nice, grassy little swale where the horses could get some grass. It was pretty wet right about now, but we could sleep up above it comfortably enough, and the horses could use the time we were getting our packs and the come-along to the trail to rest and eat.

Shade and I marked the track we meant them to follow coming back so Fort and Wraith and Reve wouldn't have to guess where to go once we took to the cut-off. It made it take more time to get back to them than just traveling as rapidly as we could would have, but Fort had followed us to the peak of the mountain so he could keep track of us and report back to Reve and Wraith on our progress. It took three days to get Nutmeg and the come-along over the top of the mountain (the come-along was the real hold-up) but at least Nutmeg and Jagr were well rested for the trip.

We had climbed quite high into the mountains at that point, probably something between seven and eight thousand feet, so the snow all around us didn't exactly surprise me. Down in the valley I knew we'd be coming up on First Harvest, but here, Thaw still dominated, first Bud just beginning. This high in the mountains the growing season would be short and intense. In one day, I'd swear we first gained and then dropped a thousand feet, with another thousand the first day of climbing and yet another thousand in downslope the third day. We probably dropped another five hundred feet from where we unloaded Nutmeg to where we made camp for the night.

Once unloaded, Nutmeg danced and slid down the shale bank on his wrapped legs as easily as if he was trying out for an acrobatic troupe and then danced up the trail as if swaggering. Jagr followed him without a bobble, and both allowed us to unwrap their legs with an attitude that said to us that as far as they were concerned, they'd never needed the wraps in the first place. Maybe they hadn't, but I was glad I'd used them. This way their legs stayed blemish free, without so much as a scratch or a scrape.

Reve tossed the lighter packs down to Shade and to me, and Wraith and Fort belayed the rest of them from separate trees, but it didn't take nearly as long, with all five of us working at it, to get Nutmeg's load down to the trail as I had expected. We did have to rope the come-along to get it down to the trail. Fort and Wraith belayed it from their individual trees, so that it had to be pretty carefully coordinated, but soon enough, we had it down on the trail as well, and then all we had to do was to get the packs and the come-along down the trail to the camp-site Shade and I had found.

That took three trips, even with all of us carrying a bag each trip, but we managed to get everything to the high ground just before dark. Shade and Fort had even contrived to snare a couple of rabbits while the rest of us finished ferrying the last of the packs from the slide to camp. We headed out just after dawn, the people more in need of another rest day than the horses, but eager to see how far we could get before nightfall, now we had a decent trail to follow.

We made good time. We were losing elevation now, gradually, it was true, and it had to be admitted that in places the trail had suffered considerable damage from erosion and the weathering of more than a century without traffic, but we traveled more south than west, now. I think we all felt that the end of the trail would soon come into sight.

We had reached Nogaynos. Our maps assured us of that. And, if they were to be believed, we had penetrated well into the northern mountains that bounded the land of the magicians. Now all we had to do was to find one of the old mages' deserted strongholds, and we'd be set.

If occupied, surely those who lived there could tell us where to find an unoccupied holding we could renovate and live in, and if not occupied, well, perhaps the holding would do for us. If not, my books assured me that we would be able to find more, now that we had finally arrived in the land of legends and myths, dreams and fantasies.

# XXXVII

## KING MARC

**"I** AM WORRIED ABOUT YOUR BROTHER," King Marc mentioned to Garve`, as his son settled into a chair on the other side of the tea table. "At times he seems very like he did before his trip south, bored and restless and generally out of sorts, but at other times he seems distracted and lethargic."

"I know," Garve` agreed. "It must have something to do with that failed coup."

"Oh, I'm sure it has," King Marc assured him. "Nehl thought Jiden meant to kill me and put him on the throne and he has been forced to realize that Jiden never intended to do any such thing, and that if he'd been here that night, Jiden would have tried to have him assassinated right along with me and you. He's having a hard time making sense of it. That much I know. But there's something else going on I don't know about."

"What?" Garve` asked blankly.

"It's something Freddy knows about," King Marc told him. "Freddy made some hard decisions while they were down south, some smart decisions, and got them out and away from Bardons' place before they could be killed, and Nehl's just beginning to realize it. And Freddy made what was, for him, the really tough call to leave Nehl behind and come home when Nehl wouldn't listen to reason. The old Freddy," he pointed out, "wouldn't have done that."

"No. . ." Garve` agreed with him. "That surprises me."

"It surprises me, too," King Marc allowed. "But Freddy did it. He walked from Southren to Quattar with a single guide, and carried his own pack on the trip as well. General Meric told me all about it."

"Freddy?" Garve` almost squeaked it.

"Freddy," his father assured him. "And, the captain of the longship told me that Freddy rowed a shift on the oars every day, as well. That's why he's looking as muscular and fit as he is."

"And why his hair's so white," Garve` nodded, trying to consider what such a turnabout for his younger brother meant. "So Freddy wasn't involved in the coup?" he more asked himself than his father.

"Oh, no," King Marc shook his head. "He was involved, all right. But the failure of the coup seems to have shaken him up, made him look at things in a different light. I think it quite possible that the coup didn't happen quite the way he and Nehl had planned for it to go—and not at all the way they had been told it would. At least Freddy realized that if he and Nehl had been here when it took place, that Jiden and his people would have tried to kill Nehl and Freddy as well as you and me. It made Freddy think, apparently. Too bad," he added, almost under his breath, "that it didn't do the same thing for Nehl."

"Freddy's always been smarter than Nehl," Garve` commented, more to himself than his father.

"He's younger, and third in line for the throne," King Marc reminded him. "He wasn't nearly as spoiled as Nehl. Neither of you boys were. Margrete made Nehl stupid."

Garve` didn't address the concept of how anyone could make anyone else stupid. It wasn't something he was equipped to deal with.

"Maybe Nehl is finding it hard to deal with the failure of the coup. I know I've been having difficulty with the whole idea that Councilor Jiden and two other noble families were willing to try one." And Garve` shook his head in incomprehension.

"I think that was King Bane," his father told him. "I think he put Jiden up to it. I don't think it's an accident that Jiden's trade comes out of the south, or that D'Arcys and Bardons live in the south."

"You would think that they'd know better than to deal with the bastard," Garve` commented, almost bitterly. "After all the Amadeans he's killed or taken captive."

"Bane's men haven't taken any of the wealthy," his father lessoned him.

"They take the farmers and the ranchers who live in the foothills and the villages to the south and the east of the mountains. Most of them are poor, or middle class at best. The wealthy ranchers and the families with large, richly producing farms are able to keep enough hired men around to fight off the Caelian raiders, at least the smaller groups of them and are not often harassed. Add the natural arrogance and stupidity of both the Bardons and the D'Arcys, and their complete and bloody-minded disregard for the less fortunate and I doubt they can even conceive of the possibility that Bane could be dangerous to them. They probably think they're putting something over on him!"

Garve` blinked, considering it.

"Has Meric ever thought of putting a bunch of men on one of the abandoned farms or ranches?" he wondered. "They could work the land while they're on the lookout for the raiders, maybe even raise enough food to feed themselves while they're at it."

"That's a great idea!" King Marc grabbed a piece of paper and started to write excitedly. "They could keep half a dozen horses there, too," he added, jotting a note down to himself to remember the idea. "It's more expensive feeding the horses than it is providing them to the men in the first place," he told Garve`. "If the men could raise some hay, some vegetables, some pigs, a few cattle here and there, it would go far to alleviate the expense of maintaining the troops. And if we could keep twenty or thirty men in each farm-hold, they could make a stab at taking on the average raiding party. Or at least hold on until reinforcements could arrive."

"How are you going to get reinforcements there?" Garve` wanted to know. "What are you going to use as a signal?"

"Bells," his father returned. "You know how you can hear church bells for miles? Well, we're going to transplant a bunch of church bells to the south, and your bait farms would be just the place for them."

Garve` sat back in his chair, pleased that he had given his father an idea the King thought was a good one.

"We'll need more archers, though," King Marc qualified. "We need to be able to put at least eight of them in each of the bait farms with horses so we can get them around to where they're needed quickly enough to make a difference. If we have eight archers in place, and sixteen more coming from each of the nearest farm-holds, we'll have a fair chance of wiping a normal raiding party out."

King Marc sat back in his chair and regarded the half-formed plan assessingly. After long moments, he added.

"I'd like to see that. I really would. Wiping a few of those murdering bastards out would give our people a real morale boost, and it might even make the Caelian think twice about sending their men to raid us."

Privately, Garve` doubted it. The Caelian had been raiding the southern Amadean foothills for generations. The southern farms (and ranches) yielded rich rewards to those who would work them. The grasslands along the lower slopes were lush, making two ton of hay to the acre and sometimes even more, with just enough water in the winter to bring the grass up strong, and hot, dry enough summers to harden the grain off and ripen it for harvest earlier than most other climes in Amadea.

The early hay brought premium prices as people in need of the feed had to pay whatever was asked in order to keep their livestock until the coastal valley hay came ripe, and pretty much the same could be said for their vegetables and their berries. Their dark-berries, sweet-berries and red-berries came in a month before anybody else's, too, and their gold-fruit, large and small, went for staggering prices both fresh and dried.

The southern-most plantations made sugar, while honey came out of the foothills and the mountains. People in the coastal valleys kept hives in their orchards and sold both honey for cooking and candy and beeswax for candles. Not that the Caelian cared about such things, King Marc reminded himself. No, they wanted grain and meat and slaves, and of late, they'd just been killing people out of hand and not bothering with slaves and their raiding parties were getting larger.

Instead of a dozen, they were arriving in groups of twenty to thirty. Why? He wondered. What were they up to?

They'd been doing the raiding the same way, in the same numbers for most of the last century. Now they were suddenly changing their tactics? It didn't make sense, unless they had something else in mind. Though what, he had no idea. He stared at his son thoughtfully.

"What do you think?" he wanted to know.

"I think you ought to see if Nehl knows anything," Garve` offered. "Jiden's gone," he reminded his father. "You're not going to get anything more out of his family. They're too afraid they might incriminate themselves if they say anything about him. But Nehl must have known something. And if he was working with or for King Bane, maybe he can tell us something about the man."

King Marc considered that.

"I can ask him about that bridge he signed off on," he murmured, mostly to himself. "I wonder what Jiden told him about it to get him to do it."

Garve` wondered if Jiden had needed to tell his brother anything. Had Nehl even known what he was signing off on? But he didn't voice his doubts to his father. Let him find out, he thought. Nehl had already conspired to get his father killed. You couldn't get any farther on his wrong side than that. Maybe if King Marc talked to him about it and Nehl snapped, their father would be forced to do something about him—something more than just talk.

"No idea," he said aloud. He changed the subject. "What are you going to do about the conspirators?" he inquired. "I know that the men who spearheaded the effort are all dead, but what about their supporters who are left?"

"I've already pulled the Jiden kids out of the household and sorted them out between Lord Liam's and my mother's households," his father told him. "I've been wondering who I could put the D'Arcy children and the Bardon children with."

Garve` laughed a little.

"Put the D'Arcy and the Bardon boys in farm-holds in the country where they'll have to work for their living," he suggested. "Not rich places, either. Lower middle class all the way. Strong work ethic, Temple-going, hand-me- down wearing, god-fearing, close to the earth types. See if a life of no work, no eat can make a change in them."

"That is an excellent suggestion," his father praised. "What about the girls?"

"No idea," Garve' told him.

His father considered for a long moment, and then offered, "Healers, teachers, herb women?"

"Can't hurt," Garve' shrugged.

"Well, it can't hurt the girls, I wouldn't think. Might be a real detriment to the ladies."

"We'll find out," his father told him, with distinct satisfaction.

"Tell me something," Garve' requested, watching him. His father raised his eyebrows and Garve' took it as a signal to continue. "Why take the children away from them? Just to punish them?"

"Not at all," King Marc told him. "I take them away in the hope that by having them raised by more reasonable, ethical people, they will learn some- thing besides arrogance, stupidity, selfishness and cruelty. And maybe meet some real, decent people with whom they can forge friendships and perhaps even marry. The D'Arcys need an infusion of new blood in the worst way. Did you know that they only have five children between all the cousins, these days? Including second and third cousins? And that Bardons only have seven? Again including second and third cousins? Not that Jidens have many more. Eight altogether, and only two of them girls."

"Isn't that a little cruel?" Garve' wondered.

"Why would you think that?" his father wanted to know. "These families dump their kids on nurses and nannies the moment they're born and then send them off to their fancy schools almost as soon as they're potty-trained. If the kids see their parents more than twice a year, and for more than a few moments at the most, they feel they're truly unfortunate, and they're right to feel that way, since their fathers are more apt to have them whipped than they are to speak to them gently." Garve' winced.

"They'll get a much better education in those farm-holds than they would in those private schools of theirs, and they'll be treated a lot better, too." Garve` had to admit that his father might have something there.

"Margrete never allowed anyone to lay a hand on us," he pointed out, in all fairness.

"Well," his father allowed, "she knew that if I ever found out that any one of you boys had been abused, that I'd eliminate the problem and her along with it and I'll make certain that the people who take these aristo kids have the same understanding." Garve` nodded.

"She hates you, you know. Margrete." His father shrugged.

"Let her," he said. "Her father and brother murdered your mother, and don't you ever doubt that she was in on it. I only learned what they'd done within hours after giving her my vows, and by the time I reached my wedding bed, I'd killed them both, so she has her reasons, just as I have mine. She shouldn't have tried to marry me."

Garve` nodded to his father, speechless.

"Marry who you will and when you will," his father lessoned him, "but take heed when you marry. The wrong wife can be a cross you'll bear for years, a burden you can never quite get rid of. If you'll take my advice, you'll choose your wife for something more than her looks."

"Someone like Vere di Brevard, perhaps?" Garve` asked him lightly.

"Only if you can learn to care deeply for her," his father retorted. "She is too fine to be yoked to a man who doesn't appreciate her."

"Right," Garve` ostensibly agreed. Internally, he thought, if he could bring Vere di Brevard to the altar, he'd find himself replacing the problematical Crown Prince in the succession before he could say jack rabbit, and let Nehl pose the slightest of threats to her, and he, Garve`, wouldn't have to worry about the succession ever again. His father would put a period to his brother's existence. A large one. Unfortunately, he admitted, if just to himself, marrying Vere di Brevard might pose a problem—no one knew where Vere had gone or even if she was still alive.

Ah well, he told himself. He'd keep looking for her. Quietly. It wouldn't do for Nehl to kill her before he could get her to the altar, and Nehl would do it if he found her before Garve` did. Then again, if his brother did manage to kill her, he wouldn't have to worry about the succession ever again. His father would make certain Nehl didn't live to kill anyone else.

He watched his father pull out stationary and pen and set to work to write letters. A glance at the head of the stationary informed him that his father was writing to General Meric. Fine. He'd retire to his own rooms and write some letters of his own. He wanted to solidify his position with his father while Nehl was out of favor, just in case Vere couldn't be found. Or, he admitted, just to himself, was dead.

Nehl, he thought, privately, had put his foot in it with the coup. It wouldn't take much for his father to eliminate him from the succession for good and all, and if he did, well, Garve' was next in line. He just had to make certain that he had his father's favor when King Marc reached the point where he couldn't stomach Nehl as his heir another moment. Not, he thought to himself with a secret smile, as he made his way to his rooms, that it would be all that difficult to do.

# XXXVIII

## THE TOWERS

W E FIRST CAUGHT SIGHT OF the tops of the towers, twinkling in the sunlight through the trees. For a long time we couldn't see anything else, just the glitter of sun off those glass panels, a pane here, another there. The trail, such as it was, all overgrown so only the feel of it under our feet told us that it had been trodden down by many feet over many years, descended steeply through the trees. First it slid along the side of a hill, then stepped down in a switchback, only to skid directly over another steep downslope before it decided to impersonate a super duper staircase.

Through that section, we'd walk sideways for about ten feet, then turn and walk sideways ten feet the other direction, all the time slipping and sliding downhill until we'd abruptly fetch up on a flat spot like a staircase landing, before starting down another section of hillside to the next 'landing'.

The four-footed critters, Nutmeg, Jagr and the wolves, had a lot easier time of it than I had. Even with his pack, which was a good deal lighter these days, Nutmeg still had the advantage, and, of course, Jagr carried no pack. And the wolves claws provided enough purchase to offset any disadvantage their now relatively light packs might produce. But me—all I had was two feet, a pack as heavy as any of those the wolves carried, and the come-along to manage. It wasn't easy. I slipped and slid a lot and landed on my butt more than I liked.

At the bottom of the last 'stair', we reached a wide spot free of trees from which we could see out and down on the side of the mountain near the towers. From that spot, where we stopped for a breather, we could see the center of a roof that alternated between some kind of slate tile and skylights between the glass roofed spires of the towers. The place was massive.

Farther on, we could see the tops of tall stone walls, and much farther on, beyond the walls, and far below them, we could see the ocean. The wolves shared congratulatory grins at the sight. Those grins said as far as they were concerned, we had arrived.

I felt too tired to grin. Around the curve of the hill, I could see that the trail dropped yet again. I didn't want to guess how much farther we had to negotiate these steep hillsides to reach the foot of those towers. Three miles? Four? I stood up and dusted off the seat of my pants. And even if we reached the walls of those towers, could we find the gate? And assuming we could find the gate, which might be assuming a bit much, could we get through it?

I wasn't at all sure that we could. I sensed magic from those old stones. I could feel it, even way up here. And if I could feel it from this far away, there had to be a lot of it, and strong magic, too. It felt dangerous to me. And what about people? Were there any? Would they be friendly if there were?

Welcoming? Or would we be no more nor better than trespassers, as far as they were concerned? Or even worse, unwelcome invaders?

Well, I thought, starting down the next descent, we were going to find out. This was the first major house we had come to on this trail so far. The rest had been cabins and cottages and they had not been in good condition, with broken windows and rotted roofs and vegetation grown up everywhere around them. At least this place might have people.

Fort and Shade slipped around me and let the steep grade carry them faster than I was comfortable, on my only two feet, traveling. Nutmeg, tired and leg weary, wasn't interested in going any faster, either, but Wraith and Reve soon slipped by me as well, with Jagr, too young to carry any weight and therefore free of any pack, right on their heels. I resigned myself to being the last to reach lower ground, because I could see where the stream came out below me, and beyond that, green grass. I figured as soon as Nutmeg spotted that grass, that he'd speed up as well, and I was right, too.

By the time I got to where the stream came out, the wolves and the horses had stopped to drink the icy water. I'd filled my canteen up on top, where the spring came out of the rocks, and still had plenty of water. In Amadea, the streams weren't always as pure as one would hope. Apparently the water situation was better in Mahdi than it was in Amadea.

I'd wait on the water, I told myself, and headed on down to where the wall curved towards the valley. I didn't see any gate on this side.

Wild roses grew along the walls, here and there, hiding the wall and making me think of tales of Briar Rose and Sleeping Beauty. Below the highest levels of the wall a small valley stretched, down to a good-sized creek. I regarded it thoughtfully.

The gate in the interior wall, when I reached it, was closed and warded with a tapestry of power, made all of iridescent threads of many colors, white and red and blue, yellow and green, lavender and purple and pink. The wards ignored the horses but rebuffed the wolves, although not violently. They just sort of flicked their noses in warning.

I approached carefully, sitting down on the ground (fortunately not wet) in front of them and started studying. Before long, becoming curious, the wolves had changed and pulled on clothing to protect them from the sharpness of the wind, joining me in staring at the wards.

When I reached out slowly, to pluck at the white thread, it flickered, and then allowed me to draw it towards me until, working with all the delicacy I could manage, I had separated it entirely from the tapestry over the gate. I stuck it on the gatepost—it seemed wrong just to drop it—and then reached out carefully to draw the pink thread towards me. It came, just as the white thread had. After that, I sat and studied for long moments. Red next? Or lavender?

In the end, I chose the lavender thread, pulling it carefully from the woven wards before me. When I had managed to completely separate it from the tapestry, I stuck it on the gatepost and then selected the violet thread. It went on the gate-post next to the lavender thread, and

then I pulled out the red thread, sticking it on the gatepost between the
pink thread and the violet thread, before I separated the blue thread
from the rainbow tapestry. The yellow thread went on the other side
of the gatepost, with the orange one. The green thread went between
the yellow thread and the blue one. The pale green thread went closer
to the yellow, while the deep forest green thread fit closer to the blue.

At which point, the gate opened. We all stood outside it and craned
our necks so we could look inside. The drive, at about the same width
as the gate, curled around in a circle that meandered through what
I would have called maple trees and blue spruce, with a huge high
mountain pine here and there soaring towards the sky. I supposed
that however we had descended those last not quite twenty miles or
so, we were still fairly high up in the mountains. Four thousand feet?
Possibly? Or three?

Climbing roses and the occasional bush rose punctuated the
remains of a rustic rail fence underneath the trees, a rough sort of
lawn filling the semi-circle enclosed by them. If you took the drive to
the right, you'd see more lawn—if you could call it that--and roses to
the right of the drive, carrying on right up to the far wall before you
finally fetched up in front of the house. If you took the drive to the
left, you'd see paddocks and a carriage house and finally stables on
the far side of the trees, and more rustic lawn and roses before you
finally reached the front of the house. If you could call a baronial
affair like this a house.

The massive center section soared up for at least four stories, if not
more (I couldn't tell). A balcony sheltered the front door, guarded,
itself, by an ornamental carved stone balustrade that continued on
to span the roofs of square stone two story porticos to either side
of the front entry. Looked at with a bit of a jaundiced eye, those
porticos could form a very effective barbican guarding the entry.
The walls looked thick, possibly four feet? Or even five. What front
windows could be seen looked more like arrow slits than windows,
and the buttresses to either side of the center section of the—house?
looked like nothing so much as great, dark granite outcrops of rock,

making the glass domes forming their roofs behind the battlements and crenellations incongruous in the extreme.

Nutmeg spotted the grass and, apparently deciding it looked more delicious than the grass he'd been enjoying outside the walls, pushed past us to plant himself in the center of the semi-circle and drop his head to graze. Jagr, deciding he didn't want to be left out, hurried to join him. Nothing happened to them, so I tried stepping through the—now--open gate. Nothing happened to me, so the wolves followed me in. I closed the gate behind us and latched it, but I didn't do anything about the wards.

I couldn't make up my mind whether the place looked abandoned, or merely unkempt in the way a place might be when it was too big for its caretakers to manage. I could well believe the latter, given the size of the place. Choosing the right hand path, I made my unhurried way to the front door, figuring that choosing the direct path across the lawn and over the remnants of fences would merely make me appear a manner-less barbarian. We wanted to make ourselves welcome here, I considered. No point in getting off on the wrong foot.

The door flung open the moment I placed a foot upon the first of the three shallow stairs leading to the portico, and two while-haired people, a man and a woman, both of whom looked old enough to be my great grandparents and enough alike to be twins, hurried out to greet us. The female of the pair jumped up and down like a kid and clapped her hands joyously.

"You're here!" she repeated several times. Well, yes, we were.

"Our wandering chick has come home!" the male of the pair exulted. Huh.

"We've waited ever so long," the female announced. "I'm Rheet. That's Peet."

"How very nice to meet you," I told her, a bit nonplussed by their greeting. Had they been expecting us? How could they have? It made no sense to me. "I'm Vere. And these are--"

"Mahdi wolves!" Rheet caroled. "The Mahdi wolves brought you home!" She appeared quite excited by this, clapping her hands together and barely managing not to jump up and down, as if this was an important point.

Well, I thought, that was a fair conclusion, but very perspicacious of her, since they were two-legged at the moment rather than four-legged, and dressed as human travelers, complete with backpacks. I introduced them.

"Get your packs and come in!" Rheet invited as I finished the introductions. "Oh," she added, "we've waited so long for this day!"

"Come in!" Peet added happily. "Come in!" he repeated. Confidingly, he told Rheet, "A Nogaynos mage and Mahdi wolves! How perfect!"

I hefted my pack and followed them into the dark entry, not understanding.

Why was my arrival with Mahdi wolves 'perfect'?

The entry seemed more of a tunnel than anything else, something like six feet deep and not a bit over four feet wide, with another door at the other end. It had to have been set up that way for defensive purposes. Rheet noted my attention to the double door arrangement.

"It's an airlock," she explained to me. "Because of the poison air, you know."

"Surely that's no longer a problem," I faltered, surveying the wide entry hall.

"Oh, of course not," Rheet assured me. "But it was when we decided to stay on. But we never did get much of it here—too far from Caelian."

I nodded to her explanation. That made sense, as far north as we were. But the connotations of her statement stunned me. How old were these people? A hundred and fifty years old? Or more? If they had been forced to hang those airlock doors to keep out the poison air from the Caelian attack?

Wraith and Reve and the boys dropped their packs along the wall. I set mine slowly down beside theirs, trying to take everything in as I moved.

"So the Caelian warriors never got here?" Wraith wanted to know, his eyes curious as he gawked at the wainscoted walls to either side of us. Sprigged silk wall-paper above the wainscoting looked as delicate and elegant and as tastefully done as any wall in the Amadean palace.

"Never," Peet assured him. "They started dying almost as soon as they crossed over the Lupine."

"But the people fleeing the poison air told us what was going on, and then the people behind them, running away from the Caelian warriors told us the rest,"

Rheet said. "That gave our mages time to seal off the areas inside the walls and make certain that the house was air tight, before they took the children and left.

They always intended to come back as soon as the danger was past—that was the plan, anyway--but they never did."

"And you—stayed." My voice faltered. Just how old were they?

"We didn't want to go," Peet explained. "This is our home." He led us under the massive tiered stone staircase that supported the center of the structure.

"But the children had to be taken out," Rheet said, as if I needed convincing. "Dying of the poison air would be bad. Being captured by the Caelian would be worse. At least this way some of the houses could be saved."

"The houses?" I queried. This house, if you could call it that, looked untouched, not merely by an invading force, but by the use and abuse of the years, as well, and if I was to go by what they had said so far, this house had been standing for a couple of hundred years at the least.

"The mages and their children are the essence of the houses," Peet told me. "We're just caretakers for them. We have just enough magic to get by," he added, "housekeeping spells, and mending and repairs, some earth magic for the gardens, a little spirit to help with the animals, and places to hide where the Caelian will never find us."

"Mages and their children and grandchildren have been filtering back for oh, at least a hundred years," Rheet said. "But very few of them come this far north, or this far west. So we've been alone all this time." Her last statement sounded forlorn. She distracted herself by opening the door to a large dining hall that looked out into an enclosed garden filled with greenery.

I thought such an area was often called a 'conservatory'. The hearth in the wall opposite the glass dominated that end of the room, and the long, side walls featured more of the delicately sprigged silk with its pale background above white painted wainscoting. Impressive. I nodded my approval to Rheet as her eyes raised questioningly to mine.

Rheet opened the door in the long wall to our left and led us into the kitchen. We followed her into the cheerful, sunny room and stared around it, gawking at everything from the raw timber staircase along the interior wall and the pantry built into it, to the great hearth in the exterior wall opposite it, containing both brick ovens and a cast iron stove complete with a hot water reservoir. Pots and pans hung from the mantel over the hearth, and had been stacked to either side of it in open shelving above wood boxes below. A door opened into the dark interior of the wall to either side of hearth, the first a tidy small sleeping alcove, the second lined with shelves and cupboards.

A still room, perhaps? I wondered, before we turned to the tall, narrow windows forming a bay in the wall standing at right angles to the hearth wall, just beyond the scullery sink and the drains to either side of it under the smaller, square, more ordinary windows. A generously sized dining table and a half dozen chairs looked out into the enclosed garden beyond the windows, with a door opening into the garden just beyond the table. The interior wall at right angles to the outer wall had been painted yellow above the white wainscoting and the area under the staircase had been enclosed to form pantries, leaving only a space at the head of the staircase open to give entrance to the area under the staircase.       An ancient plank work table at the center of the room created a cooking island, and the room was so spacious it held everything without the least bit of crowding.

It wouldn't have surprised me to find that the room was somewhat larger than twenty-five feet across—twenty-six? Twenty-seven? In fact, its entire ambiance was one of generosity, spaciousness and light. I could well imagine meals being prepared here for fifty or sixty people, easily.

We could be comfortable here, I thought, eyeing that table under the windows. We'd have plenty of room to work in this kitchen, and plenty of cupboard space to store food for the winter. Undoubtedly there would be a root cellar underground where food could be stockpiled, for a large household like this. If only we could stay, I thought wistfully.

# XXXIX

## HOME

"WE CAME FROM THE NORTH," Reve told her, "so we've been traveling to the south."

"We've come more than thirty-five hundred miles," Fort told her. "It took us two years to get here and this is the first house in Nogaynos we've seen that hasn't been in ruins."

Rheet and Peet turned to face each other, their eyes wide.

"That far!" Rheet exclaimed, sounding awed as she led us back to the area under the stairs and showed us the comfortable sitting rooms to either side of the main staircase. We all peeked into the rooms, obediently oohing and ahhing over their luxurious furnishings.

"I was raised in Amadea's Palace City," I told them. "I had to travel north out of the city in the beginning, and then west, before I could turn south, skirting the great prairie and the ice pack, so I came a little farther. I met up with the wolves just outside of Mahdi, and wintered there before starting south again."

"Amadea," Rheet and Peet exchanged glances at that and started us up the stairs. "But however did you know to come here?"

"I was adopted," I shrugged. "Someone paid my adoptive parents to raise me, leaving additional money to be given to me when I came of age, but my adoptive mother spent a lot more of the money than she was supposed to. When I started to get old enough so that she faced having to turn what was left of it over to me, she decided she didn't want me around any longer and turned me out so she could keep it."

Very carefully, Peet asked, "Do you think such things are happening to other Nogaynos children who lost their families?"

"In Amadea? Certainly," I answered him. "In Mahdi? I don't know. I don't know many Mahdi and I have never been there. I've skirted it, maybe, but I haven't really gone into Mahdi."

"We have Nogaynos blood," Reve told Peet and Rheet proudly. "We're Smoke wolves."

Their pride indicated rather strongly that Nogaynos children had fared rather better in Mahdi than I had in Amadea. I deemed it time to change the subject.

"But however have you managed?" I wondered aloud.

"Oh, that's no problem," Peet assured me. "We keep half a dozen head of cattle on hand, we have some sheep and a few pigs, a pony to help with chores, and a couple of dogs and cats to keep down the rodents and help with the stock. And then we have the gardens and the orchards. Then again, the woods are full of deer and wild cattle and we hunt them now and again, when we want to put more meat in storage."

"And we have magic," Rheet told us, her voice hushed over the last word, and prideful. "We have cleaning spells, and spells to keep the meat and the greens fresh, and spells to keep the roofs sound and the glass from breaking."

"Vere has magic too," Reve assured her. "She can use 'travel'!"

"And air, and earth and fire and spirit!" Shade informed them, bragging a little.

I patted his shoulder, not sure we ought to be telling them these things.

Especially since I was anything but proficient at them. "I have a great deal to learn," I pointed out.

"Oh, then you'll want to see the library," Rheet announced, bouncing. She and Peet seemed pleased by the idea that I had magic. (Or that I wanted to learn more.)

We reached the top of the staircase, and she showed us around quickly.

"Those are the state guest chambers," she gestured to our right.

"There's the state guest parlor and three guest chambers—front room, side room and back room next the kitchen tower," she elucidated. "Dining hall, great hall and dais straight ahead and to your left," she added.

"Are there any guest chambers for people who aren't state dignitaries?" I wondered, thinking about us.

"Of course," Rheet assured me. "The bachelors' rooms are off the kitchen side parlor, two large chambers for two to four men each with another room in front of the kitchen. The fourth room for the butler opens off the entry hall.

Unattached women guests have the rooms above and behind the scholar's chamber and the library, with three large chambers around a parlor on the other side of the keep from them. And on the first floor there are three more chambers around the side parlor, then the state dining chamber over the entry, the great

hall next to it, with the scholar's chamber behind the library and apprentices' chamber behind the dais—usually reserved for the girls. It's entered off the library."

She took a breath.

"That's twelve rooms," I counted, impressed.

"House women either have rooms on the ground floor or the third floor, according to their preferences," Rheet continued. "The House horticulturalist usually claims the ground floor buttress room on the women's side of the house for herself, for instance, but occasionally she prefers one of the third floor rooms that gives entrance to one of the dome towers, which provides her with a private laboratory for her horticultural studies. And, of course," Rheet finished, "there's the chapel on the first floor at the back of the house, over the staff dining hall. It rises through two stories and has a choir loft and a stained glass window. The window is protected by the conservatory across the back of the keep. So that's twenty bed-chambers in all, with the nursery, the chapel, the great hall, the two dining halls, the school-room over the chapel, and seven parlors besides the library. The Towers is the true home of a Magister of Nogaynos. It is truly a residence fit for a queen!"

Wow, I thought. It certainly was. This place was enormous! Orienting myself, I placed the formal dining hall over the entry hall, the chapel over the ground floor dining area next to the kitchen, the great hall to one side of the entry across the front of the house, over, well, whatever was underneath it. The interior wall of the great hall was punctuated by a great hearth as well as the door into the library, with another hearth at the back of the dais, at right angles to the larger hearth. Marvelous bureau bookcases, all done in a golden, richly grained wood accented with gold and mirrored glass cabinets flanked each of the hearths, and comfortable sofas and chairs clustered around the front of them upon rich carpets of brilliantly colored swirls and roses.

I had been in Amadea's ancestral palace, and this 'great' hall, though not over-large or overtly ostentatious, equaled anything the palace had. Oh, the house looked older, the timbered bones of its apartments darkened with age between the white-washed and wall-papered paneled stone of the walls and the carefully varnished veneer of the golden wainscoting, which was saying something. I knew the Amadean palace to be four or five hundred years old at the least, so if this 'house' was older—then how old was it? Really? A millennia? More? I wasn't sure I wanted to guess.

"These are family rooms," Rheet informed us, as she opened the door in the interior wall beyond the great hearth. "The library," she announced proudly.

I understood her pride with the first sweep of my eyes. The space had to be at least twenty feet across and a good deal more than twenty feet long, the crimson, gold and cream, pink and muted green carpet on the floor dotted about with desks and writing tables and chairs. The hearth had been situated in the massive stone wall at the interior end of the room, a pair of leather upholstered sofas with a scattering of equally comfortable chairs grouped before it. Light streamed into the space from the opposite end of the space through a wall of deep, tall, narrow windows.

Between the hearth on one end and the windows on the other, both interior walls were lined with golden breakfront bureau bookcases filled to the brim with leather-bound books. Some of the books looked so old they might even be incunabula, that is written by hand instead of printed. The room virtually begged one to select a book and settle down before a cozy fire in the hearth.

I could hardly wait to accept its invitation.

"Wow!" Shade said.

"Double wow!" I agreed. I could hardly help wandering about the shelves to peer through the glassed in cabinet doors at the spines of the books enclosed there. It certainly wouldn't be any hardship to study in this room!

Smiling, wordlessly, Rheet crossed the room to opened the door to a large bed-sit behind the library.

"The scholar's apartment," she intoned.

Another big hearth dominated the far wall, a delicately painted and enameled stove set into it, with room on the top plate for a pair of reasonably-sized hot water kettles. A sofa and chairs upholstered in dainty sprigged silk gathered around it, on another of those swirly crimson and pink rose carpets. A bank of tall windows pierced the exterior wall to the right of the door, several beds placed to the left along the interior wall. The big four-poster tester bed, its headboard pressed snugly into the wall at right angles to the door, seemed nearly as broad as it was long its deep mattress covered by a well-stuffed comforter, while a somewhat smaller bed placed at right angles to it, its head sunk into the wall against a curved panel was just as sumptuously dressed,. A privacy panel at its foot and densely woven bed panels screened it from the rest of the room.

Both beds had been bracketed by chests with bookcases atop them and crystal light-holders for reading. An exquisite painted glass partition, held in rosewood frames, with painted lacquer-work panels below, stood at the foot of the first bed, with a smaller, single bed set wide-ways across its foot. An attendant's rest, perhaps? Or a variant of a reading couch? The plethora of colorful cushions stacked along the partition suggested as much. At least it looked comfortable.

On the other side of the room, the window end, another pair of four poster beds nestled into opposite walls, their headboards sunk a couple of feet deep into the paneled stone bracketed by small chests topped by smaller bookcases. The curved panels above the headboards provided crystal light-holders for those who liked to read in bed, while the beds were all screened by richly caparisoned bed- hangings and painted partitions at their feet, for privacy. Under the windows, a table and chairs had been set up, a tea tray complete with cups in the middle of it.   Desks to either side of the door provided study areas, while bureau bookcases with fitted interiors stood to either side of the hearth.

The walls had been painted a pale lavender-pink, over off-white wainscoting, with drapes only a couple of shades darker pulled back away from the windows. The room was large, over twenty feet deep and close to thirty feet long, space enough to comfortably house a family of four—or more. A door in the back corner opened to a small bath, relief station and dressing area set into the wall and warmed by the side of the hearth. Even the palace rooms in Amadea hadn't been as tastefully and elegantly arranged—or as comfortably.

Here the luxury was simple, spacious, light and airy. Furnished for convenience, comfort, even coziness, the room invited one to sit and toast one's toes before the fire, or to cuddle up in a puffy quilt under the windows with a book in hand. The carpets scattered about caressed one's toes, and the chairs cushioned the body, enticing one to settle in and rest. Silver candelabra on the mantel to either side of an ornate coffer-fort sat under a large canvas depicting a woman in mage robes and holding a very refined and well-bred horse in front of the house.

"Your room," Rheet added, just to be clear.

The room would certainly provide for all of us, I thought, wondering if Wraith and Reve had ever lived in such style or comfort before. I certainly hadn't. It all looked amazing to me.

Peet appeared in my peripheral vision, carting my pack. He set it down on the chest beside the slightly larger bed at the left of the hearth and closest to the door to the bath. Exploring, I examined the space. I found a small water closet, complete with a small enamel sink under a mirror. The room was really tiny, tucked back into the wall the way it was, with one niche cut into the stone on the left of the door for the water closet and another niche cut into the stone on the hearth side, for bathing. What dressing area there was had been tucked into the foot of the bath.

My foster brothers would have said it was hardly big enough to 'swing a cat', though why anyone would want to do that, I couldn't fathom. But then, I could see one of my foster brothers doing it. I shook my head, just to myself, remembering them and turned my attention back to the space. The sink niche had been cut into the back wall, with copper and ceramic fittings, tiled back- splash and counters over small drawers and hidden plumbing. Less than four feet of floor space joined the utilities, the tiny windows to either side of the sink's mirror opening out to the conservatory below.

It was all quite wonderful.

"I'll get our packs," Fort volunteered, and slipped away.

"Perhaps the chambers behind the dais?" Rheet suggested carefully, in answer to some question of Reve's I hadn't quite heard, drawing us after her to show us the door leading from the library into the rooms behind the dais.

The plural was, perhaps, inaccurate, given how small the area given over to the water closet, sink, bathing and dressing space was. I would have called it a bed-sit, but, like the chamber Rheet thought I ought to occupy, this room had tall windows looking out into a glass enclosed garden, set into a curve in the opening of the wall. The tall, four-poster bed was large, lush, and, like the other bed, had a lovely painted glass partition set at the foot of it. What I suspected would be called a trundle bed set across the foot of it. The carpet on the floor was mostly grass green, the sofa and chairs upholstered in shades of green from pale to dark, echoing the green cast of the light from the garden below.

The walls had been painted a pale green over off-white wainscoting, and exquisite carved wood tables. End tables, a writing table, and a table under the windows had been scattered about charmingly. Wrought iron candelabra and candle stands ornamented with silver stood and sat on and around the chairs and tables and accented the mantel over the hearth. A sofa and chairs had been arranged on a green ground carpet facing the hearth, which had itself been flanked by matching golden bureau bookcases.      In the fore-corner, a pair of single beds had been arranged, attended by chests with bookcases atop them, bed-hangings for privacy reinforced by partitions at their feet.

The room was large enough to swallow them all up without yielding an iota of its spaciousness, graciousness, or comfort. Three narrow, deep windows in the front walls merely added to the effect. Reve walked about caressing things with reverent fingers. Wraith smiled at her.

"I'll get our packs," he said.

I turned to Rheet and Peet, thinking unhappily that this place was just too good to be true. The house itself, the warm welcome, everything about it urged me to bask in the glow of it, but I just couldn't bring myself to do it. Some- where, I could not but help think, there had to be a sting in the tail. When something seemed too good to be true, it usually was.

'Wait and see' I warned myself silently. 'Watch and wait'. If it was too good to be true, I'd find out, sooner or later. Rheet and Peet (if those were their names) had to want something from us. I just couldn't figure out what that could be. They seemed to have everything. What could we possibly bring to them? Well, other than our labor. Which, now I came to think about it, just might be my answer. I had no idea just how old these people were, but they certainly were not young, whether or not their birth predated the diaspora. I just had to be certain, I warned myself, that I wasn't taken by surprise, that was all.

"We need to get Nutmeg and Jagr settled," I told them, setting the thoughts aside for now.

"Finish your tour, first," Peet advised. "They are well enough where they are for the time being."

Well, he was probably right about that, I considered ruefully, and they would save him some mowing, while they were at it. I noted that Fort's and Shade's packs joined mine in the scholar's room behind the library and I amused myself with wondering if Rheet and Peet saw me as someone to guard, or Fort and Shade as just more scholars. Perhaps some combination of both? Or perhaps they knew something more of the relationship between Mahdi wolves and Nogaynos mages than I did? I wouldn't find it surprising if they did. After all, what I knew about Mahdi could be put on the head of a pin, and they had lived next to Mahdi all their lives.

Rheet took us out to the great hall, and then up the 'grand' staircase to the gallery over the dining hall, and showed us the rooms clustered around the center parlor looking out into a circular greenhouse garden. Unless I was very mistaken, those were orange trees filling the space. I found that very interesting, given how far north we were, and how high up in the mountains.

Then she showed us along a gallery to the opposite side of the house, and into another parlor, directly over the library. Two large square chambers opened off the parlor, with a third chamber, almost exactly half as large as the others, built directly over the dais looking out into the great hall filled the space. Each of the chambers shared the same tastefully done understated elegance I had seen in the scholar's chamber and the buttress chamber behind the dais. The space over the great hall had been left open, and even though the windows looked narrow, they were tall, and filled the great hall with light.

So far, I thought, as I followed Rheet's lead, I had seen no poor relation's meager quarters, no dark and dingy rooms or cramped, cold accommodations, no spare, stark spaces into which the unwanted and unregarded might be stashed, the way I had been in my adoptive parents' home. But with another floor to be explored, I didn't doubt that I would. Anyone who commanded a house like this one would have poor relations, probably people born to the family with lesser magic, or direst of all, no magic to speak of. In a culture based on magic, those without magic would occupy about the same space, I suspected as those in Amadea born to poor parents, or who were unlucky enough to have no parents at all.

But the attics surprised me. I found no drafty garrets there, no small, mean, dark rooms. Instead the rooms were all spacious, light and airy, a schoolroom over the two levels of chapel below it, large dorm rooms in each of the back corners, a lovely, airy parlor to each side of the house, and one large, front corner room opening out into a domed solarium situated on the buttress tower to that side of the house. The enclosed space over the two stories of the great hall had been turned into a nursery and playroom for children, with Nanny's room over the dais. Well, over the room over the dais. Nanny's room opened out to the other domed buttress tower.

At least, that was what Rheet called it. According to her the back corner room belonged to the 'Instructress', while the other back corner room had been reserved for the household daughters. The eldest got the small wall alcove room, while beds for four more girls had been arranged around the walls with the sitting area at the center of the room, complete with bureau bookcases and a couple of quite exquisite desks. The entire room looked spacious, gracious, light and airy, with tall, elegant windows looking out over the greenhouses below. The view was spectacular.

The parlor between front and back corner rooms shared the same view, just as the parlor between the Instructress' room shared the same view with the rooms to either side of it. The space over the entry hall had been arranged for meals, for a small study area, and an equally cozy sitting area before the hearth.

Sconces scattered around the rooms, the hallways and the staircases held lights that, as twilight approached, began to fill the rooms with a soft glow. I eased a finger close to the glass of the light, surprised by the coolness I found. I realized then that they were Mage lights, cool to the touch and powered by magic.

"Fire magic?" I inquired of Rheet, curiously. Rheet shook her head, smiling at my wonder.

"Just magic," she said. "Just a little touch of it in each glass that builds over time, drawing on the magic that the house channels through its walls.

Generations of magic, a thousand years, perhaps even two thousand years of magic have been settled into these walls, into the ground and the glass, the roofs and the windows. They loop," she explained. "Deepening, intensifying the magic, year after year, decade after decade, generation after generation. Water magic pouring down over the house from the heavens, earth magic pushing up from the ground, air magic and water magic nourishing the trees, the shrubs and the grass, fire magic in all the hearths to warm the house and its people, and the magic of the spirit wrapping it all around to keep it safe and filled with the riches of welcome, good-will, love and light and inspiration. Magic augmented and increased by every generation that has lived here."

"Truly," I told her, "this house is magnificent."

"Tomorrow," Rheet assured me, "we'll take you all the way up to the roof so you can see your new world. But for now, it is time for you to go with Peet to see the stables and settle your horses down there where they'll be cozy and comfortable."

Given the number and ruggedness of the miles they had come, and the relatively short amount of time they'd covered those miles in, Nutmeg and Jagr were in very good condition, but I was still pleased to see that the stable lived up to Rheet's report of it. Arranged along the walls behind the carriage house, where they formed a square, the stable provided almost three dozen stalls around three sides of a luxurious training rectangle. In no time at all, we had Nutmeg unpacked, and both he and the colt stalled up adjacent to each other, their mangers filled with hay, their troughs brimming with fresh, clear water. A combination of sawdust and straw provided them a deep, springy surface into which they could nestle when they wished to rest.

This seemed, I thought, as I worked, a good place to stay. I just hoped it turned out to be as good as it seemed. I wanted a home, at long last. I wanted a place where, now I had no other place to go, that would take me in and allow me to make it my own. But, I couldn't help but think, what did they want, this so hospitable welcoming pair of custodians? What would the price be that I paid for such a palace? Humm?

# XL

# OLD NICK'S NIGHT

KING MARC LEANED BACK IN his chair and pushed his feet out towards the fire. On either side of him, Freddy and Garve` lounged, his mother Malaya and his father, Lucius, draped over the sofa. Only Nehl was missing. Marc didn't ask after him; Nehl tended to be missing from family activities a lot, these days. His absences only seemed to make the rest of them more comfortable. Marc flinched at the thought, tucked it away to think about later. His mother sighed and stretched."Another year gone," she observed, her eyes traveling to the fire on the hearth.

"And nothing resolved," his father grumbled.

"Vere's strategies work," Marc reminded him. "And so do Garve`'s. At the start of the new year, we'll have another hundred archers in training, and we'll be mounting and training another hundred horses and men. By summer, we ought to be able to send them down to Meric to help out."

"You need five hundred each, not a mere hundred," Lucius groused.

"But a hundred is a good start," Malaya congratulated him. "Such things take time. The Caelians have been raiding us for more than a hundred years. This is the first time we've found any defensive strategies that work against them."

"Expensive," Lucius growled.

"More expensive to allow them to continue to bleed the western foothills of their people and their produce," his mother pointed out.

"D'Arcys and Bardons certainly aren't going to do anything to help," Freddy commented. "All they do is hold assemblies and balls and parties." And plot to overthrow the government, he thought, but did not add.

"I think that's a good idea, fostering their children out to learn better," Malaya observed. "Perhaps the next generation will be of more value than the old."

"I wouldn't bet on it," Freddy retorted pessimistically.

"Blood will tell?" Garve` inquired of him.

"Sometimes," Freddy agreed with the concept equivocally. He shrugged a little. "Look at us. Nehl takes after his Caelian half. You take after your Amadean-Nogaynos half. I take after—what?" he asked of his grandparents.

"Amadean," his grandmother informed him, "without the leavening of my Nogaynos blood. And Caelian, with Southern Amadean, at that."

"Comes by it honestly, then," Lucius shrugged the entire discussion away from them. "My mother was Caelian and Southern Amadean by halves."

"A D'Arcy?" Freddy asked lightly.

"Yes, if you must know." Lucius said it truculently. D'Arcys, these days, were not the kind of antecedents one boasted of.         Three generations ago, on the other hand. . . well, things had been different, then. At least somewhat.

"She was a very charming woman, and a great beauty," Malaya said firmly, cutting off that train of remembrance. She saw no profit in it.

The woman had also been a man-trap, with a honeyed tongue carrying a sting along behind it. She had been a nightmare of a mother-in-law, a master of the back-handed compliment and an artist at building lies out of a grain of truth, the kind of woman who was no other woman's friend, and who always had to be the center of attention. Malaya didn't miss her. Her death had been a relief, and not just for her.

Lucius, she knew, had been the victim of a very complicated relationship with his mother. He had adored her, but he hadn't understood her. Well, Malaya thought, no man ever would understand that kind of woman, whatever he told himself. Then again, no man ever did understand a great beauty.

Great beauties learned very young to pretend to the virtues men imputed to them, and to keep their own council over what they really thought and felt. They had to, if they wanted to survive.

"So I have a Caelian's looks and the temperament of a Southern Belle," Freddy summarized, amused by the thought.

"We are all the amalgam of all of our lines of blood together," King Marc told him. "Some of us just pull harder to one line or another."

"Which brings us," Lucius caught him up, "to the matter of the succession." Marc sighed.

"There is something wrong with Nehl," he said. "We all know it." His statement purported to face facts.

Freddy looked down at the carpet and very carefully said nothing. Garve` looked at Freddy, though his brother didn't notice it. He, too, kept his mouth shut. Lucius looked at his son inquiringly.

"He tortured a young girl," Marc told them all, sighing it. "That is a known fact. She was innocent; he knew it, and he tortured her anyway, merely to do it."

Lucius shook his head censoriously. "Not fit," he growled.

"Since he has come home from the south, no less than the bodies of four girls have been found washed up on the beaches at various places," Marc continued doggedly. "I cannot prove that he killed the girls, but they were beaten in much the same manner that Vere was beaten—they shared many of the same broken bones, and, also like her, they had been tied down to be beaten."

"That is telling," Malaya observed, unhappily.

"That's not all," Marc informed her. "During the time that Nehl was in Quattar the first time, three girls went missing. Two were found washed up in virtually the same place on the beach, and again, both had been tied down and beaten, the pattern of their broken bones again adhering to the pattern of broken bones on Vere's body, and they, too, had been bound. Additionally, during the time that Nehl was in Southren, three girls went missing. And while only two were found, again, the two who were discovered shared the same pattern of broken bones, the same marks from binding. Apparently, each of the girls was bound the same way so that they could be beaten without being able to defend themselves."

"That," Lucius grated, "that is appalling." He sounded deeply perturbed.

"And again, in Quattar, a girl went missing during the short time Nehl was there to take ship to return home," Marc continued unhappily. "She was found dumped in a gutter, and again, the pattern of her broken bones and the ligature marks on her wrists and ankles all corresponded to the marks and the broken bones on the previously murdered girls."

"That is truly horrifying," Malaya agreed, by her expression deeply appalled.

"I cannot prove that my son has committed such horrendous crimes," Marc admitted. "I do not want to prove such a thing. But in my heart I do know it, and so does Freddy."

Freddy looked up at that, quickly, his eyes shocked by his father's assertion.

"Freddy accompanied his brother south," Marc continued his story, "he guested in Bardons' home with him, and, when I sent them the news of the coup and its failure, he was responsible for getting the two of them to safety in Southren."

"Well done," Lucius praised.

Freddy colored up at that, but he didn't raise his eyes again.

"However, when I sent them the all clear, and invited them to come home again," King Marc went on matter-of-factly, "Freddy left his brother, when Nehl had a fit about the lack of horses General Meric was willing to part with to carry his boxes and the scant escort he meant to send with them and refused to come, he paid his own guide to help him to make the trip by himself. Freddy walked from Southren to Quattar on his own feet, carrying what his guide considered the bare necessities, on his back, leaving his gear for the general to send after him. Nehl had to hire a contingent from outside of the military, of men, horses, and a wagon to carry the gear, to make the trip."

"Telling," Lucius commented.

"I agree," Marc nodded to him. "I believe that Freddy learned something about his brother on that trip that made him willing to break with his brother. Something so dire that he was willing to make an uncomfortable trip on his own feet with scant protection in order to make his way home."

"The making of him," Lucius observed.

"No doubt," Marc agreed. "I'm not going to ask him what that thing was that he learned about his brother. Nehl is his brother and they have always been

close. I won't ask Freddy to betray his brother. But, it is one more straw to the load of the coincidences I've been gathering. I'm convinced. The succession must be changed. Nehl must be excluded."

"How do you intend to change it?" his mother wanted to know.

"If, God forbid, something should happen to me, Father should reinstate himself as the king," King Marc told his father. "Garve` will follow him, should Father be unable to do so, and Freddy will follow Garve`."

He wasn't happy with either Freddy or Garve` in the immediate line of succession—they were both followers, not leaders. They wouldn't stand up for anything, and he knew it—but he had no one else.

"I've already taken steps to remove Nehl from the succession. All you have to do is to ratify it along with Lord Liam and Laren. Neither the Jidens, nor the D'Arcys, nor the Bardons are at present confirmed to the Council, so you, Liam and Laren make it unanimous."

"Of course," Lucius agreed, very subdued.

"It isn't just the girls," King Marc added abruptly, "although the evidence of their deaths would be more than sufficient to justify my actions, but there is also the matter of the coup, and Nehl's involvement with Councilor Jiden. The fact that they double-crossed him and sought to put one of their own on the throne, cannot be allowed to matter.

He conspired with them to murder me, and Garve`, his own brother. Freddy knows that, as well, even though he doesn't say it. Their appalling behavior towards an innocent young girl in an effort to use her as a diversion to keep me ignorant of their real plans only makes their betrayal more distressing."

"It does," Lucius nodded slowly, ponderously, agreeing with him.

"Have you considered marrying again and removing the succession from the Caelian line altogether?" his mother wondered.

"I have," Marc allowed, "but I know of no one other than that young girl my sons so egregiously wronged who I would consider for the position, and I do not believe she would even consider it, never mind accept."

"Nehl would kill her," Freddy looked up quickly, the words startled from his lips, will-he, nil-he.

"I know," his father admitted to him. "And that is another of the stones of reason why she would not consider having me."

"But if Nehl is a murderer—" Malaya began, let it drop. Her eyes turned thoughtful.

"Yes," her son caught her up. "I have thought of it." Marc shook his head. "I do know what it is to have a wife murdered for someone else's ambition."

"What," Garve` wondered, "if one of us could bring her to the altar? Vere, I mean."

"Nehl?" his grandmother reacted as if stung.

"No, no. Not Nehl," Garve` hurried to assure her. "But perhaps Freddy? Or me?"

"I doubt Freddy would have much more chance with her than Nehl would have," Malaya pointed out.

"That would be interesting," King Marc allowed. He frowned. "But, of course, no one knows where she is."

"And that may be a blessing," his mother reminded him. "If Nehl doesn't know where she is, he can't kill her very well, now can he?"

"There is that," King Marc admitted.

"If she's in Amadea, we can find her," his father assured him.

"What if she's gotten to Nogaynos?" King Marc wondered.

His father shrugged.

"We can send scouts, come spring," he offered.

"I don't know," Malaya demurred. "Wouldn't that just bring her to Nehl's attention?"

"I'd like her for Amadea," King Marc admitted. "She could be very valuable to us."

"Does she have power?" Malaya wanted to know.

"I don't know," King Marc told her.

"I just know she's important." Lucius nodded.

"We'll find her then," he told his son confidently. "It may take a while, but we'll find her."

Garve` sat quietly in his chair and nodded with the rest of them. Well, he was thinking, if the girl was going to be the key to the kingdom, then he would just have to get her to the altar. Somehow. Then he frowned, as his thoughts caught up with him. If his father thought he was going to cut Nehl out of the succession and that Nehl would just accept it, he was mad.

The only way Nehl was going to be dropped from his position as Crown Prince was if his father had him killed. As long as Nehl was alive, he'd find a way, and however hesitant his father might be to execute his own son, he would find that Nehl wasn't quite so dainty. Nehl didn't mind killing. He would find a way, whether it be a knife in the back some dark night, or poison in his gravy, the moment Nehl got wind of this conversation, he would start scheming to find a way to kill his father, if he had to hire an assassin to do it, or put a bounty on his head.

"Well, now," his father said, drawing his attention. "It's Old Nick's night.

Midnight. Time to make a wish for the new year." He lifted the glass his butler poured out for him and lifted it to his lips. "And it is my wish--" he broke off, making the rest of his wish in silence, as was the tradition, and then quaffed his wine.

"I make my wish," Queen Malaya announced, and lifted her goblet, so that the firelight gleamed through the golden wine. She lifted the glass to her lips and drained the wine to its lees.

Retired King Lucius lifted his glass and made his wish, drinking it away with gusto, followed by Garve` and Freddy. None of them vouchsafed the substance of their wishes, but they sat together in silence, once they had drunk their wishes down, watching the fire-log before them burn to embers in the hearth.

No one gave any thought to what the erstwhile Crown Prince Nehl wished.

# AUTHOR'S NOTE

THIS ISN'T THE END OF Vere's saga, it is just the beginning. There are tales of war and daring-do to come, with more stories of Vere, and of Nora, Jo, and Val, of Shade and Fort, Laird and Ven and Petey, of Simon, Mathias and Geordie.

Read on to meet the Sun Wolves, the Stone wolves, and the Grannies, with, of course, more of King Marc and the further adventures of Freddy and Nehl, in the Lost World and Pony Power and all the chronicles to follow.

And, if you liked Vere's story, please, if you would, leave a review to help more people to find her, and Shade and Fort and King Marc and all the rest.

Most of all, thank you for reading.

*Gaia Lewes*

www.ingramcontent.com/pod-product-compliance
Lightning Source LLC
Chambersburg PA
CBHW061314190726
48288CB00002B/499